Lifelong Love

When you know better, you do better.

Taz Will

Copyright © 2013 Taz Will

All rights reserved.

ISBN-10: 1-939-764-017
ISBN-13: 978-1-939-764-010

Copyright © 2013 Taz Will

Lifelong Love: When you know better, you do better. All Rights Reserved: No part of this book may be reproduced or transmitted in any form or any means, electronic or mechanical, including photocopying, recording, or by any information storage and retrieval system without the written permission from the publisher or author, except for the inclusion of brief quotations embodied in critical reviews and certain other noncommercial uses permitted by copyright law.

This is a work of fiction. It is not meant to depict, portray or represent any particular real persons. All the characters, incidents and dialogues are the products of the author's imagination and are not to be constructed as real. Any resemblance to actual events or person living or dead is coincidental and is not intended by the author. For permission requests, write to the publisher, addressed "Attention: Permissions Coordinator," at the address below.

Keep It Funky Publishing LLC
4579 Laclede Ave #349
St. Louis, MO 63108
keepitfunkypublishing@yahoo.com
kifpstl.com

1 TREASURE

First day of summer and we all know that it's time for the games to begin. The weather is just right for a couple flare up fights so we know there may be something popping off at the first softball game. The whole hood has a vibe going through the air. We can't wait for the weekend to hit so we can go out and support our team and our hood.

Growing up in Cochran may look dangerous but to us its home. It's where we all know each other and we're all family. Everyone knows families have their issues and sometimes it might need to be resolved with a fight here or there. When it all came down to it we know that once summer is over we can start fresh, put it all behind us or let it boil over until next summer.

Oh yeah, even though this is the hood, we always have something going on with our community. From softball to basketball, boxing, camp, skating, you name it, we had it. Plus it's all free, all we have to do is show up and we can participate in whatever we want. I couldn't wait for Sunday's softball game; I know that my dream man Deangelo will be there. Everybody calls him Pandillero; not me though.

Deangelo's a pecan shade of brown, light brown eyes, dark long curly hair that he keeps braided in some crazy way. He has a smile that makes your insides melt; six four, he about two hundred twenty pounds. His body ripped in all the right places. Something about him said stay away but the attraction I feel from him was like water rolling downhill into a drain.

I know he's pretty high on the list when it comes to the drug game; shit, he at the top of the damn thing. He only eighteen but has the flyest gear, stays in the hottest whips and has every girl in the hood wantin' to be on his team. I know he ain't checking for me, shit, I'm four years younger than him but I know he will be and sooner than what he thinks.

Sunday game is jammed packed; everybody is here, even the red Bomb Pop truck showed up; Donnie's the man. Usually he sits on Ninth Street by the mailroom building across from the townhouses. On game days, Donnie pulls that truck right up on Seventh Street across from our building—Fourteen Eighteen. The line's usually long as hell but you can still see the game so it doesn't matter.

Even though we're in walking distance of Busch Stadium, we have our own games. They're way better than anything we can experience down at that lame ass stadium. Everybody brings out their grills, music and if you wanted anything, you can get it. Everybody looks out for everybody and no matter how much drama there is, we all take care of each other.

After I quickly changed into my biking shorts with the lime green stripe down the side, I tied my hot pink shirt into my black slip, pulling it to the back. I put on my fresh white Princess Reeboks and was running down the hall. I can't wait on that raggedy ass elevator, plus, Deion just got shot on it a couple weeks ago.

I ran down the steps careful not to slip on the gallons of water Ms. Phillips poured down them earlier today. We could smell the bleach and hint of pine-sol from in the house. She worked us this morning but no matter what she wanted, we always too happy to make it happen.

As soon as I made it out the doors I'm damn near popped in the head with a tennis ball, "Ray-Ray you better stop playing and watch where you throwing that ball!" I wanted to go over and smack his ass with the court stick lying on the ground. He always messing with me and I don't have time right now to deal with his simple ass. I'm trying to get to the game before the next one started.

I had to miss the first one 'cause my mom's told me I couldn't go outside 'til she came back. But as soon as I heard that little red car take off down Seventh Street, I flew out the house. Hell, I'll hear her before she pass back over Cass. I already know if she makes it back before I do everybody will let me know.

Like I said, the hood looks out for the hood. They all know I'm supposed to be in the house. They also know nothin' will happen to me so they let me be out without telling my moms. Most of the time anyway, that's unless I'm out fighting or something stupid. Then they'll make sure they tell her what's going on with me.

I'm on a mission though; I wanted to see my future and I'm too clean not to make that happen. My girls, Nova and Nina, we met with our click in the parking lot like we usually do. We sat around and waited on the old head game to finish. We already know the next game is going to be the old school versus the new school.

Then I see him, ol' Deangelo pulled right up front and center with all eyes on him and his all-white Eddie Bauer Expedition. The sun beaming off those twenty-four inch rims, the trunk was banging that new Mr. Big track hard. Errbody knew it was time to make their way down to the field 'cause the game was almost ready to start. Me and my girls were having too much fun just standin' around laughing and then I feel somebody bump into me. "What's up T? Now I know I don't see Kathy's car so why you down here, shouldn't you be up on that porch?"

I turned around and oh yes, Deangelo standing right in front of me taking his shirt off. I can still see his body as he tries to adjust his wife beater. His smell...got damn his scent always fucks up my mind making me forget everything I've ever known.

"Why, you gone tell on me?" He licked his lip and smiled; I know he fucking with me but got damn!

"As soon as Kathy pull up, so you better hope I'm out

on the field when she do."

"Yeah, right!"

"Okay, we'll see," he said with a straight face.

"Shouldn't you be getting ready? Why you all over here messing with me anyway?" I wanted to run my hand down his stomach just to feel what all that was about, I felt everybody looking at us and decided to just look away.

"You scared now huh T?" I wanted to tell him, hell yeah! From touching you, that's about it. Instead I said, "I don't care, tell her. Ms. Phillips will cover for me. Now what?"

I sat back on the car and he sat right beside me, "T, I already know Sparkle beefin' with Kim and ya'll only waiting over here to fight after the game. So if you stay down here, I'm telling Kathy on yo' ass." I can't believe he doing this to me, how the hell he know all that anyway? He know I'm not about to fight anybody anyway, that's unless somebody hit me, but still. I don't have anything to do with that so why he not minding his business and letting me mind mine?

"I'm not in that so why you worried about it?"

"'Cause you have a game what, next weekend? How you gone look if you all beat up?"

"Really? So I told you I wasn't in that but you already know that I'm gonna get beat up?"

"T, stop playing with me; I gotta go but if I see some drama over here you betta believe I'm tellin' Kathy on yo' ass. If I'm not on the field I'm gone put yo' ass up on that porch myself, so make the right choice T."

He didn't let me say anything; he walked away like he was my damn daddy or something. I should've told him to kick rocks and mind his own. Oh well, I guess I'll head over and get a seat on the bleachers. My girls have already left and found us a row, so I joined them.

That game was too exciting; new school kicked they butts today. I can't wait for them to play Murphy Blair next time. We start to walk back to the building when Sparkle and her lil click come walking around the side. Kim was already out front makin' her way to her and the rest of my girls were following behind. We all stood around while they argued for a second, then out of nowhere, I feel somebody grab my arm and start pulling me away. I was prayin' that it wasn't my momma. I didn't even want to look to see who it was.

"I told you to make the right choice T; now you have to make me drag yo' ass upstairs."

"Deangelo, I'm not doing anything but standing there. What's wrong with you?" He didn't say anything until we made it to the elevator.

"T, if you never remember anything that I ever tell you in your whole life, remember this, if you know better, you do better. You hear me?"

"Yeah," I said that so dry he had to repeat it again, as soon as we made it to my door he said,

"Now you hear that?" I was too shocked; it sounded like they were shooting.

"How you know that was gone happen?"

"T, did you hear what I just told you? T, stay outta trouble and stay in the house 'til Kathy gets back." He ran back down the hall and headed down the steps.

As soon as I made it in the house, I went to the porch; people were errwhere. I was glad my sister and brother were gone with Momma. I looked down and I could see somebody lying on the side of the building. I see Deangelo truck drive down backwards in the parking lot. He nodded at me as he jumped in the backseat and the truck pulled off. About two hours later, everything was right back to the usual and errbody was outside like nothing had happened.

I found out that Marcus was shot in the leg. He jumped into the fight to help his sister Sparkle then tried to shoot Kim. Somebody took the gun from him and shot his ass. I was too happy that Deangelo did what he did 'cause I could've been the one shot. He was sho' right; I wouldn't have been playing in a game no time soon.

After that, I was startin' to feel like Deangelo was shadowing me or something. Every time I turned around he was off in the distance. It didn't bother me one bit but it did teach me who my real friends was. Seem like the majority of them stopped hanging with me. They didn't want Deangelo telling us what to do, where to go, or making comments about what we wore. I didn't mind 'cause it kept me in his presence so I was good. To hell with what they was talking about; I had a bunch of close calls though without my girls around.

I was too happy that Deangelo picked me up walkin' down Seventh Street after I left the mall shopping. These ho's from the O'Fallon Place were on my ass. I knew they were trying to jump me. All I kept thinkin' was once I pass over Cole they won't dare step foot on our soil so let me make it. I can hear them behind me talking mad shit. I have a bunch of stuff in my bags and I know I'm not about to go back home and tell Momma I let these ho's take it from me.

Then I see Deangelo pull up along the side of me. I thought he was going to keep going but he pulled over and talked to one of the girls behind me. I didn't even bother to look back; I just kept stepping, he pulled ahead of me and got out. Once he went around to the passenger door, I knew he wanted me to get in; I walked over.

"T, why you down here by yoself? You know they was about to put it on you, don't you?" He started to laugh then took my bags and put them in the back.

"Yeah whatever; dey wasn't goin' have an easy time if dey tried. I was goin' home with somethin' to show my momma, either these bags or all black and blue." I'd rather get my ass beat down by all those ho's. At least I'd get two, maybe even three; either way, my momma wasn't gone get me. He laughed even harder like I was a punk or something.

"Whatchu doin' in the morning?"

"Skating at the Center why?"

"Good, after skating come upstairs." Deangelo dropped me off in Thirteen Fifteen parking lot then he headed off 'round the circle. I walked my happy ass into the building and in run Pie; she so damn nosey.

"Girl, Pandillero bought all dat fo' you?" I just looked at her. This trick hasn't talked to me since she was kicked off the basketball team. Now she all in my face.

"No!" I changed my mind about waiting on the elevator so I headed up the steps then I hear her say, "Yes he did." I just kept it moving; pie face bitch need to mind her business.

The next day I go to the Center for skating and had a ball, I see Deangelo come in and wave me over. "You ready T?" I don't know what he want so I turn in my skates and head upstairs. The smell that came out the boxing room had me wanting to throw up; it was musty as hell in there.

It was only a couple other people in there. I see my cousin; she loved to box, I go over to see what she doing. Next thing I know, Rook come out the back yelling and screaming at me like I pissed him off or something. Deangelo thought it was too funny when I showed him my stance and how I threw a punch. I didn't know what I had just walked into. Every day before practice ended, Rook came or sent somebody to get me. I was so tired of seeing that ring I thought I was going to kill Deangelo for getting me in it. I had my chance to show him my moves a couple months later.

Deangelo was already there after my practice so he decided he'd spar with me. I know he was just letting me win but it still felt good to know a little something.

"Dang T, I didn't know you learned that much so soon."

"Yeah man, Treasure keeps it up and she'll be in the ring in no time."

"Rook, you crazy. She's not getting into nobody match man."

"Why not? She got the skills Pandillero; what, you don't think she can hold her own?"

I sat back trying to focus on my rhythm on the speed bag, watching them continue to go back and forth about me like I wasn't here.

"Well, I hate to breakup this argument you two are havin' but, I really don't want to get in the ring with anyone. This fun and all but I don't want my face all jacked up." They both started to laugh then Rook threw his hand at me and walked away.

"Hey Treasure, I haven't seen you in a long time; how you doing baby?"

"I'm all right Mrs. Joseph. How are you doing?" I loved Deangelo mother. Whenever she came down she always give me money and I know this time will be no different.

"Where you coming from all sweaty?"

"I had practice then I had a little sparrin' match in the ring, that's all."

"What? You too pretty to be fighting, who Rook have you over there fighting so I can go break my foot off in his ass."

"It wasn't a real match Mrs. Joseph. I sparred with Deangelo, that's all."

"Child, move. Let me head over here 'cause I know good got damn well I need to go kick both they asses. Rook having you spar with Deangelo and Deangelo actually doing it..." I couldn't get a word out after that; she started moving right past me toward the Center. Once she calmed down, she came back over to our building and gave me some money so I was good.

I spent a ton of time in the Center. I hated that I wouldn't be able to participate anymore 'cause we was movin' to the county. The closer the day came, the more time I stayed over there doing whatever I could to forget that I would miss the place.

Deangelo thought that I was being over dramatic about not being able to live in the hood anymore. He said the hood was no place to live; it's just a place to be until something better come along. It was all that I knew and no matter what he said, I was going to miss it and all the people that lived in it.

2 DEANGELO

"Man, why we have to drive all the way over here on the North to see some wack ass girls' basketball game? This shit better be good; I mean I'm down for my hood and all but for a girl's game? Hell, just last year they didn't win one damn game. Now you make it seem like they the Bulls are something," Bateador said as he counted another stack of hundred dollar bills from out of the bag resting on the floor of the car.

"Man, stop whining. You already know why we going. So do yoself a fava and finish up with the count so we can be in and out of here and make it. We already late." I know I shouldn't have waited 'til the last minute but my connect is only in town for a minute. I have to take care of this, and then I'm good.

This saved me the dough on having some dumbass runner take it out to LA for me anyway. All that I can think about is seein' this game. It's the championship game and if my girl does what I know she can, then they got this one in the bag. I pull up in the parking lot of the diner at Natural Bridge and Goodfellow while Bateador get out.

My connect see us from inside so he hit the horn on the truck and unlock the doors so Bateador can put the bag inside. As Bateador walks back to the car, I hear the horn again on the truck then the doors lock. I back out and try to make it to the game before it gets too late.

When I pull up, I see Wohl Center is packed. Damn, I need to park but I can hear the game already started. I pull up in the front and jump out. "Ay Bateador, park the car. You don't wanna see the game anyway right?"

"Yeah right. Think you slick nigga; she still gone be there. You act like she jumpin' on a flight when the game over or something." Bateador get out and shake his head laughing at me but I don't care what he thinks. I know she want me to be here. Besides, I go to all her games even if she doesn't know when I'm there or not. Damn! They down by one, should I let her see me or should I wait 'til after the game?

I don't want to distract her but then again maybe she'll play a little harder if she knows I'm here? Hell with it, I'm gone show her love. I know she gone do what she have to do; it can't hurt for her to know a nigga here. "All right T, let's take this one back to the hood baby!" She looked up and gave me a smile but quickly turned away.

"No you not Pandillero! I know you not distracting my players are you! And I know you didn't drag yo' smitten ass all da way across town to see yo' auntie. So that leaves one person that would get you over here!"

"Ha-ha; what's up auntie how you doing? I heard ya'll had a game over here. I was on this side of town so I stopped by to see what ya'll was up to."

My aunt Laura, she always gives me a hard time. She knows T's not like them other chickens I'm plucking so she had to mess with me. It's funny though; everybody seemed to guard her for the same reason. I can't knock 'em though 'cause I do the same thing. She has that way about her. Everybody that come into contact with her want only the best for her and will push anybody away that they fell wasn't on their game.

"Yeah, you told me that at the last game; you just so happen to be on that side of town too. You ain't fooling nobody nephew; I know you here to see Treasure. But let me tell you this, if you think for one second that I'm gone fall back and let you—" BARRRRR.

Good, the game back on and I don't have to hear her

mouth; I already know what she gone say anyway. 'She too young for you, she not like the girls from the hood, she got great things in her future'. Hell, I know that already. Just let me enjoy the moment, I know when my time comes she'll be mine, even if it is ten, twenty years from now.

"Damn, that game was off the chain! I hate we missed the beginning; they went hard as hell. Yo, girl got skills; did you see how she shook both dey guards and the center for the layup? Damn and her three game is off da chain. They tried dey best to shut her down but she was on fire." Bateador sounded like he just watched a professional game and had to hit me with the highlights. "Ay you ready? I just got a call I need to pick up my whip and head to the drop," Bateador said as he checked his pager. "Yeah man, just give me a second so I can see how they doing."

It was a close game and I know what it feel like to lose by one point. I could see as they went to the locker room that they were hurt. "Yeah man, whatever. Tell Treasure and nem I said what's up," Bateador said as he walked out to the car. I headed to the locker room and before I could tell somebody to go in and get T, I see Laura coming my way.

"Yeah nephew, you still on this side of town huh? Don't play with me lil boy. You may be big man this and top dog that but I'll call Kathy if I have too, don't get it twisted!" I had to laugh 'cause if she wasn't my aunt I would tell her to mind her damn business and stay the hell out of mine. I'm gone give her a pass. Besides, the last thing I want her to do is call Kathy. I know if she does it'll be at least twenty years before I even see T again.

Don't get me wrong, I'm not physically scared of Kathy, that's T's mom. After working for her awhile back for SLATE and seeing her no nonsense attitude, I know she doesn't play. Plus, I don't want T to get in trouble so I'm gone play nice with my aunt for now. She knows not to come at me like that on any of my business and I know it's only for T that she is.

"Naw Auntie, don't be like that. I just wanted to talk to T for a minute, that's all. I already know and it's not like that.

You know I wouldn't do anything like that Auntie!" I smile and let my charisma work its magic.

"All right nephew, I know, but I have to look out for my baby just like I would for you," Laura said as she walked into the locker room. I can hear her telling them that they still have next year and to change so they can get in the van.

I stopped Tracy, one of her teammates and told her to tell T to come holla at me. "Ummm, why you wanna holla at hu? I'm right herrre; I can holla at chu!" she said as she played with a long string of gum coming out her mouth. This lil girl here fast as hell. The way she smiling in my face, I know the niggas in the hood telling the truth about her.

"Naw, I'm good; just tell T to come holla at me." I pulled out a roll of money and gave her five dollars, "Here and hurry up and tell her." After she finished given me the 'let's fuck' face and tryin' to count my money. I shoved it back in my pocket and threw her a wink just so she could get the hell out my face and do what I said. Sure enough, I hear her telling errbody in nat mufucka, "Treasure, Pandillero at the door. He said he wanted to holla-at-cha!" Errbody in there laughing and makin' all kinds of noise. I shoulda told that dumbass lil girl to only tell T, but I guess you can't teach a rat common sense in one conversation.

"Ay T, good game. I know you not down about it," I told her as she walked out the locker room. I put my arm around her shoulder. "Naw, not down, just pissed. All these clowns in here think it's funny. They have next year; I don't. We live all the way in no man's land now; they don't even have a team," she said. I could tell she was hurt but I was determined to cheer her up.

"So you wanna get something to eat? You know, you don't have to ride back in that raggedy ass Center van." Whatever I had to say to get her to chill with me for a minute I was going to say. "Naw, I have to shower and get some of this funk off me. I don't wanna have that nice car of yours smelling 'cause of me," she said as she continued to look down. It kinda pissed me off that she hadn't looked up one time at me since we've been standin' here.

"Don't worry about it. I can take you to the hood and wait 'til you get ready or I can take you to my crib. You can change there." Before I can say anything else, she looked up at me and turned her head to the side with the sexiest smile ever. "Nice try Mr. Man, I think I'll have to pass! I'm stayin' down my aunt house tonight, so when I get changed we can get something to eat then. Since I know you though, by the time all that happens you'll be onto the next one. You know you're a busy man Mr. Deangelo. I don't want to hold you up."

Before she could look away, I pulled her face up and stared her in her eyes. "If I recall, I asked you if you wanted to get something to eat and said I would wait until you changed. So therefore, you won't be holding me up. Besides, last time I checked, I made my own hours and reported to myself so you don't have to worry about that now do you?"

I can see in her eyes she wanted to say yes but I know she's worried about being with me. A small part of me wanted her to be afraid of me so that she wouldn't get attached. And there was another part of me that didn't want her to be afraid of me.

That's what turned me on about T. She's not like the rest of the chicks I come across. I can bag 'em and tag 'em without even sayin' a word. Hell, all they see is the nice whips, fresh gear, that I have money and I'm good looking. Not T though, she don't care about all that. She knows what she wants.

All the lame ass niggas from the hood all know that when it came down to it, she not giving it up. So they move on, which is the best thing they can do. 'Cause they all know that I lay claim to her and if I think any nigga's a threat they'll be dealt with to the fullest without a doubt. "All right Treasure, let's go to the van so we can get back," Tony, her coach said as she walked past me and gave me the 'I'm watching you stare.'

"Well, I guess I'll call you from Donna house when I get changed," T said as Laura grabbed her by the arm walking her down the hall. "All right, but why you not calling me from yo' aunt house?" I had to ask; I was in hot pursuit behind them. "Gee Gee don't have a phone so I can go down Donna house and use hers," she said as they made it to the van. "Ay wait a minute."

I waved over Bateador and walked towards him. The last thing I need is for Donna feigning ass to have my number anyway. "Ay, give me yo' cell." He pulled it out. I took it and walked back over to T. "Do me a favor; take this. Call me when you ready," I told her and gave her the phone. I can hear Bateador mumbling something as I watch her get into the van.

"Damn man, how you just give Treasure my phone like that? What my girl's gone think when they call and I don't have my phone," Bateador said as we headed to the car. "Damn nigga, stop crying and drive. You know damn well T won't answer the damn thing. If she does, so what. Fuck them dusty bitches you fuck wit' anyway." We both laugh as we pull off.

3 TREASURE

All right, here we go. Let's go out here and take this one back to the house. I'm tryin' my best to stay focused but I can't stop checkin' to see if my family made it yet. I told my momma and my daddy what time the game started, I'm hoping at least my daddy will show up. All right, it's only second quarter, they still have time. We in the lead by ten so no pressure. These chicks better than what I thought.

Halftime you would think my team would be focused on the game. They eatin' nachos and shit in the stands talkin' to some dirty ass niggas. Here I am sitting on the bench waiting on my people to show up; I can't believe no one is here yet. I can't ever get any support from them! Third quarter, how the hell we fall behind that quick? These dumbass broads not even paying attention. Fuck it! I'm running this bitch fourth quarter.

Damn, they straight played me; nobody showed up. It's all good; we down by three anyway but not for long. Yes! My three-pointer just sent the game into overtime. "All right T, let's take this one back to the hood baby!" Deangelo said, I looked up and saw him on the sideline. I just smiled and turned back around, Coach talking, these ho's smiling in the stands. Damn, he fine as hell. It doesn't get any better than that. I'm glad he came. I was about to really be mad if nobody showed up.

All right, we neck and neck. This the second overtime so if we can hold the ball we'll be all right. That last layup, I was cutting it close. That big bitch of a center damn near took my head off as I went in on her ass. FUCK! This dumb bitch Sherry just turned over the ball and they scored. I guess this was the way I was supposed to go out. I'm pissed; I damn near ran to the locker room so I can put on my warm-ups and get in the van. I'm about ten seconds or a smart look away from demolishing one of these ho's.

"Treasure, Pandillero at the door. He said he wanted to holla-at-cha!" I hear Tracy say as she walking in with this stupid ass look on her face. Before I walk past her, I move in close to her. "You remember I punched you in the nose and you bled on my new shoes so I punched yo' punk ass the next day for that? Keep on playing with me and you gone get punched again bitch!" I threw my shoulder into her as I walked away heading for the door. I know she must've done something behind my back 'cause they all started laughin'. It doesn't matter though; I bet she won't do it in my face.

'Damn, look at him—tall, nice body, exquisite face. This man knows he the shit and his gear always toppa da line.' That was all I could think once his arm went around my shoulder. I hate being this close to him; his scent alone sends waves over my skin. He made my body want to do things that I don't have time for right now. I already know if we did those things, he would be long gone from coming out to support me.

Man, what make him think I can be naked in the same house with him? I don't even know if I can control myself in a situation like that. I told him no but he surprised the hell outta me and gave me a phone to call him on. I guess he's serious about getting something to eat after all. Oh well, I'll call him when I'm ready I guess. I just want to get back so I can get out this uniform.

I hurried up and changed; then it hit me how much I hate waitin' on people. This shit for the birds. I'd rather do what I want instead of waitin' on somebody. I figured I'd walk around until he decides to call me. I walk past Fourteen

Nineteen headed down the hill. What the fuck? I called this nigga three times no answer but I see him leaned up against a car in the circle with Paula pissy ass.

Okay! I started backpedaling just to make sure he doesn't see me and headed back to Fourteen Thirty-Four before he can. Damn, here go Corey snitching ass. I know he finna go back and tell Deangelo he saw me so I might as well say something.

"Hey Corey how you doing?"

"I'm chillin' Treasure; what's up witchu?"

"Nothing much, about to head home that's all."

"You seen Pandillero Treasure? I think he was looking for you."

"Naw I haven't but can you do me a favor? Can you give this back to him? I think it might be yours anyway. I saw you give it to him earlier. You had a couple calls, here you go."

"Ay, before you go, let me see if I can find Pandillero first. Like I said, I know he was looking for you."

"No you didn't, you said you think he was!" Before he can look away, I turn and start walking faster away towards Fourteen Thirty-Four. Once I was in, I went right out the backdoor so I can jump on the first Thirty Four West Florissant bus heading to my house.

I know I have to get on the bus fast. I can see it coming up the street; hurry up. I know Corey had to find Deangelo by now. I need to get the hell from down here before he come looking for me. Fuck, I can hear a car beatin' all the way down the street and my gut's telling me that it's Deangelo. Good, the bus here, all I have to do is make it on and I'm out. The dumbass bus driver finally decides to pullover.

I can see Deangelo sitting at the light; I made sure I looked him dead in the face as I hopped my ass right on the bus. Shit, why can't this bus make one stop? Good, we made it through the light at Grand and Florissant. "What the hell are you doin' man?" I hear the bus driver yell and blow the horn. Everybody being nosey trying to see what he talkin' 'bout. I glance out the window to see if I can see anything,

"What the fuck?" I covered my mouth not realizing that I let it come out. All I can do is drop my head as I hear the driver open the door.

"Ay Big Dog, sorry 'bout that." "What's up man? You couldn't wait to get on at the next stop?" I look up slowly. I see Deangelo look dead at me. Why does he like humiliating me like this? I knew that when I saw Corey truck stopped on the side of the bus he wasn't far behind. "Naw, I was actually trying to get somebody off the bus real quick. Here take this for your trouble. I see who I'm looking for coming now," he said as he gave the driver what looked like two hundred dollars.

All I can do is get up and off. By the looks of the people on the bus, they don't want to sit around and wait while I try to influence him to let me go home. After we get off the bus, I can see Corey smile as he pulls off allowing the long train of cars behind him to go on. Deangelo opened the door with a smile on his face, closed it and jumped in on the other side then drove off.

"What's up T? I thought you was gone call me when you was ready?" he said leaning over toward me looking fine as hell. "I did, three times! Guess you were too busy," I said as we stopped at the light. He tapped me on my shoulder, "I told you I wasn't busy. What part of that you don't understand? I saw that you called, so I was waiting on you to come down. I don't ever answer a call from that number. Good thing Donna told me she saw you head to the bus stop now ain't it?" he said then headed on through the light.

"That's dumb. Why give me the phone if you knew you wouldn't answer?"

"Every time you called I was in the circle waiting to see you come out the building but you never did. Then Bateador told me you gave him the phone and was headed home. I thought you said you were staying down in the hood tonight anyway?"

"Yeah okay, tell me anything. I decided to go home 'cause I suddenly felt sick when I came outside." I leaned my head back against the headrest. We sat quiet for a minute then

I see that he passed right by Chambers and West Florissant. "Where are you taking me now? You know you passed my house!" I'm too tired to even look over at him. "Don't act like that T; that ain't even for us. We're going to get something to eat. I know you hungry. I can hear your stomach all the way over here." I closed my eyes and tried not to laugh.

After a power nap, I hear him talking on the phone so I shifted in the seat so that he knew I was awake. "That game must've worn you out T. You den slobbed all over a brother seat." I shook my head and smiled 'cause I know he lying but why waste the time going back and forth with him? "You ready to eat?" "Yeah, where are we?" Looked like the middle of nowhere; I know we had to be pretty far out. "We at my little hideaway joint out here in Truesdale." "Did we have to come all the way out here to eat?" I asked as we walked toward the restaurant.

"We not as far as you think T. Besides, if you wanted to go on the other side of the world to eat, you know if you ask I'll make it happen for you," he said as he put his arm around my shoulder. Damn, he smells good. Why do I let him do me like this? Hell, I'm here now. I might as well enjoy it for what it is.

4 MYZPHYT

"What's good Myzphyt? You chillin' tonight?"

"Yeah Pandillero. Whatchu up to? See you in na hood tonight. What bring you down dis way?"

"Shit, chillin.' Had to come through see what this lil get together was all about." I stood by talking with Pandillero, and then I see Treasure make her way to the dance floor.

"Look at T, about to get herself in trouble out there doing all that."

"Damn nigga, I ain't know you had Treasure on lock like dat."

"Get that shit outta here. She ain't on lock and damn sure not by me nigga. You see how she throwing that Coke bottle around? She knows these cats about to be all over her."

"Who you tellin', she look good as hell out derrre. Look at that nigga Chucky; he trying his best to play it off and dance wit' her."

We both sat back and laughed at his failed attempts. I can tell by the look on his face that he gettin' more and more pissed that Treasure not having it. I see Chucky grab her waist and Treasure pulled back away from him still moving with the beat. The more she floated around making it happen, the more Chucky followed trying to get her back.

I couldn't hear what was being said but the look on Chucky face told me he was going in. Then I see him grab her again so I stand up off the wall to make my way over. I fell Pandillero grab my shoulder. "Chill out youngin." I know he watching. I can't believe he just lettin' it happen.

I turn back around and continue to watch as Chucky gettin' closer and closer to Treasure. She stopped dancing, said something to him and tried to walk away. Then I see Chucky grab her arm again while he drawin' back to hit her. Bateador came out of nowhere and caught that nigga with three hits sending him falling back into the crowd of people behind them.

I see Treasure push through the crowd towards the door, I see Debbie stop her. "Come walk wit' me for a minute youngin." Pandillero look like he wasn't bothered one bit about what just happened. One minute he sound like Treasure his girl and now he act like he can give a fuck less about what just happened. We make our way down the stairs all the way to the extra steps in the basement to the old boiler room.

I never been in this part of the building before, growing up they use to tell us this where Candyman lived. I can hear Chucky off in the distance, "Man fuck you nigga! Fight me heads up; I bet I whoop yo' ass nigga!" He kept talkin' shit as we walk down into the room. It's nothing but old heads standing around like I'm walking in on a secret meeting or some shit.

They all just laughing and taunting Chucky wit' shit like, "Man, Bateador would beat da shit outchu boy." "Don't chu know he took home silver?" "Why da hell you think they call him Bateador? It damn sure ain't 'cause of no hood shit." "I got six thousand on Bateador. Who want to take the bet?" They all continued putting in their two cents on how it will turn out.

Pandillero didn't say a thing 'til he walked over closer in the room. "So Chucky, you think you wanna warm up before you whoop Bateador ass?" They all laughed harder; Money Man was on the ground laughing. "Man, fuck ya'll niggas. I'll fight anyone of ya'll bitch asses! Ya'll niggas got me fucked up!" They all laughed again. I see Pandillero take off his shit and hand it to Bateador. "Nigga can't fight so yo' bitch ass gone shoot me nigga?" Chucky said.

"Nigga, I'm not gone shoot yo' punk ass, but this is gone be the fight for yo' life. Hell, if you beat me or knock me out you can live. If not, then this is it for yo' ass now ain't it? So you betta fight, 'cause yo' life depend on it nigga." Pandillero took his strap and gave it to Bateador while they all laughed some more.

"Man, ain't nobody gotta shoot yo' young ass nigga," Rook said, another old head from back in the day who used to be a professional boxer.

"See, ya'll young niggas should've taken advantage of all da opportunities dat da hood had for ya'll. See, I know you can't fuck wit' any nigga in here wit' throwing nem hands, damn sho' not Bateador. I know fosho you can't fuck wit' Pandillero and I guess yo' young ass about to find that out real soon now ain't chu?" They all laughed more at the thought of what was about to take place.

"So, let me ask you something. What made you wanna hit her?"

"Who nigga? What the fuck iz you talkin' about?"

"Who" Pandillero said, *Whop, Whop, Whop, Whop,* he sent four to his ass and moved back before he had a chance to figure out what happened. Chucky was dazed but he regrouped quick; this time he looked ready.

"Dhat bitch Tre..." *Whop, Whop.* He couldn't even get her name out before Pandillero sent two more to his grill.

"So, I guess you gone make this as hard on you as possible huh?" Pandillero said as he danced out of Chucky attempt to grab hold of him. "Naw, nigga, thought chu said you wanted to throw hands?" Lil C said. I didn't know what to think. With the last two shots Pandillero hit Chucky wit', I can see his mouth start to bleed but he wiped it off and was back talking shit.

The two of them went on with Chucky not being able to land one hit before Pandillero decided to put it on him. He hit Chucky with so many combinations it was like he was moving in fast forward. I can barely see the hits but I can damn sho' hear 'em and I know that shit hurt. Pandillero could've knocked him out and there's nothin' Chucky can do to stop the shit from happening.

I mean he letting his ass have it, watching this like watching Ali fight a lil nigga off the street. I mean a lil nigga, small person, dwarf or whatever they called. The look on Pandillero face said he wanted to punish that nigga though. He wants to do as much damage as he can before this nigga met his doom.

Chucky can barely stand up; his face bloody and starting to swell like his eye already has. "Watch this," Pandillero said. He hit Chucky so hard; I swear I heard the bones in Chucky sternum explode as he fell to the ground gasping for air. I see spatters of blood come from his mouth as Pandillero walked over to Bateador and started putting his shit back on. Errbody laughing and making comments about what happened and how stupid Chucky is. I watch Pandillero walk over next to Chucky.

He leaned down and said, "I hope now you know in the next life not to fuck with another man's Treasure!" He walk toward the door, "Ay youngin, you ready to get back to the party?" As we headed out the basement, I hear a muffled sound that I know was the last of Chucky. I didn't know Pandillero could throw his shit the way I just saw him. I figured that's why he had Bateador around. We chilled out at the party a little bit longer, then he says he out. I sat back and thought about everything that had happened 'til the party ended.

* * *

"Excuse me Treasure; Debby wanted me to tell you that she was waitin' downstairs on you." Damn, this girl fine as hell! All this time that I've known her the first thing I have to say is that somebody else waiting on her? Damn! "All right, thanks," she said as she walked toward the elevator. Hell, fuck it; they just gone have to wait. I'm going over here with her. They can wait 'til I get back.

"Hold the elevator!" I yell out so she can wait up on me. Good, she still here. "Now you know this elevator take forever," she said then giggled and looked away. "Yeah I know but I was actually hoping I could ride down witchu so I can get a chance to rap witchu for a second," I said waiting for her to respond but she didn't say anything.

She turned and looked at me with her eyes squinted as if she was trying to read my lips. Damn, her eyelashes are long as hell, the top and bottom. Her eyes are deep, like she can see through my soul and pull out every corrupt thing that I have within me. Good, the elevator door opened, but damn, any other time dis bitch is jammed packed. Now it's empty as a mothafucka.

"So you said you wanted to rap, so rap!" she said as she stared at me like I was getting on her nerve. "Damn ma, I know you not as mean as dey say you are but you sho' put a nigga on na spot." I smirked and waited on her to respond, she didn't again. "I was actually wondering what was up witchu and my peoples?" I know this will get her to say something back. "Who Debby? Nothing—"

"Naw, not Debby Ma, JT," I quickly stopped her. "I saw you kicking it wit' him the other day but I thought you was wit' my fam Pandillero on the low. So I wanted to know what's up."

She looked at me, gave me the most seductive smile I've ever witnessed. She pulled her lip in on the side using her tongue then tilted her head and took in a deep breath. "So you wanna rap wit' me about not one, but two other men? You know the last time I checked all that was my business and I don't get in yo' business so why would you be in mine?"

Then she let out a laugh that was so intoxicating that all I can do is laugh wit' her and shake my head. If I can hold on to this moment, I would. I'm kinda mad that Fourteen Thirty-Four is only a seven-story. If it was a twelve-story like New Jack City, I would've pushed every damn button on nis mug.

As the doors opened, she stepped out and I couldn't control myself so I reached out and grabbed her wrist. "Ay hold up, I know I shouldn't be in yo' business but I don't wanna be stepping on any toes 'cause I wanna get to know you. I mean, it's kinda fucked up that we been knowing each other this long and never had a conversation 'til now.

I know all dese niggas down here be sweatin' you and I really don't give a damn about dem. I know that even if you ain't fuckin' wit' JT, it's kinda the word in da hood dat Pandillero den cut some niggas short for trying to holla at chu. So I figured it must be 'cause you with him, are you was wit' him when he did them niggas in. That's my fam and all so I want to know what's up before I try to come at chu."

She smiled then pulled her arm away; before she can say anything, I hear Debby yell her big ass mouth in the door asking her to come on. "Well, I don't know anything about his business or what he does. I've known him just as long as I've known you. I think we haven't had a conversation 'cause I remember I had to kick yo' cousin ass on the side of Fourteen Eighteen. Ya'll tried to jump me and my brother on our way to school back in the day.

I'm not wit' JT; I been knowing him since I went to his son birthday party when ney lived in our building. He fun to hang out wit' and he never tried anything besides a hug here and there. JT is way too old for me and if my momma found out she would kick his ass. So I hope I told you enough of my business. You have a good night. It was nice rapping witchu," she said, then smiled and started to walk away.

"Well hold up. If it ain't too much to ask, let me walk wit' ya'll over there." I wasn't about to let her get away. I had to get another minute of her time. I know I have shit to do but fuck that it can wait 'til I get back. "How you know where we going?" she said as I opened the door for her. "Man, dis da hood. I know what's popping and what ain't." "So Debby told you huh?"

She stopped and looked me in the eyes. I felt like I was on trial. All I wanted to do was tell the truth, the whole truth and nothing but the truth. "Yeah, she told me." We both laughed as we walked out the door. After we made it to Fourteen Fifteen, I decided that the conversation couldn't just end there. I had to make sure that everything was good up at the party.

I still remember what happened with dat nigga Chucky a couple months back. I know I'm not about to let shit like that happen again. It was like half the hood was dere, I let her breathe and make her rounds. I stood back and watched her from across da room.

She was different. All the rest of dese hood stars was on the prowl for dey next baby daddy. She seemed like she was bored and if I'm not mistakin' like she looking for somebody. Then I knew what it was; I see her walk out to the porch and sure enough, out the side of my eye, Pandillero followed out a couple seconds later.

Damn, this nigga be popping up errwhere. I never paid attention but dey right, dat nigga ain't ever dat far away when Treasure in da hood. Hell, Debby said she was coming down when she left work, which is sexy as hell to me. She only a junior in high school but she worked downtown at the bank.

All dese ho's in da hood either turned tricks or sit back waiting on ney welfare check to come through, not her. She goes to school and work at the bank. I think she work at a fast food joint too. But hell, she still gets hella props from me.

Look at dis nigga smiling all in her face and shit. I know dis nigga doin' it in these streets; I know she ain't about that but what does she see in his old ass? I know he too old for her. Damn, they're looking at me. I smiled and threw a nod at 'em. Man, I'm trippin.' Let me chill out before I forget that nigga family and snatch up my girl on his ass. Now he wanna come over here smiling in my face.

"What's up Big Dog? I ain't know you were in the hood tonight," I said as this nigga came over looking like he wanted to lay a check down are something. "You know I'm always around. But what's good witchu though fam? I saw you walk over with Debby and T; you good?" I know dis nigga ain't trying to lay claim like that with me but I'm up for the challenge. "Yeah man, I was trying to see what's up wit' Treasure. She ain't given a nigga any play dough. I just wanna get to know her shit." Fuck it. I want dis nigga to see my hand so I can see his next move.

"Aw, that's what's up youngin. T cool man; I don't know if she gone fuck witchu like that. You know, all these lil niggas down here be trying to get at her. They realize she ain't fucking wit'em like that and dey start talkin' shit about her," he said as Treasure came back in.

Just like feigns to corner boys on the first of the month, you can see niggas tryin' to be the next in line to throw game at her. "Look at dat nigga LA; I can tell you what he saying from here. 'Ay Treasure, what's up? Can I take you to get a box of rice? Hold up, all dis money in my pocket. It may look like a lot but this really a twenty wrapped around forty ones.' Silly ass nigga there!"

We both laughed as he continued joanin' on err nigga that tried to holla. And sure enough, she ended up walking away in the end. "But look here youngin, I'm out! Make sure she get back to Gee Gee house safe and let me know if she holla at you are not. Like I said, I doubt it but give it yo' best shot cuz," he said, as he walked to the door. Before he could get out, I see Wyneisha and Karen dusty asses rapping with him then he put his arms around them and walked out the door.

I don't know if I'm a little buzzed or not but did this nigga just give me da green light on his girl or am I just trippin'? I had to laugh 'cause we fam but I know that nigga know better than that. Then he gone doubt my skills? Me? Naw, that nigga up to somethin' but it don't matter 'cause I know Treasure saw him walk out with them two dike bitches. Everybody in the hood know they do threesomes more than dey brush dey teeth.

But fuck dat nigga. About an hour later I see Treasure heading toward the door by herself. Debby then disappeared. Yeah, she my cousin but I know she a drunk who like to fuck. Plus, I seen her earlier wit' that dark skin nigga she been fucking wit' so she good. Damn, she gone. Let me shoot down the steps to meet up with her.

As I make it to the door, she not outside, I must've beat the elevator. I walk back in and hear people gettin' off but I don't see her. Where the hell she go that fast? This girl like a phantom. One minute she here, the next she nowhere to be found. I don't know. Fuck it. I'll see her again.

I start back toward the parking lot to head back to

Fourteen Thirty-Four then I hear, "All right youngin keep yo' head up." I know it's that nigga Pandillero. I look closer into his old school. This nigga got a straight muscle car for real, he rarely bring out his white seventy one Plymouth 'Cuda hardtop. Damn, that's a nice ass whip, that nigga keep it clean. Damn, derrre go Treasure right there.

She didn't look at me but I know it's her. She 'bout da only one that nigga would be closing the door for. Hell, if she let him, he probably put her in a booster seat and strap a helmet on her ass too. I laugh and tilt my head up at that nigga as he smiling pulling out of the parking lot.

"Damn, youngin, I asked you to do one thing and I clearly see you couldn't do that," he said as he turned up the radio and pulled off. Yeah, he won this round but the next one he can call it a wrap. All I can do is laugh my way back across the ball field. Yeah, dat nigga got me this time but oh boy he better know its game on!

5 TREASURE

Let me hurry up. Debby drunk ass been screaming for me for about ten minutes now. I hope she don't get too lifted tonight. I'm damn sure not up to tracking down somebody to help me carry her ass back home. Last time her drunk ass threw up in my cousin Navigator, it cost me fifty dollars to have the detailers clean that shit up. Then the next day this trick say she gone pay me back when she get her check. I still ain't seen that money and it's been almost two weeks. I wish Trey Loc was here. I hate that he went to that damn boy's home. We used to have so much fun together.

Now I'm hanging out with Debby it wouldn't be that bad if she didn't drink as much as she do. As I lock the door, I see her fine ass cousin coming towards me. This dude always been fine but now it's like he just morphed into this thug-like model. He has a sepia brown skin tone, about six feet, maybe one hundred sixty pounds of pure fuckin' thug passion.

One thing I'm not into is all the tattoos he has going on. Kind of remind me of Stacy. His hair's always freshly cut and lined just right. I doubt if he will ever be on Deangelo level in the game but he doin' his thing from what I hear.

Is he really about to say something to me? "Excuse me Treasure; Debby wanted me to tell you that she was waitin' downstairs on you." I'm not even going to make eye contact with him. I know he has those hazel eyes looking right at me just like Stacy ass. "All right, thanks," was all I could manage to say before trying to make a mad dash to the elevator.

Come on damn thing so I can go on about my business. "Hold the elevator!" Damn, I knew it wasn't going to be that easy to get out of this. Now here he comes again. I know what he wants but I'm really not in the mood to be nice tonight. I see him round the corner. "Now you know this elevator take forever." Okay, that's enough. Maybe he'll get the hint if I look off. "Yeah, I know but I was actually hopin..."

Really? All this time I been knowing him, now he wants to rap with me? He must really think I'm some damn fool. Shit, look at those eyes. I never really looked at him before, especially not directly in the eyes, but damn. I'm glad I haven't 'cause this something I can stare at all day long. I'm trying my best to keep up with the conversation but all I keep thinking is, 'Why does he waste his time slinging that bullshit on the streets? Why not take what he was blessed with and do something in modeling like Shane and Blane?'

I said something back to him then went back to thinking to myself. 'Hell, if he can't make it in the modeling field I'm pretty sure he can do something in porn.' Before I knew it, I burst out laughing. It made me laugh more that he thought I was laughing at whatever he was talking about.

I was weak by the time we made it off the elevator, I tried to part ways with him but he insisted on walking with us. Then he had to see what was going on at the party. I know his game so I chatted with him for a minute going over. Then before the door could close I made my way as far away from him as possible.

I know that ain't who I think it is with that bitch Cora sitting on his lap. I move further away and try to play it off but I can feel his eyes in the back of my head following me around the apartment. Hell, I know what he wants so why keep pretending? I head out to the porch and I don't have to wait long before I heard, "What's up T? Whatchu doing down here?"

I just looked at him and smiled. Damn he fine. "Nothing much, told Debby I would come over here with her so I did." Why do I want to lick his damn lips? They look soft as hell.

"Is that right? Why you got on that lil ass skirt? Does Kathy know you walking around the hood like that?"

"I don't know. You wanna call her and ask?"

"Hell naw!" he said as we both started to laugh.

"Whatchu got to hide T?" he said as he leaned into my side. Damn, why he always smell so fucking good? Every inch of my body wants to have that smell embedded into my pores.

"I need to be asking you that question Mr. Man. You the one made a beeline out here after me." I was waiting on his comeback.

"Shit T, you know me, back to you though. You said you came over here with Debby but you didn't mention that Myzphyt came with you too. I know you feel that nigga eyeing us right now." Instantly, we both turned our heads and looked over at Myzphyt and sure enough he was pressed up against the wall. Even in the dark, I can see those big hazel eyes reading our lips.

"That ain't nothing I have to hide; he walked over here wanting to know my busines—"

"Like what?" he said cutting me off.

"Like if I was witchu or JT 'cause he wanted to get to know me. I told him I wasn't wit' anyone and that I wasn't feelin' him like that."

"Look at you T, breaking hearts all ova the hood. But check this, whatchu doin' when you leave here?"

"Nothing. I'm leaving from down here soon as my sister gets off work. She's coming to get me to take me home. You know I have to go to school tomorrow," I said, as I smiled and bumped into his shoulder.

"What? I thought you had to be at the bank tomorrow for your first couple hours then after lunch you had to be at school?"

"Naw, they changed our blocks. This a new semester. Next semester I only go to one class in the morning then I work for the rest of the day. Can't wait for that!" I said as I smiled over at him.

"Hell T, it's seven now. You need to be heading home now so you can go to school in the morning. You know if Kathy find out you miss class she gone beat dat ass!" He laughed. I shook my head and laughed under my breath.

"My sister will be down at ten. I'll still have time to sleep, so I'm good."

"Well, do dis. Call yo' sister, tell her you got a ride and meet me downstairs when you ready. I'll take you home. That way, I know you'll get enough sleep for tomorrow."

"Naw, 'cause if I call her and can't find you I'm gone be up shit creek. And I would hate to have to get a ride from one of these vultures down here. The last thing I need is for them to know where I live."

"Come on T, have confidence in yo' boy, I'll be downstairs like I said. You have fun. I'll see you in a minute. Try not to hurt nobody T. And don't bend yo' ass ova!" He went back in before I could respond; he thinks he slick as hell.

Let me go back in here. Well damn, before I can make it to the door, here comes LA. He used to be cute then he lost his eye playing around with a gun trying to be tough and shot his self. Now he just a handicap corner boy who never know who's standing on his left side.

Damn, that was mean, but to hell with him. When we was younger, he made fun of me 'cause my bike had a banana seat with clickers. I know that's petty but I still remember, so let me make this quick 'cause I see he trying to pull out his money. Like I'm gone drop to my knees and bust his head for him just at the site of it.

It looks like I may never get out of here; maybe dey put something in the drinks to make them believe that I was here to fuck. Where da hell is Debby? Damn, I hate when she do this. All right, there she go. Look at Damon sneaky ass; this black bastard always trying to play Debby out.

I told her he tried to holla at me but I guess she was drunk and forgot 'cause she still been hugged up with him. Oh well, "Ay Debby, I'm heading out. I have school tomorrow." I tried to tell her but all she did was flicked her tongue out at me and bent over in nis nigga face. Hell, fuck it. Her cousin here.

Let him deal with her drunk ass; I'm out.

I made a stealth-like move to the door, damn near ran down the hall. I pushed for the elevator as I headed for the steps. I see Deangelo as I come out, he opens the door for me but for some reason is looking around, then he finally closes it. As he walks around I hear him say, "All right youngin keep yo' head up."

"Why you messing with him like that?" I was trying not to laugh; he came inches away from my face waiting.

"Why you running from him like that?" We both laughed 'cause I know he was trying to feel how hard I was breathing without me knowing.

"I wasn't running from him. I took the steps; that's all." He looked back over at me again.

"Yeah, okay T." He pulled out the parking lot. I heard him tease him even more.

"Deangelo, whatchu tell him?"

"Nothing, walk you back." I kinda felt bad for him 'cause in that moment I knew Deangelo had played him out.

He knew he was taking me home so why tell him to walk me back to Gee Gee house? I wonder what he would've done if Myzphyt would've been with me when I came out. Hell, I wonder what Myzphyt would've done when I walked to Deangelo? Either way, the outcome could've been uncomfortable for me.

He could be an evil person at times when it came to these fools down here. But to me, he'll always be my true love. Yeah them other ho's just fillers and I know he keep it wrapped tight and get tested on the regular. I'm not even worried about them passing shit to him.

The ride to my house we listened to the radio and had small conversations here and there. As he pulled into the driveway, I could tell something was on his mind I figured it wasn't in my lane, so I let it go. "Damn T, for real, can you do me one favor? That's all I'm asking is one favor."

What? This is not like him. Where is this coming from? He's never asked me for anything, especially not like this. "What is it?" He looked down trying to get the words formed that will help him get this favor completed.

"Yo' mom's not here right? I know I shouldn't be asking you dis but I need to hold you tonight." He slowly looked up to see my reaction; I don't know what to say.

"Look, if you want, I can wait on you to do whatchu have to do. Then we can head to my crib out here and I'll take you to school in da morning. I promise, I won't do anything but hold you. I won't even let you do anything to me no matter how hard you try, I promise."

I stared off at the house weighing my options. It took me longer than what I thought. "Nothing Deangelo, I'm telling you right herrre and right now, don't cross a line that we won't be able to come back from. I mean it!"

Hell, I feel like I'm about to set myself up for way more than I'm ready for. "T, I got chu like I said, I promise." I went into the house, called my sister, told her I was going back down Gee Gee house and I had a ride to school in the morning. Then I was back out the door, we pulled off. All I keep thinking is, 'I thought he said his place was around here.' We all the way out in Lake St. Louis.

"I thought you said go to your place around my house? This is nowhere near my house."

"I have a house in Moline but I didn't wanna take you there. So, I'm taking you to my other house."

"Why, you haven't had a chance to get it decontaminated yet?"

"Yeah, ha ha T!"

We both started to laugh, as we pulled into the driveway. I can tell this house is huge. It has all kinds of flowers and bushes neatly trimmed all the way around the driveway. As we walked in, I had to take a moment to take it all in. He grabbed his mail from off the table by the door and started to fumble through it as he hit on lights from a remote he picked up.

I walked through the house going in and out of rooms. The colors are soft and neutral; the mood is charming while still luxurious. The second level master suite is enormous and still seemed private. As I walked over to the fireplace, I jumped back 'cause it seemed like when I touched it the flame began to burn. "Scared you, didn't I?" Deangelo said as he walked over towards me sitting my bags down on the bed.

"The bathroom is through there. I'll use the one in the basement. Just push this button here when you finished and I'll come back upstairs." Before he could walk out I said, "You have a beautiful home." "You do too!" He smiled and walked out the room closing the door behind him.

What the hell does that mean? Is he making fun of my momma's house? Damn, I forgot he may have cameras in here. Shit! Let me take this towel and wrap it around me good. If he do have cameras, all he gone see is this big ass white towel getting wet the hell up. Better yet, let me take a bath so he really can't see shit.

I managed to get in and out without showing a single bra strap. That'll teach him if he does. After I try my best to ring the towel out, I hang it on the bar in the shower. I head into the room and push the button he showed me.

I was trying to figure out if he had a TV in here then I heard a soft knock on the door. "T, you good?" "Yeah come in." Damn! Damn! Damn! Why the fuck did he have to come in here with no shirt on and some damn boxer briefs? First thing that came to my mind was an image of that big ass roll of hamburger meat from Aldi trying to fall out the bottom of the damn things. Fuck, what am I gone do? Is it hard? Damn, what if that thing is soft, I can't even start to imagine how big it gets when it's hard.

"T, you hear me? Damn T, do I need to put on something else? I can already see yo' mind in the gutter. Snap out of it."

"Whatchu talking 'bout? I'm not paying you any attention. I was wondering if you had a TV in herrre, that's all." I tried to play it off. When I finally decided to stop talking to his dick I looked up. I see he has his finger pointed up towards the ceiling. As I followed, I can see the TV up above my head right above the bed. I looked back over at him.

"Really? So, whatchu do when you don't want to lie on yo' back and watch TV?"

"T, stop playing. You think I didn't think of that already?"

He walked over and picked up the remote sitting in front of me. He pushed something; I saw a huge chunk of the wall move back then down and out came a TV. He used the remote to adjust it towards us as he turned the one above us on. Before he can change the channel, I see different parts of the house. I knew he had cameras and it looked like they errwhere.

"Which one you wanna watch T?" I pointed to the one on the wall.

"You not scared that thing will fall and kill you in yo' sleep?"

"Nope." He made his way to the top of the bed; it was huge. It has to be twice the width of a Super King and the stuff on top I know is all custom made. He pulled the sheets back and waved me in.

"Can you see the TV T?" I felt kinda awkward 'cause I can see it fine if I put my leg over him and put my head on his chest. But that's pushing it too fucking far doin' all that.

"I could better if I was on that side."

"I can't have you by da door."

"Why is that?" Here we go with another one of Deangelo life lessons.

"'Cause I'm a man that's why! Anything come through that door gone have to deal with me first, not you T. So let me adjust the TV. Let me know when it's good; don't forget I can still turn the one on above us." I let him adjust the TV; I don't really plan on watching it anyway after hearing what he just said. I'm ready to close my eyes and leave my worries in his arms.

After we watched TV for a minute, I felt my eyes slowly fall closed. I don't know if it was the safety of his broad shoulders and hard arms that put me to sleep, or the feel of that long piece of meat pressed into the back of my ass. Maybe it was the softness of his freshly showered body that did it?

Before I knew it, he kissed the back of my head, "Goodnight T," and wrapped his body around me like a glove.

I don't know what it was that put my uncertainties to rest but I know it wasn't long before I was soundly asleep.

"T, you need to get up. T, come on sleepy head," I heard him say as he effortlessly used his arm to roll me over facing him. "I'm up!" I said, not thinking for one second what my breath must smell like this early in the damn morning.

Then it hit me; I'm in the bed with Deangelo and I'm all in his face talking with dragon breath. "SHIT!" I jumped up, grabbed my bag and headed to the bathroom. I was too mortified; first thing I did was brush my teeth. "T, you know you crazy as hell. Ain't nobody studding yo' Cheerio smelling ass breath!" he yelled into the bathroom at me. Then I heard him laughing and closing the door. After I swiftly got dressed, I head downstairs to find him on his way back up the steps from the basement.

Damn he look good, all I can do is smile. This house is even more beautiful now that the sun is shining through. I can see the lake is right there, it look like he has a boat dock out there. I love boat docks for some reason, especially if you can dangle your feet into the water as the waves pass by. Something about the movement in the water sets your body and mind at peace. I always feel like no matter what's happening everything will continue to move forward like the waves.

"You ready T?"

"Yeah! Why you use the bathroom in the basement anyway? I know I saw a bathroom in just about every room in nis joint," I said as he walked me out the house.

"I just didn't want you to try and take advantage of me that's all." We both laughed.

"You wanna leave yo' stuff here before I take you to school? We can stop by your house if you want," he said before closing the door.

"Naw, I can take it with me to school. I know you don't want my clothes lying around. Plus, I don't want my momma to see me come through the door with a damn overnight bag and you waiting outside."

"You can leave it here. Trust me, I don't mind. You

sho' right about Kathy. But you sure T, I can pic—" Before he can finish I started to the car, I know we can do this all day long.

As he drove me to school, we talked a little, and then went back and forth about me eating breakfast. I let him get me a sandwich and an orange juice from the restaurant nearby. When we pulled into the parking lot at school, I became instantly embarrassed again and slid slowly down into the seat. He *would* decide to drop me off in a damn Lexus. Why me man? Why me? I just had to ask.

"So what was that about last night? Something's up witchu. You making me think you have some trouble brewing and I might not se—" I couldn't finish what I was about to say so I looked away. The image of him lying in a casket came to the front of my mind.

He moved over and grabbed my hand. "Naw T, I'm good, I just needed to celebrate witchu, that's all." Celebrate, what the hell he means celebrate?

"Celebrate what?"

"I got the call earlier that I was picked up for the next season on that pro team in Greece. You da first person I thought about celebrating with. I heard chu was in the hood, just didn't know how quick you move though. I was shocked to see you come to Charlene spot. So, since I couldn't spend da day witchu, I had to ask for the night. So don't worry about me T, I'm good. Shit, I'm great now! If you would let me get you a celly I could be even better."

"You just wanna keep tabs on me. I can get my own cell if I wanted one Sir!"

"Why you always have to be so difficult? All I'm sayin' is you can let me get chu a cell ph—" I cut him off.

"So, I guess you'll be leaving soon huh?" I don't know whether to be happy or sad about the thought of not seeing him my senior year. Who's gone be there for me now?

"Don't know exactly how soon, but you know you can always call me. Dat's another reason I'm getting' you a cell. Hell, we can chill every day together if you got time for yo' boy," he said, as he laid his head back on the headrest. I had to get my mind off it.

"I can get my own; I do have a couple jobs to afford it. I'll get one when I'm ready for you to keep tabs on me, you 'bout the only one that will call me. Anyway, do you have cameras in the bathroom too?" I said as I looked over at him. He smiled and met my gaze, I don't know if it's because of what I said or asked him.

"Of course, but I turned the ones off inside when we came in just in case." What the hell he means just in case?

"What does that mean?" He started to laugh.

"Not whatchu thinking. I just didn't want you to be on there just in case someone else was looking in, that's all." That took me for a loop; what does he mean someone else? I have more questions now than I did before I asked the question.

"So somebody else can see what's going on at your house? Why you want that?"

"T, you worry too much. I would never do anything to put you in jeopardy so I turned them off. Can we leave it at that?"

"Yeah, whatever." I turned back around and looked out the window. Damn, I wish everybody would go inside the school but of course they had to stand around gawking trying to see through these tinted ass windows.

"What's wrong T? You don't want them to see you getting out my hooptie? I can pull off and wait on nem to leave if you want!"

"Ha-ha funny man. You know I don't want these lames trying to get in my business. Why you always have to do stuff like this to me anyway?" I said as I chuckled then took a sip of my drink.

"Yeah, whatever T. Come here." He placed his arms around me holding me tight. All I can think is, 'Don't ever let go.' Then he kissed the top of my head. I turned facing the door. It feels like I'm standing on a stage about to bust my ass. As quickly as possible, I stepped out the car, closed the door and damn near ran away. Before I made it to building nine, I looked back and waved Deangelo bye.

6 MYZPHYT

Man, nese streets been good to a nigga, I can't complain one bit. Running my own lil crew, yo' boy on the rise in these hood politics fosho. New whip, pockets on swole errday. Shit, I have to pat myself on the back for how good this shit is. Here we go. Just the person I needed to see to make this day even better.

"What's up Treasure? You need a ride?" I said, as I pulled along the side of her. Straight, she didn't even break her stride. She just gone keep mobbing like she don't hear or see me talking to her? Good, she stuck at the light. Now she gotta talk to me. "Treasure, I know you hear me. What's with all the attitude?"

The way she just looked at me I should be ducking from the drive-by shooting she just sent my way. "I'm sorry you think I'm a ho but I'm not! Only ho's respond to tricks screaming out a damn car window at 'em. So if you have something to say, I would suggest you show me some respect and approach me like your father or mother should've taught you how!" she said, as she quick-stepped across the street.

Now normally I would just keep rolling, but not today. I'm about to find out what all that's about. I thought we were better than that. This girl know she think she tough as hell. I shoot through the light, park the car and jump out as she come blowing past me.

"Ay, my bad. I just wanted to give you a ride, dat's all. I didn't mean any disrespect by it." She steady on da move. I feel like we damn near running down na street trying to keep up with her.

"Well, like they say, if you don't know better, you don't do better!" she said as she continued to walk down Ninth Street. I wasn't about to let her do me so I continued to try and get her to slow up and talk with me. She was most definitely on a mission.

"Can you hold up a minute so I can talk to you though?" I said, as I tapped the side of her arm.

What the fuck? She just stopped dead in her steps like I hit an off button or something. Let me stand back before she turns around swinging on me. "Look, I'm tired. All I wanna do is get to where I'm going. So like the old saying go, 'can you please just leave me be so I can do that." She turned around and looked at me.

"If you so tired, let me drive you where you trying to go. No sense in you walking there!" She snapped her neck to the side.

"No sense in you still talking to me after I just dissed yo' ass damn near three blocks ago. Read my lips, whatever you selling, I ain't buying, whatever you trying to buy, I damn sure ain't selling. So goodbye and have a blessed day!" She walked off to Fourteen Thirty-Four toward the backdoor.

All I can think is, 'Damn we made it down here fast'. My car all the fucking way up on Cole and Ninth Street. All right, I see I have to take a different approach with her now. I know fosho all them niggas was lying like a mufucka saying they hit that. Not unless they smack the shit out her smart-ass mouth! That's about the only hitting they did wit' her.

Hell, I can only imagine what she said to that nigga Chucky to make him wanna put hands to her mufuckin' ass. Man, let me get back to my car I need a drink after fucking with her ass!

* * *

Let me go down here see what's popping at Debby crib. I heard she was having a lil get together. I bet they just sitting around drinking. Aw shit, Debby straight got it jumping in herrre tonight. Damn, I ain't seen Treasure in a couple days but who am I kidding, I wasn't looking either. Especially after the way she did me dirty the last time I saw her.

I'm surprised Debby and Treasure stuck up ass ain't at the club some damn where. Soon as I mention her name, she walks in the door. But hold up, that body suit just turned my frown upside down. She thick as a bitch! Got damn, I see why dat nigga Pandillero keep her close. Nigga still stupid for giving me the green light though. I don't care how many times she turns me down, after seeing all that I'm about to holla at my girl right now!

"Hello Treasure, how are you doing this fine evening?" I say in my best prep boy accent. Damn and she got that damn zipper showing just enough of them big old tigo bitties. If I had the chance, I would lick, slurp, hell *suffocate* myself on nem things right about now.

"Real funny. Hey Myzphyt, I'm doing well how about chu?" Damn, this girl must be a schizoid or something. I know she got all the symptoms. If I looked it up in the dictionary, they probably have her picture with a big ass caution sign on it.

One minute she nice, the next minute she a... fuck it, BITCH! Hell, with a capital B.I.T.C and H! "Aw, you must've had some rest huh? Do I need to back up so you won't beat me up?" She dropped her head down and started to laugh.

"My bad. I told Debby to tell you that I apologize for doing you like that. She said she did, I was even looking for you a couple days later so I could tell you myself. It doesn't matter though. I do apologize for the way I behaved that day. It was a bad day for me that's all. I didn't have any right to take it out on you. I did mean what I said about screaming at a woman from a car though. I should've said it in a different way. So my bad, I hope you accept my apology."

Dang, I wasn't expecting that from her. Yeah, this girl has to be crazy. Let me just say yeah and get the hell away from her. Shit, look at that smile and those eyes. They just won't let my damn legs or mouth get out what I need to say and do. It's like those long ass eyelashes are a cage that lock you in when you look at 'em. What da fuck? Does she have some mind control shit going on with those things?

"It's cool ma. Like I said, I just want to get to know you better, that's all. Trust, I know next time not to ride up on you or anyone else like that for that matter." We both laughed and continued to talk. After about two-three hours, it was like we was best friends are some shit.

I don't know what it is about this girl but like I said, now I know why Pandillero keep her close. I also know how I'm gone straight clown all dem niggas that been lying saying they hit. I can't fucking wait. This shit like a burning wad of gas-soaked paper in my pocket. I just can't fucking wait.

My Body by LSG came on the radio. I can see this her song so I asked if she wanted to dance. Once again, she shocked the shit out of me, damn near yanked me into the middle of the floor. I didn't want her to freak out on me so I decided not to pull anything greasy like grab her ass.

I figured I'd just put my hands on her hips and see how she reacts before I get too close. She feels good as fuck, her body soft and silky. I'm too happy she wore this getup 'cause I can feel every single move of her hips.

Aw shit, she actually wrapped her hands around me; her body feels excellent. My shlong getting harder by the second. She's fucking with me now. Why she have to turn around and put that ass on me like this? She knows my dick hard.

I can tell by the way her sexy ass keep looking back at me as she grinds to the beat. I gotta get back in control before I lose one right here in the middle of the floor. All right here we go, please don't let this song end. Play it for about three more years, at least!

7 TREASURE

Damn, I'm tired. Now I have to walk my ass all the way down Gee Gee house, do dey hair, then jump on the bus and go to work. If I wasn't so damn cheap, I would have a fucking car right now. But fuck that. Why get a car just to have a bill to pay? Ain't nothing wrong with the bus. It's cheaper than a car note, insurance, property tax and gas, so let me get my walk on.

What the fuck? I know ain't no dumbass hollering at me from a car like I'm some prostitute or something. Is that Myzphyt? He really lost his damn mind. I'm just gone keep going like I don't hear him 'cause I don't have time to teach a boy how to be a man.

That's what his father was supposed to do. But I know he probably don't know his daddy so his momma should've filled him in. Dang it! I would get stopped at the dang on light with him steady chasing me. "Treasure, I know you hear me. What's with all the attitude?" All the attitude let me tell this bastard something real quick. Now let me get across this street before the light change.

What the fuck? He just doesn't get it, does he? Now let me guess, he think I'm about to get in a car with his ass. Hell the fuck no. He ain't gone have me doing five to ten. Talking 'bout just take the charge for him and say it's my shit in the car. Hell, it could be stolen.

I'm gone just keep walking. I don't care what he talking about, what the fuck? Breathe Treasure, Breathe! Did this motherfucka just touch me; I know he didn't just touch me! Please Lord, stop me from what I'm about to do if he just touched me! Breathe Treasure, Breathe! Good, I'm here. Damn, that was quick!

Now let me tell him something real fast so I can be done with this shit. Now that that's over, let me get up here, knock they hair out, 'cause the bus come in two hours. I need to hurry up. Fuck I'm tired! After I put two perms in and started on my lil cousin head, all I could think of was how I just did Myzphyt.

That shit was foul. The more I sit back and think about it I see how fucked up I did his ass. I know damn well I wouldn't want somebody to treat me like that. Even if he was in the wrong with how he came at me. I could've handled that way better than what I did. I need to do some damage control before I leave from down here. As I headed out the door to catch the bus I ran up the stairs to Debby house hoping that Myzphyt was down there.

"Hey Debby is Myzphyt around?"

"Naw, girl, I don't know where he at. Come in so I can call him?"

"Naw, that's okay. Can you tell him that I apologize about earlier for me?"

"Why what happened?"

"Nothing really, I just wasn't in the mood and he was there so I took it out on him. Can you tell him that though? I gotta go before I miss the bus."

"All right, I'll tell him," she said as I waved bye and made a mad dash to the bus stop. Good, just in time.

* * *

"Hey Debby, what's up?"

"I was calling to make sure you was coming to my lil thing Friday?"

"Girl yeah, I'll be there after I get off work."

"All right. Dat's what's up. I'll see you later den girl." It's been a couple days since I saw Myzphyt. I was down there the next day after work. I looked for him to apologize but he was nowhere to be found. I hope I see him before I head over Debby house so it won't be awkward. Plus, I need to see where his head at before I go around him.

Whatchu mean to tell me Debby not drinking tonight? Now that's the person I miss hanging out with right there. Hell, there goes Myzphyt. I hope he not too mad at me. I wonder if I should go over and apologize to him now? Hell, to da no! He ain't about to give me a dose of my own medicine. I'm gone chill out and have a good time tonight. I deserve it all the ripping and running I been doing.

Well, well, well he not that mad. He on his way over here. And by the way, those hazel eyes of his looking he not mad at all! "Hello Treasure, how are you doing this fine evening?" Hell naw. Why he trying to sound like that? He knows he needs to quit.

Damn, look at those eyes. They make the cookie throb like it got its own heartbeat or something. He knows he sexy as hell around nis bitch. I wonder if he still with that one trick Cherell? It doesn't matter. I know damn well I'm not interested in his ass like that no way.

Shit, I knew it was coming so let me just apologize and hope for the best. Good, now that's out of the way I can chill out. I never realized there was something behind all the tough guy slash pretty boy vibe he gave out. I always thought he was a jerk who thought he could get any and everything he wanted. He probably does think that but he still pretty cool, laid back I guess.

Aw shit, I know they not about to play my jam. Damn, I love this song. Do I wanna dance? Hell, he doesn't have to ask me twice! Soon as we hit the floor, I start feeling nat shit. I don't give a fuck who looking. Aw, he one of dem types doesn't really dance just stands there.

All right, you wanna just stand there, I got chu. I move in closer making sure he feels my body all up against his. I slowly sway back and forth rubbing every inch of myself across him. Okay, he's hangin' in there. I can feel that boa constrictor making a move. Let's see how he handles this!

I turn around and slowly lean forward with the beat bending more and more, dipping my back and working my ass into his body. I can see he enjoying it and I know that boa constrictor den turned to a python now the way it's trying to slip in between my cheeks. Let me help it out. I whined my way up and down slithering my body across his. I guess that did the trick 'cause he sho' put an end to that. All I can do is giggle under my breath and give him some room to breathe for the rest of the song.

"You know you wrong for that right!" Myzphyt said as he walked me back to my aunt house.

"Whatchu mean? I told you I apologize. I thought we were good."

"Come on Treasure; don't try and play like you don't know what I'm talking 'bout. You got a nigga in straight pain trying to keep it together still! That's messed up. You know dat right?" I laughed and kept walking.

"Well I must say, I had a good time tonight and I have to admit it was partly 'cause of good company." I stopped before getting too close to my aunt's door.

"I'll take that. I had a good time witchu too. So when can we do this again away from the hood Treasure?"

"I don't know. It depends on the next time I see you."

"Why's that?"

"That'll let me know if I wanna hang out witchu again or not. It just depends."

"I'm cool with that! Well goodnight Treasure. I'm gone try my best to make sure you see me soon," he said, as I looked up into those delicious eyes of his. Damn, why in the hell is he making me feel like dis?

He slowly leaned in and kissed me on my cheek but he didn't pull back. He whispered, "Don't go disappearing on me." I could feel his warm breath caress my face. Fuck it. I wrapped my arms around his neck and kissed him slowly. I can feel his tongue twirl around in my mouth as we went back and forth.

I felt like I was floating when he lifted me just barely up off my feet and wrapped his arms tighter around my waist. I bit down just a touch on his bottom lip as he gave me a small kiss back. He slowly began to release me back down to my feet.

Damn, that was good. I smiled and opened the door as he nodded at me before I closed it. Why the hell did I just do that? I know teasing him is not what I need to be doing right now.

8 BLASÉ

I know she not in this class. She got all AP classes. She can't be in this class with these dumbass niggas. This like a third grade math class. She must be like me, in here for the ninety minute nap before heading to her next class. Yep, I called it; she walked in, put her head straight down on the table.

What, it ain't even five minutes in. I can see she straight sleep in dis bitch. Fuck, she finer sleep then she is awake. I need to move my seat so I can get a better look. What I wouldn't do to lay her down in a bed right now. Even without setting her body on fire from yamming the hell out of her, just being near her would make my day.

After about a hour in, this dumbass teacher decided he wanted to start teaching these clowns something. And of course, they're not paying him any attention. I sit back and laugh. I would be sleep right now but I have to wait until baby girl wake up so I can talk to her for a minute. "Miss Waters, Miss Waters!" the teacher called her without getting a response.

I tapped her on her shoulder and pointed at him as everyone in the class looked back at her. She slowly turned her head up with a look of pure anger in her eyes. She looked at him and shouted out, "WHAT!?" The class erupted in amusement not believing that she would respond the way that she did to him. I shook my head wondering why she just get thrown out of class.

"Welcome to the class Miss Waters; please take out your book and follow along with us." To my surprise, the teacher backed down, took a different tone and decided to play nice. I guess when you that pretty no man is a match when you're upset.

"Mr. Brooks I don't mean to be rude but we both know that I'm only in here 'cause the advance chemistry class was full! I'm tired and don't feel like following along or arguing about it; so let me be frank. I'll complete whatever work you assign but I need to sleep. If you don't like that you can send me to the office so I can get another class that I don't have to be bothered in. Besides, it's not my fault that these broke schools have more remedial classes then they do advanced. That's something for the superintendent to work out!"

She sat straight up waiting on him to respond while the entire class sat in shock turning their attention to him as they waited with her. "Class, turn to page one fort..." Everybody exploded in laughter again; I think I heard somebody call him a bitch ass nigga. Another girl asked how he let her talk to him like that. I looked over at her; she had her head back on the desk falling back to sleep.

This girl is something else. The way she just handled his ass I got to get to know her; she just my speed. Plus, I don't see her with anybody in school besides her people and Sammy. I did see her riding with Tim nem before and some nigga in a bad ass white Lexus GS 300 Sedan blacked out, sitting on some thang's, system jumping.

Hell, I know he gotta be in nese streets. Now that I think about it, since that day, I haven't seen her riding with Tim nem. But she always wit' Sammy in her ride. I wonder why she doesn't have her own whip.

"What's up cuzzo? Finally getting yo' sleepy ass up? I know that class boring as hell ain't it. All dem dumb mufuckas in there!" My cousin Safari said, as he met me in the hall.

"I actually didn't go to sleep today. This shit was funny as hell. That one girl, I think her name Treasure; she went off on Mr. Barnes ass. Boy, I ain't ever seen somebody go off like that on a teacher. She funny as hell for that!" I said as we made our way through the halls.

"Damn straight? I heard she mean as hell! We've been in school with her since forever. Here it is junior year, she don't ever come to shit, stay to herself. I don't even remember her having a fight or hell, even an argument with anybody."

"I do remember hearing she had a fight with Kevin bitch ass when she first came here, something about him fucking with her. They said she just got up and started handing it to his ass. That bitch ass nigga had to use a...damn whatchu call it? Umm...abacus, yeah, an abacus to hit her with but they said she shook that shit off and commenced to beating that ass even more," I said, as we both laughed harder, damn near doubling over as we made it to the lunchroom.

"You know, she be right out there with her peoples. That's Trey Loc lil cousin. That nigga be screaming that shit all through the halls when he sees her. You know that nigga silly as hell. He be running off errbody that try and holla at her. Not to mention them Eight Hundred niggas she with all the time. They around her like they bodyguards are something.

She doesn't move from one class to da next without one of them with her, especially that nigga City. I don't think he family though. I think he most definitely with her," Safari said but before he could go on, I wanted to know why I hadn't picked up on that before. But hell, then again, that girl's like a sniper, scout or hit man or something. She can only be picked out when she want to be. Other than that, she stays to herself and only speaks when spoken too.

I have to get to know her before she disappears for good so I know dem Eight Hundred niggas be hoopin'. I been hearing 'bout the games they have over at their house so I know I can get an invite. "Ay, what's up with ya'll?" I said as I walked over and dabbed 'em off. I can see Treasure, sort of, standing off to the side just out of view behind City and Damon. They moved closer together like a blockade protecting the fort. "Ain't shit up. What bring ya'll on this side of the cafeteria?" Tony, her lil brother said as he looked around at errbody then back at me and Safari.

If I didn't know any better I would say dese niggas sizing us up. All the attention on us and all their small talk stopped. "We been hearing 'bout these games. Niggas keep saying ya'll smashing niggas on na court. We trying to see when the next game so we can bring our squad through see what all da hype about," Safari said as he walked closer and gave his b-boy stance.

We all started laughing. That's except for Treasure and City. I really can't see her but I sure don't hear her. By the looks this nigga City giving me if I didn't pay attention before, I am now. This nigga look like he wanna go at it and I ain't even had a chance to say shit to her; yet. I know dis nigga a boxer and all but if he think for one second he intimidating me he has another thing coming.

"Man, ya'll can bring the whole GGV. It ain't gone stop that ass whipping ya'll gone get on da court!" Damon deep voice ass said. He the only nigga I know in the ninth grade sound like he somebody grandfather.

"All right, don't sleep on yo' boys. We nice but enough of the talk. When the next game?" I said still thrashing that nigga City right in the eye so he know I don't back down. 'Eyeball all you want lil nigga. You ain't scaring shit here!' I said to myself.

"We can put a game together Saturday. I think it would be best if ya'll have some chance and we met at Lemaster's. That way ya'll can't run back to Glasgow Village saying we demolished ya'll 'cause we had the home court advantage!" Darrius said as he stood up off the table.

"Man, wherever, but I prefer to kill ya'll niggas on ya'll own court. That way ya'll don't have a reason to feel uncomfortable," Safari said.

"Aight then cool. I'll hit that nigga Mike up and let him know the details. We can see what ya'll GGV niggas got on the court!" Tony said.

"Now ya'll sure ya'll wanna take it to the house 'cause it ain't no chance in hell ya'll winning shit there!" Damon said, then he dabbed off City as we walked away.

"I told you cuz, that nigga City be on her ass; you see how that nigga was looking? I just knew I was gone have to flat line his ass the way he was throwing them hostile ass vibes out!" Safari said as we made our way back to our usual table.

"Man, fuck that nigga. They not together; I know that! But I also know if that nigga could change that, he would. But you know a nigga like me about to snatch that up ASAP!" I said as we both laughed and sat down. I couldn't wait for the weekend, with this fucked up ass block schedule I won't be in class again with Treasure 'til next week.

I don't ever see her in the halls. Hell, I don't even know what building her locker's in. I don't even know what time she gets out this bitch. Seem like she make her own hours. I know one thing; I'm gone let these niggas have it and then afterwards holla at Treasure. I don't care if these niggas pull a strap out to try and stop me.

They lived in Dellwood. It's too damn quiet over here, bunch of white people out walking their dogs down these long boring ass streets without sidewalks. Most of the houses look the same. I never been over their house before but by the line of cars, music playing and smell of barbeque, I know I'm at the right place. Good, my people here. Hell, I didn't expect it to be jumping like this.

As I got out and walked to the back I can't help but admire their house. The yard is huge and green as hell. You can tell it's well taken care of. And the house is no smaller; it has to be extra rooms in there. The brown and white really makes it stand out from the rest of the houses on the block. To my surprise, the backyard is even bigger than the front. These niggas have a full court basketball joint setup out here.

People are errwhere, some sitting at tables eating, others walking around, some even dancing to the music. Good, another team on the court, I have some time to holla at Treasure before the game. I know if I look for her I won't find her so I decided to look for that nigga City. I was shocked when I didn't see him.

"What's up Big Dog? You finally showed up. I thought you sent yo' peoples in ya' place," Tony said as he walked over and gave me a pound.

"Man you know how it is; I had to make a couple moves before I headed over. But you talking 'bout me. I don't see too many of yo' peoples out here!" I was hoping he would take the bait.

"Aw yeah, like who? I see errbody except that nigga City," he said shaking his head side to side.

"What's up wit' yo' boy. He doesn't wanna get this ass whooping we about to lay on ya'll?" I started laughing waiting on his response.

"What? Nigga please! His love struck ass here. He just in Treasure room. I bet if we walked toward the court that nigga 'bout looking out the window at the game. He probably trying to tell her not to go but she ain't hearing it. Besides, I just saw her ride pull up so he'll be—" Before he could finish, I see City coming out the backdoor looking like he ready to kill somebody.

I look back up the driveway and see Treasure getting into a brand new all white Range Rover. It's sittin' on way too much. This mug still has temp tags in the window. It has to be fresh off the lot. As the car drove off all I could do was shake my head. I knew it wouldn't be simple but I thought I would at least get a chance to talk to her for a minute. "See, I told you Big Dog, soon as this game over with, we next. So don't go running back to the GGV without getting this ass kickin' we 'bout to put on ya'll!" he said as he walked away.

On my way home, all I could think about was her. It's something about this girl that make a nigga wanna give chase. Even if it meant getting the door slammed in his face. Hell, even if it meant dealing with a nigga like City. But either way, it's worth it to find out more about her. I have to give it to them lil niggas. For them to all be shorter than me they quick as hell. The game was close but they did they thing and held they record.

That's just for now though. I plan to be at every game until we smash them and I get to know Treasure. I need to hurry up. I'm supposed to meet up with my brother in the city. Say his connect put him up with this heavy hitter. I'm about my money so I sped down highway Two Seventy jumped off on Riverview and headed down Hall Street to the highway to meet up with him.

9 TREASURE

I should've taken my ass home instead of staying in that bitch 'til three this fucking morning. It's all good though. I'm doing all overtime hours now. I can still smell them damn onions though.

Look at all these dummies in here. If they shut the fuck up and learn something maybe they won't be in this remedial ass class. On the other hand, I'm kinda glad that I'm not in that AP class 'cause I know I would be getting my ass kicked trying to keep my eyes open. Good, a desk open. I'm finna sleep this time right out.

All I can dream about is Deangelo being gone and not having my buddy around. Even though he plays me every chance he gets, when I'm with him, we have a good time. The thought of feeling his body up against mine has my head all fucked up right now.

That is one sexy man! I'll take a beat down from Momma every day to feel the way I felt that next morning. Shiiiit, no the hell I won't. That woman crazy. If she eva find out I'm out that bitch quick, fast and in a hurry! I ain't going to any hospital for anybody. What the fuck, is somebody touching me? I know some dumbass mufucka ain't finna ask for their seat!

Where this Morris Chestnut looking dude come from? He fine as hell! I wanted to laugh 'cause all that came to mind was RICKAAAAAAY! What the fuck he pointing at? What the hell? He woke me up for this dumbass teacher? Before I knew it, I screamed, "WHAT!?" Damn, why did I just do that? I know I'm about to get put out this bitch but fuck it, I don't care. "Welcome to the cla..." Mr. Brooks said.

I know this muthafucka ain't trying to put me on front street like I'm dumb are something! I let his ass have it! Hell, if he gone put me out anyway I might as well tell his ass off. What the fuck all these blockheaded bitches looking at? That's all they do, come to school and bullshit. Well damn, he smarter than he look. He didn't throw me out so I guess I'm going back to sleep. Good, the bell, up just in time to be the first one out dis bitch. I hope Ethan ready. Who am I kidding; I know he waiting outside the door for me. Yep!

"What's up man?"

"Nuttin', killed it on the supposed to be pop quiz," Ethan said as we made our way to our favorite spot in the cafeteria.

"Hey Damon, how you doing?"

"I'm good Treasure. How's the jobs treating you these day?" Damon has that Barry White thing going that has these lil girls have a fit over him.

"You know somebody needs to make that money! Why not me?" We all began to laugh.

Damn, here comes that Morris Chestnut lookin' dude. Ummm, he has to be about what, six three, probably one eighty or something. His cousin can get it fosho, looking like Lance Gross and shit. Where do they come from? To be this fine, I know they got these fools up here going at it over them. Why Mr. Chestnut keeps trying to look at me?

Hell naw, I know Ethan getting mad. I can tell by the way he rocking back and forth. What the hell? I know that ain't why they came over here. They out they damn mind if they think they gone come to the house and run our damn court. Too bad I already told Deangelo I would hang out with him.

"Now, ya'll sure ya'll want to take it to th..." Damon said and dabbed off Ethan as they walked away.

"Hell naw, they think they gone run us on our court?

Yeah, okay!" Tony said, as we all began to laugh.

"What's up Treasure? You chilling wit' money bags this weekend?" Ethan said walking towards me then leaned against my side.

"Now you know that's my business so why you even going there Mr. Ethan?"

"Aw, that nigga City thought he was slick didn't he with that sly shit! Nigga, you know that's what she was gone say! I know if I knew then you knew not to ask!" Damon said as we all laughed.

"Hell, I had to try, right!" Ethan said as we all laughed harder.

We stood around for the next lunch laughing and joking before we decided we spent enough time hanging out. Don't get me wrong, we only skipped classes that really didn't affect us like shop, keyboarding and newspaper, basically electives. We all are smart; you couldn't hang around us if you a dummy! What the hell would we want to be around somebody who couldn't keep up with us? It just didn't make sense, so we made sure we did what we had to do when it came to school.

Dang, he called me like fifteen minutes ago saying he was at Chambers and New Halls Ferry Road. I been sitting here babying Ethan ass trying not to hurt his feelings. Don't get me wrong, Ethan's a young tender, got that George Wilson look goin' on and shit. I've been knowing him too long though. I don't wanna be hurt when he starts slanging that thang from chick to chick.

I know he mess with girls now but he ain't been in a real relationship and I haven't either really to be honest. I just think it's best if we keep things the way they are, that's all. Let him get his heart broken by somebody else. Oh, it's gone happen. That's just fact. I don't wanna be the one to do it to him though.

After telling Ethan that I was out I head to the car. I'm moving so fast Deangelo didn't even have a chance to look up from his phone to open the door for me. Usually, I won't get in a car with a man if they don't open the door. Deangelo only let me do it when I was at school. But I see Mr. Chestnut out the corner of my eye. I know I'll be telling Deangelo to stick around so I can get a better view.

Deangelo pull off heading for who knows where. It don't even matter either 'cause as long as we together I know we gone have a nice time. He always takes me to different places. Places that I wouldn't even think about going. I know this trip will be no different.

I sat back and let him drive with no care in the world. We ride and vibe out to the music with just simple hellos being said. After we stop at this Spanish restaurant and eat, we head further out on Highway Forty and stop at what look like a cowboy place.

"Don't think you slick T! Who you running from?"

"Whatchu mean?"

"T, you sneak past me and jump in the car peeping ol' boy in the driveway. You know better than that. You don't have to run. I could've still opened the door while you peeped him out."

"Man, I don't know whatchu talking about. I was just ready to go. You the one too busy on the phone."

"Yeah aight T. Let's not try it again though. Next time the door will be locked so you have to wait on me to open it."

"What we doing here?"

"We about to have fun; whatchu think?"

"Yeah, okay. How much fun could this be?" I said as he reached into the back handing me this cute pink and black cowgirl hat.

"What's this for?"

"I know you like it right. Yo' boy got taste?" I have to hand it to him; I do like it and it matches the long pink strapless summer dress I have on. I can hear country music playing over the speakers as we make our way to the first available pool table. I wait while he gets me a soda and him a bottle of water then pay for the games.

"You found yo' stick yet T? Don't take all day. You know it don't matter what stick you get I'm still winning right?"

"Whatever. I know today is my day, I been practicing just in case we found ourselves shooting again."

"Aw, look at you T!" After getting my tail kicked a couple games, I figured since he always putting me in awkward situations I would return the favor. I grabbed his hand and lead him to the dance floor. Well damn, if I would've known this shit was so damn complicated I would've sat my ass down.

We laughed so hard at the fact that we couldn't get the steps and just how serious these white people took the whole thing. After making fools out of ourselves a couple songs, we decided to throw darts and of course, I won in that, then we headed back out the door.

10 BLASÉ

I've never been this excited to get to Mr. Barnes class. I don't care what he talking about, I'm about to talk to her today and I don't care who has something to say about it. Good, she here. Let me get that seat right next to her.

"Excuse me, this seat taken?"

"You don't see the air sitting there already?" Really, that's how she gone come at me?

"Naw, I don't but I guess the air won't mind if I have a seat now will it?"

"I guess not!" This girl is something else.

"Hey, my name is Blasé."

"Yeah, I know who you are. You the Blasé from the GGV. You the same Blasé that was talking mad game about running the court. And the same Blasé who went back to the GGV like the rest of them. Without a win! Did I miss anything?"

"That's how you gone do me? All right, I see now you like to come out swinging, huh? Well I'm also the same Blasé that'll be back and run that court sooner than you think."

"That's what yo' mouth said the last time," she said as she looked over at me with her head tilted to the side waiting on me to reply.

"You funny, you know that right, a real comedian." We both started to laugh. Good, at least I got her to laugh. Maybe this won't be as bad as I thought it was heading.

"Well, if you so confident Mr. Blasé, I know they having a game same time this Saturday. So I guess you gone put that plan into action."

"Well, you don't have to guess. Just know it and when we shut it down, you can let me take you to dinner."

"I didn't say all that Mr. Blasé, but when you eat those words, maybe I'll let you take me to dinner and maybe I won't." She is too cool for me. I can go back and forth with her all day without a problem. She keep eyeballing me the way she is, I may not wait to see her ass at the game.

We talked in class about all kinds of stuff. It made me really realize just how short the class was. Before, it felt like time was creeping past to the point where I was tired of sleeping so I had to wake the hell up. But now it's not long enough. I can't get enough time to talk to her before it's time to go.

After talking with her for the rest of the time, before the bell even rang, she said she was out and left. I would walk with her to lunch but every time I look up them Eight Hundred niggas be popping out of nowhere and shit. Hell, I see why.

I wouldn't want anything to happen to her either. That's the thing about the View. These females be trippin'. They fight every damn day over stupid shit. I guess that's why she only hangs with her people and Sammy so that she not in that dumb shit. Plus, I know these chicks be hatin' on her so I bet that's why them niggas walk her to class like that.

By the way they say she beat the shit out of Kevin. She must know how to fight. Plus, I been hearing some shit about her and Sammy but I know how stories can get flipped. I don't pay it no mind.

I can't see the shit they say about them happening like that anyway. Shit, with a mouth like hers, hell, she better know how to fight. On the real, somebody that beautiful should never have to fight a day in her life. Matter fact, if that nigga Kevin didn't transfer schools I would go beat his ass right now for that bitch shit he pulled back then.

*   *   *

All right, I know we about to kick some ass today. I got my real squad. I already know the shit they 'bout to pull so I hope these lil niggas ready.

"Man, is this girl gone be here? The one yo' ass been all smiles about?" my brother Randy said as we turned down their street heading to their crib.

"Yeah, she said she was, why?"

"'Cause if she looks as good as you say she does then I might just pull her from you real quick."

"Man, get that shit outta here. You can't pull shit, don't nobody want yo' old ass. She would run right over yo' ass and not even look back."

"Damn, its jammed pack. This dey house or O'Fallon Park after the parade?"

"Yeah, this it. I'm telling you it's nice, but fuck all that. Let's see who up next."

"I'll be there in a minute let me make a couple calls real quick." As I walk to the back I can see Treasure through the big open windows. Look like she talking to somebody, I head on to the back and holla at errbody.

Good, we on. "What's up Sam man, you not playing today? Don't tell me you niggas scared?" We all began to laugh, them Eight Hundred niggas even laughed. I wonder why they called that shit when it's only seven of these niggas? Oh well!

I heard Damon say, "Naw, somebody had to sit out! So whoever loss in one-on-one had to sit that ass on the sideline."

"Straight. So damn Sam, I guess you lost huh?"

"Yeah man I got my ass kicked this time, but it's all good. You laughing now but you won't be later!"

"Whatever, so who beat chu?" Debo asked him.

"Our ringer beat his ass and shut that shit down in nis bitch!" James said as they all laughed more.

"Don't tell me ya'll niggas that scared ya'll have to bring in a ringer," Mike said.

"Naw man. Our ringer said it was a must that they played in this game," Darrius said as he slapped his hands together to exaggerate his point.

"Man, so I guess it's a secret that we don't know who it is right? 'Cause ya'll still ain't said a name yet!" Safari said as we all stood waiting to hear who.

"Man, would ya'll calm down. The game 'bout to start. Ya'll can find out then," City said as they all started laughing and walking to the court.

"Damn, man, I thought you were gone miss the start of the game. Took yo' ass long enough to get out here," I said to my brother when I saw him walking down the driveway.

"Man, that nigga talking 'bout the price den went up 'cause the connect said so. What the fuck he mean 'cause the connect said s...?"

"Man, I'm about to start dis game and you come down here with that? That shit can wait 'til we beat these niggas!"

"Man fuck you. I'm finna get me something to eat and find yo' girl," he said as he walked over to the barbeque pit. Damn, is that Pandillero coming out the basement door? With...Treasure? What the fuck? Damn, this a small world. This the nigga I met a while back with my brother. Hell, this the connect my brother was just talking about.

"All right ya'll niggas ready to start," Damon yelled out at us. We all walked over to the court.

"So where dis mystery ringer at ya'll got," Safari said as he looked around.

"Behind ya'll. Who ya'll thought it was," Darrius said as we all turned around. There her fine ass goes. She got on some ball shorts and a sports bra. Abs for days, headlights for weeks and ass for years.

"Ya'll playing right?" Safari said as we all began to laugh.

"Yeah, we playin'. Now our ball since shit so funny," she said as she grabbed the ball from Mike and passed it to City. We all just stood there 'cause she looked pissed about something.

"Damn, ya'll finished watching or can we get this shit over wit'?" she said as she found her spot on the court.

"Fuck it. Let's play," Safari said as we started the game.

Hell, I can't even get a hello, fuck you, nothing? This girl knows she can flip the switch on a nigga quick without even givin' a damn.

"Come on Mike, if you can't check her den let us know! She hitting so many threes in yo' face I den lost count," Debo yelled at Mike.

"Fuck it. I got her," Safari said as he picked her up coming down the court. The next thing I know, Safari damn ankles break and she hit another fuckin' three.

"Damn, I thought you said you got me? We have a first aid kit in na house or would you prefer the ambulance," she said as she walked past Safari. We were hurt from laughing at this nigga. She knows not to bring that shit in the hole though.

"Aight T, let's bring it home baby!" I heard Pandillero say from off the sideline. Baby? She wit' dat nigga? I know something up 'cause he watching her like a hawk. I see my brother go over, dab him off and start hollan at him. Damn, the game close. Couple more buckets either way and its game over. We down right now but it's nothing. Fuck, they scored again, three more points they way and we out.

What th...? Hold up. "Come on man, how you gone stop the game like that?" Debo said, as Treasure walked off the court with the ball tucked under her arm. I see her walking toward my brother and Pandillero. She doesn't look too happy; let me see what's up.

"Excuse me; I don't know who the hell you ar...."

"Aw, my bad. That's my brother. He just here to watch the game. I hope that's okay." I tried to explain while everybody is standing around now. We have all eyes on us out here.

"Thank you for talking for your brother but I think he has a name right," she said as she gave me the 'I didn't ask you shit' look and turned back towards my brother. I look around at these Eight Hundred niggas, they look like they about to hand it to him or something.

"My name Randy...."

"Randy, fuck all that! I know you new over here but let me explain something to you real quick so we can finish kicking yo' people ass over ther—"

"T, I already told hi—" Pandillero tried to stop her from going in, she looked at him. He threw his hands up and then she turned her body and looked my brother square in the face. I can see these Eight Hundred niggas all come in a tad bit closer behind us while City made his way on the side of my brother.

"Like I was saying, since you den fucked up my game let me tell you how it works over here. Anything that you have to say to him, you can say it when you hit Chambers and Imperial! Other than that, please respect my momma house and my family. We out here to have a good time and just so we don't get this confused that does include that schoolyard back there. So I would truly appreciate it if you said hello and goodbye to him...." She looked at Pandillero.

"...while he's here. I promise you though Randy, when you hit Cham—bers and Im—per—rial I have no problems witchu saying whatever it is you need to say to him. Randy, I wish we could've met under better circumstances. I hope that there are no hard feelings, 'cause yo' brother is pretty cool. But you know what Randy? I really don't give a fuck about how you feel since you seem to be so disrespectful!" she said ending the conversation without even worrying about a response.

"Hold up lil mama! I'm not one of these lil niggas and far fro—" I look up and out of nowhere see Bateador standing right in front of Randy.

"What's that now Randy? Come holla at me for a second. This spot right here not the place to voice your grievances homie!" Pandillero tapped Bateador shoulder.

"Li nan B. fre Sa negro jwenn pwen an!"

"Vini non sou Pandillero li di ke li pa youn nan sa yo' niga lil."

"Kite ki chi pou kont li nonm!"

They both said something in another language. Sounded crazy as hell to me. Took us all by surprise hearing the shit come out they mouth. She walked over to Pandillero, pulling him aside so no one could hear what she had to say. Then I see Pandillero go over and grab a bottle of water.

Bateador seem like he disappeared into thin air. She makes her way back to the court.

"Here you go. Ain't like ya'll gone win no damn way," she said as she threw Debo the ball. The minute the ball came into play this dumbass nigga Mike lose it. She came right from behind his silly ass and takes it from him in mid-dribble. She went straight past him down and shoots the three to win the game.

Before the ball fell from the net, she was on her way back into the house. I see Pandillero get up and head for the backdoor shaking his head and laughing. Errbody else on the ground laughing about what the hell just happened. I can't believe dis shit myself. They straight used her as a ringer for real—and won? All these big ass niggas and we let this girl, Treasure-I-Didn't-Even-Know-She-Could-Play, beat us?

"Damn Big Dog, how you gone go back to the GGV now?" Tony said.

"Yeah, shit ain't so funny now is it?" Sam said.

"I think these niggas need to move 'cause it ain't no way in hell dey gone be able to explain nis shit," City said, as they all was on the ground laughing.

Then to top it off, all we hear coming from the radio is, "Na na na na, Na na na na, Hey, Hey, Hey, Goodbye!" Then it sound like the record scratched and they played "Bigg, B, B, Bigg, Bigg Eight Hundred! Bigg, B, B, Bigg, Bigg Eight Hundred!"

These niggas got a theme song? Hell naw! The whole yard weak laughing. All we can do is join in with them. After about another hour, we headed home. Randy was pissed that Treasure went at him the way she did. Not to mention he bitchin' about fucking up with them niggas.

I told him to squash it 'cause she was right. That's why they came down hard like that. But we both know shit could've been worse. Hell, I told him not to worry about shit before the game started. He always have to try and do shit his way all the time.

12 DEANGELO

“What’s up wit’ ya' T?”

“Nothing much, about to get in nis game. Whatchu doing out this way?”

"Came to holla at you for a minute. That’s about it.”

“Yeah, ‘bout what?”

“It can wait ‘til you finish hoopin.’ Who ya’ll playing anyway?”

“Some dudes from the GGV, that’s all, they go to school with us. We're still waitin’ on ney team to show up. Plus, they said they would let me know when ney here. So go ‘head what’s up?”

“You sure?”

“What? Is this something bad you about to tell me ‘cause this not like you?”

“Come on T, it ain’t bad, but um—memba I was telling you about me getting picked up for Greece?”

“Yeah, what about it?”

“Found out when I’m leaving out.”

“So when you leaving?”

“After Labor Day, right before yo’ senior year.” I can see that T was trying not to look up at me. The whole time I started talking she been walking around making like she was busy. I walked over to her in the living room and put my arm around her shoulder. We walked down to the basement so she could go out the basement door toward the court.

"So how long is training? What, couple months then you going on break and—"

"Naw T. I won't be back in a couple months. I'll be there for at least a year straight before I can come back. I might be able to slide out for a minute but that won't be 'til after, you know." Then I hear them tap on the glass door letting T know the game about to start. T kept her head down and looked at the floor for a minute. Then she looked back up at me just in T fashion.

"I'm happy for you. I know you gone kill it over there. Let me get out here." As she stepped forward, I pulled the door open and stepped out before I let her pass.

"I'm gone stick around so I can holla at chu some more. Plus, I wanna see if I taught chu anything on this court." I knew that would cheer her up. I can see by the look on her face she wanna ask me to stay but she would never do it. "Cool!" was all she said as she stepped around me and headed to the court.

Damn, that's that lil youngin' Blitz. Yelp, I see his fat ass brother over there Randy. That's who T was ducking from, that nigga Blitz. Hell naw, the Lou is hella small. I see dey shocked to see T. These fools be talkin' mad shit when they find out she in a game but when she gets to doing her thing the laughing stop.

I taught my T right. She can hang wit' any nigga and give 'em a run for dey money with no problem. Hell, I would put money on it if she was anybody else. But I would never gamble with my girl on no level. She better den that.

"Aight T, let's bring it home baby!" I always gotta sho' some love for my girl. Plus, I know that lil young nigga hate that shit! What's his name, County? I know he got a crush on T, I ain't worried. The nigga younger than T; he ain't shit to be worried about. T clowning today; she's puttin' it on these cats. Look at this cat think he finna, do any better handli—HELL NAW! She just put a cross on this nigga, made his legs stop working. I wish my peoples were here to see this shit. He gone think I'm lying when I tell him about this here.

"What's up Pandillero? I ain't know you would be herrre. I was just hearin' 'bout chu before I ate and shit!" "What's up Randy?" I dabbed him off then moved over to finish watching the game. I hope this nigga get the point and shut da fuck up. Talkin' 'bout he was just hearing about me. Yeah nigga, I know. You got a problem with the hike but you gone get over it.

"These yo' peoples?"

"Something like that, I see yo' brother got some skills out there on the court."

"Yeah man, that's all dese niggas do. I was waiting to see dis bitch he been telling me about from his school and shit he trying to get at."

"Aw yeah, what's her name?" I already know he talking 'bout T. I just wanna hear him say the shit though, some bitch. I should knock his head off his shoulder for even letting nat shit come out his mouth like that.

"Shit'd I think her name Trisha or something. Man I on't know, don't get me to lying. But um, what's the deal with the price on the next packag...?" I was about to bitch slap the shit out that nigga for coming at me like that. He knows damn well he need to holla at Bateador about all that shit. Not to mention the fact he called T a bitch. And he bringing all dis shit up at her house like we at a trap some damn where.

"Hold up Randy, I'm here to watch the game that's all. Whatever you need to discuss, holla at B about! Don't ever come at me about some shit like that 'cause I don't know whatchu talkin' 'bout. That lil bitch comment you made den already pissed me off so why don't chu fall back before we have a problem."

I don't even bother to look at the nigga after I said it. I hope he fix his mouth to say something else so I can take this nigga on a ride. Hell, here she go, I can tell by the way she looking at me she mad. "Excuse me, I don't kn..." Look at T, sexy as hell when she mad. All I can do is watch.

Look at her hips. Girl got mad body and boy what I would do to that muthafucka. Blitz think he got some type of pull with her thinkin' she gone back down but wait for it. Shut down! Just like I thought. This nigga Randy lookin' shook. All these lil ass niggas ready to jump for T ass.

"T, I alre...." I knew she didn't give a fuck 'cause she's way too pissed right now to listen to what the hell anybody has to say. I'm just gone step back and let her get it out. Damn, here this nigga go.

I move back over, tap Bateador shoulder. We both spoke Haitian Creole 'cause I know none of them know what we talking about. Hell, I can tell by the way they all looking they can't.

"It's cool B. That nigga get the point!"

"Come on Pandillero, he said he not one of these lil niggas."

"Leave that shit alone man!" After hearing T go the fuck off on Randy and Bateador get at him, I knew she was gone try and check a nigga. But I got something for her ass.

"What the hell was that Deangelo? And why the hell is Corey here?"

"Look at chu T. Hurry up so we can get out of herrre. I wanna take you somewhere today."

"Yeah, try and play me crazy Mr. Deangelo. I see whatchu doing. Tell Corey I don't need him running to my rescue either." She walked back to the court. Too easy. I already know T; she may have an attitude out this world. If you just move on to something else, she'll either stand and fight or resolve the problem. I knew that all I had to do was resolve it and she would be happy to move on.

"T, you killed it out there. You should've seen the look on they face." T didn't say a word. She went into the bathroom and locked the door behind her. I sat in the living room waiting on her to come out. After a while, I decided to go out to the car and call Bateador, let him know to let that shit wit' Randy go and to tell him about the game of course.

I made a couple more calls to my people so they could put some shit together for me real quick. When I went back in the house, I see T sitting in the living room. I figured something was on her mind and she's upset. I know I have to make her feel better so I asked her to take a ride with me and we headed to the door.

"I know you not all quiet over there about what happened with that nigga Randy. Let me know what's going on with what I told you earlier." She didn't say anything; she moved that fat ass toward me and leaned onto the door staring out the window.

I decided to take her for her favorite pass time where I know she'll relax and feel a little better. I cross the bridge and head for the lake. When we pulled up, T unbuckled her seatbelt and was about to get out. I hit the lock back on her, opened my door and made my way to T side and opened it for her.

I know she annoyed but that's still no reason for her to not be treated like the woman she is. She headed to her favorite spot right as I was about to grab a blanket from out the back. I got the text I was waiting for so I closed the door and followed in T direction. We walked around for a minute; I was trying to give her space. She seemed to be in her own world so I let her lead the way.

I've never been around T this long without us saying a word or laughing so I had to end this quick. "Ay T, you wanna sit down, get something to eat real quick?" She looked back at me and quickly turned away without answering me. I went over, put my arm around her shoulders and lead her toward the dock.

She never really looked up so I didn't know if she saw the picnic my people put together for us or not. I see my peoples head back to the car so I tell T to look up and all I can get out of her was a, "That's pretty." T love shit like this. I know she must have some heavy shit going through her head right now. We sat down on the dock.

"So T talk to yo' boy. Tell me whatchu think about me going over there for a year." I passed her a bottle of water and waited on her to say something, anything for real. All she did was laid on her stomach, picked up some grapes and looked out at the water. I let her lay there for a minute while she nibbled on fruit.

That's it, this getting on my last nerve. I feel like I'm

about to lose my mind with this not talking shit. "T, can you say something," I said with a lil frustration behind it.

"Whatchu want me to say Deangelo? You have to do whatchu have to do! Do what make you happy! I don't know whatchu want me to say."

I moved some of the stuff sitting on the blanket out of the way. I eased myself under T so her head was on my lap. She was looking up at me. Oh shit, I should've thought this through. I can't have her head being this close to my dick. It's making me happy as a mug. Let me move her up so her back is against my chest. That way, I can think and talk to her at the same time.

"Look T, I know it's more than that. If it wasn't, then you wouldn't be acting like this. So, since you won't spit it out, let me! I know it's your senior year and all coming up and I know you probably worried about me not being there for you. I understand it seems like a long time but I'll be back to see you before you know it." I can feel her lungs expand then skip and do it again. I wrap my arms tighter around her to try and make her relax. Is that a tear on my arm? I know she not crying. I've never seen T cry. Never in a million years would I want to be the reason she was crying.

I lean forward pushing her off. Before I knew it, I was turning her body directly in front of me while wrapping her legs around my waist. She tried not to look up but I can see the tears as they fell onto the space in between us and down onto the blanket that separated our bodies.

I pulled her chin up, "T, what's up with this here? Talk to me, what's going on witchu?" Those walnut shaped eyes of hers trying not to open to see me. When they did, all I wanted to do was make her happy. The site of her brown eyes now darkened in red covered in moisture hurt me. I hate the feeling I have in me right now. I've done some shit in my life but have never felt like this before.

"I, I, it's just a lot to take in right now. I knew this was coming when you told me. I figured I would see you every couple months are something. At least, I thought you would be around for my graduation. You won't even be there for that. Then you'll be leaving in a couple months. I barely see you now but at least I see you.

I know we not together or anything like that but I already know you gone get over there, find some bitch and that's gone be the last I see or hear from you. Who's gone be there for me now? You da only person who has been there for all the big things that have happened in my life. I don't wanna lose that."

All I can do is pull her head into my chest and let her let it out. After I felt her slow up I gave her a water bottle and we walked back to the car. I didn't bother to ask her to come back to my crib. She sat on the couch; I grabbed some water out the fridge and joined her. I turned on the radio and laid back holding T in my arms.

What the hell am I doing? The only thing in my head was what she said and how it's making me second-guess the role I've played in her life. She right though, I don't want to lose her either. I always said when she was old enough she would be mine. She not quite there just yet.

My heart telling me to roll with it and stop all the waiting. I love T. Damn! I love T, not just 'cause I know her, but I really do love T on some wife her up now if I could type shit. She means the world to me and no matter how much I try to deny my feelings or put them on the back burner, I can't. Fuck it!

"T, if you would be up for it, maybe after graduation you can come over and see me? Maybe go to school in Greece or something?" She started to sit up.

"What?"

"I mean you might like it over there, it's a pretty cool place. I can get you set up or you can stay with me if you want T." Then all of a sudden, she shot up to her feet heading to the door and said she was ready to go home. Really? That came from out of nowhere.

"What's wrong T? Why you ready to go home?" She turned around and looked me dead in my eyes.

"You runnin' game on me; that's why! That's exactly why I didn't wanna say anything earlier. I didn't want chu to think I was one of those weak bitches you fuck wit'. So like I said, you running game on me and I'm ready to go home! Now please! If not, I can call my momma to come get me."

Really? T then loss her damn mind. Hell, no! Not today, I walked right up in her space and looked down at her. "What the hell you mean? Don't lose yo' fucking mind and forget who you talkin' to. I ain't ever treated you like some bitch off the street or tried to run game on you...." I moved back put my hands on my knees forcing her to see me. "...and if I brought yo' ass here you better believe I'm the one taking you home! Don't try and hit me with that you gone call yo' momma bullshit either 'cause you know you bluffing.

You would call a cab before you called Kathy. I know it and you do too. Stop bullshitting yoself with that..." I stood back up looking at her again. "...Now that we have that out the way, can we talk for a second. Then, if you still want to leave I'll take you."

She stood there for a minute then decided to sit her ass back on the couch. Look at her got her arms crossed and pouting like a damn baby. If T was anybody else, she damn sho' wouldn't be here. And she damn sho' wouldn't be talking all that shit she flapping her gums about.

"Look T, I'm for real about you coming over after you graduate and everything else I just told you. I'm not the one to be tied down to anybody and I know you know that. But if you think about it, we've been together longer than either of us can remember. I've never tried to force you into being in a relationship with me 'cause I wanted you to be able to live your life like I have. So, I guess I've never been in a real relationship with anyone 'cause I was building one with you."

I walked over to the table by the front door and grabbed the box my peoples dropped off for me earlier this week and took it back over to T. I kneeled down in between her legs and gave it to her.

"Here, but before you open it I just want chu to know that I truly do love you T. I love you more than I realized until this day. Even though I'm leaving, if anything come up you know you can always let Bateador know you being cold and I'll come back as soon as I get the word." I can see the tears roll down from her eyes as she opened the box. Once she saw the ring, she picked it up and read the inscription, "Forever T DAJ."

"I was saving this for when I left but I figured I'd give it to you so you know that I'd never forget about chu." Hell, how could I forget about T? Ain't a bitch out there that could compare to my T. I should know; I had enough of them to make that decision already.

Without a word, she leaned in and kissed me. I slowly kissed her back, taking in her sweet taste mixed with the salty tears on her lips. I picked her up and carried her off to the bedroom. Damn, she light. All I can do is try my best not to let one go right now.

The way her ass feels in my hands as she rides me while we kiss our way to the bed is mind blowing. I laid her back onto the bed and climbed on top of her. We continue to go at it and then I pull up to look her in the eyes. I softly wipe the trails of tears away from her face.

"You sure? I mean the way we're going at it I have to know if you sure you want to take this step and have sex with me. So think about it T; are you sure that you wanna have sex with me right now?" She nodded her head up and down; I stood up watching her sit up straight on the bed. Damn, I been waiting on this for I don't know how long. I have to make sure that this what she wants though. I know what the hell I need and it all depends on what she says.

"T look, I know a lot has been said and you may not be thinking straight right now. We don't have to do this. You know tomorrow is another day and with that comes change. So, are you sure T?"

"What does that mean? Tomorrow you may change your mind on loving me? Or you may change your mind on me meeting you in Greece? What does that mean," she said staring into my eyes like she was trying to read my mind.

"It means that if we go through with this, our relationship will change and we both will be in uncharted waters. Before you make this decision, you need to consider that there's going to be a change that we may not be expecting. So if you want, we can stop what's happening and chill out."

She sat there for a minute then slid to the edge of the bed and stood up. The radio was still on and I can hear *I Wanna Know* by Joe, filling up the room. She began to shed every bit of clothing she had on to the sound of the music.

I watch in awe at the site of her. Before she took off her panties she said, "I'm sure I wanna have sex witchu, what about chu?" That was all I needed to hear. I wrapped T up in my arms and lifted her body right back in the air.

I felt like I didn't have enough hands to explore her body. I laid her back down and damn near tore her panties off. I couldn't wait to taste what T has been saving for me all this time. Just like I thought from the moment my tongue hit her lips. I can feel her body tremble in my hands, I took my time. I wanna hit every nook and hidden valley within her trap.

I let the words from the song guide me and explain to T what I was truly feeling. My tongue can't move fast enough across her clit. Damn, this the best pussy I've had in my life. I can do this all day if she let me and never stop. The taste of her warm silky flow was melting in my mouth faster than I can get it out. This the best dessert I ever had.

She so wet, I have to see what it'll feel like; I slowly slid my finger into her. She too tight for my dick. I know I'd rip the lining out this muthafucka. I eased in another finger and tried my best to prepare her for me. Shit, I can't take it no more.

I know she den came twice already. After I felt her body jerk, I slurped up her sugary cream again then I had to get in. I kissed my way up her body. I was only able to stop long enough to suck on her breast while I prepared myself for the dive. Soon as my dick moved across her clit I was ready to murder that ass.

I slowed down; forcing myself to wait and I watched her move while I played around with her warm insides with the tip of my dick. Then I couldn't wait any longer, the seductive way she bit down on her lip and looked up at me. I can't control myself, I inch myself in gradually as she began to lose her breath. I can feel her walls trying to stop me from breaching her paradise.

Shit was starting to piss me off. I'm too experienced to be about to nut. I let the thought of being clowned by a virgin get to my head and pushed thru. She screamed a tortured sound and I stopped. I know she was in pain and I snapped back realizing it was my T not some random virgin.

Not like I had one before but still. I leaned in and covered her mouth with mine. Moving down to let her breathe I sucked in her nipple flicking it until I felt her muscles clinch down on me. I started back moving a little not going in any further. I worked it like this for a minute.

"You all right T? I'm not hurting you am I?" She didn't say anything, just moved her head from side-to-side. Her eyes rolled back in her head. I crept in slower and slower until I thought she couldn't take any more. I worked her with a little bit more and the more she screamed in ecstasy I knew to give her a little bit more.

She tight as fuck. My dick can barely move and this damn sleeve is not helping it at all. I was like a miner in her pussy. Digging for whatever was hiding down in there. It was turning me on more that I had to coach her to breathe. Seemed like I had to keep reminding her but the only way she would listen was if I backed out. It was feeling like she was getting tighter and not molding around me like she should've been. Not that I'm complaining but damn, I'll neva get out da pussy at dis rate.

After about another hour of heart stopping passionate mind-blowing bliss, I felt my body do some shit it has never done before, like a deep down in my bones type feeling came over me. All I can feel is heat, adrenalin and pressure come from my toes all the way up to my head then to the tip of my dick. I pulled out before I came just in case. I feel like I'm frozen or having a seizure. I can't stop pulsating. What the fuck? The thought of how it would've felt busin' inside of her had me goin' again right after the first one.

I roll over with T in my arms for a minute. A little while after, I made my way to the bathroom to get some towels. When I turned around from getting the towels out the closet, T was standing there looking sexy as hell, nothing on. All I can do is watch as she comes closer to me.

It was like this was the first time I'd seen her naked. I walked over and gave her a long kiss and start checking to make sure that every inch of her body was real. I had to make sure this not a dream and the way she kissed me back let me know this all so real. The moment I reached down and found the right spot, my finger was covered. I can feel her insides roll down my finger and puddle into my hand. I knew that I'm wide-awake.

She turned and walked to the shower. Damn, look at that ass move. My dick was right back rock solid and dragging me in her direction. Round two, I had her backup in my arms pinned against the shower wall as the water made its way down our bodies. I placed her back down then broke for the room to get another condom, and then picked up right where we left off.

I lost count of how many times we made love that night. The next morning came and went. By the time me and T woke up, it was two o'clock in the afternoon, we was still naked. I had T wrapped up in my arms making sure she didn't go anywhere.

All I can think about is everything that went down and how I just realized how much I love her. My mind is racing. Whatever change today brings I hope that it won't stop me from being just like this with T no time soon.

13 TREASURE

What the hell he means he leaving in a couple months? For a whole damn year? FUCK! That's all I want to scream right now. But you know what, pull it together. Let me just sit here a minute to get my mind right before he come back.

Damn, I was hoping he would say something came up and he had to go but of course not. Whenever I need to be put on the spot Deangelo's always the one to do it. From the time we got in the car I just kept thinkin' about what it would be like without him being around. Yeah he damn straight I'm not mad about that fat fuck, fuck him!

He's been there for me ever since I can remember. Stood up for me when niggas was talking shit behind my back. Squashed beefs for me when hood rats thought I was messing wit' they supposed to be man. He gave me heads up on all the niggas even the ones I talked to. And just like he said, they all tried to pull the same shit.

Big games he was there. When we moved he was the one who told me to keep hooping. Hell, he took me to the court every chance he could. My first job he was there; every job he was there. Taught me how to drive, even let me use his car to get my license. He made sure I was taken care of. I didn't need for nothing and he has never asked for anything in return. FUCK!

Good, just the place I need to be to think let me hurry

up and...what the fuck? Okay, now he wanna play. Why I just wanna scream, 'Hurry up and let me out the damn car din!' Why the hell is it so hard for me to stop myself from crying right now? I thought I left all this shit back out on the court.

Just keep walking; think Treasure and think before you look like a damn fool in front of him. The last thing I need is to be making ugly ass faces with snot dripping and shit all up in his damn face. I'll never live that down. Do I wanna sit down and eat? What the hell? Where we going now? Who the hell is that?

Ain't that cute, somebody having a picnic. Why we can't be like that? Instead, here I am trying not to cry with a damn friend. A fucking friend! After all this time, all I am to him is a FRIEND? My dumb ass stood on the sideline just watching 'cause I'm a fucking FRIEND. Why the fuck am I feeling like this? I been knew that all I am, was, or will ever be is a fucking FRIEND to him!

Look up for what? See, this the shit I'm talking about. He always does romantic shit like we together. Making me feel like he love me, then he play me out and put me right back in that FRIEND category. That's all right, even though I'm happy as hell that he did all this, I'm just going to say, "That's pretty."

I wanna show his ass just how pretty it is and feel him inside me. Just make love to him right here and now. I know, FRIEND, that's all I need to keep telling myself so I won't get this situation confused. Let me just lay down for a second before I lose my damn mind. I already know the deal though; he gone get over there and move on with his life.

Ain't shit here for him but jail or the grave! FUCK! I don't know what to think now; I can't ask him to stay. I know that if I do and he stays what will happen. I can't and won't do that to him; what the fuck kinda bullshit is that? How that sound? 'Um can you please stay here for me FRIEND? You have a lot to look forward to. Like going to jail or getting killed over some dumbass drug shit. Oh yeah, did I mention our FRIENDSHIP?' Yeah, that'll be fair to him.

Damn he strong. I'm sure glad that he pulled me up

'cause I don't know if that was another leg I was just laying on or his dick. Shit, this feel good, if this what a friend feel like. Hell, I don't want or need any fucking more; just let me have this one. Have this one who's leaving me. The one I'm not going see anymore.

He's not gone be there for me like he used to be. I can't hold these gates any longer. Maybe he won't notice or say anything. I'm trying to patch this shit back together but I don't think I can. I should've known he was gone make me face this head on. I can't hold this in any longer I know I have to tell him what I'm feeling.

It's hard as hell to get these words out without slipping up and telling him how much I love his ass. That felt good though, even if it wasn't all of what I wanted to say. After getting back in the car, we sped backup the highway. Well, I know he not taking me home seeing he just past my exit. Guess I haven't wet his shirt up enough with my crybaby ass.

I need to tell him how I really feel about him; I just can't though. I know he don't give a fuck about being with someone. It's way too many desperate bitches out there that'll do whatever he dream of. Just to be wit' him or to be seen with him and they won't fight him back. I know he know I have my limit and there are way too many limits for somebody like him.

He needs to be free to do what he wants when he wants. I guess I wish he could just commit his heart to me and leave all them ho's alone. I know better than that. I can't be the one heartbroken and lonely waiting around on him. I've been waitin' for him long enough. I guess I'm really scared of him leaving me heartbroken. Or treating me like them ho's he fuck with. I think that'll hurt me the most. Why even throw myself into traffic like that anyway?

I guess all that hiding how I really felt about him has all boiled over at the thought of losing him forever. I may just be a friend to him but he'll always be my true love no matter what. Damn, I love his house. It's so calming; make you wanna just lie back and relax with the one you love. Let me sit down; I need to think. This has to be my new favorite spot, on his chest listening to his heartbeat. I think if I lay here in his arms long enough I can remember the sound.

Am I dreaming or did he just say what I think he said? I have to sit up and ask him, "WHAT?" He did just ask me to go over there with him after I get out of school. Oh really, he can set his FRIEND up a spot while she sit around on the sidelines in another country doing the same shit to her there as he do here? Fuck this. I need to go home, I can't figure this FRIEND shit out for nothing.

Only thing I know is I don't wanna be a DAMN FRIEND! Maybe if I say it without telling him how I feel he'll understand. I couldn't get that shit out my mouth before I changed my mind. I'll let him think whatever and threaten to call Momma if he doesn't take me home.

Who the hell he talking to like that? He sho' right though. Hell, I would try to find a bus before I call Momma. FUCK! I have to talk to him now 'cause I know he won't take me home until I do. After I sit back on the couch, Deangelo starts telling me shit that I been waiting to hear for a minute. But why now when he about to leave my ass? Did he just say he been building a relationship with me? Oh yeah buddy, what kind, a FRIENDS only relationship?

Ain't this a bitch? What the hell is this and why the hell is he on his knees in between my legs like this. I can feel my juices starting to flow. His scent is doing something to me that my body is ready to welcome. I'm not about to hold anything back. Deangelo is way too close for me right now. All I want to do is suck on his bottom lip and taste the words coming out his mouth. That's it; here come the tears. "Forever T, Deangelo Alejandro Joseph" Look how cute he is; he was thinking about me.

I knew he loved me already but I guess it's a little more than as a friend. I want to kiss him but he probably will hurry up and take my ass home then. Fuck this, I can't resist him anymore. I hope he kisses me back, that's all I can hope for. I bet this how crackheads feel the first time they hit dope. I've only heard about it and this has to be the feeling they're talking about.

I feel like my soul is looking down at my body right now. The way his hands feel moving from my thighs up to my ass. The feel of his arms holding me makes me feel secure. I know there's no way in hell he'll let me fall. I can't think of a better place I'd rather be right at this moment. No, don't stop!

"You sure? I mean the way w..." Am I sure? HELL TO THE MUTHAFUCKIN YEAH I'M SURE! As good as I feel right now, I can't even get the words out my damn mouth. The only thing I can do is shake my head up and down. What now? All this talking is starting to get on my nerves. Hold up, he think that I expect for him to change by the morning? I'm not Boo Boo The Fool. I know he's not going to change in a couple hours. I don't know if I'll be hurt or not if he changed his mind on me going over there. Hell, I don't even know if I want to chase up behind him.

He so concerned about changin' his mind; he better hope he put it on me. 'Cause waiting this long if it's not worth it I know I sure in the hell will have a lot to consider. To be honest, at this point I'm so ready I feel like I'm about to lose my mind if he don't finish what he started. Please, let's stop with all the talking and work me 'til I can't think any fucking more.

After talking to Deangelo and thinking about everything he said, all I can think was, 'Yeah, whatever.' I stood up, slid my shirt off, stepped out my shorts, unsnapped my bra and said, "I'm sure I wanna have sex witchu, what about chu?" Before I know it, he picking me up, kissing me harder, touching me faster. It's like he was hit with a bolt of energy.

With every touch and kiss, I fell a pulse come from his body to mine. Yes, get these panties off baby! My cake is so fucking wet. As soon as his tongue touched my clit, all I could do was hold his head to keep his ass focused. He licked my nana, flicking his tongue all over my swollen jewel. Then he peeled back my lips and licked up and down for a minute and down in my soaked hole. I felt the tip of his moist tongue trace the edge of my pussy. I let go and released the flood gates.

I felt his finger slide in my drenched hall then he took

his thumb and slid it up to my clit. Teasing it, not too hard and not too soft. I can feel the floodgates detonate and my purse getting wetter and wetter. That's not stopping Deangelo though; he catching every bit of me. Sucking and gulping it down before it has a chance to make it past my lips. Deangelo on a mission tonight. I've exploded so many times, I don't know if I have any liquid left inside of me.

He kissing me all over as he make his way up my body. What the hell? I can't breathe; his dick is so damn thick and hard, I don't think...damn, breathe! "You all right T? I'm not hurting you am I?" 'Breathe Treasure, BREATHE!' was on repeat in my head as he dug deeper in me. All I can do is scream out to catch my damn breath. I didn't know it would hurt like this, feel like I'm being ripped open. He didn't move and I felt my body tense again and shake vigorously. His tongue on my nipple and the squeezing of my breast sent my juices flowing again.

The more we went at it, the more I was getting into it. I wanted him to stop holding back. He probably thought I was about to pass out with all the trouble I was having catching my breath. Every time he started back up, the more I didn't want this to be over. Forever couldn't be long enough for me to feel this fucking good. I felt his body get harder. Then he started to vibrate, I know he about to cum. I rode the wave with him for as long as I could hold on.

After he made his way to the bathroom, I had to go at it some more. Hell, if we going at it anyway, might as well make this moment last for as long as I can. I went right in behind him and by the looks of his man, he ret-to-go. I led him to the shower and we went at it again. Then again in the kitchen, then again on the steps, then again in the living room. Hell, I was surprised that I was able to hang in there with him as many times as I did.

I guess after I figured he had been holding back I had to see what every inch of his man would feel like. To my amazement, it seemed like his dick grew bigger each time we started over. My ass was beat by the time we fell asleep. I didn't have any worries or regrets; my entire lower half was sore but so da fuck what. All I wanna do is feel his body next to mine for as long as I can.

14 DEANGELO

"Whatchu sitting all the way over there for T?"

"What?"

"You've been acting all funny since we left the house."

"I told you I was sore. Feel like you broke something." I chuckled and shook my head pulling her face to me kissing her lips. She moaned as I looked at her, her eyes still closed after I pulled away.

"I ain't break shit; I tow my pussy up though! I told you we could've stayed in the tub longer. You wouldn't be that sore if you weren't so fuckin' hard headed." She didn't say anything she adjusted in her seat for the thousandth time.

"You thinking about last night?"

"Are you?"

"Damn straight; what else would I be thinking about?" I pulled her over towards me again. I needed to feel her so I moved my seat back and had her sit over in my lap. She crumbled into my neck as I rubbed up and down her thigh. Who the hell would've thought it would've gone down like that? Sho' not me, caught me by surprise like a mufucka.

"So whatchu wanna do today?"

"I hope eat. You do remember pulling in front of this restaurant don't you? I hope you not daydream-driving over here."

"Come on now T, I'm talking about after we eat?"

"I don't know. Besides, I may have changed my mind about hanging out witchu today."

"Yeah? Okay, yo' mouth can tell me anything but yo' body can't." We both started to laugh as I kissed her sucking her tongue into my mouth. Once I kissed that crazy shit she was yappin' out her mouth she was back in my neck, I think she was trying to hide but the shit wasn't workin'.

"Well, Debby called left me a message; she wanted me to swing by the East Coast with them tonight. I already know you not down with that though?"

"That's how you gone do me?"

"Yeah, that's what I thought; I already know how you feel about showing up with me. I guess we can figure something else out."

I didn't bother to answer her. Shit, I would love to show T off on my arm. If that's what will make her happy, so be it. I'm down for that. I helped her out and we made our way in. After we enjoyed our food, we were back in the car in no time. I figured we would hit a movie then stop by the East Coast Lounge. Plus, my dude was having a party there tonight.

My eyes lit up seeing T come into the living room in a tight rose dress and heels. The way it fell just enough off her shoulder made me want to cancel our plans and stay in.

"You sure you wanna head down here T? I mean, we can chill out if you want to." She turned slow in a circle stopping right so I can see her ass, and then looked back over her shoulder.

"Why not? I mean you did want me to wear this didn't you? You having second thoughts on whatchu picked up for me?" Then she walked towards me and put her head on my shoulder.

"Why you doing this to me T? You look good as hell in that dress and you know I'm not having second thoughts. Just different ones." We both laughed and headed to the door. After the short dress change, we were making rounds at the club. It didn't take long before I heard the chatter boxes get to running off at the mouth about us.

I sat back with my boys and watched T do her thing

around the room. The way she moved turned me on. I should've put it on her before we left, I know she would've been walkin' all funny and shit like earlier so I didn't. All I wanted to do was leave and get her home with me. The East Coast a hood lounge so we pretty much know errbody in this bitch. Usually, I won't take T to anything in the hood.

I mean, not come in the door with her or leave out for that matter. Not that I didn't want too. I didn't want her to be that close to the shit I had going in the streets. That's just for her own safety. Plus, I don't want people to be all in our business, especially not these ho's. They the main reason why I try and stay away from T when she down here. These ho's like to talk too much shit and keep up way too much drama.

They all talk; half of them I wouldn't touch. And the ones that I have, I most definitely didn't want T nowhere around them. I already know they'd do and say whatever they can to be with me. T would be the one that would have to deal with it. I'd rather them assume what we have then to let them in on it.

"Damn Pandillero, I see you riding wit' cho' girl on yo' arm tonight. Can't believe this nigga wife'd up on us and shit," Yoppa said as they all began to laugh.

"Man stop playing. If that's the case that nigga been wife'd up if you talking 'bout Treasure, ya'll niggas already know. This nigga ain't slick," Flight said as they laughed even harder.

"Whatever, ya'll niggas crazy." Before I can turn back around, I feel somebody sit down on my lap. I know by the smell of freshly smoked weed it ain't T.

"Dang Pandillero, how you just gone come through herrre wit' Treasure like dat? Dat's messed up."

"Really? Now why is that?"

"'Cause I thought me and you was kickin' it tonight?"

"Why you think that?" Cindy started whispering in my ear, she a bona fide freak. She whispering shit so nasty into my ear I forgot she was sitting on me. Once she finished, I just laughed.

"Girl you crazy. I gotta pass tonight though."

"Why?" I wanted to tell her 'cause T a thoroughbred and she a mutt. They not even in the same category. I don't have the time to explain to her why the two shouldn't be used in comparison. Plus, I didn't want to have to throw her ass out of here when she started acting crazy if I did.

"'Cause like you said, I walked in here with T so that's who I'm walking out of here with." I politely helped her sad ass up off my damn lap.

"All right den, but chu know dat's messed up 'cause dat ain't eva stopped chu in da past." I laughed some more as she walked off. I didn't have to look around to find T 'cause her eyes was locked right into mine then she looked away. I can see she frontin,' laughing and shit like what she just saw didn't faze her. I'll cross that bridge when I get to it. Hell, if she keeps moving that ass past me I'm not gone let her get a word out before I put it on her ass. I know exactly how to take her mind off this shit here.

The whole time we was there, I could tell them skeezas was trying to get at T. They were coming like clockwork. It was to the point I literally put a chair around me to keep them ho's away. I looked like I was a lion tamer or some shit. Then the more I thought about it, this a regular night for me in the hood.

Bitches come flocking like pigeons when I walk in. Only thing is, they don't need to hear a clap. They just see green and will tear each other apart to try and get something they'll never have. Hell, if they knew any better they would be going after T. She already has what they trying to get.

I chill out and let they asses come, one by one. I'm turning tricks away faster than I can keep up with. It was to the point that when they came by the table I wouldn't even look at dey asses. Then they would walk away. I see T on the other side of the room and it look like she don't look too happy.

I go in a little closer to see what's going on. Before I make it, a scuffle breaks out and bouncers are errwhere. I look around for T and don't see her. I go to the front and nothing. I start to ask around but errbody saying she went in another direction. I see Bateador come up so I ask him but he look like something wrong.

"Ay Pandillero, it's some niggas in the alley, they got Treasure. They say if you wanna see her again to come around the back." Fuck it. I pop the trunk, grab my Desert Eagle and make my way to the back. I should shoot my damn self for dragging T into this shit. I have to stay focused on what's going on.

I walk back and see two niggas. One of them had a gun to T head; it was pure hatred on her face. She looked different for some reason but not scared; she looked extremely pissed the fuck off. I guess it rubbed off on me and made me even more furious. The dumbass niggas didn't know it was another back door to the club. Before they can even say anything, Bateador dropped one.

As soon as he looked, I dropped the nigga holding T. We didn't say anything; I grabbed T up and put her in the car. The further away I took T, the harder she began to breathe; I knew what had just taken place was starting to set in. I fucked up by taking T and all I can do now is try to get her to understand what happened.

After I turned off Lucas and Hunt onto Halls Ferry I heard T start crying, then she screamed for me to pull over. I didn't think anything of it so I pulled off to the side. Next thing I know, she got out. I jumped out behind her trying to talk with her about what happened but she kept walking. It was just my luck a cop was coming down the road.

I watched T as she flagged him down; I headed back to the car and pulled off. I waited at the convenience store to see if I saw her in his car. When he came past, he pulled in and she wasn't with him. I went back down to find her.

I drove around for about an hour before I decided to go by her house and see if she made it. I didn't give a fuck if Kathy was mad or not about me looking for T that early in the morning. I went straight to the door, but before I hit the doorbell, I hear a ball bouncing coming from the back. I was too happy to see T still dressed up and shooting the ball in the dark. Then it hit me what she just did and I was hot.

"What the hell T? You could've at least let me take you

home after what happened tonight."

"I don't need you to protect me Deangelo. I'm fine; I just want to be left alone."

"Yeah, obviously you don't and nothing happened either, right?"

"Look Deangelo, you don't need to protect me. You need to be worried about protecting yoself! If it wasn't for yo' lil ho Cindy coming over there fucking with me I wouldn't be in this mess right now."

"What the hell Cindy have to do with this? She sat on my lap and so what? I know you not fighting over no shit like that."

"Really? You think that's what this is about? Well, let me let you in on the secret. Cindy, you know the ho you fuck wit'? Yeah her, she came over to the table talking mad shit about you and her. When I wouldn't bite, Shannon decided she heard enough and hit her. I was about to leave when nem niggas pulled me out the door.

The whole time they asking me about you saying shit like, 'Yeah this her, she ain't said a word yet. Cindy said she wasn't gone say shit. I saw her come in with da nigga. Dat's her. She da only one he been looking at all night. We got dat nigga now. I bet chu mad you came wit' dat nigga ain't chu? Should've let Cindy have his ass.' Bullshit! So stop worrying about me and get yo' shit together!" It all started to make sense. The next time I see that bitch Cindy, she better already be dead 'cause she sho' don't want me to get a hold to her ass alive.

"That still don't explain why you got out the car though T."

"Like I said, I just want to be left alone." I walked over and held her in my arms. We walked to the curb and took a seat.

"Look at chu T, a straight soldier or some shit. All this pop off, gun to ya' dome and all you worried about is me?" I laughed and leaned over on her. She laid back in the grass and put her arms straight back like she was about to make a snow angel or something. I looked back at her. She looked tired like all the light was pulled out of her.

I felt her tense up as I moved over the top of her, I told her to relax. I put just enough of my weight on the top of her for her to know I was there. I kissed her as thoughts of losing her came flooding into my mind. Her legs wrapped around my legs as I deepened the kiss matching her slow grinds, "Talk to me T. I know you feeling something about what happe—"

"Yeah Deangelo, I'm pissed, pissed that I didn't see them before they had a chance to pull me out the door. Pissed dat bitch Cindy was trying to set chu up. Pissed that I was sleeping and not seeing what she was up to. I mean I saw her on you; I saw her walk away and talk to them. Hell, I saw all of them look over at our table. I saw how they were lookin' at chu. I saw how they came over by us. I saw that bitch pointing all in my face and shit. I mean, all the signs was there and I stil—"

"T don't worry about that shit, what's done is done. You don't know them or what happened. So you don't have to worry about that shit no more." I kissed her again as she closed her eyes I sat up next to her.

"It was more than two of them Deangelo. I didn't want you to bring me home 'cause I know I saw four of 'em wit' her. That's why I stopped the policeman just in case they were following us. It took me so long to get home 'cause I went the back way. I don't wanna bring shit to my momma house. I can't." I can hear in T voice she tired so I let it go.

I sat there thinking about if I loss T and how this shit could've gone another route. I don't know what the hell I would've done if that happened. Then all I could hear was T's breathing even out. I look back at her and she was slowly falling to sleep right there in the grass.

It was like she had no care in the world. I carried her in the house; I put her down without staying long. I know if I stay I'll just be adding more flames to the fire. Once I got in the car I jumped on the phone and it was just like she said. Bateador filled in the missing dots and I was on my way to handle it.

After all that went down, I decided to put some distance between me and T. She called a couple times but I didn't answer. I tried to talk with her and explain but she didn't wanna hear it. I made sure I had eyes on her though, just in case. I was about to leave out so I had to make sure errbody knew I was done with T.

I couldn't leave her and it might be dangerous even with the niggas I had to look after her. I started kicking it with this chick that had just moved to the hood. When I heard T was down, I made sure she saw me with her. But this dumbass broad just had to run up on her. I should've known something was up by the way she ran off. Next thing I know, T beatin' the shit out of her like it's no tomorrow.

I jumped at the chance to put up the front so I had to do T in while all eyes were focused on us and the situation. I know it 'bout hurt T but I had to do it. There's no way in hell Kathy was goin' to let me drag her ass away from her senior year. Those dumb mufuckas in the hood know they can spin a story too. I heard the bitch was pregnant; we loss the baby 'cause of T. The chick knocked T out, she knocked the chick out, all kinds of shit. It was a mess but I had to do what I had to do to protect her.

15 TREASURE

I wonder what he thinking? I bet he like, 'She don't know what the hell she doing.' Or, 'She lazy; she don't do nothing in bed.' I wish I could read minds right now. I don't know if it was good or bad. Shit, I feel like I'm sittin' on a brick over here. I wonder if I did it right or if he liked it? I don't know. I feel good just sore as hell, whatever, if he had a problem, then that's on him.

Why he think I'm sittin' far away from him now? This the same place I always sit. What he think I'm supposed to be all up on his ass now? Am I? I guess so since he den pulled me on his hard, heavy dick havin' ass. Why bring somebody to a restaurant and ask what they wanna do.

I really wanted to go to the East Coast. I already said I'd go. I'll be surprised if he willin' to go with me though. We made our way back to his house and I wasn't shocked to see two boxes sitting on the bed waiting for me when I came out the shower. I was hoping he would be waiting naked as a jay bird but I guess he keepin' his promise and not doing anything 'til later.

I already know by the designer labels on the box that this shit expensive. Inside was a pretty rose dress and it's just my size. The heels, I do love me some heels. I've never had Manolos before but these out of this world cute. They set the whole outfit off. My legs looked too fire with them puppies on my feet. I can't wait to show 'em off.

Deangelo always find the perfect gift for me. I know he probably has someone picking it out. At times, I feel kinda bad that I don't get him anything in return. What do you get someone that has everything they want already? He already has my heart and now my body, so what else is there for me to give him? I don't know but if he was to ask maybe and yes I say maybe I'll give it to him. Shit, he might be into some real freak nasty shit that I don't know about. I may have to run the other way if he asked for me to piss on him or some crazy shit like that.

I make my way back down the steps and head into the living room. I can't expect anything different from Deangelo, he fine as ever! I love a man that can dress and he looking so, so, fucking sexy. He asked me something but the look in eyes asked me to turn around, so I did. I made sure he could see me from the back; I wanted him to get a good view. Plus he promised me earlier he was going to bend me over when we made it back. I had to get closer to see if he would do it now and not later. I can smell his cologne and I wanna get a real up close taste of it. I rested on his shoulder and took a moment to enjoy.

"So you want me to go in first?"

"What T? Don't do me like that."

"I know you don't want to really be seen coming and going with me. You don't have to front like it doesn't matter."

"Naw, it ain't like that. I just don't want shit to happen to you 'cause of me that's all."

"Deangelo save it, 'cause we go hella places together but when we in the hood you front like we hi and bye'n or something."

"Yeah, that's the difference. It's the hood; you know they talk."

"So what do you wanna do 'cause I'm not trying to hear that, when they not talking? I see you hit the locks and if you want me to go first, I guess I'm supposed to climb out the trunk or something?" He didn't say anything. He smiled at me, walked around and opened the door. He grabbed my hand leading the way into the club.

We walked hand-in-hand straight into the lion's mouth; as soon as that door swung open, all eyes was on us. I can see why he doesn't want to come in with me now. The talking started right then and there. I can feel nothing but eyes watching our every move. Deangelo thought he was being funny trying to prove to me that it wasn't a problem for him to be seen with me. Seem like we did a couple laps before he pulled me off to the side.

"Now, did we miss anybody? I know they all can see that I came in here with you now. But if not, you wanna go back around?" Hell, I wanted to leave. Being this close, I wanted to kiss him and jump into his arms, ride the shit out his ass.

"You think you cute, right?"

"Think! T stop. You betta ask around. I know I'm the shit. Why you think these ho's staring at chu with the shit face?" He looked me up and down then ran his hand along my thigh while lickin' his lips. His touch, even though it was simple and quick, sent a tsunami straight to my panties.

"Probably the same way these niggas, yo' niggas might I add, staring at you. 'Cause I'm the shit! Now what?"

"All right, keep it up and we up outta here!" he said, stopping me from walking away before I put my hands in a place that they did not need to be. Yet!

"Why you say that?"

"'Cause I'll sho' dem niggas what they ain't gone have. Whatchu think about that?"

"Yeah, whateva."

"Whateva my ass. The way you looking in that dress don't go too far 'cause we only gone be herrre for a minute, then we out."

"I hear you," I said as I headed to my table and he went to his.

He never really wanted me around the people he messed with for real besides Corey and the rest of the ones we grew up with. Other than that, he didn't want me near the rest of them clowns, especially not Stacy. I already know he was kinda mad that Randy ass was at the house when he came by. But he knows I didn't know he had shit to do with him so he never pressed the issue.

I was having a good time laughing and dancing. Even after I saw that bitch Cindy sit on his lap, licking all in his ear or whatever the hell she was doing. Nasty ho, bitch worse than Kisha. Every nigga in the hood then 'bout ran through her ass. She think she slick, keep looking back at me like I'm supposed to get mad or some shit.

That ho crazy if she thinks that shit bother me. It don't. I already know the deal. She'll never have what I have with Deangelo no matter how much filthy disgusting shit she promises him. I just looked over at him to let him know I see him.

Then I watched that burned flour smelling bitch walk around. I know she was talking about me 'cause she looked over at me and they did too. I should've stood up so they could get a better view, I just ignored her though.

Before I knew it, two of the dudes she was speaking with were asking me if they could buy me a drink. All I kept thinking was, "Yeah bitch, I could have them too." I turned them down with a simple hand and turned in the other direction. I don't want shit that bitch got and if they talking to her then I don't want them either. I damn sho' don't need them to buy me a drink, especially not alcohol.

It kinda made me laugh when I thought about Deangelo's reaction if he saw me taking some alcohol from one of these niggas. He would probably take it way too fucking serious. He would also be all in my ear about drinking alcohol and how it leads to other things that you not supposed to put in yo' body blah, blah, blah. Only drug dealer I know that's so anti-everything. Don't drink, don't smoke, don't this, don't that. His ass only drinks water and most of the time it has to be bottled at that.

Right as I'm about to let him know I'm ready to go, it's like the pressure in the room changed. I know something about to go down. Cindy came hot tailing it over to the table. Dis bitch walked right up to me, put her finger across the table toward my face and asked me what I'm looking at.

The shit so uncalled for; I hadn't even looked in her direction for at least an hour. She had to come all the way over here to press me about that. I turned around to see who she talking to, then around the table asking them who she talking to. Of course, they egged it on by bursting out laughing in the bitch face, making fun out of what I did to her. She went on and on about how I need to stop looking at her. I'm mad she got my man. She sexes him better than I do. Quack, quack, quack, is all I heard coming from that duck.

It didn't bother me that she was making a scene. I sat there and took it. Then I thought more about her little encounter with Deangelo. I wanted to push her buttons so she can give me a reason to fuck her up. I sat up right on the edge of the table where I knew I was right within her reach and she in mine. It must've taken her by surprise 'cause she backed her punk ass up. I stared her ass down.

"You know what? You doing all this for Deangelo and he not even paying you any fucking attention. Why don't you take yo' tired ass back over there and do something else. You don't want none of this trick! Yeah, you think I'm a punk 'cause you what five or six years older than me and I don't get into this ghetto black bitch shit you pulling. Don't let me fool you.

You can put cho hands on me if you want. I promise you gone be in for a surprise. Matter fact, why don't you take yo' old washed up, nappy headed ass home with those four bastards you have running around by deyselves." I guess I pushed the right button 'cause she started talking mad shit again. This time she kept her distance; bitch knew better. Then, as I sat back in my chair, she picked up a drink.

Next thing I know, Shannon hit her sending her ass up against the dart machine. Errbody in nat bitch was going toward the fight. I'm trying to go in the opposite direction and making no progress. I felt somebody pick me up, sling my ass around, then I see the back door and I'm outside. I know it's not Deangelo 'cause whoever it is smell like Cheetos and weed. Plus, this a fat nigga. I can feel his stomach arching my back.

I figured it's a bouncer but I wasn't in the fight so soon as he let me down I punched his ass right in the face. My heel broke, giving me just enough time to move as his big slow ass tried to knock the shit out of me with a backhand. I know that if I run, there's no way in hell fat bastard gone catch me.

I kicked those heels off and took off. Just as fast as that run started it ended. I felt another nigga come from the side of the car and grab me by my hair. It was like some shit off a cartoon how fast he snatched my ass back. As soon as that happened I see Corey going past the alley so I screamed out to him. I know he heard me 'cause he took off in my direction. I can't see if he has a gun, so I yelled out.

"They have a gun on me!" He slowed down and I see him pull something out but move off to the side. That bastard that I hit slapped me on my ass hard and told me to shut up. I hear him tell Corey to tell Deangelo to come around to the alley. Then they started talking shit and before I know it, I see Deangelo.

I'm too mad at him for coming and I don't see Corey so that made me even madder. I didn't want anything to happen to Deangelo trying to save me. He was too close to being out of this mess and off to living out his dream. If he was to get hurt all that hard work and traveling would be out the door. Then it would be over.

The only thing I hear first is two shots; then a rally of shots, and then nothing just clicks. I think I'm in shock, I can't feel anything. It's like time stood still. The only thing that snapped me back is Deangelo giving me my shoes and running with me in his arms to the car. He sped off so quick I don't know if he hit, if Corey hit, hell, if I'm hit. Then the night plays back in my head and I'm hot, I need to get away.

I should've seen the shit that was happening around me. Then I remember the other two dudes they were with them and I thought about where we were going. I can't let them know where I live. I panicked and told Deangelo to pull over and soon as he slowed down enough, I got the hell out the car and headed back down the street. I'm scared as hell, when I see a car coming; I just know it's them. I can hear

Deangelo coming behind me.

When I see it's a police car I flagged his ass down quick. I know that'll send Deangelo the hell away. I figured he'll be okay, if they following us then they see me talking to the police. And they probably think I'm telling him what happened.

Once I see Deangelo pull into the convenience store I thanked the officer for the directions and took off through the Matador apartments. I've never run that fast in my fucking life. I'm hitting streets in my dress like I'm in a hundred-meter dash while hitting the club. I forgot all about the fact that I don't have on any shoes.

I don't give a damn though. I can't get what just happened out of my head. As I walk through the path heading to our backyard, I'm happy as hell to be home. And glad that I don't see my mom's car. I sat there for a minute while I washed my feet off with the water hose.

I tried to get as much of the rock and glass I had stuck in them out. At some point, I stopped trying and grabbed a ball and started shooting. I need to think and this the perfect thing for that. I zone out into my own world seeing how many times I can hit in the dark.

"What the hell T? Yo..." I don't even have to turn around; I already know who it is. I was praying that he got the hell out of North County but of course, he didn't. I don't need this shit right now. I tried to get him to give me a minute to think but he wasn't trying to hear me.

I let him have it. When he put me in his arms, I felt better, not a whole lot, but better. We sat down and he had jokes. I fell back and let my body land on the grass. If this the type of shit he deals with on a daily, I don't know how he do it and still have jokes. When he climbed on top of me I felt better instantly. I was beat; my body was catching up with me. I pushed him off and he picked up my feet, looking them over, and then started rubbing them making me close my eyes. I talked to him for a minute before I heard him waking me up.

I called him a couple times after that but he didn't respond; I took it for what it was worth. I got my answer the next time I saw him, he did me even dirtier in the hood. After that, I was wishing to never see his ass again.

16 MYZPHYT

"Ay Debby what's up with yo' girl Treasure? I ain't seen or heard from her since they say she went heads up with that chick Pandillero be coming through here with."

"You know Treasure ain't one to be tracked; I don't know where she at. Dat bitch lucky I didn't know who she was. I was wondering why she was asking so many questions after I saw Treasure walk by."

"Whatchu mean she was asking questions," I asked her. I had to get down to the nitty gritty.

"Like who was she and is she da one everybody keeps saying wit' Pandillero. Shit like dat. Plus, I could tell by da look on her face when Sandy silly ass told her that Treasure was his girl on da low. I should've known that she was gone try and step to her. I just didn't think the bitch had it in her.

If I would've known that she was going over there to fuck with Treasure, man, I would've whooped her ass right therrre on GP and told her to leave her the fuck alone. Fuck dat. Dat's my dog right therrre. That girl don't even fuck wit' nobody. Dis bitch gone try and run up on her and shit."

"I was shocked to hear she actually did fight da girl. I thought she was all walk away, say whatchu wanna say, type person. I just knew dey was lyin' when ney said she was fighting her."

"That's Treasure dough. She don't start shit and she

would walk away and let chu say whatchu want. That's how I know dat tramp had to put her hands on her first. It just ain't like her to fight somebody, especially over no nigga like errbody trying to say she did," Debby said, as she walked into the kitchen.

"Well, if you see her or talk to her, tell her to call me damn!" I said to Debby as I walked out the door.

Man, why da hell did I say I would come all the way out in North County just to play some pool? Shit, I'd rather be across that bridge at the Casino, way in the back right now. Fuck it. I told my niggas I would come by so I figure I'll just chill out with them for a minute and head out.

It's popping in this mufucka I see all my peoples over by the pool tables. But damn I didn't know they got down like this out here. They got errthing you need in here: pool, darts, dance floor, bowling and damn, where do all these bitches live? They killing them dry-scalp-having ass ho's in the hood. I gots to get out more!

"I see my brother kicking ya'll ass over here on nis pool table huh?" I said as I walked over.

"Man, Shakes ain't kicking nobody ass. This nigga just lucky, that's all," Vic said as he dabbed me off.

"Oh shit Myzphyt, look what I see over derrre!" Shake said.

"Where?"

"Look at the third lane from the door. Now tell me dat ain't who I think it is." I look and say it ain't so.

"I'm out! I'll see you niggas later!"

"Whatchu just got here!" Shake yelled at me. I don't even respond. I stopped by the bar, grabbed a drink and made my way over to where she was.

"So this where you been hiding out?" I leaned over and whispered in Treasure ear.

"I don't hide Myzphyt!" she said as she turned around and continued.

"Whatchu doing all the way out here anyway? Who you hiding from?"

"Can I at least get a hug before we get into all dat?" She

stood up and tried to give me some bullshit hug. I pulled her in closer and held onto her so she can't move.

"So you ready to tell me the verdict?" Before she can answer, I hear a squeaky voice.

"So who's your cute friend? Charles Divin?" her friend asked her. I didn't want to let Treasure go so I looked over at her.

"Naw, this Treasure!" They both laughed.

"He silly. This Myzphyt, Myzphyt that's Sammy."

"Nice to meet you Sammy. You mind if I talk to Treasure for a minute?"

"Take your time."

"You want something to drink Treasure or something to eat?" She smiled as we walked up the steps.

"No, I'm good but thanks for asking."

"You know you looking awfully good in that fit you have on. I can see that work you putting in paying off."

"You silly; whatchu talking about Myzphyt?"

"Hell, you about the only girl in here in real Louis Vuitton with, let me see, hold up." I reach down and take her shoe off then put it back on her foot.

"Why you take my shoe?"

"Yep, real red bottom heels on." I look back up and take my time searching her legs. Wondering what that lump of gold would taste like as I make my way back up.

"Stop playing; whatchu know about some damn red bottoms? Besides, this was a gift, that's all."

"I heard that. I guess all that shit I been hearing ain't true at all if Pandillero breaking you off like dat."

"Come on Myzphyt, let's not go there." We laughed and continued on our way. Still with Treasure in my arms, I walked her over to a table that was kinda in the cut.

"So?"

"So what Mr. Myzphyt?"

"Come on, you have me over here on eggshells waiting. Don't act like you don't remember what I just asked you."

"Well, if you're asking if I've decided if I want to hang out with you then I would think you know the answer to that already. We are sitting here aren't we?"

"You still haven't let me know if we can hang out. It was just by chance that I'm here with you now."

"How about this, we see how this night turns out and then ask me again. It's been a little minute since I last talked to you, you know."

"I'm cool with that, hate that I can't get a definite answer though. Besides, the last time I have to say, you really did disappear on me. That's messed up too 'cause I been looking for you, calling no answer. I can't believe you doing me like that."

"I didn't disappear. I just needed a break from down there, that's all. Don't try and act like you worried about me anyway."

"I was and I am worried about you. I heard what happened. I even called you hellas to find out if you was aight but you never returned any of my calls. I asked Debby about chu. She said she hadn't heard from you and that she had been trying to call you and shit."

"Yeah, I guess I been busy."

"I don't know. You look like the swelling has gone down a bit, but chu can still see a little puff under yo' eye. At least the scratches have gone away," I said, we both busted out laughing.

"Yeah, I guess my hair has just started to grow back too huh? They did say she snatched me bald right?" We laughed even harder. I knew Treasure could handle her own but I had to tease her.

"Here I thought you was da nonviolent type and you out there toe tagging chicks just off the humbug and shit. Dey say that chick so lumped up I thought I'd pull a muscle laughing at the thought of you fighting."

"Stop, you know that's not me to be fighting. That's why I said I need a break 'cause I know better than to act like that."

"I feel you ma. I'm glad to see you okay though. I been hearing shit in the hood but as long as you good, I don't give a fuck about what they talking about."

"Well, I'm glad you have my back Mr. Myzphyt. Now what brings you to my part of the woods?"

"Aw shit, now that I know where yo' part of the woods is I might as well get me a long-term cabin out in this mufucka."

"You really on a roll tonight aren't you?" she said as we laughed some more. After a minute, her friends all came over and before I knew it, my people joined in. We had a good time sitting there getting to know each other.

We played a couple rounds of pool then threw darts. I guess all these county girls like darts 'cause they kicked our asses. Then we made our way to the stage and watched everyone make fools out their selves singing along in a karaoke contest we decided to have. I tried to get her to let me take her home but she wasn't havin' it. We made plans to hook up in a couple days and I was good with that. Hell, I was already making plans. I wished I knew what the hell she likes to do. Whatever that was, I'm more than willing to make it happen.

*　　*　　*

We been kicking it together for a couple months now. I mean, if it wasn't for her having to go to work, we would damn near be joined at the hip. I have noticed she was into that romantic type shit. I made some plans and spent hella bread on putting something together for her. I couldn't wait. This time I'm not letting her get out of riding with me. I can't mess this up.

I convinced her to let me at least pick her up from Gee Gee house; I was on a mission to make sure everything was right. The whole day I was so damn happy even my crew picked up on it. I was a little pissed that the count was off a little but I didn't let that get to me one bit.

"What's up Treasure; you ready to go?"

"Before we go anywhere, I'm gone need to see some license, registration and insurance! And you need to pop the trunk."

"Damnnn, you gone do me like that? Whatchu don't trust me?"

"Yeah, yeah, yeah! You want me to go or not? 'Cause if

that's too much I can always." She turned like she was about to head back into the building.

"Man hold up!" I grabbed my shit and popped the trunk.

"Here, you want to check under the seats to?"

"Hell yeah. I was doing that anyway; you don't have any hidden compartments in here do you?" she said as she looked around then back at me.

"You a trip. You do this wit' errbody you get in the car with?"

"Nope, just people that I know living that life!" I opened the door for her and jumped in, then pulled out.

"So I know Pandillero keep his shit sitting in the front seat waiting on your inspection then huh?"

"Let's not get into my business Myzphyt and no he don't! I didn't have to worry about that with him. You know that already, now don't chu?"

"You brutal, you know that right?" She didn't say anything; she smiled and enjoyed the ride. We didn't have to go far. "What we doing here? I know you don't think we finna check in do you?" Treasure said as she turned toward me.

"Come on now, I know better than that. Can you have just a little trust in me? We just here to eat; then we back out the door!" I grabbed the ticket from the valet and walked her up to the restaurant. We sat at a table right next to the window. I can tell she has never been here before by the way she looking around. The room turned giving us the perfect view of St. Louis from the air.

"So you like it?"

"This is nice. I didn't know you had it in you Myzphyt."

"That hurt!"

"No, I just, let me start over. Yes, I like it." She adjusted in her seat.

"I think every time I see you, you look sexier than the last." There she go, a smile that makes this room feel like it's standing still.

"You come here often?"

"Nope!"

"So how you know if the food any good?"

"I didn't say I've never been here. I just don't come here often, that's all."

"Look at the riverfront. Even though it's dark you can still see the water," she said as she rested her chin in her hand and leaned toward the window.

We talked the whole time and then after we were done we headed down Broadway. As we pulled up to the house I can see she taken back by the size. Before she can ask me anything, I jumped out and opened the door. What, she rolling with it? She didn't ask one question as we made our way down the long path to the boat dock.

I see my peoples wave us on board so I helped her up onto the boat and we sat back and chilled. "You cold?" "Not really." That was all I needed to hear I jumped up and covered my body around her letting her fall back into my arms. After we finished up on the boat, we headed into the house.

"I know this not where you laying your head so don't even think about fronting like it is!" she said as she walked around checking out the layout.

"Who said I was gone front Treasure? I don't lay my head here; this my peoples house. They let me chill out here from time to time."

"This a stunning place they have here. I've been hearing about it since forever. I didn't know they turned this place around like this."

"Yeah, after my grandma died we all chipped in and turned it into a bed and breakfast. But tonight it's just me and you here if that's okay witchu." She turned around and smiled then leaned up against the kitchen island. Damn, she sexy. The way her body is screaming at me I can't ignore it any longer. I feel like I'm about to fulfill a fantasy that I been dreaming about for years.

I walked over and pulled her into my arms letting my mouth take her in, she tasted so damn good. I pick her short ass up and sit her on the counter. I kissed down her neck, caressing every inch of her. The more she into it the more it made my blood boil. I can't resist once I had her warm, soft, round breast spilling out of my hands. I look up at her head draped back with her eyes closed. I made my way down, lifted up her body just enough to slip off the string trying to stop me.

I exposed her succulent firm thighs and moved her legs apart; I had to get a better view. Her waist hella small, probably sixteen inches, it's her ass that had her sitting up like a mule. She had at least forty plus inches around dat mufucka. I was in disbelief, her pussy fat and I can already see she getting excited.

I started rubbing my fingers over her wetness before I opened her up like a book. Fuck, she wet as a mufucka! I pulled the stool over and took a seat so I can get real comfortable. I plan on being here longer than an appetizer; I plan on enjoyin' all the benefits of the buffet in front of me.

My finger immediately drenched with her sap. I can feel her tense up a little and let out a moan that made me want to hear it again. She bit down on her lip and looked down at me. I wanted to see her make the sound this time. I slowly slid my finger out brushing up against her hard clit before it was all the way out. Without taking my eye off her, I tried to swallow her fat ass pussy whole. I wanted to cover every inch of it in my mouth.

I enjoyed the taste of her and the look in her eyes while I was doing it. I put two fingers in her and started moving my fingers in circles, rubbing her pulsating clit wit' my thumb. There it goes. The sound I been waiting on her to make. All her warm gooey filling oozed into my mouth. I watch as her body shakes, her back arched and her head fell back again.

After I made her cum again I had to get in. I helped her down from the counter and quickly took her to the bedroom. Once we was inside, before I knew it she pushed me down onto the foot of the bed. She let her dress drop down to the floor then she climbed on top of me and helped me with my clothes. My dick was standing straight up. I slid on a rubber and guided her right down on top of me. Oh shit, I'm about to scream like a bitch, she too damn tight.

Every inch that she makes disappear is making me wanna dig my damn toes into the floor. This some good pussy here! I tried my best to ignore my body telling me to let go. I know if she keeps at it the way she is, I'm not goin' be able to ignore it anymore. I picked her up without taking one inch of me out of her and flipped her onto the bed. As we kissed I held her tight in my arms. I laid her back and found my way back to drinking up her juices as she came over and over again on my tongue.

"Wake up sleepy head, I gotta go!" I heard Treasure say. I rolled over and she fully dressed by the side of the bed. I have to take a minute to enjoy the view of her; I can't believe she ready to go so soon. I reach over and pulling her back into my arms.

"It's too early to go. Plus, I want chu to spend the day wit' me. We can leave tomorrow."

"Sound good but I have to go! So get up; I'm already late!" Before I let her go, I kissed her hoping she'll change her mind. She slid out the bed again and headed out the door.

"You know it's messed up that you won't let me take you home right?"

"I already told you I have stuff to do plus, I see my sister car so I better hurry up." She lean over and kiss me. I jump out, open the door and watch her walk off into the building. All day I'm feeling like I'm riding a wave that's never ending. I know I have other things to do but the way I feel I have to go back to the house and get this off me. Every time I blink, I flash back to what happened, which made my dick hard as hell. I need to take the day to drain as much of this nut out that I can if I wanna focus on anything else.

The next day I'm in the hood so I go check on the count. I been so wrapped up in Treasure the last two months I haven't been around like I would've. I head to Eleven Twelve building and before I can even get out the door I hear, "What's up youngin? How you been boy?"

"Shit, couldn't be better thanks to you. What's up witchu dough Pandillero, Bateador?"

"Hell naw, just gone throw that shit at me like that

huh? You hear dis nigga Bateador, thanks to me. So how she doing?"

"Who, my mom's? She cool, why you ask?" He played me so I'm gone play his ass right back.

"Really? Who else nigga T. I already know ya'll was out there at umm...What's the name of it Bateador?"

"Top of the Riverfront," Bateador said.

"Yeah, that spinning restaurant shit, so I know you know how she doing. Nigga trying to play like I was asking about Ms. Sherry, hell naw!"

How the hell these niggas know about that? I know my peoples didn't tell 'em. And I know Treasure ain't fucking with him like that. The way Bateador just spit that shit out sound like he was there or some shit.

"How you know we was there?"

"Man, stop playing. Don't you mean that was where ya'll went first? This nigga trying to be bashful like we don't know about his ol' I wanna be romantic ass. Hell naw," Bateador said as they both began to laugh; shit, he got me there.

"Look at the youngin, I can see he stepping his game up. Boat rides, staying out at that big ass overnight joint his people run and shit. Too bad it ended early; must not have been worth staying that extra day huh?" Pandillero said as they both stood clowning wit' each other. I see these niggas be on some mercenary shit now. They have to have eyes on her to know all this.

"Like I said Pandillero, I'm good, you should know. Hell, if you don't know, then like I said, thanks." I leaned back up against the whip and smiled at that nigga. I watch him mug me down with fire in his eyes at the thought of my words.

"Come on youngin, you know I have eyes and ears errwhere around nis bitch, especially when it comes to T. So let me get real focused right now and put this bug in yo' ear! I know she 'bout mad at me right now, but that's right now. You my peoples and all, but don't think for a second that'll come into play if some shit happen to T. Make sure you keep yo' mind right. And whatever shit you have popping off in these streets, don't come in any distance of T and we straight," Pandillero said as he turned and walked away like a mad pussy-whipped bitch.

He's straight trying to put the check down on me. Bateador still looking at me waiting on me to say something. Fuck that nigga though; he can't get mad at me 'cause I'm not going to report back to that nigga like this bitch ass nigga Bateador do.

"Come on man, we been tight what, six or seven weeks now? She don't have to worry about any chicks running up on her or niggas either if that's whatchu mean."

"What the fuck lil nigga. You forgetting who you talking to?" Bateador said as he beefed up and started to come towards me.

"Hold up there Bateador," Pandillero said as he grabbed his shoulder and walked back.

"Let me holla at him for a minute." Pandillero walked up on me man-to-man.

"Just so I'm clear lil nigga, I will kill you in a heartbeat if something happen to T! The next time you mention any of my business for one ear to hear I'll drop you where you stand. You can try me if you want to and Ms. Sherry will be passing out a shitload of obituaries for all the niggas that have a problem wit' it."

He turned around; Bateador was still mugging me, they jumped in the whip and pulled off. It's all good. Fuck him! Hell, I would be mad too if I fucked up with Treasure. Now that I know where we stand, I know to keep that nigga at arms distance.

* * *

"Man, you should've let me whoop that lil nigga ass back there," Bateador said.

"That ain't shit. He just chasing that pink ghost right now, that's all. I can tell by the smile on that lil nigga face T gave it up to his punk ass."

"I don't give a fuck what he chasing; lil nigga need to learn his place and watch who the fuck he running his mouth off to." I didn't respond; I turned up the music and we made our rounds. The thought of T given that nigga my pussy already have me wantin' to body his ass. I'm so fuckin' pissed wit' her I wanna go snatch her ass up right now and fuck her up.

17 TREASURE

"Hello!"

"Hey T, it's me. Can you come outside real quick? I need to holla at chu for a minute."

"Yeah, all right. Here I come." I wonder why Deangelo calling me if he outside. Why didn't he just come in? I walked over to get in the car. Deangelo wrapped his arms around me and hugged me. Not just any hug but a hug that said this will be the last one, like he saying goodbye. I waited on him so I can get in; then my stomach start to turn.

"What's wrong witchu Mr. Deangelo?"

"I got a lot on my mind T." By the sound of his voice I know this a conversation that I don't want to hear. Not today, tomorrow, or any other day for that matter.

"So you gone tell me or am I supposed to guess whatchu wanna talk about?" He didn't say anything. He put the car in drive, turned up the music and drove off. We drove out to my favorite spot. Once we made our way to the water, he stood there looking in the sky like he was making a promise or asking for something. I moved closer to him and grabbed his hand and waited 'til he looked back down.

"So the way you acting I have to assume that there has been a change that you want to tell me about but can't get it out." He turned and looked at me then at the ground.

"T, I have a lot of shit going on with me right now and

I want to do what's best for you. I just don't know what that is right now. I can't lie to you T; I need to take a step back. I'm not saying I regret anything but I need to work some shit out and I don't want you to wait around on me."

I let go of his hand and headed back to the car, I don't need to hear anything else. I already know where this going sad thing is, it took him three punk ass days to figure it out. I can feel my face heat up I'm not going to let him see me cry. Three days ago he was tellin' me he loved me and blah, blah, blah. He avoid my calls since the shit in the alley and on the third punk ass day he hit me wit' this. Seven years we been rockin' together, we spend less than twenty four hours as a couple and it take him three days to change his mind. Ain't that a bitch!

"T, I want to expla—"

"Just open the door Deangelo please and take me home," I say as calm as I can. I smile and touch his shoulder as I make my way back into the car. "T, can we—" I cut his ass smooth off by turning up the radio. I don't give a shit that this is his car. I don't wanna hear it, so fuck what he has to say. As soon as he pulls in the driveway before he even came to a complete stop, I jumped the fuck out the car and damn near ran back in the house without even looking back.

* * *

"Yeah Gee Gee, I'm headed down there now to do they hair but I'm not going to be down there long so go ahead and get them washed up." I haven't been in the hood in a minute. I was tired of people asking me what happened and making up bullshit ass stories about it. I been jumping on the express bus which took me out of my way but I don't give a shit. I didn't want to run any chance of seeing him or nobody else for that matter.

Later that night, we all decided to go bowling, so I called up my girl Sammy to see if she wanted to go. Of course she was down. Just like clockwork, we all arrived at the bowling alley. We had a good time playing a couple games, laughing and joking the night away.

"So this whe..." I hear Myzphyt say all up in my damn ear. I don't even have to see him; I already know it's him. I turn around and sure enough it's him standing there looking just right and smelling even better. Those eyes, those eyes.

Even though I didn't want anything to do with the drama down in the hood, just looking at his eyes is making me forget all about that bullshit. Before I know it, my body was pressed up against his as he held me in his arms making me forget all about what the hell Sammy was saying.

*   *   *

Time sure does fly when you're having fun. We've been hanging tough since I been at the college, these six or so weeks flew past. Tonight, I don't care what we do as long as I see what the hell that python move like. After we ate dinner, we went on this long boat ride that I didn't want to end. He held me in his arms so tight I enjoyed the hell out of it.

After the ride, we headed back up to the house, it was huge. I know his grandmother owned it. After she died, the place caught fire. I didn't know they fixed it up the way that they have; the inside was quite for a bed and breakfast though.

I had to tease him about it. When he told me the place was empty it was game on. I need something to get Deangelo ass off my lower lips. That sample I had that one night has my insides dying for some more.

I've been thinking about this all night. I wonder how long it'll take him. Shit, he looks good standing over there. I leaned up against the island and made sure he got a real good look at me. I can see his eyes scan me from top to bottom.

Next thing I know, we going at it. The moment he picked me up and sat my ass on that counter, I was dripping wet. I know exactly what I want and there's no stopping each and every avalanche I'm about to create. The shit he was doing with his tongue helped me let go. He's working it like his life about to end.

After we made our way to the bedroom, I was tired of waiting. I dropped my clothes and helped him out of his. He wrapped that hard monster up and I slowly slid down him. I was trying my best to keep going. I adjusted and swayed my hips back and forth, moving sideways.

I finally reach the bottom and I can grind on it in

circles. I'm working his stick inside of me trying my damndest not to scream Deangelo name. My legs were resting on the side of him so I can bounce up and down on him better. I'm riding his ass like he trying to run the hell away.

I can see his mouth as he trying not to make a sound. I know he feeling it once he opened his eyes. I see the burning inside of him. Myzphyt had to get control of the situation. He stops me and lifts me on the bed and decided to return the favor. We went at it a couple more times before we were sleep.

8 BLASÉ

We spent the next couple days clowning each other about how that shit went down. We been hearing it in school since we been back. News sho' do travel quick around this bitch. It's all good 'cause I hope I see her today in class. Shit, I haven't seen her in weeks. Now that I think about it, it's been about seven, eight weeks. She straight be in and out this place I guess. If I do see Treasure today in class, to be honest, I don't know how to approach her after that shit went down.

I can tell she was waiting on me to come in; she din turned her desk to face the door. "Sooo, Mr. Blasé. How did that game turn out fo' ya'? Did ya'll shut it down like you said ya'll would?"

"No, we took a L. Didn't know what we was running into. They had this ringer who came through and broke us down. Before we realized it, the game was over!"

"You don't say!" She laughed and turned her desk back the right way.

"So why you didn't tell me you play ball, or hell, that you would be playing in the game?"

"Now what fun would that have been? I had to see why you were so positive; you just knew you would run the court. I see ya'll have skills though. I have to say, for a minute there I was starting to get worried. Then I realized that yo' cousin Mike was the weak man so I just played him."

"Man, you talk about skills. I would've never in a million years thought you was ballin' like that."

We continued to talk about the game for a while then she looked over. "But on the real, let your brother know that I didn't mean any disrespe—"

"Don't worry about it, I had already told him to watch the game and not worry about anything else. He cool though; if not, he'll get over it. How you know Pandillero though? I see you two must be pretty tight the way he let you go hard on him. Do you know Bateador too, seem like those two tight?"

"Come on Mr. Blasé don't mess up a conversation by asking me about my business like that?"

"My bad. I just wante—"

"Look, that's my business. So, let's just move on and keep it on the up and up." She laid her head in her hand and looked over at me. Then she gave me a smile that made me want to lean over and kiss her soft pretty lips. We stared at each other for a second then she slightly bit down on her lip like she was all of a sudden shy.

"I think you owe me a dinner Mr. Blasé. So when you gone pay up?"

"Today if you like! Hell right now if you ready to go!"

"You know what, I *am* ready to go. I don't have work today anyway but don't you have class after lunch?"

"Yeah but I can skip them though. I can play catch up tomorrow from my peoples' notes."

"What classes do you have?"

"They AP classes."

"Well, I can't have you missing any classes like that. Now, if you would've said woodwork or pottery then yeah. But I'll just have to catch up with you on another day."

"It ain't a probl—"

"It would be for me if you missed those classes so." She wrote her number down on a piece of paper and handed it to me.

"Call me later and we can settle the tab."

"Aight then cool."

I couldn't wait to get home, I tore ass out of there. I

figured I could get home knock out some of this homework. Damn, I'm glad I didn't skip 'cause I would've missed that test in chemistry. Let me clean up and give Treasure a call.

I make my way to her house, jump out and go knock on the door. Her brother opens the door with a slick ass grin on his face. Before we can say a word, she walks out from behind him. "You ready to eat?" She walked to my car smelling good as hell. Look at that ass move on her. Damn I think she get thicker, finer and sexier every time I see her mufuckin' ass.

"Yeah, you like Italian food. I know this spot we can hit up," I said as I walked toward my side of the door. The next thing I know, she look at me, turn around, then start heading back toward the house. I hear her brother burst out laughing as he open the door wider moving out her way. Without a word, she was back inside. I turn almost sprinting back to the front door.

"What was all that about?"

"Ay man, don't blame me. Blame my pops for that! She don't play when it come to shit like that!"

"What I do?"

"Man she old school, both my sisters are. You know; the opening doors and pull out chairs crap. My father always say, 'You have to treat a lady right and do that type shit. If not, she a ho that is good to go!' That's what that's about man." He looked back over his shoulder.

"Hold up, watch this!" He held his finger up at me.

"Ay Treasure, Blasé herrre for you." I see her come back around the corner.

"Aw hey Blasé, how are you today? You ready to go," she said like it was my first time seeing her. Damn, this girl is crazy as hell. Something telling me to run back to my car and tear ass getting the hell out of here. But I should know better, so I play along.

"Sure, you ready?"

"Of course, why else would I be standing here?" She made her way back out the door.

I look back at her brother and laugh at him circling his

finger around his ear letting me know she is crazy. This time I hustle over to her door, open it and close it behind her.

"So the mystery of Eight Hundred is solved." She asked me what I was talking about, like she didn't know already.

"You! You're the eighth person forming Eight Hundred. I was wondering why dem niggas was called Eight Hundred when it was only seven of 'em, but including you, that makes eight."

"I guess. To be honest I never thought it was a mystery seeing that we're together all the time you know, all eight of us." We talk all the way to the restaurant, all the way through dinner and all the way back to her place. We had a good time. I jumped out and opened the door for her as we stood in the driveway talking even more.

"Well Mr. Blasé, I had a great time tonight!"

"Hell, I'm just glad you came out with me. If my dumb ass was smart, I would've thrown the game from the beginning so that we could do this." We both laughed standing out on the side of the car.

"Naw, what fun would that have been? Don't try to make that an excuse either for that beat down ya'll had!"

"Ya'll won fair and square. I really did enjoy my time witchu though Treasure. I hope this won't be the last time." I pulled her closer to me sat her on the car.

"I guess we'll see now won't we, Blasé!"

Damn, my Johnson getting harder and harder every time she move up against it. I wrap my hands around her waist and kiss her on her moist lips as she slips her arms around my neck. I don't want to let this moment end. I pull her closer helping her down as we kissed the night away. I feel her start to pull away. I gave her a simple kiss on the temple.

"Thank you!"

"For what?" she said as she leaned back into my hands.

"For making my day!" I slowly released my grip so she wouldn't fall back. I walked her to the house and cruised home on cloud nine. I was a happy man after that. We spent several days and nights talking, having fun and enjoying each other's time.

19 TREASURE

Dang, had I known these last six weeks at Harris Stowe welcoming thing would be no different from high school, I wouldn't have even signed up for it. Seem like the majority of the people was just there to join some click. The others had they nose so stuck up in the air they didn't even notice what was going on around them. I sure can't wait to see Mr. Chestnut today though. Ethan walked with me as I headed out the door.

"All right Ethan, see you later!"

"Where you heading? Thought you had to go to work?"

"Naw, I'm off today, I'm gone go clown Blasé real quick then head home."

"You know you wrong, right? Aight, see you later," he said as he headed to class.

Let me hurry up before he gets there. All right, let me just move this this way so he know it's about to go down! "Sooo, how wa..." I said as his tall, dark and lovely looking ass came in the door. I can tell by the way he look he knew this was coming.

After messing with him for a while, I decided to let him know that I really didn't mean any harm or hostility towards his brother. I know they were guest at our house so I should've handled the situation a little different. With me just finding out about just how soon Deangelo would be leaving, I was pretty upset from the jump.

I wasn't surprised to know that they knew Deangelo. Hell, anybody high enough up on the totem pole had to have some kinda connection to him at some point. I was a bit stunned that he tried to be in my business with Deangelo though. I haven't even thought to question him about his ties with him.

We talked some more then I had to find out when he was going to pay up. Hell, why not? I'm single. Why not get to know him a little better? It hasn't stopped me in the past so why would it now? Besides, after my last little chat with Deangelo I know there's been a change so why sit around waiting on him? Myzphyt is another story, yeah we been hangin' tough the past couple weeks but I still don't see a problem. After deciding that I couldn't let him miss class for me I gave him my number so we could make plans for later tonight.

When the bell rang, I went home and went straight to bed. Right on cue, Blasé called and I finished getting ready and laughed with my peoples 'til he arrived. I saw him as he pulled up but of course my nosey ass brother jumped up to get the door.

I grabbed my purse and was right behind him. "You ready to eat?" I said as I took in the smell of his cologne and walked past him. He said something but I was too distracted by the fact that it looked like he wasn't going toward my door. I stopped dead in my path, turned smooth around and went back in the house when I realized he didn't have a lick of manners.

Look at these fools, they jumping from out the window, they think it's funny. 'Welcome back.' 'That was quick.' 'How did it go?' They all got jokes today. They know I don't play that shit. That's why they laughing right now. "Ay Treasu..." I see my brother got jokes too huh? Let's try this again and start from the beginning, "Aw, hey Bl..."

I know he 'bout think I'm crazy as hell. It doesn't help that I can see my brother big head ass mocking me out the corner of my eye. After we talked and ate, then talked some more. We were back at my house standing outside his car. He look fire leaning up against the car like that and I keep getting a slight whiff of his cologne. It's playing with my lower lips every time the wind teases me. Uh oh, don't pull me in like that baby; make me wanna call you 'Papi' with that type of control. Why the hell does this feel so fucking right? I can't resist any longer looking at his lips with him being all up and on me like this.

After pushing myself to the limit I had to back away from his smooth ass. Something about where this was going was feeling too damn fast. So, we said goodnight and the next couple times that we met up after that I was feeling good about Mr. Blasé.

20 MYZPHYT

"What's up Treasure? What time you get off today?"

"I'm already off heading down my aunt house. Why, what's up?"

"Nothing. I wanted to know if you wanted a ride."

"I'm walking out the front now so no thanks."

"Good thing I'm already here then, huh?"

"Whatchu mean you already here?"

"If you look up and quit searching through that big ass bag you'd see me." I see her look over in my direction and just admired the way she moved. The way her legs shined in the sun her calves in them heels only topped it off. Even in her business outfit her body is banging, that fabric holding shit together so good it don't make sense.

"I know you was *not* about to walk with those things on."

"No, I was looking for my flats in this big ass bag as you called it," she said as I gave her a hug and kiss. We were back in da hood before we knew it.

"So what's up with later?"

"I have to head home, take care of some stuff, why?"

"Shit, I was trying to chill witchu that's all. How you getting home?"

"My momma already here. I'm just meeting her then I'm out."

"So when we gettin' up again?"

"I don't know. Senior year around the corner, I have a ton of shit to get done and I don't know when I'll be down here again." I know why she don't wanna stick around with all the shit that I heard happened. Not to mention the fight is still following her around.

"Well peep this; my birthday is in three weeks and my peoples throwing me a lil something down at Spruill's. So give me the best birthday present by going with me."

"I guess I can do that!" She leaned over and kissed me. I jumped out and watched her fat ass bounce all the way into the building. I don't know; something about Treasure's off since all that shit went down. She seems to be feeling me more, but sometimes it seem like she pulling away from me.

I don't know why or if I should even trip off it. Hell, I have bigger problems to deal with right now. As much as I want to work it out with her and make her my girl. On the real, I have other shit to do.

What the fuck? "I know this is not the count from the weekend?"

"Yeah man, dem old heads was on us all weekend talking 'bout don't come through 'til they cleared the games up and shit. Any other time they don't give a fuck but they was on us this time." I was about to let Ken have it but I already know what the problem was. And it had nothing to do with no hood softball games.

It's Pandillero! I know Bateador would've been the one to shut out my crew, but he wouldn't have done anything if he didn't get the go ahead. It's all good though, I can make that up in a minute. Quick shuffle of the deck and I'm back on. Like I said, fuck that nigga. He ain't stopping shit. Nigga still mad about me throwing that shit up in his face and not reporting back to him about what Treasure was up to that's all.

"What's up Unk?" I walked over to my uncle Showboat and dabbed him off.

"Shit, heard you been getting hit for a minute boy. Those numbers you bringing in looking real weak; you know that right?"

"Yeah man, fam then locked me out. Seem like we beefing or something."

"I don't know whatchu did but you might wanna fix it before Mike take yo' shit."

"Man, you gone do me like that?"

"Come on now nephew; you know the game. I'll holla at you later."

"Showboat! Showboat!" I can't believe this shit man. I know that nigga Pandillero mad but I didn't think he would take the shit this far.

"Hey Myzphyt it's me. I was calling to tell you that I can't make it to your party but I can hang out with you that day. Give me a call, bye!" There goes my day. I only been able to catch up with Treasure a few times over these last weeks. I know she has a lot going on in school and work but she keep running from me every chance she get.

"What's up Treasure? It's good you finally making time for yo' man."

"Really? It's good to see you Myzphyt. Don't act like this the first time I then seen you this week."

"You been actin' funny and shit, I don't know what to think with you no more. Now you not even coming out with me tonight for my birthday. That's kinda fucked up."

"I'm not acting funny and it's not like I don't want to come out with you. I just can't. So you ready to go?" I didn't respond. I know why she don't wanna come out but I let it go and spent what little time with her that I could. We hit up Dave and Buster then sat down and had fun eating before we headed back to the hood.

"I hope you had fun Mr. Myzphyt and I hope you have fun tonight at your party."

"Well, if you came out, then I would really have fun."

"I told you already that I can't."

"You can't or you won't?" I was getting tired of her playing like she was so busy.

"What's that supposed to mean?"

"It means you can't come or you won't come 'cause Pandillero might be there? Don't play Treasure. I already know why you don't wanna go! That shit that popped off with you and that nigga Pandillero still got you shook. I already know that, I'm tryin' to understand 'cause it happened in April, here it is August. This nigga ain't even been fucking witchu since, unless you lyin' to me. You still hiding out in the county, staying away from the hood and playing me out every chance you get."

"It don't have anything to do with Deangelo and to be honest, I just don't wanna go!" I was pissed, like my head was about to pop off any second after all I been going through behind fucking wit' her. Now she won't even come out wit' me.

"You know what? That's fucked up! I been catching hell from that nigga 'cause of you and it was worth it. But now you act like you set me up or some shit! What, you fucked wit' me just to get back at him? You know how much paper I den loss 'cause of you!"

"Myzphyt, Fuck you!" Before I can even say anything, she was out the door and in the building. I wanted to stop her but my head was too far gone to give chase.

Later that night I went to my party trying my best not to even think about what had happened with me and Treasure. I was about to get lifted and not worry about shit that happened with her, Pandillero, or the count. Shit, not even the two grand them punk ass rental cops took off me. We partied hard that night, I was feeling too good. So good we went at it two days in a row after that. I haven't talk to Treasure since and I really don't give a fuck at this point.

I started fucking with Sharon on my birthday so I decided to go chill out wit' her at Maxine crib. I was feeling frozen by the time we left out that mufucka then I hear, "Ay lil niggas let me holla at ya'll for a minute!"

21 DEANGELO

A couple days before my flight out Bateador called me said to meet him down in the hood. I rode out 'cause he sounded like it was important.

"What's up Pandillero? Jump in for a minute; I got something to show you."

"What's up Bateador, we got a problem? What we looking for?" Bateador didn't say anything back. All he did was pointed to Eleven Twenty-One. I saw people start to come out the building.

"Yeah nigga, so what? You act like these fools don't always have some shit jumping off down here."

"Yeah, but you see that youngin Myzphyt with them niggas don't you?"

"Yeah, don't tell me you had me come down here 'cause he fuckin' with some chick on the sid—"

"Naw man, I know you ain't gone hate on that nigga 'cause he fucking with somebody other than Treasure. I got word that yo' boy been dipping. Hell, before I called you I was up that bitch Maxine house hollan at Snoop. I go to the back, come out, I see that nigga Myzphyt lacing his L up with the shit he had just comp from Snoop. I knew you would want to see this shit wit' yo' own eyes so I hit you up."

Before he could say any more, I jumped out the car and was on my way to catch up with the nigga. "Ay lil niggas let me holla at ya'll for a minute!" I yelled out to them before they made it to the parking lot. They all stopped and waited while I walked up except for him. I can hear Bateador following behind me, like a chorus line, all these niggas said, "What's up Pandillero, Bateador."

I didn't say shit back; I was heated. I walked right up on that nigga Myzphyt and pulled him up against the wall. I hear Bateador tell them other lil niggas to get the fuck outta here and then they all started heading back in the building. I can smell that shit coming off his young ass as he question what's going on.

"Shut the fuck up! So I see you just said fuck me right? I thought I explained myself to you the last time I saw you not to fuck up and that I was watching you. Didn't I?"

"What the fuck you talking 'bout Pandillero, you tripping wit' me 'cause I'm wit' dis bitch Sharon and not Treasure?"

"Nigga, you think I give a fuck about you cheating on T? Who the fuck I look like to you? She gone find that out on her own anyway. I told yo' ass not to fuck up. You already know the rules of the game. By the smell of that dip, I can see you don't give a fuck. Since you den fucked up and started using that bullshit, yo' ass is done! No more pac for you or yo' peoples. And if I think you talk to or ever go around T again nigga, I'm gone make good on my promise to you about Ms. Sherry!"

"Hold up Pandillero. What's the problem?" I didn't even look back. I tightened my grip around that nigga throat a little bit more. I already know it's his uncle Showboat.

"The problem is yo' nephew then fucked up yo' money. That's the problem," Bateador said as he cut him off.

"Come on now Pandillero, whatever it is we can deal with this without all the hostility. Some youngin's just told me to come down 'cause it look like Myzphyt was down here beefin' wit' ya'll. Let me holla at chu cuz so we can work this shit out." I released my grip and let that nigga breathe.

"Don't forget what I said lil nigga!" I turned and walked toward Showboat.

"Ain't shit to talk about. If you can't keep yo' own nephew from getting wet then you can't handle the pac, so we done! Find yo' shit somewhere else." I jumped in my whip and waited for Bateador to finish talking to the nigga, and then he came over.

"Look, I don't give a fuck how much those niggas beg, make sure they don't get a damn thing from nobody. Let Cap know the deal."

"I got chu Pandillero. You know this might pop off though right?"

"Hell nigga, if you can't handle it while I'm gone then I can call in some hitters to look out for you."

"It ain't that nigga. I just wanna make sure I got the go to cancel dem niggas if they feeling froggy."

"Man, handle that shit. I don't care who it is if they wanna take it there."

"I got chu Pandillero."

22 TREASURE

Senior year is right around the corner. I know Deangelo will be leaving soon. I need to get the hell out of here myself, sooner than later. I know the hood is talking about that shit that happened in the club, and then the fight didn't make it no better.

I'm baffled that the police haven't showed up at Momma door yet. I try my best to keep it moving and stay as busy as I can. Just in case, at least I know ahead of time if they looking for me. I keep feeling like somebody watching me, every time I turn around feel like eyes on me.

I don't know if I'm just scared behind that shit or losing my damn mind. The only person I can talk to about it is probably not answering my calls. I don't know what to do. Myzphyt keep calling me to chill with him and to be honest I'm not in the right mind to be hanging around in the hood. That's the last place I want to be right now.

I try to play it off but I think he know what time it is. He has to know that I'm keeping my distance. He cool and all but I don't see a relationship coming out of this thing we have going. Besides, he's trying too hard to be like Deangelo and I know how that turned out for me.

"Hey Myzphyt, it..." I hope he's not mad but I can't fuck with him like that. The last time I did some shit like that I ended up with a gun to my fucking head. I'm not going to put myself back into that position. I don't care who wants me to go somewhere with them. Fuck that shit! That shit for the birds.

All I have to do is get this paperwork finished real quick so I can knock out school. Once they told me I had enough credits to graduate early, I hurried up and signed up. It seem like lately every time I'm with Myzphyt he seem like he high. I don't fuck with dudes that get high and I know he knows that. I've been pullin' back even more now that I picked up on it. I already know if Deangelo found out he would have my ass even if he is mad with me right now.

I wasn't surprised that Myzphyt was mad at me for not going to his party. Hell, I really don't care. I'm trying to be nice seeing that I was leaving real soon anyway. I still haven't even told him that I was going and to be honest, I was glad that I didn't. After spending the day with him I can feel the hostility growing. I tried to ignore and just have a good time with him.

"You know what? That's fucked up! I been catching hell from that nigga 'caus...." Then he went too far. I wanted to smack the shit out his ass for the way he was talking to me. I know better than that. Plus, it wasn't worth it. "Myzphyt, fuck you!" I ain't got time to argue with his silly ass.

All I can think about is what he said. I set him up? Basically, he called me Cindy. I wanted to tell Deangelo how his stupid ass came at me so bad. I know he'd take the shit too far. I never ran back to him and told him shit anyway. Some kinda way he always finds out, like he a fly on all the damn walls in the hood. It sound like he already pulling strings with him anyway. Talking 'bout he been catching hell 'cause of me. Bullshit!

23 BLASÉ

"What's up Treasure? I wanted to ask you something real quick!"

"Nothin' much, what's up Mr. Blasé?"

"You know Homecoming right around the corner; I usually don't go to stuff like that, but if I had you as a date I would make an exception."

"Oh!"

"Oh? So can I take you to Homecoming with me?" I can tell by the look on her face that she's not going. Why in the hell would I wait until the week before to ask her and I've already been making plans since last month? I should've asked her to go first, what the fuck was I thinking?

"Well Blasé, I actually won't be in town that weekend. I made plans to go to Memphis about a week ago. So I'm sorry I can't go witchu." Damn, I knew that was coming. I would try and get her to change her mind but I know she won't.

"All right, it's cool!"

"If you wanna dance though, we can dance now." She tried to pull me up but I wasn't in the mood. My heart was crushed and I was starting to feel like she wasn't feeling me like I was her.

It seem like we only kick it away from school and not even that often either. She always has a reason why she can't be around people we know or something. I know one thing though, I'm not about to blow my stacks. Especially with the way things looking with Treasure, so let me call up my ex real quick.

*　　*　　*

"What's up Blitz? What ya'll get into after Homecoming?"

"Shit Safari! You already know."

"Yeah I know you dropped her ass off at the crib and took yo' ass home by yo' damn self. Don't say you didn't 'cause Lawanda stopped by the after party and told me. Probably sat up crying over Treasure all damn night didn't you?"

"Man, get out of here wit' that shit! I told you we didn't get into shit, hell yeah I dropped her ass off. Crying over Treasure, yeah okay." We stood around laughing and joking while we waited on the bell.

"What I miss?" After class I see errbody outside my locker like they having a good time. I didn't hear the bell ring so I was the last one out of class.

"Shit! Just clowning 'cause that nigga Mike just got slapped by his gal," Safari said.

"What happened?"

"She said he was lying on her, saying he hit or some shit like that. Next thing we know she slapped his ass. Now he running behind her and shit like a lost dog," Debo said as they all made even more noise. It must've been the perfect day for shit to hit the fan.

I tossed my stuff in my locker and up walks Lawanda. She was upset about how I dropped her off so I let her get it off on me. Errbody thought the shit was funny, I already know she fronting; and then she hugged me.

"I'm just messing with you boo."

"I already know you not tripping like that. But I'm about to head to lunch so I gotta go."

She kissed me and next thing I know I see Treasure that nigga City was right behind her cheesing and shit like something was funny. I pried Lawanda off and started to go after her. Lawanda grabbed my arm. I don't wanna make a scene.

I tried to get away from her as soon as I could. I know that my boys thought the shit was hilarious 'cause of all the chaos they started by laughing, banging on lockers and shit. Lawanda got mad when Safari dumbass said 'I got caught,' she had a full-blown fit. She started cursing and hitting me like she was losing her damn mind.

I had to pick her ass up and take her outside to get her to calm down. By the time I look up, I see Treasure headin' to the parking lot. I tried to make a break for it after her but as I came down the breezeway, City and Damon was there.

"Too late nigga! You busted!" I heard Damon say. I slowed down and walked over to dem niggas.

"What she say?" They both looked at each other then back to me.

"WHO?" They had a serious look on their faces like they really didn't know who I was talking about. All I said was all right then and walked away as they began to laugh and talk shit.

I saw Treasure from a distance after that. Then I heard that she wasn't even in school anymore. I know that had nothing to do with me she was way too smart for that.

I tried to get information out of her people but those niggas wasn't budging. Then Sammy act like she didn't even know who the hell I was talking about. Like I made her up or some shit, like she was a figment of my imagination. That's sho' what she was starting to feel like too. Like she was just a memory, something that I made up and no one else knew anything about her.

Seem like the shit was all in my head. I thought I would see her around or if nothing else at graduation. But they called her name and she wasn't there. I wish I would've had the chance to know more about her or to spend more time with her. I guess the old saying is true, if you know better you do better!

If I could've only explained to Treasure what happened maybe we could've worked it out, or maybe if I would've asked her in advance to go to Homecoming none of this would've ever happened. Who knows; if I could change it I would.

25 TREASURE

"I hope you ready for Memphis this weekend. We about to have fun!"

"Sammy I already know. This our last year of school too. I'm gone miss you man when I leave. You know I only have a couple more weeks 'til I graduate so we have to clown Homecoming weekend!"

"Girl, who you telling? I sho' hate that I passed on getting out early now. I missed the deadline to get my paperwork in by a couple damn hours. If my daddy would've signed the shit, I wouldn't have had to wait on him to get off work. I'm too mad! I'm gone miss you too though girl. So whatchu gone do when you get out?"

"I don't know yet but I know what we doing this weekend."

"Parrrtay!" We both sang together then said our goodbyes and headed to class. I could've told Sammy about my plans. I didn't want her feedback or her to run her mouth to anyone about it. I just skipped over it and went on about my way. While I was walking to class, I saw Blasé heading in my direction. I slowed up and gave him a hug.

"What's up Treasure? I wanted to ask you something real quick!" After I turned Blasé down about going to Homecoming, I could see that he was hurt. I didn't want to stick around for the rest of the day thinking about it. I grabbed up my shit and took a long walk back to the crib.

We had a blast in Memphis. It seemed like the weekend just flew past and we was back in school. Everybody was talking about who went with who and who wore what. I was the least bit interested in any of that. I have to say I was surprised to hear that Blasé went with his ex-girlfriend Lawanda.

I didn't really expect for him not to go. Hell, if he would've asked me before we made plans to go to Memphis I would've went with him but he never did ask me. I thought that he would have at least asked me or told me that he would ask her I guess. Then again, we not a couple so I can't be mad.

"What's up Ethan?"

"Nothing, you ready?"

"You know it! Why you going this way?"

"Damon wants me to stop at his locker and get his book so he doesn't have to go down here after lunch."

"You know I hate going to building four, they too damn ghetto down there."

"It's cool. I got chu. We'll be in and out." We make our way to Damon locker. As soon as I see him close the door, I start heading toward the door down the hall.

Something told me to look up and soon as I did I see Blasé standing there kissing Lawanda. He looks over at me like he shocked to see me. I feel Ethan put his hand on my back and we don't miss a beat heading out the door. As we made our way out I can hear the laughter and beating on the lockers. It was like they just saw the best show they had ever witnessed. I was so embarrassed all I wanted to do was get out of there.

"You all right?"

"Yeah, I'm good. Why?"

"I was just checking. I know you saw yo' boy back there."

"Yeah Ethan, I saw him. It's not a big deal though. I'm out; I see a ride. See you later!" I didn't even wait on him to respond. I picked up my step and stopped Tim before he pulled out the lot.

I was home so I went straight to my room and went to

sleep. I wasn't about to waste any time crying over something that wasn't mine so I slept on it. Soon as the bus let out everybody came running to my room asking me what happened. After I told them to mind their damn business, they got the point, all except for Ethan.

He challenged me to a one-on-one game so I took the challenge and forgot all about what had happened. After the game, we sat on the porch.

"So you gone give him another chance?"

"Nope!"

"You sure about that?"

"Yep! Besides we not together anyway."

"Fuck that nigga. His loss, right." I fell back and put my head on his leg, looked up at him and smiled. We sat out 'til the sun went down and did nothing.

Blasé tried to call me a couple times but I avoided his calls. I didn't have time for it and he wasn't going to slow me down. I only went to school a couple times senior year, mostly to test out of shit, then I was out the door. I had my cousins Excursion so I didn't have to wait on anyone to take me home.

I saw Blasé twice when I did, I made sure I faded to black and rolled out as soon as I could. That was the last time I saw Blasé. I wasn't mad at him or anything but like I said, I was embarrassed about how everything went down. I hope he's well and all his dreams come true, I just have to move on with my life and let others do the same.

26 MYZPHYT

I was locked out the hood after that and my peoples were feeling it too. I decided to try and convince my uncle to hit them niggas and make a move that would take over the whole operation.

"Myzphyt, you don't know half of the people I know. Stop pushing this shit so hard. Let me think for a minute and we'll go from there."

"Showboat, I know you not scared nigga. Let's make this shit happen. I know you can find out where the next drop gone be so let's make a mufuckin' move." I tried my best to get my uncle to roll with it. It took him a minute to get back with me but I was too stoked when he called and said he was ready and gave me the details.

All I could think about as I sat a couple blocks back away from the warehouse was how I was going to make that nigga Pandillero pay for locking us out. I was also happy that my family would be on top of the pyramid from here on out, which meant more money and more dope to smoke and sell. I was feigning to get this shit done. I saw my uncle in the passenger seat as the car he was in drove closer towards the warehouse. Then they parked.

My hand was twitching waiting for them niggas to come out. I didn't even pay attention to the Bomb Pop Truck that drove past us. Next thing I know, the truck stopped and all I can hear is a non-fucking-stop scream of rounds from AR's rip through the air. All I can do is jump out the door and bust as I ran to close the distance. They stopped firing and the truck sped away.

The closer I got to the car the harder I bawled. I know my uncle was sitting there. I wouldn't have even known that it was a head that was candy coated across the door if I didn't. It's unbelievable the damage the rounds did to him. There's nothing left of his head. All I can see was his chest and a mangled arm draped out the door.

"Get in Myzphyt; we gotta go! Get the fuck in nigga!" I heard Lil Tony shout. Marcus pulled me in the car and we drove off. I couldn't go to my uncle funeral and see the closed casket sitting in the room. All my family crying and not understanding what happened. It was all my fault and I wasn't ready to face that. I smoked everything that I could get my hands on to try and get rid of the pain.

Seemed like shit went downhill since that shit happened. I was popped about a month later. With my uncle gone, I didn't have anybody to turn to for real. Spent almost a month on lock 'cause my other uncles told errbody not to get me out. They was pissed about what all happened so I was on my own. When I got out I was cleaning myself up then fucked up and was in a car with my boys and got hit with another charge.

Spent a year down, all I could do inside was spend my time getting high just to pass the days. When I came home, my mom's was the only one looking out for me. Even the lil niggas that used to run for me was running the other way.

So, I did what I knew best, got high and started robbing niggas. I was kicking in houses, whatever I needed to do to get a fix. It wasn't until I was pulled over for drivin' with no lights they found my stash. I was able to get treatment instead of going upstate.

With all the shit that has happened to me, all I can think about is if I could take back anything in my life, it would be losing Treasure the way I did. I hate that I didn't go after Treasure and apologize on my birthday. I shouldn't have went at her the way I did. I should've been more understanding and let her know that I had her back. Maybe she would've went with me that night to the party. Hell, I hate that I never spoke with her again after the shit with Pandillero that night.

If I was thinking, I should've tried to get her to spend the night with me instead of going to the party at all. My mom's still keep in touch with her people. Sound like she long gone. All I dream about is how she doing and if she good.

I wish I could talk with her or even write her. I already know that nigga Pandillero would find out. But fuck him I'd risk it just to know anything about her right now. Seem like she all I got to look forward to, but like they say, 'If you know better, you do better.' If I knew what I know now, I would've handled that shit way better than how I did.

27 BLASÉ

"I know that ain't Treasure going into Blueberry Hill is it?" I hurried up and turned my head looking out the window trying to see if Safari really does see her. I had to find out if it was her or not so I told Safari that we needed to make a stop.

I parked and jump out, we went in. As soon as I took a look around the room I could hear a high pitch squeaky laugh that I know was all too familiar. We looked at each other and both said, "That's Sammy!" We laughed and made our way toward the laughter. Of course, just like old times, Treasure was sitting at a table with her back to us. Sammy was laughing so hard all she could do was giggle as she tried to get Treasure attention to look at us.

"What's up Sammy? Treasure, long time no see," Safari said, as he walked around and slid out the chair next to Sammy.

"Sup Sammy? How you been Treasure?" I said as I stood waiting to see what reaction she would have after seeing me. She gave me her infamous smile.

"Hello Mr. Blasé. How's life with what's her name?" Straight for the juggler always with Treasure.

"Aw, enough of all that talk. We not in high school no more. Man, would you sit down?" Safari said like it was his table.

"Ya'll don't mind if we join ya'll, right?" Before

Treasure could say anything Sammy said nope and licked her tongue out at Treasure. I sat down next to her.

"Where you been Treasure? I didn't see you at graduation. Yo' ass just said fuck it huh and dropped the hell out." We all began to laugh 'cause he know damn well she too smart for that. If anything, she went off to college early or some shit.

"Nope, my girl only in town for a lil while. She been awa—"

"Sammy, I can speak for myself and don't even think to tell my business," she said as she twisted her head at Sammy.

"Like I said, she only in town for a minute and we just out having a good old time. It's funny seeing you two here though," Sammy said, as she looked over at Safari.

"Yeah, we were in the area and were looking for a spot to eat at. I guess you can call it luck that we ran into you two," I said, Treasure sat there trying not to look in my direction. Good thing this place had a dance floor though. After sending messages to Safari without saying anything, he asked Sammy to dance and off they went.

"So we just gone sit here and not say anything?" she said as she turned facing me.

"I was just thinking the same thing but I'm also still in shock to see you. What's it been, almost a year, that's not including the rest of the school year you dipped out on."

"How about we start again. Hi, my name is Treasure and you are?" she said as she held her hand out. I knew this girl was crazy but she always surprises me with just how much.

"Come on Treasure, we just gone pretend like nothing happened? I mean you never gave me a chance to expl...."

"Look Blasé whatever happened, happened. It was meant to be so let it be."

"I know that but—"

"See, that's that! You said enough, you know. That's good enough for me. As long as we both know better, we both will do better so let's move on from that."

I wanted to press the issue but I didn't want her to

leave so I rolled with it. After talking about little things for a while I found out she was only going to be in town 'til after her birthday. I have to say, being with her for the short amount of time that I was sent me back to the good old days when we hung out.

I was surprised that I managed to get her phone number and a promise from her to hook up with me the next day so I was good. We hung out a couple times each week. I was starting to feel kinda down that she would be leaving in the next couple days. I figured I would do something nice for her before she left.

In true form, Treasure showed up to my crib looking sexy as hell. I still don't know where she's been all this time. The way her body is looking, I know she been hitting the gym on a regular. Once we was finished eating the bomb ass dinner I made she looked over at me.

"You know Blasé, I have to be honest with you; I don't want you to get the wrong idea. I've been having a nice time with you and all but when I leave here, that's it. I'm not looking back! I'm going to move on with my life and leave this all in my past." I could tell by the sound of her voice that her mind was made up. There was nothing I can say at this time that will change her mind. Hell, she was leaving out in two days.

All I want to do at this moment is wrap her up and hold her for as long as I can. I stood up and slid her chair out from under the table and pulled her up into my arms. I don't want to waste another second so I carried her over to the wall. I started to go at her like I was on death row and this was the last time I'd ever be in her presence as a living man.

I kissed her, making sure she was down for the cause. Once she kissed me back I was in heaven on earth. I unbuttoned and took off her shirt, her bra was no problem. Once I saw them girls sitting up close and in my face, I wanted to sample both of 'em and she had more than enough. I couldn't stop; her girls had to be at least a thirty six double D. I had to taste her and I don't have time to put her down. I lifted her high enough in the air to swing one leg at a time over my shoulders.

Look at that. I start to lick my way down spreading her Ashera apart with only my face. I was able to fuck her wringing wet pussy with my tongue. The taste of her joy had me turned up to the fullest; all I wanted was more. The more she dug her nails into the back of my head the more I teased her walls and clit.

I didn't know she would taste this good. The feel of her insides made my mouth beg for more of the milk she was about to deliver to me. I let her give it to me until I couldn't take any more. I slowly brought her down. As soon as I had her mounted on the wall good I stepped out my clothes and laced up.

I had to move fast. I don't know how long I can hold out. My dick went straight in her tight, wet, hot Ashera and my toes began to curl from all the friction. The way her body moved up and down, the warmth and excitement of hearing her moan made me want to go even harder and deeper. I put her all the way down onto her feet then turned her around.

I've been waiting to tap that ass for way too long to skip out on the chance to now. I bent her over and started to work her. The more she arched her back the deeper I dug. Oh shit, she grabbing her ankles. Fuck! This Ashera too damn hot. I smacked her on the ass. Hearing her scream with pleasure made me want to give her more. I grabbed her waist and tried to kill it! I mean, I tried to put a whole in the wall with my dick through her body.

I couldn't hold it any longer. My load was coming and it was nothing I could do to stop it. I felt like my legs were going to give way. I pulled out, lost my shield and watched as it landed all down her ass. The site of my load moving down that pretty valley and covering her wet pussy made me instantly ready for another go. So, off to the bedroom we went. I was exhausted by the time we finished. I needed an IV to get liquid back into my body. I went to sleep with Treasure on my chest.

28 TREASURE

Walking through the airport, all I thought about was how happy I was that I had a first class ticket home. Everybody else was complaining that they wouldn't be back to they spot for days. Not me. I'm out this bitch today. Damn, is that? Nah, it couldn't be him. Let me hurry up before I miss my damn flight.

Soon as I saw that damn Arch all I could think about was how much I really missed home. It's been a long time since I been here but I know that this lil month that I have here is going to fly past. Soon as I walk down the ramp towards the baggage claim I see all my peoples. They're making all kinds of noise, got balloons and all kinds of shit. I even see they already picked my bags up for me. After many hugs and hellos, we were out the door.

"Hey Ethan, told you I would be back before you missed me," I said to Ethan as he walked me to his car.

"I been missing you since the minute you walked out the house the last time."

"Man, stop. You know you ain't worried about me."

"Treasure, don't do me like that. You know I missed you and if it was up to me you wouldn't be leaving again." He draped his arm around me as we took our time going to his car. Instead of taking me home, we decided to make a stop at my favorite spot. We spent hours just walking and talking before I realized it, we was back at the house sitting on the ground in the middle of the court.

"All right Treasure, let's see if you lost anything on this here court," he said as he went over and grabbed a ball from under the porch.

"Lost what? Don't let the smooth taste fool you. Ain't shit loss here," I said as I ran into the house to hit the court lights on. We played game after game until damn near three in the morning. I didn't realize how much fun I had with Ethan. I think out of everybody he's the one person I can really let loose with.

The next day I woke up hella late. It's almost four in the afternoon. Of course, I hear Sammy in the living room talking to my brother so I jumped up to see my girl. "What's up Sammy?" I said as I walked over and gave her a hug. "Girl, nothing! Here to take yo' sleepy ass to eat. I know you 'bout hungry, heard you had a late night last night," she said as she began to laugh like she really know what the hell she was talking about.

After I changed, we made our way to Blueberry Hill, found us a spot. We started going back and forth talking about how those cute bitches from school all fat now and most of 'em pregnant. We laughed hard just thinking about it. I can see Sammy looking behind me like she trying to say something. I turned to see who it was. There stands Safari and Blasé right here in the living flesh.

Umm, he looks even better now than he did in high school. It's a shame I never had a chance to see what he was working with. Look at Safari. Cocky ass, he just gone take over our table. Guess this a party for four now. Sammy think it's cute inviting them to join us.

Why is he staring at me so much? After listening to her and Safari go back and forth way too damn long, they decided it would be even funnier to leave us here. AWKWARD!! I can't take him just sitting and watching me any longer.

"So we just gone sit here and not say anything?" For a minute, he didn't say anything then he said he was thinking the same thing. He started trying to explain to me what happened.

I didn't want to hear it though. I have very good eyesight and what I saw with my eyes was enough for me to be finished with the situation. He was free to do what he wanted.

Once the ice was broken, we loosened up and started to enjoy each other's company again. I'm only in town for a minute and I wasn't going to let the opportunity to test out Mr. Blasé. Every day that I had a little free time he would come through. I was starting to get worried that maybe he was thinking the time we was spending together was more than what it really was. He said he had 'big plans for us' and he wanted me to come over.

I was surprised to learn that he could throw down in the kitchen. And it ain't anything sexier than a man that can cook. We had a good time. I know that I have to tell him the truth about where this thing of ours heading. It seem like since I walked through the door I just can't find the words or time to say it. Once we was finished eating I decided I might as well spill it on the table and get it over with.

"You know Blasé; I have to be hone..." I sat there trying my best to read his reaction but I can't. I look down at the table hoping he'll hurry up and say something. Once he got up, I thought he was going to put my ass out but he didn't. He turned me facing him and effortlessly picked me up.

Okay, let's see where this is heading. I wrapped my legs around him. He kissed my bottom lip then sucked it into his mouth. He tasted so good; I sucked on his tongue.

We continued to kiss as he placed me up against the wall. My shit came off so fast I don't even know how he got it off. The way he licked my breast turned me on instantly. I was begging for more. Oh shit, what is he doing? I didn't know he was this strong. Hell, I better brace myself on the wall just in case he let my ass go.

The way he eating my pearl is driving me insane. The site of him holding me in the air while he does it is making me flow harder than a flash flood. I was trying to force feed his ass even though he didn't need to be forced. I was so turned on by the shine I created all over his nose, mouth and chin. I can't wait for him to strap up and let me feel it. My feet never touched the ground. His arms held me the whole time he made his move.

As soon as he went in, I thought, 'Please don't stop, harder, faster, slower.' I can't make my damn mind up. Then he put me down and before I can get my balance my face was planted in the wall. He was hitting it from the back.

The more we went at it, the further down the wall my head went. I was touching my toes. In no time I can feel the wall touching my back and his dick is trying to do the same. The stuff we did that night had me on another planet. After I saw that he was good and sleep I snatched up my stuff ran out the door and called Sammy to pick me up.

"Girl, its five o'clock in the damn morning and here you are creeping out Blitz house. I guess it wasn't whatchu was thinking it would be, huh?"

"Girl, it was more than what I thought it would be. I just didn't want to have to say goodbye to him, that's all."

"So I guess when he start calling yo' ass like crazy you not gone tell him goodbye then either, right?"

"Nope and I would appreciate it if you didn't say anything to him either if you see him!"

"So what if I do see him? What am I supposed to say?"

"Whatchu think? You ain't seen me since and ain't heard from me either. What the hell? Damn, that looks like somebody. Slow down Sammy; wait on this car to pass us."

"Girl, what car?"

"The one that's behind you. I saw it pull out when you picked me up."

"Girl, look at yo' paranoid ass. That car din turned now."

"I'm for real; that looked like somebody I know. Yo' ass going so fast you not paying any damn attention."

"Whatever crazy!" Sammy said, as we continued on our way.

29 DOMINIC

First real day in Fort Lewis, why in the hell do we have to get up so damn early just to go to PT? I haven't had to get up like this since basic, damn near two years ago. "Monroe, get yo' ass up man. We have about three minutes to make it over to PT." I walked over to Monroe and shook the shit out his rack. "Damn, Xavier, I'm up. I was waiting on yo' ass. You the one in there taking all day," he said as he sat up and put on his shoes.

We quickly made it across the street and up the rusted lead chipped steps into the gym. Good, we not that late. We still have time to bullspit.

"Dang, who is that coming down the steps?" I asked Monroe as both our eyes followed the baddest chick in the room to her spot. I can't take my eyes away from her. I can feel my mouth drop open as her girls bounce hard like she don't have on a bra or something.

"I don't know man but that chick with the short hair is fine as hell. And she look like she see yo' boy. Don't know about you but I'm most definitely going to get a better view!" We both laugh as we made our way to the back of the formation behind them. This girl was bad, about five four, honey brown complexion; thick as a plum. Even in her PT shirt, I can tell her sports bra is having a battle trying to hold down those bouncing melons.

Just thinking about it has my man waking up; I better take my mind off it. I know these cheap PT shorts not gone hide my man for long. Let me concentrate on this fat pig in front of me for a minute to calm myself down. Man, if this gal bend over one more time and show me all that magma crust between her legs, I may just throw up and head to sick hall for the day.

"Xavier, you ready?" Monroe pushes me like he's been saying something to me the whole time. "What?" I snap back at him and back into the room.

"PT over, you ready to go to chow?" Monroe said as we stood up.

"Yeah man, we came at the right time. Heck, I think we may just like it here in Washington after all. If we thought Fort Gordon was off the chain we may have found us some winners."

"Shit, you don't have to tell me, I already know X. I bet I get that chick with the short hair. She was eyeing me the whole time. Caught her looking at my dick like she wanted to suck," Monroe said as we sat at our table.

"Yeah, whatever. That gal she was with, she was thick as hell. I wonder what rank she is. I hope they not some stuck up officers or something."

"Shit'd man I don't give a fuck what she is. The way she was eyeballing me, I know as soon as I get the chance I'm on it for real," Monroe said as he sat back in his chair.

Monroe always has been a cocky mothersucka. He think 'cause he box and hit the gym, every chick he come across is looking at his man. I thought that nigga learned a couple months back. Fool was in the barracks screaming like a chick 'cause of the burn coming from that muchucka when he tried to piss. You can't tell that nigga nothing though when it come to cat. He thinks all cat good cat. This nigga even got a dang on tat that says that stupid stuff. I just laugh at him and shake my head.

"Ay ain't that her in line?" I ask Monroe as I jab him in the side.

"Yeah, they're coming this way too. Told you ol' girl

wanna suck!" We both laugh as they stop at the table.

"These seats taken?" she says as she sits her tray down and pulls out the chair before we can even respond.

"Naw, I'm Monroe, this Xavier. Ya'll must be new; if not, where ya'll been hiding all weekend?" Look at this fool; he always trying to mack. I laugh at him and stand up and pull him up as they sit down.

"I'm Harmony, this Payton, I came in about one, and she came in about two this morning. They didn't have a room for us until three then we were late to PT, which was at five. But fuck them; they should've told us ahead of time." We all begin to laugh and continue to talk while we eat. Harmony is from New Jersey and she has the attitude to match. She's not bad looking and seems to be really interested in my boy.

Payton didn't say too much. She seems like a book nerd though. The whole time, she was studying this bull crap book they gave us when we arrived. We all tossed it to the side but not her. She was reading it like there was a promotion buried within the pages.

"Hey, so who was the other girl with ya'll at PT this morning? Where she at, she don't eat breakfast?" They both looked at each other and began to giggle.

"Who, Waters?" Harmony said as she looks over at Payton.

"Yeah, I guess. She short, she has her hair cut like down around her face, kinda high in the back."

"A bob," Payton said.

"Yeah, I guess. What's up with her?"

"I don't know. Like I said, we all just met early this morning. All I know is she from St. Louis. She seems cool. They put us in a room together and I think she said she was admin or something. Why you checking for her so hard anyway?"

"He not, but back to you Ms. Harmony," Monroe said as I gathered my tray and we all headed out the door.

30 TREASURE

I don't know why I'm thinking about Deangelo. After our last little talk I didn't want to see or hear from him any damn way. I guess he got what he wanted and changed his mind about even wanting to know me anymore. It was just on a whim I was in the hood and saw him. He walked right past me all hugged up with some new chick.

He looked me right in my face and they walked past like he was throwing acid on me. I took my time and walked back to Fourteen Eighteen so I could see my aunt. This tramp comes screaming at me talking 'bout she his woman and I need to stay away from him. I laughed at her and stared her down as I walked past her to go up the steps.

Then this heffa pulled me by the back of my shirt like I was a child. Before I knew it, I was feeding that bitch every left and right I could. I tried to stomp that ho head in the ground. She went down and was screaming for help. Instantly, the lobby was packed. I hear my auntie nem coming down the steps. Then I feel somebody damn near body slam me against the wall knocking the air out of me. I look and it's Deangelo ass. He had me hemmed up like I was one of these niggas or something.

He yelling at me so loud I couldn't even comprehend what he was saying. One thing I knew was that he was protecting that bitch. My peoples was pissed, they pulled me from out his grip. I could see the anger in his eyes and hear the detestation in his voice. Who was that person? I've never seen him act like that, let alone towards me.

I can't lie, it hurt but I was done at that point. Embarrassed was not the word, I was more humiliated about the way I acted than anything. She did have it coming for sure! I could've let her say what she needed to say. Even after she put her hands on me, I could've tried to reason with the bitch. Fuck that! Bitch need to keep her hands to herself! She can talk all she wants and it ain't a problem. But don't put yo' hands on me. My aunt said she think the trick name Tiffany; she was supposed to be pregnant by him. It all made sense for his actions but he needed to keep his bitch in check. I'm not giving him a pass for the way he treated me. But if she is or was pregnant I know he was just trying to protect his child.

I know she new down there, while she was trying to find out who I was, she should've asked if she should fuck with me. The hood was all talk for a minute with shit like I fought with her over him. I was mad 'cause she was pregnant by him. I tried to kill her baby, all kinds of shit. Whatever, I know what happened and that's all that mattered.

Eighteen months earlier.

"What's up Ethan? I know you not sitting over there mad at me are you?"

"Man, why you have to go and pull some shit like this? And you just now telling me a couple days before you go? That's fucked up!" Ethan said, and then he laid back on my bed as I finished packing my bag. I walk over, sit beside him and put my hand on his leg.

"I know this a lot to take in but I have to go—" Before I can finish, he pops up and looks so angry. If I didn't know any better I'd be scared.

"Man, fuck dat nigga. He left; get over it! Don't take it out on us 'cause you can't talk to him or whatever the hell you mad about! You know just as well as I do, he 'bout laid up with some chick. That nigga ain't shit. He wasn't shit but a drug dealer when he was here and he ain't shit over there! So get over him. Man, back out of going into this bullshit ass Army!" I knew he was right, but who is he to judge me like that? He can't hit me below the belt like that.

"You know what Ethan; I don't care how you feel about my business. I'm not doing this 'cause of him and you know it! I have to get the hell out of here now, not later. I know if I stick around I'll be just like the rest of these people, lost!"

"Damn Treasure, I know and I'm sorry but I'm so fucking pissed right now. Couldn't you have told me when you joined? Why wait 'til two days before you leave. I didn't have a chance to..."

"I just didn't want anyone to change my mind; I know it's fucked up. And I know I'm wrong for not telling you but I been busting my ass! You know it, I'm tired Ethan. I can't keep turning my wheels. I have to go."

I sat staring in his eyes as the tears began to flow. I knew that it would be hard to do something this spontaneous and out of character but I had to go. I didn't have to but I wanted to. Shit, I needed to shake some shit up in my life. Ethan softly wiped the tears from my face and before I knew it, we locked lips. In that moment, my mind, body and spirit realized that I may have missed out on the perfect one for me.

Two days later.

"What's up Ms. Lady? Where you headed?" As I turn around I see JT old chocolate ass standing there fucking me with his eyes.

"I'm headed back to the hotel. I just came down here for a minute before I headed out of town."

"I know you not about to leave without telling me goodbye right?"

"Really? You worried about me leaving? Tell me anything JT." I turned heading out the door.

"Hold up Ms. Lady. Let me drive you down there."

"Why?"

"Girl, stop playing with me. You know I can take you down there." Seeing that the hotel was right across Cole Street on the other end of the projects, I jumped in. Before the radio came on, we was sitting out front. "Thanks JT, see ya' later," I said as I opened the door and stepped out. I didn't want him to think for a second it was cue for him to walk me in or anything else. "All right Lady; you take care," he said, and then pulled back off.

Months had passed since I had talked to my family or anyone for that matter. My moms and my godmother showed up at my graduation from Basic. I wished they could've come to my graduation from AIT but I know money tight. I was shocked when drill sergeant gave me a first class ticket home. Hell, everybody else had Greyhound tickets waiting on them.

He think he slick trying to make it like he bought the damn thing, yeah right. He must've thought that was gone persuade me to fuck him before I left. Yeah, okay! I wouldn't fuck him with somebody else pussy, all the hell his punk ass put us through. He looked out for me though. I was in a leadership position until two days before graduation.

That ugly ass Acting First Sergeant fired me 'cause I went to the real First Sergeant and told him all the slick shit she was talking to me. Bitch been hating on me since I been here. Every time she see me in civilian clothes she got a hating ass comment, "You think you cute. You glad I don't show up in my civi's, blah, blah, blah." Fuck that hater. I ain't even mad. I'm out dis bitch, headed back to the Lou for a month before I ride right back out.

I wonder how Myzphyt doing; not like I really care after he said all that bullshit last time I saw him. I haven't heard or even tried to write Deangelo since the package. I know that he must be having a good old time over in Greece. It's like he just said fuck me and erased me from his memory bank.

Current day.

Man, this plane shit, I don't know how I'll get use to it.

I hate taking off and landing but this turbulence have me thinking this bitch about to go down are something. This place expensive as hell. Cost me a hundred dollars to get to post from the airport. Why the hell they don't have post vans; this shit is ridiculous. Dang, it's almost three in the morning. Good thing it's not that many people here.

"Why you wearing your dress blues?" some girl asked me. I turned around. She look like she from New York somewhere.

"They said when we left AIT that we had to report in our dress blues."

"Yeah, they told me the same thing but I figured oh well, I'll just play like I didn't know. Besides, the Specialist told me that they do that as a joke on new recruits."

"Don't matter; I'm just ready to go to sleep. That ride was hella long; I hope they don't be on some bullshit when we get therrre."

"By the way, I'm Harmony!" she said holding out her hand.

"Waters, nice to meet you." After talking with her I found out a lot about Harmony, like she thirty. I couldn't believe it; she look no older than eighteen, twenty max.

What the hell they mean PT; we just got in the damn room! This some bullshit right here. We make a mad dash down the fire escape like stairs to where PT formation was about ready to start. "Good thing we slept in PT's huh?" Harmony said while we made our way to the back. PT was nothing; it was like some remedial type shit nothing like basic or AIT.

It was a bunch of fat asses that failed their PT test so they had all the new recruits join in with them. Instead of going to breakfast I decided that I'd go back to the room and get some sleep. I told Harmony and some other chick I would see them later. Dang, I could swear that look like somebody I know parked across the street. Let me walk over that way so I can get a better look. Damn, guess not, they pulled off before I could get a chance to go over there. Oh well.

"Waters, look like you have a secret admirer asking

about you," Harmony said smiling shaking her head at the same time. I was kinda annoyed that she was making such a big deal out of whatever she had heard. I already know she was goin' give me all the details.

31 DOMINIC

"Ay man hurry up we need to get to the NCO club before it's too late. You know they stop mufuckas from leaving off this hell hole post at a certain time." I yelled into the bathroom to Monroe as he took his dang time. Walking down the steps I remember I left my watch.

"Hold up I need to run back upstairs for a sec!"

"Man here you go rushing me and you the one going back upstairs. Hurry up," Monroe said as he headed to the car.

"Excuse me can I talk to you for a second?" Monroe called out.

"What's up? Do I know you?" she said as she headed to the parking lot.

"Naw Shorty you don't know me I'm Monroe, but my mans been checking for you for a minute. You like a panther around this bitch, I mean post, excuse my language.

I wanted to know if you and yo' girls where planning on going to the NCO club tonight? It's supposed to be packed. I know my mans wanted to speak with you for a minute if he had the chance." After she finished laughing she looked away. I see a car with somebody in it I don't know if it's her man or not. Frankly I don't give a fuck if it is.

"Actually we headed that way now so I guess we'll see ya'll there. By the way, my name is Treasure or Waters if you prefer Monroe right?"

"I guess we will and its Charles. I'm use to using last names around here. But it's nice to finally meet you." I hold out my hand and shook hers as she looks off in a distance then turned and walked away.

"You know you fucked up right?" I look over at Monroe as we drove into the parking lot of the NCO club.

"What I do," he said as he began to smirk like he was caught.

"Man I saw you talking to Shorty in the parking lot nigga don't play me! You trying to fuck? I mean just let me know so I can stay the hell away or pick up my game so you don't have a chance." I had to let him know he ain't ahead of the game by no distance.

"Man that was nothing; I was putting in a good word for you while you over there thinking I'm *that* nigga. I know you feeling her so I ain't trying to do shit with her. Besides, I'm trying to get at that fine ass Harmony. She a freak! I can feel it. Plus she from New Jersey so I know she got a head game out this world.

Yo' girl, she got too much attitude for me with her country ass. Check, she said, 'see ya'll dherrre.' country, down south ass. I should've asked her how many r's I'd need to spell there the way she said it." We both laughed at his attempt to mock her accent.

"I mean she cute as fuck got some big ass melons, a fat ass and small waste but she always looking all mean and shit. I figure she what, thirty six D's, twenty, forty five give or take? Nice ass shape but I don't have time for no attitude! I deal with that enough with First Sergeant no dick getting ass. By the way, I'd knock the dust off First Sergeant old ass if she let me. You can have that headache all day if you want it." Monroe said as we laughed and walked in the club.

Okay there she go, forget it, I been waiting to talk with her for too long. And I don't know when the next time I'll see her. "Hey Harmony, Payton and—?" I waited for her name but she turned away as if someone had called her. Shoot, shorty do have a way about her. I guess she not feeling a nigga like I thought she would. But I'm not gone let her off that easy.

"I'm sorry I didn't catch your name," I said as she looked back at me and gave me the look of death.

"I'm sorry I didn't *throw* my name out so how could you catch it?" She stared me down as if she was waiting to see if I could keep up in a race. "This is Waters," Harmony said as they began to laugh while Waters just sat nursing a drink that she didn't seem to like.

"What's good Harmony, Payton, and Treasure?" I hear Monroe say as he walks up behind me. Why the hell this nigga know her name? First name at that and I don't? She told him her name but not me, what the hell is up with that? I have to reel this back in, she not gone do me like I'm one of these bum ass niggas in here.

As the others headed to the dance floor I sat watching her wondering what the attitude was about. But hell, ain't no time like now so she just gone have to deal with it.

"Excuse me Ms. I Didn't Throw My Name. I'm Dominic. I don't know what I did to get on your bad side but I sure hate that I did." I watched her look at me and give me a gorgeous smile. Her wet full lips slightly pulled up on the sides showing just a glimpse of her teeth. Before she spoke she bit down on her bottom lip pulling her teeth softly across it. Almost as if she was flirting with me. I'm starting to think she may be bipolar. Just a minute ago she seemed to want to bite my head off. Now I think she flirting with me.

I don't know how to read this girl here but something about her wants me to figure it out and make whatever her problem is go away. "My name is Treasure or Waters if you like; you're not on any of my sides. I was just messing with you 'cause for the last couple weeks I been hearrring about someone trying to track me down.

Then Mr. Monroe stopped me earlier and said the same thing so when I saw you walk-in with him, I figured it must've been you. I hope I didn't hurt your feelings. I was starting to feel a little bad about messing with you. Thought maybe I took it too far," she said as she smiled and looked at the others as they came back to the bar.

"Ay, we found a table, ya'll coming or ya'll gone chill here?" Monroe said as he stood with his arm wrapped around Harmony as if they had been knowing each other for years. We both stood up and I followed behind her. The way that thang was moving in that dress I'd bet my last dollar she don't have on any panties. I'd probably give my last breath to explore what she don't want any panties to touch.

I pull out her chair and sat next to her, the smell of her perfume was pulling me in. The softness of her back as my finger brushed up against it made my man want to stand to attention. The floor was quickly packed as *Left, Right, Left* by Drama came on. You would think all these Army squares would hate that corny song.

"So Treasure is your first name?" She smiled and looked over at me.

"Naw, people call me Treasure, it's my middle name, my first name is Terentia." She lowered her eyes then looked away.

"Terentia, that's a beautiful name for a beautiful woman." I can hear her giggle but she didn't turn and look at me.

"You mind if I call you Terentia?" Her head turned abruptly with a slight frown on her face. I don't understand what I said wrong. Then her face softened and she began to smile.

"Sure! If you want, I mean it's still my name," she said as she continued to stare into my eyes. I guess she was trying to figure out why I want to call her by her first name.

After a couple songs worth of small talk I found out really not a dang thing about Terentia. She talked but she wanted to know mostly about me. Every time I asked about her, she gave me a short quick answer. Makes me think she running from something or she doesn't want to get attached to anyone.

Then there it was, my golden ticket, I sat back and had no problem doing it with Terentia as the others danced away to the beat. When it happened. *Just Friends* by Musiq Soulchild began to play as I watched her face light up like it was her jam.

All I can think is thank you Dj for playing this song!

I quickly asked her to dance and we made our way to the floor. When I first heard this song last week I thought about her. And now I'm here on the dance floor watching her swing those sexy hips to the beat. The way she moving got a nigga in over his head. I pull her close wrap my hands around her small firm waste and groove out.

My nose wide open as she put that thang all up against my man. All I can think about is her like it's nobody else in this joint. To my surprise, after it ended we stayed on the floor and she showed me what she was working with. I was like a kid in a candy factory. I don't like to dance but the way she moved against me I didn't have to do much.

Then she picked it up as soon as she heard, a down south booty shaker come on. That ass was moving full speed ahead. All I can think is she got to have some freak in her to move like this. I'm too geeked to find out how she work it for real now. After a couple songs they slowed it down and I guess she decided she had enough. She turned, looked at me and began to walk back to our table so I followed behind her.

"Dang Terentia, how you gone do me like that, I thought we were having a good time out there?"

"I was but I hate this song and plus I'm tired I'm actually ready to go I need to get some rest," she said as she began to fumble around with her purse. She avoided eye contact almost as if she was about to cry are something. Shit, maybe she is bipolar. She dancing and having a good time one minute. Now she has a tremble in her voice won't look up and ready to go. I don't know about this girl my mind telling me to run while I still can. But who am I fooling; she had me when she didn't throw her name so I could catch it.

"Well I can take you back if you like. I drove plus it will give me some time to get to know you a little better. If that's all right with you?" She gave me a sexy tender smile. Before she can answer the others came back and she turned to them letting them know that she was ready to go.

"What? It's still early it ain't nothing to do back on post." Harmony said as she began to pout.

"How about X give you a ride back and I ride back with them. If that's okay with ya'll?" Monroe said as he leaned over and gave Harmony a kiss on her neck. This nigga know he sly as all out.

"Is that okay Waters you cool with riding home with Xavier? We know who you with so if we get back we know who to send the MP's after." Harmony said as she looked over at me with this overly protective mother look on her face.

"I'll take you straight back to the B's no stops. You can call them when we get there if you want," I said trying to reassure her. She looked like she wanted to say, "Trick I came with you! So you taking me home!" Then she smiled and looked at me.

"Straight back, no stops and don't think for one second you getting any!" We all laughed said goodbye then I walked her to the car.

"So what was up with that back there? You seemed like something was on yo' mind when that song came on." I tried to focus on the road. It was hard trying not to focus on how her smooth caramel calf muscles and thick thighs would feel wrapped around my shoulders.

"Nothing I just don't like the song," she said as she sat piercing out the window in a world of her own. I need to go slower I'm gone milk this moment for what it's worth.

"Come on sexy don't be like that. I know you not shy so can we have a conversation that's more than two or three words from you?" This girl is a piece of work.

"Well if you really wanna know, that song reminds me of someone who I don't talk to anymore. I'm not shy and have no problem talking to you but right now like I said I'm tired. The drink they gave me was strong as hell and I shouldn't have drank the little bit that I did 'cause I'm not a drinker.

By the way, first you was trying to catch my name and now that you have you won't use either of the options I gave you. Or the one you asked me to use. So what's the deal with that?" she said as she turned toward me waiting for a response. I can see this girl is more than a handful. She's beautiful, honest and sexy as all out. With a smoking bad body and has a smart mouth that I'd love to hear screaming my name if she let me.

"My bad Terentia I just call it like I see it. You sexy as that thang and I'm feeling that attitude you have going on with you. I just want to get to know you better that's all." I smiled as I pulled into the parking lot, looked at her soft cognac colored pecan shaped eyes then she suddenly looked away.

"I was not about to kiss you if that's what that's all about. Besides, your breath might smell like that Absolute you been chugging back all night." For a second I thought she might get out pissed off. Then she turned smiled and burst into laughter. We laughed and sat there talking for another hour.

"So it's still early you want something to eat, watch a movie, TV are something Terentia?" I had to ask her, every minute I get to spend in her presence is all good with me.

"Stop playing, you know everything on this post closed," she said as I helped her off the bench we found ourselves sitting at.

"Well I know you stay in those old barracks but we stay in the new ones. We have a kitchen plus we went to the Commissary earlier and picked up some food. You may not know it yet but yo' boy X here can do his thang in the kitchen. We have the finest selection of bootleg DVDs with all the new releases. All you gotta do is trust ol' Xavier here. And before you say it I already know I'm not getting any." She smiled.

"You sure my Absolute breath won't bother you? I'd hate for you to try and take advantage of me since I've been putting back *sooo* many drinks tonight."

"Ms. Terentia I got you!" I held out my arm and we walked to the room. After I whipped up some burgers for us she got comfortable in the brown and white side chair I picked up and I popped in the movie. I couldn't resist being that far away from her I sat down on the floor beside her.

"I can't let you sit on the floor and I'm in your chair." She started to get up.

"Terentia I'm good unless you just don't want to sit there by yourself. I can sit with you if you like." I leaned my head back and gave her a smile as I waited on her snappy smart reply.

"This chair ain't that big now," she said and laughed.

"Stop playing we can make it work. Or we can sit on the bed together. Hell, we could lay down if you still tired," I said hoping she won't get mad and want to leave but I had to try.

"Okay, I see you slick as you wanna be Mr. Dominic." She nudged me in my head and we both laugh and watch the movie.

As the movie came to the end I can hear that she was fast asleep. Damn, this girl is even more beautiful in her sleep. I can stare at her all night and not get jaded. The last thing I need is for her to open her eyes and see me looking intently at her. I slid my hands under her and carried her the short distance to the bed. She light as hell, what about a hundred ten pounds.

My man getting excited just at the thought of holding her in my arms as we made love from one room to the next. Her body a work of art and I want to be the aesthetician to find out everything there needed to be found out about it. I know in due time my chance will come to do all that though.

32 TREASURE

I need a break something to let me kick back and relax. Harmony thought it would be cool if we checked out the NCO club so I agreed to go with her. I can't wait to go out tonight. I'm going to have my first taste of alcohol, see what all the hub bub is about. Hell, big brother not around and I don't know anyone here so no big deal. Just the thought of Deangelo gave me a flash of what he would say. Then all the memories and bs he put me through helped me keep focused. "Excuse m..." some guy called out.

Who is this big head mufucka? I didn't know they made fedora hats that size. I can't help but laugh under my breath as he came running behind me. I have to hand it to him, besides having a big ass head he does have a Roy Jones look to him.

Oh and he over here to tell me about his boy, how classic is that? Now why the hell would I want to be bothered by someone who's not even man enough to step to me as such? Whatever let me get this over with we heading to the NCO club anyway.

As soon as we made it through the door I had Harmony get me a drink. Seeing it'll be damn near eight months 'til I turn eighteen I'm not old enough, I know she don't mind. I took one sip and wanted to pour that shit out on the ground. This the bullshit people talk about? Fuck that, I looked at Harmony and told her I was finished. She thought the shit was funny so her old ass decided to mix it for me.

After ordering some cranberry juice she poured some into it and finished that awful shit off in one gulp. I can still taste that shit in the cranberry juice so I don't wanna drink it. I decided I'd watch the ice melt in it.

We sat looking around the club from the bar, it's jammed packed. Then I see Head walk in the door with some Nathan Owens looking guy. I don't wanna take my eyes off him. He about six two probably one hundred eighty pounds and built like a god. Nice outfit look like something straight off a mannequin.

I can tell he from somewhere down south just by the way he move. Slow but confident, not worried about shit and he know what he want. Before I know it I see Harmony smiling and cheesin' so damn hard I just about threw up. For her to be that old she sure is happy to see that Monroe dude.

"Hey Harmony, Payton and..." And? I looked around to find And wondering where the hell she at. I know I'm wrong for that but hell; I have to put him to the test, see if he run away or not. He silly talking about he didn't catch my name. I wonder what he'd do if I just look at his ass? Damn, Nathan Owens don't have shit on him, he look even better up close then he do from across the room. I can tell he has a fresh cut, I wonder how his hair would feel rubbing against the insides of my thighs?

Let me get my head out the trough and talk to him before he walk the hell away. Look at her, I didn't ask her to tell him shit, it's not like he don't know my name already. Hell, he been asking about me since I got here so I know he know my damn name by now.

Here go Head, I mean Monroe again, he think he the shit and can't nobody tell him he ain't. He must be from Michigan or something; he has a slick ass cat daddy appeal to him. They would leave me here with him. I don't know if I should say something or not. He look like I just fucked up his whole night. Why I have to go and do that?

"Excuse me..." Okay so he not mad, maybe he was just

waiting on them to leave. Maybe I didn't mess his night up after all. Man, if it was up to me he'd be on all my insides all damn night. Look at all that tongue moving across his teeth and lips after he say something. Damn, that shit sexy, all I can do is smile and enjoy the view.

The next thing I know I had to catch myself from biting my own damn lip off. It wasn't long before the others came back and said they had a table. I was debating on if I would take that nasty ass drink but hell I paid for it. I might as well take it with me even if I don't plan on drinking one damn sip from it again.

"...call you Terentia?" I can't believe he asked me that. I think that's the first time anyone has asked to call me by my first name. Even people back home don't call me by that. I told him it was okay then started to think about just how fucking tall his ass was. I'm only five five but man I love me some men over six feet. That shit is so fucking sexy. Like they can just pick you up and handle your ass.

Let me stop, this man is doing way too much with that tongue of his. Sexy as all out, tall, medium complexion, chiseled—I mean I hope. I really can't tell but by the looks he should be. I should touch his stomach see what the hell he hiding under there. I need to snap out of it, let me focus in on what the hell he talking about.

We talked as the others danced and I found out he was actually from Little Rock. He's the oldest child of three. Don't sound like he's too fond of his family's situation back there so he joined up. I was amazed to find out he spent damn near two years in AIT. These dudes are actually pretty damn smart.

He said they did something with communications, satellites and programming and shit like that. Hell, how in the hell am I supposed to listen. All I want to do is straddle him in that seat and kiss his ass 'til his dick magically slid in me.

No they not! Was instantly all I could think when I heard my shit, I had to sing along, I wonder if he dance, he look like he don't. I know them southern guys don't play that dancing shit. What, he actually asked me to dance, let's do it! I'm all over him trying to polish that Louisville slugger he working with. I can feel it move more and more down his leg. As the songs continued to play I was in my own world with his hands around my waist.

Oh well there goes that wet dream I'm done, that song brings back way too many memories for me, I don't even like it anymore. As we made it back to the table I can tell he don't want to stop. That song just took me by surprise. I didn't even know that hearing it would make me feel this way.

Damn, what happened? I miss my buddy more then what I thought I did. Not to mention the way I'm feeling, is that really just my buddy or is he something more than that? I don't know what it is but I have to get the hell over it. Good thing the others are here, maybe he'll forget about what just happened, plus I'm ready to go. It feel like I'm about to be cold. Of course Harmony trying to get fucked so she den pawned my ass off with Xavier. Which really ain't a big deal but I had to let him know not to try and pull no greasy shit.

Why is he looking at me like that? I wonder what he thinking. I hope he not trying to kiss me, this so uncomfortable. Why he try and play me saying I been chugging back Absolute all night? I had a sip and that was it. I busted out laughing, that caught me all by surprise. We talked for awhile then I put precaution to the wind. I decided to grab something to eat and watch a movie with him.

This a new person, the old Treasure would've made Harmony bring me back. She damn sure wouldn't be going into a room with a man she don't even know. It feels good though to let my guard down for a minute. I just hope that I don't regret it.

We ate and he turned on a movie then sat on the floor beside me. His response for why he did that was too cute; I can't say anything after that. Next thing I know I was waking up the next morning in his bed. I look over and he sitting in the chair with his head leaning to the side. I grab my stuff and make my way out the door before he can get up.

"Ooh Waters, bring yo' lil fast ass right on over here baby," Harmony said the moment I walked in the door.

"Yeah don't try and be all quiet trying to creep up in

here at what, six in the damn morning! Un un, come here baby, come here!" I just laughed and walked over to her side of the room.

"Yes mother, did I miss my curfew?" We both laughed as I sat down on the end of her bed.

"So tell me where you been Miss Lady. And don't leave anything out I want all the slimy details!" I told her what happened and of course she don't believe me. I jump in the shower and that just sent her mind into total chaos. I spent the next couple hours going back and forth with her and then I went to bed. I wasn't going to persuade her so I gave up and let her think what she wanted.

33 DOMINIC

"So where we heading tonight ladies?" Monroe asked.

"Well, we're headed to Seattle to see what's popping out there; *WE* don't know where ya'll headed."

"Well Sandy, you already know where *WE* going, to Seattle. So be ready in about an hour, ya'll can ride with us, ya' dig?" Monroe said as he grabbed Harmony from behind and carried her off laughing and joking.

"What's up beautiful? You missed me today?"

"The question is if you missed me?" I lean over and grab her hand moving her closer to me and kiss her.

"Does that answer your question?" Dang she taste good I can do this for the rest of my life if she let me. Just her standing in between my legs make me wanna take it there. I mean really take my time and work that tail over. She might need some good stick in her life. Maybe that's why she looks so dang on mean all the time. I can solve her problem if she let me get at her body. I put my arms around her waist making sure she can feel my mans greet her. She put her head into my chest.

"So you sure you wanna go to Seattle with those knuckle heads tonight. *Orrr* do you wanna hang back and chill?"

"That sound cool but I already told Harmony I would go, plus it's what, a hour away? You know they probably gone get wasted and try to drive back here."

"Heck they grown, but I can't have something happen to them so it's cool. What you think about spending the weekend out there?" Please say yes! Please let her say yes! If she don't it's cool but hot DAMN if she say yes I know it's gone be like that this weekend most definitely! I slid my hands down to feel that round apple waiting for her to say something.

"I don't know, I guess we'll see now won't we?" I already know it's a go now. I'm gone make sure to let Monroe know to stress the importance of staying and them getting a room. Of course I know Terentia not goin' want to hear their loud selves go at it. They try and sho' out all that noise ain't real.

Nigga think he really be doing something too, she don't make it no better with all the faking she do. If you hitting it right you won't be able to get one got dang word out her. Shoot, if she can talk you need to shut that off and go to work. Seem like those two be having full blown conversations. All I do is laugh and turn up the TV, half the time it seems like she just saying stuff to get at me. Monroe already told me she'd be down with the toss like we did back at Gordon but I don't pay it no mind.

"You ready to head back Ms. Terentia?" I slid down off the side of the car.

"Sure I doubt it if they gone be ready in an hour though, whatchu think?"

"From what I hear they gone be ready in about fifteen minutes, tops!" We both laugh as I walk her to her barracks and then I head back to get ready. Just like I thought, Harmony was coming out the door as I was making my way up to the room. All I did was laugh as she laughed like she read my mind.

We hit about four clubs and just like I said we checked into rooms. The way Terentia been throwing that ass on me all night I know she ready. Her body been telling me since we been here. After we headed in and got comfortable we watched TV for a minute then she turned on the radio and the lamp.

I'm getting excited just wondering what she about to do; it's not like her to step out like this. Whatever it is I can't freaking wait. I couldn't have planned for it to happen but right on cue the Dj Gods was shinning down on me and played our song.

Terentia walked over to me and pulled me to the bench at the foot of the bed. I can tell she about to let me know what's up. The way she moving and….hold the horses, she taking her clothes off? O BOY! Look at that, I had no freaking idea. We been kickin' it tough for almost eight months and I'm too happy she lettin' a nigga get some.

She grooving out to the beat as she strips making sure I'm in full view of what's happening. She dipped down and slowly came up. All I can see is that pink monkey caught in between her thighs. Her panties still on the floor with her hands.

I'm ready to bury my head in it like an ant eater. Use my tongue to drain that thang dry, I know it's wet; I can see the shine already. She stepped out of her thong, turned, walked over and the feel of her body is just what I need. She moved my hands away from her as she continued to do her thing. Rubbing up against me sitting on my lap, I'm getting a full blown lap dance. All I can do is sit here and take it. When the song ended she gave me a quick kiss on the lips, picked her stuff up off the floor and headed toward the bathroom.

"What, where you going?"

"That's all you get," she said as she heads toward the door. Before she can take another step I pick her lil ass up and carry her to the bed.

"So that's how you gone do me," I said as she laughs and tosses around while I continue to squeeze her thighs. I know that's her soft spot, the slightest squeeze has her laughing her head off.

Her body is ripe and ready for picking. I run my fingers all over her body kissing her in every spot I can. Leaving the best for last of course. After I finish touching, licking and kissing the front of her I work my way to the back. I think I found another soft spot. The moment my lips touched her back that ass perked up just enough to arch her back and I had to do it again.

I concentrate on her back to find out exactly where she'll react the most from. I roll her back over licking and kissing her softly. Making sure I let her know that she in the right place and it's time. I work my way down, I can't wait to get to her hideaway so I can make it mine. I raise one leg up kissing it from the crease of her thigh all the way to her toe then I sucked each and every one of them while she giggles. When I was finished I placed it off to the side then worked the other leg the same way in the opposite direction.

I was in a daze looking at that diamond up close; it was by far the most mouthwatering thing I've seen in my life. I wanna make her beg me to put it on her. Soft, smooth and fat is all right in my face as I kiss it and begin to open it up. When I had it positioned in the right spot with my fingers I went to town on it. I can feel her clit get bigger with every lick. I worked it slow, then fast, then in and out with more pressure than less I can taste her body react.

Her taste has become my favorite flavor and I'm about to get full off of as much of it as I can. I feel like I'm in a pie eating contest I waste no time to get her back there over and over. I can feel her insides clinch around my tongue then there it is my flavor. I made sure I put in work before I kissed her thighs and made my way up to her mouth.

We kiss as she start to take off my shirt; I pull up after I took it off. I stood on the side of the bed watching her as she waited for me to undress and join her. I waited taking in the view of her willing and wanting body move up and down with the rapid beat of her heart. "You all right over there?" I had to tease her, she turned her head like she was shy, and she closed her eyes.

"No!"

"You need something?" She turned over onto her side staring at me but not saying anything. She sat up on her hands and knees making her way over to me. Um, um, um look at all that ass, I can see it from the front she so thick! Once she reached me she grabbed for my pants but I moved back.

"You not trying to take advantage of me are you Terentia?"

She laughed and stood up off the bed, "Nope!" she said as she walked right past me to the bathroom again. I grab her again and smack her on the ass.

"Now you see what it's like. Now yo' tail all hot and bothered you wanna run into the bathroom."

"Well I don't wanna take advantage of you do I Mr. Dominic?" I put her back on the bed and performed the whole act all the way over from the top. I need to make it as wet as possible to help her out. I'm finally ready to get my man wet; I put on a glove and crept my way in.

I can hear how wet my feast is, her walls resisting my man something terrible. I'm about to lose it, I can tell it's been more than a minute since a nigga been in here. I back out use my fingers for a minute trying to make some room. She ain't ever had a nigga bringing as much drama as me to the cat. Of course it ain't working I feel the tightness trying to stop them from even going in.

Forget it, I'm just gone use the head and work it, see how much she can take. After awhile she started to let me in so I make do 'cause I have to feel that ass. By the looks of things I have a long way to go. The way her legs shaking making me proud as I don't know what with the way this going down.

I slip up and bomb rush her and the way she screamed my name I don't want to pull out but I have to ease up. I long stroke her for damn near forever. I still need to feel her up against me and I'm a long way off. The way she moving around I know I have to take it down another notch so I let her get comfortable.

The more she tries to throw it back, the more I smack that ass and she retreat. I have to go back to the long stroke 'cause my men on the move. I want to enjoy every second I can with her lips wrapped around me. I thought the condom was going to get trapped inside her as hard as I came; I had to grab hold of it to make sure. I held on for dear life to that thing. I thought it would never stop. It was so full it started coming out the top so I rolled it off and threw it on the floor. I'm too weak to move and she breathing like she about to pass out, it took us a minute to come down off our high.

"What you over there giggling about?"

"You!"

"What about me?"

"I heard that!"

"Heard what?"

"Let me show you." She climbed on top of me and began working her body on me. My mans stood right backup and was ready for the ride.

The next morning I wake up early 'cause we don't have anything to wear. I made my way to a couple stores and picked up some stuff. While I was on my way back I ordered room service so they'll be there when I make it back to the room. I put the stuff away and setup breakfast, Terentia was still sleep.

My gut said she was the one. The peaceful look on her face made me want to be whatever she need to keep it the same. I sat there beside her just looking at her; I look over and see her bracelet on the dresser. I pick it up and look at the ring that's attached to it. I never realized how many diamonds was on it. It seem like it should've been a wedding ring instead of a charm. Forever T DAJ was on the inside of it, I put it back down.

"You just gone sit there staring at me? You know it's rude to stare at people right?" she said as she turned over away from my gaze.

"It's rude to be this beautiful and not expect people to stare," I said as I kissed her cheek. After we finished eating I gave her the stuff I picked up. We met up with Monroe and Harmony in the lobby.

"What the hell? Where ya'll get clothes from?" Monroe said as we stepped out the elevator.

"Dang Waters you could've gave me a heads up if you knew we were staying. That's messed up you brought you something and didn't tell me." Harmony said as she threw her neck around.

“Naw, it ain’t that just some stuff I picked up earlier, we gone stay until tomorrow,” I said as I wrapped my arms around Terentia waist while we walked away. I hear Monroe yell, “Whatever man shit still fucked up.” I didn’t look back to say anything to him. I kissed Terentia on her neck as we made our way out the door.

34 TREASURE

"Hey Waters you wanna go to Seattle tonight, I heard about this club that we have to go check out."

"I haven't been to Seattle since we been here, I already know its hella far, like an hour ain't it?"

"Something like that, but hell it's not like there's anything else we can do around here. Just come out with me I need somebody to ride with and we can celebrate you turning the big eighteen. Please!"

"Once again, I don't wanna celebrate my b-day, why don't you ask yo' man?" She frowned and threw her hand at me.

"Who Monroe? Child he's not my man! Just a good looking, wicked pussy eating, dick slinging, back breaking..."

"Okay Harmony I get it you don't have to go on." We both laughed and started to make our way back to the barracks.

As we rounded the corner we saw Monroe and Dominic in the parking lot so of course we had to go over. Every time I see Dominic he looks better and better and the way he looks at me sets my ass on fire. The smell of his cologne makes me feel like it's penetrating me and the closer I get the better it feels.

After listening to Harmony and Monroe go back and forth Monroe carried her off to the barracks. They think they slick, we know they about to go fuck. Once they were gone Dominic had to ask me if I wanted to spend the weekend with him out in Seattle. I wanted say, HELL to the YEAH but I don't want to seem too thirsty.

Dominic says something but I see a car go past and I could've sworn I recognize the driver. I'm trying to focus on the car and listen to him at the same time. I can't believe I've been away from the Lou for almost a whole year.

I really can't believe that I haven't even tried to reach anyone back home, not even my family. I sent my mom a postcard after I arrived. Just letting her know that I made it but I didn't give a return address. I don't know if I'm getting home sick or just losing my damn mind. But it seems like every time I look up I see somebody I know from the hood. Feel like I'm paranoid as fuck, but hell I'm just gone keep it moving and let this journey lead me where it leads me.

I have to say the clubs in Seattle are jumping; too bad they all close early. Nothing like that six a.m. roll out time in East St. Louis. It's dark when you go in and the sun is coming out when you leave. After we left the club we headed to the Fairmont and this place is jaw dropping, it's elegant and welcoming. The staff extremely friendly too, not like the Lou one bit.

I hoped we won't be sharing rooms with Monroe and Harmony; I overheard him say something about the Cascade Suite. Once we were all on the elevator Monroe quickly pulled Harmony off. I started to follow when Dominic held me tighter and pushed another floor.

"Where we going to the roof?"

"Naw baby, we going to the room, you think I'm about to spend my time with you and those two in the same room?" I felt a little silly so I turned around and kissed him as the doors opened.

After looking around the rooms, chatting and watching TV I was tired of pretending that I don't want to get in some trouble so I turned the TV off. I turned up the radio and turned off the lights leaving only the lamp on the dresser on. I walk over to Dominic and give him a front row seat. I'm hoping something come on the radio soon so I can begin the show. Soon as I hear, "Doom, doom, doom, da, doom, doom, da, da, da..." I knew they was about to play my jam, I was ready! I danced around taking off my clothes.

I drop down low releasing my cat; I slowly raise my ass up, hands still on the floor right in front of him. I let him peak for a bit, uncrossed my legs and let it hang for him. I teased him a little more by making sure he didn't touch anything. I straddled his ass and sang along while I moved 'til the song went off.

It didn't matter that I wanted him to touch everything. I know he good the way his thang stretching his pants. I kissed him real good; the taste of his lips made my brain feel like it's sizzling. Slowly I pull away from him, pick up my stuff from the floor and walk towards the bathroom. All of a sudden he was right in front of me like he teleported or some shit.

"What, where you going?" I wanted to say, 'Nowhere Big Daddy!' But I chose to mess with him some more and told him that was all he was getting. He had a surprise for me though; he had me laid out on the bed in no time. He kissed me from head to toe, front to back. And baby when he hit my spot on my back, I think I came about three times back to back. I don't know if he gets down with dinner. He took his time and when he was starving he tore my ass up. His tongue did things that I've never felt before, I'm in trouble.

I know if the tongue game this good I have something coming for me with the dick game. I feel like I'm looking at a monster when he finally stopped fucking with me and put it on me. I can't take that thing, it's like something you only read about, easy twelve and thick, oh gosh it's thick. I tried my best to take it but it's no way in hell I'm going to get use to that thing no time soon.

"XXXXXXXXXX!" I was on the run when he tried to shove that thing up in me. I felt tears rush to my eyes; he stopped moving but tried to stay in place. I moved my ass right up clawing his arms trying to relieve some of the pressure he burying in me.

"I'm sorry baby; want me to take it out?" His mouth

captured mine, how the hell he expect me to tell him hell yeah? I forgot all about the tears streaming from my eyes as his tongue claimed my mouth. His hand found my nipple and his mouth sampled my neck as I caught my breathe. He licked my tears and sent butterfly kisses to the side of my eyes calming me.

"It's too big Dominic, I can't take it." I hear him chuckle even though he tried not to let me hear him. He kissed the tip of my nose then my lips pulling them into his mouth sucking on them one at a time.

"You already taking it just relax and let me show you." He pulled my leg into the crook of his arm and slowly eased inside me a little more. My stomach felt full, my mind was screaming more but my body was begging for a visit to the ER. His body held me in place, his weight made me feel secure, and his tongue made me relax and enjoy his slow dive.

Right as he was about to cum I hear him try to hold back a, "SHIIIIIIT!" under his breath. I can feel it shootout and the heat alone made me do the same. It made me laugh more 'cause he really didn't curse. Not in front of me at all. But I have heard him go back and forth with others but just not while I was around.

"I didn't hurt you right?" He pulled me back on top of him, I'm beat I can barely hold my eyes open I told him no.

"Why you so quite?" He moved me so he can see my eyes.

"I'm tired and thinking ho—" He asked me to finish. I didn't want to but I know he won't let me go to sleep without me telling him.

"Thinking how much I love you. It feels like we've been together longer than seven months." He rolled over and started twisting my nipples in his fingers as he kissed my neck up to my ear and back.

"It's been eight months Terentia. I'm glad to finally hear you tell me that, I was starting to worry." I asked him why.

"I tell you I love you every day, been that way for the last seven months. I guess you needed some good D to fall in love wit' a nigga huh?" I wanted to laugh but I was too tired.

"I love you Dominic, I've known for some time. Please X, I need to rest. That thing is nothing to play with, you said you not mixed but baby, somebody got down with a horse somewhere in yo' ancestry." We both laughed.

"Let me taste it, I won't put it in. Just close yo' eyes and tell me how much you love me." Needless to say he lied; I told him how much I loved him as he licked me up and down. Then he hit me with just puttin' the head in.

The next morning I wake up and he nowhere to be found. I look all around, even the other rooms. I crawl back in the bed and went back to sleep. When I woke up he was sitting next to me and I can smell the food from the other room. "You just gone sit there star..." I tried to turn over just in case I was jacked up or my breath was stinking. "It's rude to be this beau...," he said as he kissed me holding his lips just above my cheek, damn that felt good.

After I finally decided to get up he passed me some clothes that he bought for me. I was a little taken back that he did that. This one is special. Something about him made me at ease, or relax and not go so hard, whatever it is I like it. We hit the shower after we ate and went a couple rounds. Then Harmony and Monroe called for us to meet them downstairs so we can head back. I'm all smiles and by the way Harmony looking at me, she know why.

"What the hel..." Monroe cried before we can even get out the elevator. Then Harmony chimed in like I played her out or something. Not my fault Monroe didn't think about you this morning. Maybe you should've laid it down last night and he would've had you on the brain this morning.

Hell if I get close enough to Dominic I can still smell a light scent of me in his goatee. Dominic quickly shut it down and surprised all of us by saying we were going to stay another night. I was too happy. I didn't even bother saying shit else to them as we walked out. Me in front and Dominic pressed around me from the back.

We did a lot of sightseeing and shopping, seemed like everything I glanced at he was trying to give me. The more I resisted the more he pushed. I decided to stop this all expenses paid spree by not going into the damn stores at all, but he wasn't having it. We had a great day just the two of us, it felt good to kick back and relax; we didn't leave until late that next night.

35 DEANGELO

"What's up Snoop, how you been boy I ain't seen you in a minute! That last pac must be doing nem pockets right huh?"

"Ain't shit Pandillero, nigga got a Shorty now so I had to come off them corners, let the lil locs run it for me. But from what I'm getting that pac is beaten the shit out them niggas out there!"

"What's up Snoop, what's up Pandillero?" here this nigga Trey Loc go with some pretty boy looking ass nigga.

"What's up Trey Loc I ain't seen yo' ass since the towers came down! What's good witchu?"

"Shit chilling, but my family herrre wants to get a couple sacks." Now I should beat the shit out this nigga for bringing some strange ass nigga over here. Talking 'bout a couple sacks, since he T cousin I'm gone give him a pass.

"Man you know I say no to drugs, besides, I know all yo' family and he damn sho' ain't one of 'em!" I eyeballed this nigga waiting on him to say something.

"Oh my bad, I'm Terentia husband," he said standing there with this smug ass look on his face. I know he didn't just say what I think he said.

"Yeah this Treasure husband Dominic, but I guess you wouldn't know that huh?" Trey Loc really trying to push my buttons and get him and this nigga ass whooped ain't he.

"Aw, my bad homie didn't know you was T husband, but like I said, I say no to drugs." I look over at Snoop waiting on him to respond.

"Aight Trey Loc, let me finish hollan at my man herrre for a second and I'll get that fo yo' boy."

As they walked away I looked over at Snoop, we laughed at that clown ass nigga. T husband? What the fuck? This nigga then wife'd up my T *and* he smoke weed? What the fuck is wrong with T? I know she know better than that!

"Ay nigga, give that nigga the Returning Customer!" I told him as I walk back to my car.

"Ay Big Dog, you sure? You know if ol' girl find out or—what if it's for her?" Snoop had the never to fix his mouth and say. Instantly I'm heated as I walk back towards him.

"What the fuck lil nigga, did I stutter? I don't give a fuck if she find out or not! I know her better than you, she ain't fucking wit' that shit! Just do what I said or yo' ass gone be back on nem corners sooner than you think!"

As I make my rounds I see T for the first time all damn day. She must've just made it here, this girl know she can keep a nigga waiting. Damn! Fuck! Got Damn, she look good as hell, wait, is that a baby she getting from her momma? I know T ain't had no damn baby. That must be one of her people kids.

Shit with that outfit she have on damn sho' don't look like she had a baby. Just like T to sho' those tight ass abs and that ass sitting right in them lil bitty ass shorts. She lucky that fat ass tiger ain't showing with them things on. Ooh wee she still fine as hell, fuck that, let me make my way to find out what's going on with my girl. Damn, here this nigga Bateador come.

"What's up Pandillero? I see yo' girl back in town. Word is she married and that's his lil girl. Bet yo' ass didn't see that coming!" He laugh while giving me dap.

"Naw man, she took me by surprise, I mean I just heard she was married and actually met this nigga a minute ago." I told him as we leaned back on the car watching T across the park. She thicker than she was back then. Don't look like she got a lick of fat on her ass, body look toned. How did I let her get away?

"Yeah man, I heard they moved back here somewhere out in the county, but how you meet her ol' dude? Where dat nigga at, how you wanna handle it," Bateador said as he stood up looking around the park.

"He some punk ass pretty boy mufucka that I wanted to thrash when Trey Loc took him to Snoop for some weed. I still can't believe that T fuck wit' a mufucka that smoke dope or anything for that matter. So I'm glad to hear T back in town 'cause you know how my vote goes for ol' boy." I looked over at Bateador and smirked.

"Hell yeah, I know that niggas a done deal," he said.

"You damn straight, I already told Snoop punk ass to give him the Returning Customer. Dis lil bitch ass nigga gone try and question me about it like he second guessing a nigga or something." Bateador was looking around.

"Aw straight, well let me go holla at this lil nigga for a minute 'cause that maybe a problem right there." Bateador was heading over to where Snoop was standing. I ignored him and didn't bother to stop him; I was way too focused on T.

Oh really, I see T and pretty boy, look like its trouble in paradise. Don't look like T too happy with whatever that nigga just said. This nigga got the nerve to walk away while it looks like she talking to him? And this nigga den jumped in the whip and left. Man, these young niggas make it too easy, let me make my way over and rap wit' T for a minute.

I know this park ain't that big but got damn; you'd think all these niggas would get tired of seeing me. These ho's coming out the woodwork trying to throw that dried up ran through ass pussy at a nigga. All this small talk and ducking from these busted ass ho's getting on my nerve. They done made me lose track of T, damn! Fuck it there she goes, all these mufuckas just gone have to wait 'til I come back.

"What's up T, long time no see. Who's this pretty lil momma here?" I reach for the baby and hold her up.

"This is Shay and it has been a long time Mr. Deangelo how you been doing?" she said as she stands back and looks at me up and down then try and reach for the baby. I pull the baby back away.

"Aw yeah, she's a cutie, she look just like you. I take it she yours and ol' boy's huh?" I hold the baby up and admire her and all of T's wonderful features.

"Yeah she's mine Mr. Man! So what's up with you? I now you didn't come all the way over here to take my baby away from me!" she said as she adjusted her shorts.

"Of course I did! The whole hood told me about her, I had to come see with my own eyes. Plus I wanted to rap with you and catch up seeing you disappeared on me what it's been two, three years. I have to say, for someone to have had a baby what three, four months ago you sho' fat as cluck out here!" I laughed knowing she about to go off at the sound of me calling her fat. She look at me and gave me that sexy ass smirk and didn't say a word.

"But on the real, why you disappear like that? You didn't call a nigga and don't say you couldn't reach me 'cause I was on yo' peoples for the nine-one-one. But when you wanna get ghost you sho' do it."

"First I got yo' fat! Hatter! And I didn't disappear I had to live my life remember. I didn't try to reach you 'cause I had to let go of this plac—" I cut her off.

"Come on T, you know we better than that. Besides, I see you still think about me." I glance down at the bracelet with the ring I gave her hanging from it as the charm and smile.

"Twenty one got chu looking good as hell, I see you still working out. Got the stomach showing them tight abs. Yo' tail barely covered in those lil bitty shorts. Why you got that stuff on anyway? You look good and all but if ol' boy knew any better he wouldn't have let you out the house like that. I know I wouldn't!"

"Thanks for the compliment I guess? You said that you wanted to rap with me about something so rap!" She tucked her hand with the bracelet in her back pocket. I know she getting tired of the back and forth.

"What's up with yo' boy? I know you not f'ing wit' a

nigga knowing he do drugs? It's been a minute but I also know that you not getting down like that right?" I say as I try and calm baby girl 'cause she look like she's about to cry.

"If you trying to tell me he smokes weed I know. And he doesn't all the time, even though it's none of your business you know. I don't get in your business so let's try and do the same on yo' side Mr. Man," she said glaring at me through those gorgeous brown eyes.

"T don't play with me, fuck, I mean f ol' boy. I'm more interested in if you doing it or not," I said as the baby start to cry out. I start to rock her back and forth, yo' boy knows a little bit about kids.

"Like I said Mr. Man, that's none of your business!" T snapped and start to reach for the baby again. Good! Here go Peaches, T cousin. Before Peaches can get a word out her mouth I said what's up and handed her the baby. I grab T by the arm and pull her across the street before she can resist. And out of the eyes and ears beaming in on our conversation.

"T don't fuck with me I know it's been a minute and you all grown and shit so let me ask you this one more time. Do. You. Fuck. With. The. Shit. Or anything else? Please don't play with me right now either. Save that slick shit for somebody else before you answer!" She pulled away so I let her go.

"No Deangelo I don't fuck with anything, for somebody who always in my business you should know that. But I guess you have to ease your conscious and make sure your protégé is doing whatchu taught her," she said as she tried to walk away. I didn't want to grab her again; she was one snatch away from pissing me off to the fullest. I stepped in front of her and leaned in real close so she could feel my words in her ear.

"You right T I am checking on my, whatchu say? Protégé. To make sure she good. Just so we clear, weed ain't the only thing yo' boy do. So don't stand there and fuck with me like I don't know! Now let me keep it funky with you baby! If I find out or get the slightest inkling that you do that shit or anything else I'll kill yo' smart ass myself. Then I'll adopt baby girl and raise her not to do the dumb shit her momma did.

So you can try me if you want to T, but you know I ain't one of these niggas out here who say one thing and do another. That's my word. And if you think I'm playing you can get smart and try me and I'll end you right now. Don't open yo' mouth with you using that shit being a smart ass! Try and at least buy yourself sometime if you are so you can try and get the fuck out of town and disappear again.

And yes I did say try, 'cause you know I'll do it. I damn sho' ain't worried about a witness 'cause they can get it too. Choose yo' words wisely T and don't try and walk away from me again!" I stood back and watched her inhale what I said. To my surprise she don't look bothered at all but that's T for you, she won't buckle under pressure.

"Well Deangelo Joseph, like I said I don't use anything. If you want I can piss on you and you can get it tested if you like. Besides, I know the hood told you I'm still in the reserves and work as a flight attendant now full time. I actually just got back in town and came by here before I went home.

I know you mean well but like I said it's my business, I'm tired of you playing these mind games with me! You've been doing it all my life. That's why I disappeared as you call it." She stepped closer to me, damn near putting her breast on my ribs.

"Let's not forget, I ain't been cold yet; you think you'd get the point after all this time. My husband makes sure that I'm good, me and his child. So leave him the hell alone! Please remember my husband and my life is my business so if you could please stay out of it I would appreciate it. You know what else Mr. Deangelo Joseph I'm sick of this T shit. So you can call me by the name my mother and father gave me!

Better yet, you can call me Mrs. Xavier, that way you know I'm married and not that T person you created. Don't think that I don't know how you been pulling strings in my life all this time either. That's the real reason I left if you want me to keep it funky. Don't think I forgot for one second who you are or whatchu do. You're really not that different. Pushing this crap in the streets the way you do. And before you fix that hole in your face to say how drug free you are save it. I already know.

I ain't the one you need to be worried about. I heard about your sister Rhonda, how she doing these days? Save the captain rescue Terentia crap for her, she needs it more than I do you know. Now if you would excuse me, I'm tired of your promises and need to find my husband before he's a returning customer. By the way, if anything happens to my husband I'll probably never forgive you. So keep that in your mind Mr. Man!" She looked at me and if looks could kill I'd be one dead mufucka right now. I can tell she offended so I threw my hands up. She straight had the nerve to bump into my shoulder hard as she walked off.

Damn, I ain't seen T in too fucking long, why I have to go at her so hard? Think I fucked up! But fuck it, she did say probably. And I got the answer I wanted so now it's time to body ol' boy and get my T back. I don't give a fuck about ol' boy anyway. Baby girl should've been mine from jump, so it ain't shit for me to raise her as my own.

But why the hell did I push T that hard? Something about her is different I know. Hell, a nigga been down with her since she was walking around the hood with pony tails with barrettes hanging from the ends. I damn sho' ain't finna let no dope smoking ass nigga ride in out of nowhere and fuck T up. I ain't let it happen before and I damn sho' ain't gone let it happen now. I know she dated here and there but for her to run away, get married and then have a baby all wit' out me knowing! Damn! It's all good though, I got this in the bag.

"Damn Pandillero, look like that lil talk with Treasure didn't go as planned. I thought she was about to fuck you up, you may need to ice yo' shoulder down in the morning nigga! She dipped out so fast I thought you sat her ass on fire!" Cap said as he walked over and dabbed me off.

"Naw, that's nothing! What's good witchu fam we still hoopin' this weekend right?" I said trying to take my mind off T and the way she acting. Protégé, you damn right protégé, I chuckled under my breath.

I continued talking to Cap for a minute and chatting it

up with a couple of other niggas. And of course after running off these damn birds that like to flock over with the pussy in hand, I walked to my whip. The whole ride I was thinking about T and trying to digest what had happened and my next move.

I know I can't just show up and put my cards on the table. I need to think, quick though. I know one thing, if she disappear she using that shit, let me put the word out so I can keep track of her. Plus I know a connect that can get me the low on where she working so I know what she up too.

36 TREASURE

Let me hurry up and pick up Shay so I can go down here to this reunion. I'm so sick of my momma calling me every five minutes asking, where you at, how long you go be, it don't take that long. Damn, would this woman leave me alone? Mullanphy Park is off the chain, look like errbody from the hood here. I see a bunch of new faces and seem like all the old ones.

What the fuck happened to Aaron, he used to be fine as hell. Guess that dope took its toll on a lot of these fools, seem like every one of them then fell off. They used to think they was doing it back in the day, now they all look like they sleeping on somebody couch. They say you can never get time back. To some it does miracles but I can clearly see for the majority of them that was not the case. Here comes my momma.

"Hey mo..."

"Girl shut up and give me my damn grandbaby taking all damn day to get here. I should punch you in the face having me wait dat long," she said as she grabbed Shay and walked off. Well okay. I make my rounds speaking to all the people that I know then I smiled as my baby wrapped his arms around my waist.

"What's up wifey thought I was gone have to put out a team to come find you!" Shit his body feel good from the back, make me wanna throw that thang up grab my ankles and take it 'til I can't no mo.

"Whatchu up too?" I said as I turned around and gave him a kiss.

"Nothing just came by to drop Trey Loc off. We hit the mall up earlier and he let his girl take his car so I brought him down here to get it." Every time I see Dominic lips move I want to taste him until I'm full with everything he has to say. Damn I love this man!

"So what you get me?"

"I guess you gone have to get yo' tail home to find out now aren't you?" he said as he grabbed onto the bottom of my shorts.

"Where the heck you get these too little shorts from, while I'm at it you think you slick don't you?"

"What's wrong with my shorts?"

"Same thing that's wrong with this sports bra of a shirt you have on. I just said they too little I know you heard me!"

"Man stop, you sound like you worried about something."

"All right Terentia, don't make me F one of these niggas up out here. And I know by the way half of 'em mugging me that you used to date 'em. I wanna meet that one nigga I been hearing so much about. What's his name Phillip, Paul are something?"

"Why you wanna meet him?" What the hell? Trey Loc can't keep his mouth closed about shit! I should slap the fuck outta him when I see his ass.

"I wanna see the dumb nigga that let you walk away. I wanna thank him for helping me meet you and give that nigga a loser's fee for real!" he said as he laughed and licked the side of my neck.

"All right, all right you ready man 'cause I'm about to bounce," Trey Loc said as I turned around.

"Aw what's up Treasure I didn't know you was standing therrre!" he said as I slapped him in the back of his head.

"Ahh what was that for?"

"Who else would he be standing here with jackass," I said as I turned and mugged the shit out of Dominic for thinking the shit was funny.

"Aw boo don't be mad. You know you the only one I would be with now stop playing and give me a kiss I'll be right back."

After talking for a minute with Myzphyt mother I see Dominic and Trey Loc talking to...no he not! What the fuck is Trey Loc thinking, he really want me to kill him? Damn, I can't believe he would do that to me. Why would he introduce Dominic to Deangelo like that?

That bastard, I forgot all about Ms. Sherry talking to me. She saying something about how Myzphyt back in jail and this and that. But hell that ain't anything new, I heard he been in and out of jail since I left. Even heard he was doing that water bullshit, whatever the hell that is.

"All right Ms. Sherry I see my momma must be looking for me she has my baby."

"Oh you know she is too cute, dey already brought her by herrre to see me. I saw dat cute lil boy you married to. Look at chu Mrs. Treasure. I'll tell Myzphyt I saw you okay." Yeah whatever, I have enough on my mind then to deal with yo' crazy ass son. I waved bye and made a dash over to get my baby.

"All right baby give me a kiss I'm about to go!" That was no problem.

"Go? Now where you finna go and why the hell you over there talking to them?"

"I had to get a lil something now I'm about to shoot back to the house to watch the game."

"A lil something, what the hell you mean a lil something I thought we..."

"Come on Terentia, I'm not about to go through this again with you so stop with all the dramatics. I'll see you at home. I love you. Bye!" What the hell just happened, did he walk away from me like that?

"Girl she just been passed around from hand to hand with Gee Gee. I snatched her up and said let me take her to her momma."

"All right thanks Momma." Look at my mini me, she still a surprise to me, I thought I lost her in the delivery room. She all better now, I said thinking back on how scared I was when she was born not breathing.

"What's up T lo..." I know he didn't just take my damn baby from me. I knew I should've left with Dominic so I could cuss his ass out in private. Now I have to deal with Deangelo and his bullshit. I already know he has something to say about Dominic smoking weed, why else would he come over here.

He knows he needs to stop with all this like he doesn't know she mines. My momma and Gee Gee then let errbody down here know that. Why is he fucking with me and not giving me my damn baby back? I know he not trying to call me fat.

Now he wanna act like nothing happened, he flipped out on me first. The last time I saw his ass I had to chase him away. Now he wanna act like he hurt 'cause I rouged out on his ass. Let me tell his ass off real quick so I can get home. I sho' don't like where this conversation is going. How the fuck he gone get an attitude and give my baby to Peaches like that.

Damn, this feel like old times, he dragging me off again to chastise me like I'm his damn child. I'm so sick of this shit. Here he go playing God in my damn life, if he did anything to Dominic I'm goin' kill his ass. I need to hurry up and call Dominic 'cause if I know anything I know he 'bout had Snoop lace the shit he gave him. What the fuck, he thinks I smoke now?

He really has loss his damn mind, let me go! I snatched my arm away from him ready to throw down with his ass. I don't care what he say or do at this point. I'm glad Dominic not here to see this. The last thing I'd want is for him to get into some bullshit I been trying to put behind me for this long.

Damn, he still smells good as hell even though he got me mad as fuck. Being this close to him sending me right down memory lane like it was yesterday. Let me just tell him what he want to hear so he can leave me alone. I'll never speak to his ass again after this. All those threats he throwing out there don't mean a damn thing to me.

Yes Boo Boo, Mrs. Xavier, let that roll around in that thick head of yours for a minute. I can tell my words are getting to him. I don't care; he's played a role in my life that's all too complicated. I love my husband and I don't want to deal with his half loyal ass again. I don't care that I hit him with the fact that his sister Rhonda was a strung out dope head. Hell, I don't care about anything when it comes to his ass any fucking more. Let me hurry up and get my child and get home.

Damn, why won't Dominic answer his fucking phone? I jump on highway Seventy West and roll out heading home. I keep trying Dominic but it's just going to voicemail, fuck it let me leave a message. "Dominic don't smoke that shit you got at the park today, I'm pretty sure it has something in it. Call me back when you get this message I'm on my way there!"

I hate leaving messages but hell, I don't want to take any chances of him smoking that shit. I get Shay out the car and damn near fly into the house. I see Dominic laid out on the couch sleep. Let me check his damn pockets, yeah I check his pockets and will let him know. If he has anything in there I don't need to see, then his face should be one of 'em.

Good this got to be it, ha ha bitch, down the toilet it goes. After I walk out the bathroom I crawl up on the couch and put my ass in my favorite spot, right up against my dick. I feel Dominic pull me in closer and kiss the back of my head as we both fall off to sleep

37 SEBASTIAN

Damn, who is shorty coming in the hanger? She fine as hell. That wife beater having a hard time controlling them big ass girls she got hiding behind it. Look at those hips, baby killing me. I never knew a wife beater, some straight leg fitted pants and blue heels look that fucking sexy put together. I know I been gone a minute but who the hell is that? I have to find out who this girl is, she thick as fuck in all the right places.

Her skin looks soft as hell like she need to be wrapped up in my arms instead of in this place. Oh she saw me staring at her; fuck it, errbody in this bitch looking. Baby girl looked dead at me and threw me a smile so I know she checking for me. "Ay who is lil mama that just came in?" I asked Leon as she went into the back.

"Aw that's Treasure she started herrre Friday, she only work part time are some shit until she go to the post office," he said as he moved the ladder to clean the plane windows.

"Why she work here part time though?"

"She a flight attendant and in the military so she only come in when she feel like it I guess? I on't know, you know dat nigga Barney would do anything to be around a woman that fine. Hell, I would too; I would call the post office and try to get her fired so she could work herrre full time." We both laughed I watch as he climbed up the ladder then leave.

During my break I usually go out to my car and get a

nap. This ten to six is a bitch with my lil son at home during the day. Damn, I sure will be glad when I find him a daycare for the time I have him. Hell, if I could get a couple hours sleep it wouldn't be so bad. Lil man keep me up all day then my silly ass soon to be ex wife take her time coming to get him. But hell I made my choice and she made hers so I guess I can deal with it for now. Today I think I'm going over in the break room and see if lil mama back there. I have to know what's up with her.

As I come out of the restroom I walk to the back and head for the vending machine. Damn, there her fine ass goes. I wonder if I should say something to her. It's too many scavengers around her right now. These niggas stalking and giggling like hyenas in nis bitch. It's cool; I'll holla at her later. On my way out I see Barney.

"Ay man, you made coming to this hell worth it so thanks."

"I don't know whatchu talking 'bout Seabas but if it's what I think it is, trust, you had nothing to do wit' it," he said we both laughed and I headed to the car. After break I see her go onto one of the planes it look like she by herself. I go in the office and see what was needed on the one she went on.

Good here we go, I grab the sheet without really reading it, and as long as it's something inside I'm making my way over there. "Ay, I'm going over to A157 call me on the radio if you need something!" I told Kevin the supervisor.

"Damn, Seabas you volunteering to do work, what's going on?" he said as he glanced over at the plane.

"Aw never mind, I see exactly what has you in the mood to volunteer your services. Do yo' thang man. I hear she not too friendly though, you might want t—"

"Yeah man save it!" I cut him off, walked out and headed to the plane before she had a chance to get off.

"All right wake up; I know ya'll only come inside to sleep so wake up!" I laughed and walked toward the aisle. To my surprise she was actually cleaning and by the looks of things she was doing her thing. I walked to the galley and hit the lights. I see her stand up and look at me like she wanted to throw me back down the steps. Without a word she stood there waiting on me to say something.

"Damn, *lil-momma-why-you-act-so-funky?* I was just playing around witchu; don't go biting my head off sweetheart!" She continued to stare at me. If I thought her body was banging I must've been sleeping. This girl is beautiful hands down. Her full lips made me want to suck on 'em until they deflated. Flawless caramel skin, deep big brown cat eyes and it look like real long hair.

Made me want to do things to her that can only be done right in a tropical getaway between her, me and God. Damn, this girl is bad. I'm not even gone get started on what's hiding under that shirt. I already seen 'em in that wife beater earlier and I'm a breast, ass, hell body man and she got all of it. Her hips killing me right now, she has to be at the least-forty five inches around that ass, her waist small as hell though, maybe twenty inches round. I can't wait to get at her and take my time getting the feel of her.

"How you doing Ms. I'm Sebastian people here call me Seabas. I know I haven't met you before, I been on vacation for a minute. But had I known you where here, I would've ended that immediately! Got damn, I got a smile from her," I said waiting on her to respond but she didn't she stood there looked at my extended hand and leaned on the side of the chair.

"Lil Ma, don't be like that at least let me get a name from you, I know you want to! Hell you already smiled, at least give me your name."

"My momma always said not to trust a man like you with my name 'cause they always want more than that!" she said as she looked down like she was about to start back doing what she was doing.

"I don't know what a man like me is but if you wanna call your moms, I can talk to her and let her know that all I want to know is your name." She looked at me and began to laugh quietly like she didn't want me to know.

"My name is Xavier, I mean Treasure—" she started to say.

"Damn Ma, don't do me like that, which one is it, Xavier or Treasure? 'Cause I can't believe a woman as stunning as yourself would have a last name as her first. Now if you would have said your name was Unique or Down Right Fine then maybe I would believe you!" I smiled and winked at her.

"My name is Treasure; I'm used to people calling me by my last name so it's something I have to get use to again. So save all ya' Ma's and just call me by my name," she said as she put a magazine in the back of the seat.

"Well its nice meeting you Treasure—"

"Who said we was meeting, last I checked meeting involved having a conversation and getting to know one another. I never said I wanted to meet you or anyone else around herrre. You asked for a name and I gave you one so have a goodnight Mr. Sebastian, I have work to do." Damn, this girl got a smart mouth on her. She just gone dismiss me like that without even letting me finish what I have to say?

It's cool though I got time. By the looks of it she gone be on here at least a hour. Let me regroup before I snatch her smart mouth ass up and have her begging for me to fuck her. "All right Ma you right," I said holding my hands up as I retreated. Then I saw her shoot me a look like 'Didn't I just tell you to save your Ma's.' "My bad Treasure."

This a quick fix so let me do it and get to the back to make sure Treasure still here. I haven't heard the vacuum so I know she not finished just yet. Good she still here.

"Excuse me Ms. Treasure I know you not up for a conversation or meeting anyone but can I ask you a question?"

"Sure what is it now?" Damn, Kev was right this girl do have an attitude but it's nothing I can't handle.

"Why you so on guard? I know you not that into cleaning this plane? Whatchu doing cleaning this plane anyway? I figure someone as exceptional as you would be modeling or something." She looked at me and turned her head to the side and gave me the most intimate and fascinating smile.

"You know that's more than one question right. For someone to know that I'm not into meeting anyone you sure did try and slide all that out the way."

"Ay you can't blame a man for trying can you? Besides I have a mind that says you may not say too much to me after this. So I took a shot at getting the basics out the way." I took a seat hoping she would feel at ease. She about five three or four. I feel like I'm towering over her at six five my head damn near banging against the ceiling of this small ass plane.

"Well since I don't think you'll let it go until I answer, I'm not on guard I'm married. But I guess you wouldn't know that with me wearing my ring and all. Money is just that, money. As long as it's legal and I don't have to do something that's against my better judgment, it's mine for the take.

Whatever I do weather it's cleaning this plane or not, I give it one hundred percent no matter what. This not my only job and when I save up enough I'll be in business for myself. Don't get me wrong, if I wanted I could do my own thing now; I just have a feeling the timing not right. So until then, I'll do what I have to do to make it," she said as she headed to the galley to get some more supplies.

"Well I won't bother you anymore Treasure, thanks for chatting with me. I hope we can at least have a second to meet in the near future. I understand you married, I'm separated. I know I wouldn't want my wife to chat it up with anybody either. But I'm not into breaking up a home and would just like to get to know you if I can." Before she could answer I headed down the stairs and on to the next plane.

38 TREASURE

Dang I haven't had that much fun in who knows how long. I know I need to hurry up but oh well I can change when I get there. I can't believe I've saved as much as I have working these lil in and out jobs. Flipping my money on different things along the way has me looking all right.

I just hate that I have to hide it from Dominic the way I have been. But ever since I saw that ass at the reunion, I knew I was going to have problems. I can't front though, he was right, he chose to do what he did. All I can do now is enjoy that I'm back home more and the fact that I can come home without being worried that something is missing.

Dang I been in my own lil world, damn near tripped coming out that broke ass gate. I hate when people stare at me, make me want to ask what the fuck they looking at. Well lookie here, lookie here, who in the fuck is this copper, toned Farzan Athari looking man? He is umm-umm good looking. I can't believe I've never seen him before, don't matter, I have better things to do anyway. Let me hurry the hell up and change before this fat hungry looking man come back here and I get fired before I made it a week.

Last one 'til quitting time, I can knock this off then chill for the rest of the night. Damn, I hope don't nobody come fucking with me. Seem like I have nothing but eyes on me every time I look up. Who the fuck is that thinking he funny, corny ass. Look at Mr. Athari; I can never say it enough there are some fine ass men in the Lou errwhere you turn around.

I'm surprised his tall fine ass can even fit on this lil bitty ass plane. Oh shit here he come, I can see him out the corner of my eye, what the hell he want? "How you doing Ms. I'm Sebast..."

What the fuck? Seabas, what kinda name is that? He think he funny right. I wanted to burst out laughing I smiled and stood there hoping he would leave me alone. Hell naw he wanna talk to Kathy, yeah okay she would eat his ass alive without even thinking about it. Who is he, flight patrol, why the hell he want my damn name? My name is Not Yo' Damn Business, is what I wanted to tell him. I'm only smiling to be nice but maybe if I respond he'll leave me the hell alone. I know he won't so let me shut this shit down 'cause I got a meeting for his ass. Good he got the point.

Almost finish just a lil bit more to do then I see Mr. Sebastian coming toward me again. "Excuse me Treasure I kno..." Dang, I thought I ran him off already; let me see what he wants. It's not like I don't already know. Why do all fine black men just expect for every woman to fall into their palms all the damn time. I'm on guard 'cause you too damn fine to just wanna be friends with me what the hell you think?

He said a question that was way more than one. He's just too much; all I can do is laugh at his ass. He just gone make me talk to him, he den took a seat and shit. I decided to talk to him and when I was finished I went about doing what I was doing. Yeah I just bet he would want to get to know me! Talking about he wouldn't wanna break up a happy home, yeah I bet if I gave him a chance he would careless. Hell, my home not happy now and I still wouldn't let him.

39 SEBATIAN

I was shocked that I hadn't seen Treasure for a couple days, I saw her car but no signs of her, this girl was without a doubt out of sight. I don't know how she doing it but I figured she didn't want to be bothered. On my way out the gate to take a nap during lunch I could hear that down south joint off in the distance.

Who bumping that new shit, it's not loud but whoever it is must really like the song. I hear them singing along with it. Then I see her laid out on the hood of the car. She has her eyes closed like she in her own zone. Damn, this whole time I been stalking around inside trying to catch up with her, she been out here. With my dumbass!

"So this where you been hiding the whole time?" She jumped up and looked around to see me standing up against the other side of her car.

"What? I'm not hiding from anyone; I'm minding my business Sir just like you should learn to do!" She slid down the car, opened the door and turned off the radio. I stood by and admired the slant in her brown eyes as she looked backup at me.

I continued waiting to see what she'll do. To my shock, she climbed backup onto the hood and before she closed her eyes glanced at her watch to check the time. "Don't worry you still have a minute. Plus Barney lazy tail den left, he won't be back to about six. He probably went home to sleep. He not trying to stay here all night. He'll pop backup in time to check the planes then he back out the gate." She looked over at me then turned her body and placed her head on her hand.

"You don't get rejected very often do you? Matter fact, I would bet that you've never met a stranger in your life." All I could do was look down in shame and shake my head at what she said.

"Damn! That hurt!" We both laughed. I stood and watched as she rolled back over and looked up at the stars.

"Can I join you Mrs. Treasure?"

"Hell, why not? It's not like if I tell you no, you gone walk away."

"You know it, so you might as well get used to it!" I told her as I took a seat beside her.

"What's the deal with you anyway, why you pestering me, asking around about me? I thought you said you were married? For you to be a married man, you sure do act like a friendly puppy ready to hump the first thing moving!" she said as she sat up looking over at me. Damn, this is one beautiful girl, if she give me the chance I'm gone wife her ass up next.

"You go for the throat don't you?" We both laughed, her laughter was contagious. All I could do was laugh when I heard the seductive sound escape past those glossy lips.

"What can I say; I like to keep it funky. I don't have time to lie, too easy for me to tell the truth. It's on whomever ears it enters to do what they want with it."

"I hear you Treasure, but I'm currently separated. Have been for about a year, my ex won't sign the papers. You would think she would be happy to sign 'em. I guess that nigga I caught her cheating with was not what she thought he was. As far as being ready to pounce, that ain't me at all.

But as far as I can tell, you seem like someone I would like to get to know. The way your personality come off, I don't know if you crazy and I should go the other way or you not crazy. Maybe that's why I keep finding myself asking about you." I waited to hear her response. She laid back onto the windshield and looked off into the stars again.

"You know usually when you have a conversation the other person involved talks back."

"Well I thought we did that already. Did you forget I asked you something you answered? So if you referring to the part about keeping a conversation going, then it would be your turn Sir to ask a question and maybe I'll answer," she said without looking at me or even in my direction. Damn, look at those things, they sitting just right in that shirt. I just want to put my... Fuck! Stay focused.

"It's Seabas remember, I'm not that old you know, unless you call twenty eight old. Tell me something about you Treasure. You have any kids, if so how many and how old? I know you married, how long have you been married? How old or young are you? Don't want you to snap my head off, you from St. Louis, have any family here?"

"I guess if you gone ask why not get it all out the way right? I'm twenty two. I have a daughter, she's almost a year only child, and I've been married for three years now. Pretty much all my family is here 'cause I'm from St. Louis. I moved back seven months ago and starting to wish that I didn't. Did I get everything?"

"Yeah you a young tender huh, I live in East Saint Louis, that's where a chunk of my family from. I have family all over though. Your daughter and my son the same age his birthday in December. It was kinda messed up for a minute there, I didn't know if he was mine or not.

So I had to get that good old Dana done to make sure. But to be honest I was happy as hell, my first child. I wish I could've worked it out with his moms before she did what she did. You can't change the past you can only move forward!"

"Yeah I hear you! Dana you silly for that, must be some eastside shit to call a DNA test a Dana."

We talked until it was time to go back to work. For the next couple weeks we found ourselves out on the hood of one of our cars going on and on. It was like whatever she wanted to know I was willing to share. Something about her made me want to be the best friend, lover, or associate I could be to insure that she was happy and taken care of.

40 TREASURE

I been ducking and dodging these people since I've been coming in here. Seem like every nigga in her on the prowl, they just don't get the point do they. I keep hearing about how Mr. Athari asking people about me, what the hell does he want? He looks like he can be a dangerous motherfucka if you let him near your heart.

His wife must be confident as hell to let him out by his lonesome all night long. If I was her I would've showed my face in nis bitch at least once a week. With a man that fine and has a good job, she tripping. Plus I know she know he a dog, hell I know that and I only said something to him once. The way he investigating me I already know if I was looking for a quick fuck, I wouldn't have to coax him into shit.

Damn, he scared the shit outta me. Let me turn this shit off before somebody creep up and drag my ass off into the woods on Airport Road. Didn't mean to scare me, yeah right. If that was the case you would've said something before you walked all the damn way over here. He could've kicked rocks, whistled, or something! Hiding, who said anything about hiding? This where I been ducking yo' ass this whole time. Big difference buddy, big difference!

Why the hell is he just staring at me like that? Whatever, maybe if I don't say anything and lay back down he'll get the email I'm sending him. Yeah right, when has that ever worked for me in the past? What time is it anyway, feels like this night just got longer. I knew it, ignoring some people never work, now he has to tell me about that fat ass Barney. I knew that shit before he came over here trying to school me on it.

"You don't get rejected very often do..." Why did I just say that? Let me stop, I know exactly why. I have enough to deal with with my husband. I don't need to know shit about another married man. That didn't work either, he still want to strike out again I guess.

Look at the time go by, I can't believe it but talking with Sebastian actually make the hours fly past. It doesn't hurt either that he is God awful good looking. He actually seems like a cool person, he has a funny personality that helps and a good head on his shoulder. I still can't believe our kids were born three days apart. That shit is too ironic. I should've been leaving the hospital as she was coming in. He seems to be there for his son, fucked up situation with his wife though.

I don't know what I would've done if I found Dominic in the bed with someone else. I probably would've burned that muthafucka down and been in jail some damn where. I don't know why but I'm starting to think that Sebastian has come into my life for a reason. We have way too many things in common.

He not that bad after all, I guess the old saying is true, 'don't judge a book by its cover.' I would've never expected to be this in tune with someone like him. Hell, he loud, stay running his mouth, always have a joke, like attention, stay flirting and always have to make you cheer up and laugh. He always has some song or book verse to go along with what he has to say. I think that's the best part about him. Like I said, I think I just may like talking with Mr. Sebastian after all.

41 SEBASTIAN

"What's up Treasure? You ready to celebrate with me?"

"Celebrate what crazy?"

"Celebrate my divorce?"

"What? You celebrate a divorce? Seem like you should have a funeral first shouldn't you?" I can't help but laugh at her retort, I never thought about it that way.

"Hell yeah we can do that first, then on to the celebration. You coming out or what?"

"Yeah I guess!" We had a good time that night; I actually made a copy of the paperwork and buried it in the backyard before we headed out the door. I always have fun with Treasure; she brings light into my day.

Just trying to find ways to stop her from worrying about her situation keeps me on my feet. Her husband is one dumb nigga! I don't know what the hell he was thinking leaving her here while he hours away. I try not to get into it 'cause I don't want her to feel any pressure.

Plus I know whenever he comes in town she giving it up to him. Hell, I ain't mad at her, we only been hanging out and I just got divorced. I'm not trying to be on lock no time soon. I been knocking off chicks left and right since we split. I would knock Treasure off if she let me, I can't even front like I wouldn't.

"So whatchu wanna do today?" Treasure asked me with

a sour look on her face.

"What's wrong with you?"

"Nothing!" The way she said it I know she lying seeing she just got off the phone with her man. I figured it had something to do with him.

"Stop lying what he say? He gone put his foot in yo' ass if you with a nigga? I know I would."

"No! You always got jokes."

"For real what's wrong?"

"Nothing, he said I had 'til tonight to make my mind up, or else."

"Okay you leaving a bunch of the story out you know, so go on and get it off yo' chest. Tell Big Daddy what's wrong."

"Whatever, goof ball! He said I had 'til tonight to decide if I want to still be married. If I don't give him an answer, he moving on with his life. I asked him if he found somebody and if that was what he was talking about. It sounded like he was trying to get a pass to do something. He said no but he'll make sure I won't want to be with him anymore and he was going to give me hell about getting out. That's what he said."

"So basically, Cinderella has until midnight to run back to him or he'll sleep with some ugly stepsisters? And he'll drag his ass on giving you a divorce. Did I get all that right?"

"Yeah something like that, you're an ass you know that?" We both began to laugh.

"Let's go."

"Go where?"

"To the zoo, maybe you can talk to him face to face there?"

"Oooh, don't do me! I don't do ugly Boo Boo, I don't talk about yo' beat up ass wife."

"Ex wife! Get it right." I drove through Forest Park and pulled into the boat house. After we paddled around we sat floating in the water.

"So whatchu gone do?"

"I don't know, I don't want to lose him but I have my

doubts about him keeping secrets from me. I mean he say one thing but make me think it's another. I don't know if I can keep going like this."

"Well tell him that, he should understand."

"I did tell him Einstein, he said it's been long enough and I'm dragging my feet on purpose."

"Are you?"

"Am I what?"

"Doing it on purpose. I mean he dipped what, four months ago?"

"No, I just don't know how to trust him again with all the lying and sneaking around. I guess I have to figure out how to let it go. I don't know what I want to do." We talked a ton more and let the current push us around. After eating dinner we headed back so she could pick up her baby. The next morning I called to find out what she decided but she didn't answer. I figured she was on the road heading to him. A couple weeks past and I called Treasure, asked her to come chill out with me, she accepted so I headed out the door.

"What's up stranger thought you would be long gone by now," I said as she came over to the bar.

"Nothing much, what's up with you?" she said as we headed to our seats.

"I been chilling, can't complain you know. But back to you, why so serious?" I said with my best Joker impression.

"I said nothing, stop with all the jokes all the time! I just wanna chill out and not think about anything for a second."

"Whoa Ms. Jackson if you nasty, don't bite my head off!" I said as she looked over at me then smiled, we both laughed. There she goes that's the Treasure I like to see.

"Cheer up! Whatever it is can't be that bad. You're still breathing right."

"Yeah!"

After dinner we headed to the Riverfront and then hit the Casino before we parted ways. We were like tic and tack from that point on. After prying out bits and pieces, I found out her husband had found someone. She was pretty upset about the whole situation, especially when it came to the baby. He told her that if she didn't settle down with all the working he would get full custody and force her to leave St. Louis.

She was putty in his hands, every day it seemed like he was hitting her with something else. I have to give it to him; he wasn't willing to just watch her move on. Then again, didn't seem like she wanted to. If anything, seemed like she was waiting and just like he said, dragging her feet. After making it back to her place we sat down to watch a movie then she got up and headed to her room. Before I knew it she was back out going into the closets grabbing stuff shoving it into cases.

"What's up Treasure? You going somewhere?"

"Yeah I gotta go, excuse me," she said as she stumbled past me reaching for her purse.

"What's going on? Slow down."

"I told you I have to go, now please let me just...Hello, yes I need the next fligh..." I waited until she made her arrangements and watched as the tears began cascading down her face. Her breathing began to pick up and once she was off the phone she fell to the floor. I walked over and helped her up and carried her to the couch. I grabbed the stuff she picked out and began putting it into the bags for her as she sat on the couch crying hysterically. I wanted to ask what was wrong but I decided to wait until she caught her breath.

"Dominic in the hospital, I don't know why they said he touch and go." I didn't say a word I just helped her pack and drove her to the airport.

As we got off the highway she directed me to James S. McDonnell Blvd which was strange 'cause that's for private flights. I know she has her hand in a shit load of businesses like HFW but I didn't think she was doing it like that by far. Hell, as many jobs as she work you'd think she was broke.

I saw them rush out and help her into the building before she even made it inside. That shit made me think she was the President or something. I don't know who the hell I'm dealing with. But now that I think about the way she rolled out that billing information off the top of her head, I should've known better. This girl is nothing but surprises. I tried calling

Treasure a couple times over the next month or so with no response. Then I ran into her at the airport.

"So what's up stranger?"

"Why is that always the same thing you say every time you see me?"

"I guess 'cause you always disappearing. How you been? See ya'll just now making it back huh? No private flight today?"

"You silly, I been in and out but I'm not going back no time soon. How have you been though?"

"Chillin just came to pick up my last check that's all."

"Really? So I guess that fire fighting dream is about to start huh?"

"You know it!"

"Don't you make more money working where you at now, if you was smart you'd work both jobs on they ass."

"Yes! Yes I do make more here but I can't, its day on day off. I'm not getting younger; I have to do this before it's too late. Call it a bucket list item."

"Man stop, you not that old."

"I was the oldest one who graduated; those lil boys was like early, mid twenties. They still had Similac on they face and shit."

"You still silly." We continued to catch up as I walked her out.

"So you want me to drop ya'll off?"

"Naw, actually..." she pointed to a man holding a sign with Mrs. Xavier on it, "...yeah I didn't want to stand around waiting so I hit them up on my way off the plane."

"Go on moneybags I see you, let me hold a couple stacks!"

"You are too much! Call me later silly," she said as the driver closed the door.

The more I was around Treasure the more I wanted to spend just one more second with her. It was something about her that was like a lighthouse guiding me toward her. She started becoming the only thing I could see. Things were good for a while; she stopped working some of her nine to fives.

She changed her MOS and went away to training for about a month. I was able to swing down to Dallas and hang with her for a couple hours over a weekend. When she came back she stayed on the phone with her old man. They was constantly going back and forth about his health. After damn near begging her to let me help her, she finally told me what was going on with him. Not that I gave a fuck about the dumb nigga, but if it make her happy I was willing to help.

To be honest after she told me the situation, I was more lost than she was. She left out the part about his girl friend; I overheard her asking him, "Ain't yo' lil girlfriend there with you?" Shit like that so I know he wit' somebody, never sounded like he denied anything she was saying. I didn't know how to help her. I did the next best thing, kept her smiling and active.

She called me upset about some news she received and like that, within a couple weeks she was back on Active Duty and gone. Seem like it was always something with her every day. She would change or do something totally opposite of what she previously did. The more I stuck around her, the more she seemed to be running or trying to hide.

She moved into the middle of no man's land. Nothing but a cliff on both sides and at the bottom of a cul-de-sac. Through her front window she could see any and everyone coming and going. Not to mention she was always watching over her shoulder thinking she sees someone. I just played it off most of the time. It was cool though, she was stationed in Jefferson City so every chance I had I went down to see her.

42 DEANGELO

It's been a minute since I saw T at the reunion, I know she won't mind if I swing by the airport and swoop her up. My man said her car broke down and it's been in the shop. And pretty boy must be out of town 'cause ain't nobody spotted him in almost six months. There my girl goes, wait a minute that can't be T!

I wait for the light to change and watch her cross the street to the bus area and call Bateador, "Ay...yeah look, call Doc and tell him I'm on my way...Calm down nigga I'm good tell'em..." I pull up in the bus area and get her attention. After asking her to come over and her refusing to even look up, I throw the whip in park and jump out.

"Ay T come take a ride wit' yo' boy!" I'm trying to stop myself from touching her so I hope she comes willingly. If not, I'll drag her by her fucking throat if I have too. "Naw, I'm good." She stood up grabbing her bags trying to walk away. I popped the trunk on the Mercedes and snatched up her bags and tossed 'em in.

"I only asked to be nice but don't make me go there with you T! Get in!" I pointed her to the door, I could hear her breathing pick up. She walked over to the door as I opened it and slammed it behind her.

"Why every time I see you, you have an attitude with me?" I asked as I sped off toward the highway. She didn't respond.

"I think I know what's up and I'm damn sure about to find out!" I felt her look over at me.

"Why every time I look up I see you or somebody that knows you? What's so damn hard about you staying the fuck out my life?" Hearing those words come out her mouth kinda hurt my feelings. But if what I think is correct, I won't have any feelings for her to hurt. I smiled and turned up the radio. The whole ride she sat in the car not once asking where I was taking her. I pulled into the shopping area and she looked up.

"You know this not where I live so why are we here?" Ignoring her smart remark I sat there and looked at her, she damn straight I know where she lives.

"Damn, T you look tired, I'm not stopping you from doing anything am I? Where yo' boy at? How he doing?" She jumped up from her seat like an electrical shock had gone through her body. She unlocked the door and before she could get another foot out the car.

"Man T close the fucking door!" I looked at her with fire shooting from my eyes. She thinks she just gone walk away from me without me knowing the truth. I don't give a fuck about her pissy attitude. It don't compare in no way to the hurt I'm feeling if what I'm thinking true. I'm feeling myself about to cross the line; I grab a hold to the steering wheel to stop myself from snatching her crazy ass back in the car.

T being T, she looked me in the eye for what seemed like infinity then quickly got out the car. Man, this girl gone make me catch a case out here if she try and run off. She slammed the door shut then threw her arms down to the side and waited on me to make a move. Look at Lil T, I know she not trying to fight nobody. All I could do is chuckle as I walk over and sit against the hood.

"T, you might be crazy but you not that crazy. You do remember I won gold at that little Olympics thing now don't you? I know you do 'cause you was right there."

"Yeah I remember, but you do remember that I was supposed to get that little black belt. Yo' ass pulled me out before I could get it, you do remember that right? So please

Mr. Joseph let the smooth taste fool you and try me." I had to shake my head and chuckle, she dead ass serious. She wanted me to know that she wasn't about to run so she walked around directly in front of me.

"Now what, you drag me all the way out here with a stupid ass grin on yo' face and it don't look like you wanna fight. Can you hurry the hell up and tell me what the deal is so I can get the fuck home?"

"You already know why we here, you remember what I told you right, the last time I saw you?" She stared at me with an amused but pissed look on her face. I was hoping that she would be terrified, at least that could give me a hint of the outcome.

"So that's what this is about, you want me to piss on you right here or somewhere else? You know what; I said if you was into that kinda shit I would have to reconsider. But how I'm feeling right about now, you about to get what yo' freaky ass want." I laughed; she dropped her head cupping her face in her hands and looked back at me after a minute.

"All my damn life you been fucking with me. Keep me just enough in pocket so you can have your own personal play thing. Guess what, I'm tired and if that's what it takes for you to leave me the hell alone, and then let's go!"

Before I knew it tears stream from her eyes, all I wanna do is enclose her in my arms and apologize. But I haven't heard my answer yet so I have to push that to the side for now. She could be playing me so that I won't go through with it. Then again maybe I fucked up, hell maybe I didn't, I'm damn sure gone find out.

"Look T, all I'm trying to do is look out for you an..." Before I can get another word out she wiped her tear drenched face.

"Don't give me that shit Deangelo, every chance you get you fucking with my life and the people in it. The only peace from you I had was when they hid me out at different bases, thanks to you of course. I made sure no one but my momma and sister knew where I was at. I knew that you could buy off the rest of my family so I didn't even bother to contact them.

It was you the whole time that I was running from Deangelo. I know you didn't forget about the last time I saw you and why you came to see me have you. Not to mention every nigga I've ever fucked with; remember Myzphyt, huh? You fucked with him so much his ass was all paranoid and shit from it. You fucking with him had him thinking that I was Cindy or some shit.

Yeah he let me in on the little hood secret, why most of the guys I was talking too managed to end up doing more than weed. He called it the Returning Customer. Let's not forget about Blasé! You remember him? I don't know if I should be happy or sad that his brother decided to go pick up the package that night. I know you meant for him to be killed.

What he do Deangelo, besides chill with me? He didn't do drugs! Oh I forgot, I can't deal with anyone who sells drugs except for you right. Then you got the nerve to sit here and ask about my husband? You know he's a good man and yeah he do smoke weed but what gives you the right to lace his shit? It's 'cause of you he in and out the fucking hospital!

It's yo' fault my baby may lose her father, what the hell did she do to deserve that! It's yo' fault I had to go through two days of hell then get shipped around the country. By the way, you need to stop that selective amnesia you have going on. Last time I checked, if you loved me so fucking much you wouldn't have left me like you did. Don't worry, I already know whatchu gone say, it was for the best right.

Well maybe if yo' ass would've asked me for my fucking opinion none of this shit would've fucking happened. So FUCK YOU Deangelo, save that bullshit for somebody else. Let's get this over with so you can leave me the fuck alone. You would think after all this time you would've found some fucking body else to hound and control."

It took everything within me to hold back from choking the shit out of her. I mean to the point that all she could do was gasp for fucking air. All I ever did was protected her; I didn't tell those weak niggas to take that shit. Yeah I could've asked her from the beginning what she wanted to do.

And I was all over that shit before she disappeared. She the one that sent me away.

Fuck all that, depending on what Doc say, I might be killing her ass today anyway! I stand up and wave her in the direction of the office. When we get in, the receptionist looks at me and points me into the side exam room. We walked past all the people waiting and closed the door behind us. I hear a knock at the door then stepped outside and talked with Doc.

"Ay, I want you to run everything. I don't give a fuck if you have to drain every last drop of blood from her body. I want a full run and I need that back within a couple hours!" Doc looked at me like I lost my mind. The last time I was here I had my sister in the choke hold and Bateador had her man at gun point following behind me.

"Mr. Joseph, for everything the results will take a couple days. I can get as much as I can for now and as the other results come in I can send them over to you. I take it the drugs are what you want now. I'll put a rush on it and have them back within a couple hours!" Doc said as he headed into the room.

I waited a minute then walked in after I heard him finish talking. I stood by and watched tears fall faster and harder from T's face as Doc took another vile of blood. After he took the last one and put a cotton ball over the hole she tried to stand up. Not before Doc could pull out his tweezers holding her head still he plucked a couple hairs from her tough ass.

As we made our way back to the car, T was speeding in the opposite direction. I caught up with her, she snatched her body away. This only pissed me off more, I wrapped my arms around her waist and lifted her with ease off the sidewalk and placed her down on the hood of the car. She crying again, this time even more than before.

"Now I don't know what those tears are about. You either don't want me to find out the truth or you scared of needles. Which one is it?" She didn't say a word she had her head down and continued to sob.

"Well we have a minute before the results comeback so

I suggest we hash whatever this is going on between us out. Before you tune me out, just know I'm willing to answer any questions you have honestly. Besides if the results come back not in your favor, I plan on killing you anyway so let's talk. This might be your last time!" I can hear her laugh, maybe I'm wrong and she is just tired. Fuck that, I want proof.

"Why me Deangelo why do you keep doing this to me?" I lifted her chin so that we were eye to eye.

"I've been in love with you since I called myself coaching your softball team. I bet you don't even remember that do you? I think I was about sixteen then but lying sayin' I was eighteen. I didn't know you was four years younger than me until I worked with yo' moms. That's when I backed off 'cause I knew you wasn't ready to deal with a man like me."

"Deangelo that still don't explain all the crap you've put me through!"

"Like what T? That nigga Myzphyt? I told that nigga from jump if he wanted to be down with you with no interference from me he better have his mind right! That nigga fucked up when he started getting wet and believe me baby I had nothing to do with that! Dem niggas was fucking around with that shit long before I found out. Don't get me wrong, I knew something was up but I never would've thought he would go that far.

But who are we kidding, they don't call weed the gateway drug for nothing. That's why I never wanted you to be around a nigga that used. I only want the best for you and the best for you is someone with a clear head that can take care of you. All I've ever been worried about was you and that you was good." I wiped the tears from her face.

"So what about Blasé, what did he do?"

"T look, I knew them niggas had got into it with some Vaughn cats. I called Randy, let him know not to fuck with them and left it at that. I found out about an hour after I talked to Randy that them Vaughn niggas was waiting to roll on him. I called Blitz to try and get them to turn around.

The next day I found out that this nigga Randy was dead, he went by his self. I guess Blitz couldn't reach him in time. Bateador put a nigga on it to clean them Vaughn niggas up for that bullshit they pulled; you can ask Bateador he'll tell you. But T check, can we please finish this conversation out of this heat? At least let me get you your last meal!" I looked down at her and waited as my charisma worked her over. She began to slowly scoot off the hood; I grabbed her around the waist and helped her down. I opened the door for her and closed it as she got in.

"All right where you wanna go?" I asked as she stared out the window.

"Home!"

"Cool, you want something to eat first?"

"No!" I sped down highway One Seventy, jumped onto highway Two Seventy and headed to Bellefontaine exit. Before I could put the car in park T was out the door heading up the steps. I took my time, made a quick call and grabbed her bags from the trunk along with her purse.

As I made my way up the four steps I can see T pacing back and forth. I stopped and smiled as I handed her her purse so she could retrieve her keys. She opened the door and walked to the back. After awhile she came back out and grabbed her phone out her purse sitting on the table then stared me down.

She looked at me like she wanted to know why I'm still here, and then she turned and went back in her room. I made my way around, looked in her daughter room, kitchen, closets and bathroom. Then walked back in the living room and waited on her to come out. I hear her yell my name through the door. I can feel the steam coming out her ears as she made her way into the living room to put me in my place.

"WHAT THE FUCK DEANGELO! WHY DID YOU HAVE LAURA PICK UP MY BABY FROM PEACHES?" She screamed at me like she ain't standing right in front of me.

I smiled and looked away; before I know it, she smacked the shit outta me. I mean she hit me so hard I almost forgot who she was. My face was on fire. All I can do is smile even harder as I try to regroup and calm down. Damn, I ain't think she had it in her.

Before she can get off another hit I snatched her up, carried her over to the couch and got on top of her. I watch as she tries to get me off. The more she move the more I adjust and stop her from getting me off of her. She continues struggling and it made me laugh that she was so ready to throw down with me. The look on her face told me that I don't want to let her go just yet.

"You know you shouldn't put your hands on anyone unless you're ready for them to put their hands on you!" I can see she on fire so I eased up. Seem like it took her over an hour to calm down. Once she did, I got off of her and sat beside her on the couch and looked over at her.

"Look T, like I said I only want the best for you and maybe sometimes I go about it the wrong way. But that's the only way a nigga know how. Like I told you a long time ago, if you know better, you do better! I'm not used to this with you.

Had I known how to handle the situation better, then trust me I would've handled it better. You had a hand in this too though. You should've come to me if you wanted or needed to say anything or get anything off your chest."

She looked over at me, "Why do you only remember whatchu want to remember? As I recall, you the one who changed, you also the one who had yo' girlfriend try and jump on me! So don't say I had a hand in this when you started this."

"T I had to make sure you was okay and I would never have someone try and fight yo..." Before I can say anything else I hear a knock at the door. I watch as T went over to answer.

"Hey Laura, thanks for picking up my baby. What's all that though?" she asked Laura as she grabbed baby girl out of the stroller.

"Well I was asked to pick this up before I headed over here. You all right though? I know my nephew not giving you a hard time is he?" T didn't even look back, she shook her head no, rolled her eyes and took sleeping T into her bedroom.

"All right then I'm getting out of here. See ya'll later,"

Laura said as I stood up walking her to the door.

"Here you go and good look Auntie!" I handed her six hundred dollars as she smiled.

"Anytime nephew! Anytime!" she said then walked out and I closed the door behind her. I see T walking back out the room.

"I know you hungry, I had her stop and pick up some bomb ass soul food from this spot that I have to hit up every time I'm out this way. Come on T, have something to eat. I know that airport food ain't holding you over this long. Plus I know you didn't spend too much on food the whole time you been gone.

Hell, by the looks of your kitchen it don't look like you do much in there either. Why you live here anyway, I know you like more space than this townhouse. Tell me this T, why do you work so damn much? And if something is wrong with yo' car, why won't you just get a new one? It's not like you don't have the money."

"Whatever Deangelo, there you go again not minding yo' damn business!" I hear her say as she makes her way out the bathroom and into the living room.

"You know what, while we on yo' damn business, have I ever said anything about the bullshit you be up to? Huh? Have I ever questioned you about any of the skank ass bitches you den fucked with? Did I put my nose all up and in all these tricks you den ran over in St. Louis? No! What about the head job you got from my cousin Barbie? Did I ever say shit to you about that? No!

Have I ever said anything about your son? Yeah, thought you had that little secret didn't you? Well it's not a secret now is it? Then you putting on that front like you so surprised to find out I had a baby. You can save it!

Have I ever questioned you on that shit you do in the streets? Oh I forgot, you don't touch it. You just play the hood brokerage nigga and sit back while people kill themselves. Not to mention the fact that you use the shit to manipulate my family members. Well let me tell you, you not manipulating me anymore. So stay the fuck out my business motherfucker!"

She walks over and plops down on the arm of the couch waiting on me to respond. I walked into the kitchen, grabbed a fork, went back to the table, sat down and began to eat. I can tell it's pissing her off, I looked for the remote. Once I saw it sitting on the end table across from her, I walk over grab it and turned the TV to the game.

"Man you can miss me wit' all that!" As I sat down I look up at her and she beaten the shit out of me with her eyes. I don't know if it was 'cause she had been crying or not but her eyes looked different for a second. I see her out the corner of my eye stand up and walk over to the table. Before I have a chance to put some food in my mouth, she flips the tray over in my lap. I jump up trying to catch as much of the food back in the tray without it spilling on the floor.

"Come on T, why you trying to push me to fuck you up right now? I know you upset but we better than this. I told you that I did what I did 'cause that was the best way I knew how to handle it! Whatchu want me to say, you right? T, you right!

You've never been in my business and I admire that about you. I know you not blind and I know I did some fucked up shit to you. If I can recall, whenever I found out one of them ho's was trying to fight you or come at you 'cause of me or not, I nipped that shit in the bud. I know I may have been the cause of some of yo' scraps.

I can promise you, when word got back to me, I handled that shit. I've always been handling shit in regards to you. You right about that shit up in Washington, I was late with that but when I did get word, and I took care of it!

I always tried to keep my distance from you but sometimes a nigga can't keep his self in check. I den been at damn near all of your life events! From yo' games, to yo' graduation in basic down in Ft. Sill. I was even there when you graduated in what's that, Ft. Lee! You looking like you don't believe me or something, I can show you the tickets and graduation program sheet.

How else you had a first class flight back to the Lou. You thought that bald ass drill instructor just magically handed you the ticket. When ya'll got back to the dorms or whatever right there about two buildings away from where they had the ceremony, he gave it to you. You damn sure haven't been spending any money.

I don't have a fucking son, you den bumped yo' head with that shit. That girl was not pregnant; I had just met her ass, stop listening to the hood. You right, I was hurt when I saw you wit' lil mama. But seeing that you did disappear when you left there, I just have to roll with it? Fuck that, I'm gone go on and say it. Yeah I am hurt 'cause she should've been mine. Fuck that, she is mine! I don't care who got something to say about it.

Plus last I saw you, you called the MP's on me, you know I had to leave Washington. After that you was nowhere to be found. Then I heard you was in Nevada but before I even had a chance to try and get out there you was out." Before I could say another word I looked down and read a email from Doc.

So far Mrs. Xavier is clean; I will send you the other results when they come back. She does not have alcohol in her system.

I looked backup at her, "So by the look on your face I guess you not gone kill me now are you? Have I been punished enough for you Deangelo, or do you want to hurt me for the rest of my life?" Damn, I just knew I would have to bag and tag her ass but now I'm too far gone. What if I pushed her away for good? Fuck! Think nigga! Think!

"Look Terentia, I love you, I always have and I always will. There's nothing in or out of my power that I would or wouldn't do to protect you. I know I fucked up and I understand that you may need some time to forgive me. If you can find it in your heart to do so that is. I understand that you want me to stay out of your business. I'll respect that and I'll try. I can't say that I will honestly.

I hate that you being cold to me like this, if you change yo' mind and want to get at me you know how to find me. Before I go just do one thing for me, after that you can holla at yo' boy if you want. If not, it's all good I'll still love you. You know if you ever need anything for you or lil momma, my baby girl in there, you can get it. Can I at least have a hug before I go? I know I have food all over me but some crazy woman flipped a plate over on me."

I smiled and looked her in those heartrending brown eyes. I saw her lips begin to quiver; I wrapped my arms around her tight hoping she wouldn't make me let her go. Damn I love this girl. I just wish I didn't push her as hard as I did. Maybe if I fall back and let shit workout she will come back to me forever.

Fuck, why did I doubt her? I felt the ease in her breathing as she calmed down and stopped the flooding gates washing from her eyes onto my shirt. She began to pull away; I yearned to keep her close just a little while longer. I watch as she looks up at me. I can tell she exhausted and I can feel pain pulsating off her straight into my heart.

"Deangelo, do whatchu gone do. I told you I'm done, I can't go through this with you. Please just leave! Leave here; leave me and my family alone!" I feel my heart fall to the bottom of my soles with each step I make to the door. I know that this will be the last that I'll be this close to T again. I feel like I'm sliding down a slide filled with razor blades. As I close the door, I finally land in a pool filled with alcohol.

I make it to the car and hear something fall from my pocket as I pull out my keys. I reach down and see its T's ring; she gave me back her ring. I put it on the tip of my pinky and pulled off, fuck it; I'm on this side of town already. I might as well go out to my place in Lake St. Louis, I head west. All I could think about was how I fucked up with T. What if she never forgives me? What if she hates me? She managed to keep up with this ring for all these years. Shit, she could've sold it and got at least seventy five thousand off of it.

Hell I would've wanted her to do that, it hurts more that she gave it back? Damn! I yell out as I get off on my exit. I go in the house and jump in the shower. When I got out I made some calls while staring at the ring on the island in front of me.

43 SEBASTIAN

For her twenty fourth birthday I wanted to do something big for her. I planned a trip to Hawaii and we set off for a week in the sun. For the first couple days we did everything we could possibly do from snorkeling, swimming with dolphins, to horseback riding on the beach. I know for her birthday I have to do something off the meat rack. After she came back from her full body massage with wrap something or other. We took a helicopter ride to join on the daily cruise. We had a blast. We drank, laughed; we even joined in with the hula dancers.

I was happy just to see that she was happy, after we pulled back in we made our way to a magic show. I hit up a couple stores along the way. She said she didn't need anything, like I didn't know that. We made our way back to the room and she was surprised to see the cake I had for her with all the trimmings. We chilled out for a while then headed to the bar on the beach. I ordered a drink and juice for her while we headed for the water. We sat mostly looking at the moon bounce off the waves.

"Why you here with me?"

"Why not?"

"Stop playing with me, whatchu want from me? It's been a minute now and we still haven't even kissed but you still sticking around. You haven't put all this together for nothing so what is it?"

"I don't know. I like hanging out with you and Shay. I didn't try anything 'cause you've been going through so much. Didn't want to leave you by yourself to deal with it alone I guess, you know I have to keep you smiling." It felt good to tell her what my intentions were and the more we sat there talking the more open she was. That made it easier for her to relax and enjoy our time.

She looked over at me and smiled then sat on my lap facing me. I already know she don't have on panties so the heat coming from her rocked my body. I kissed the top of her breast then all over her neck and face. She pulled me in with her hands drawing my lips to hers.

We kissed with so much passion and intensity I thought I'd never free her mouth from mine. I was in no waiting mood so I lifted myself up; she quickly stood to her feet. I watched as she walked off toward the water, with one foot in she turned and looked back at me.

"Are you coming?" She don't have to ask me twice.

"Hell yeah!" I took off down after her, fully clothed we both went in. I picked her up seeing she wasn't only shorter than me but she afraid to swim. Her thighs around me like she holding on for dear life.

"We have to go to the room!" The one night I leave my wallet, damn!

"Why?"

"I don't have a condom." She kissed me again and nibbled on my ear. I carried her out and we walked back to the room dripping wet.

Once we made it to the room we jumped in the shower, I walked her to the bed and laid her down. All I was thinking about was getting lost in her sauce. I licked and sucked her butterfly. I can hear her breathing coming in short gasps, her body started to get tense each time I changed directions with my thumb. Once I found her spot it was a wrap.

I can taste her leak out onto my tongue; I made sure I coated it with as much of her syrup as I can. Then she jumps up, it look like she has to use the restroom. She squeezing her thighs together and rocking back and forth. Then I see that's not the case, her knees started to buckle.

She tried to play it off and kneel down on the side of the bed. I went over to pick her up. She not about to get away that easy. I know that one must have been a doozy, I better get mine off before she fall her ass to sleep.

Before I can get her up she sat up on her knees and grabbed my dick with both hands. I thought I'd lose my mind the way she went at me. Her mouth was so warm with just enough suction at just the right time. I can feel the juices from her mouth run down my dick and drip off my balls. It's feeling so good; I held the back of her head, why did I do that?

She went at it even more looking up at me from time to time. Slurping and even gagging a few times when she went too far. I felt my body want to break free so I pulled out and forced her on the bed. "Laugh at that," she said, I decided to bend her over since she tried to knock me out the way she did. I went deep ignoring her walls trying to keep me out.

Only thing I can think is this had to be minus the pain what a bear clamp would feel like the way her lips are locked around my dick. I can't think of anything else to compare it to. The view from the back was more than enough, but the sound from her flow guiding me motivated me to get it wetter.

I made sure I broke her off real good and she got at least two off before I switched up. Not to mention the in between snacks just to keep my mouth wet. The sun was coming up when we finished our last session before falling asleep. I held Treasure in my arms and was not going to let go.

After that, we spent the rest of the time there finding different spots to enjoy each other without being arrested. Then we headed back to the room to go at it more. After we returned from our trip we were even closer. For the first time I saw Treasure open up and she looked happy so that was good enough for me.

44 TREASURE

After the move and going back on Active Duty I found myself enjoying the company of Sebastian. Even if his constant jokes and over happy personality did get on my nerve from time to time. It was like nothing ever bothered him. I never saw him show any emotion besides happy. It made me think he was putting up a front. He was still good company to keep around; when he wasn't working he was with me and Shay. We had fun and I was beginning to feel a little better.

"Hey Treasure, Whatchadoin?" he said as I began to laugh at the way he said it.

"Nothing, whatchu calling me for? I thought you was on your way down?"

"Nope! Not gone be able to do it! Not me! Un, un!"

"Would you stop playing and tell me what the hell you want?"

"Calm down Madonna don't lose control. Naw, I was calling 'cause I forgot I had to go to court later today. I have some stuff to take care of the next day so I won't be able to come down. But since your birthday is right around the corner I planned something nice for you. Get yo' bags packed we out this bitch. Don't say no either 'cause I know you took off that whole week around it so I'll talk to you later. BYE!"

I know he didn't just hang up on me like that, "Hello! Hello!" That tall goof ball straight hung up on me, I can't believe him. What the hell he means pack my bags; how he know I wanna run off with him anyway? I tried to call back a couple times but he kept sending me to voicemail. I didn't hear from him again 'til he called me and told me to make my way to the airport so we could leave.

When I found out we were going to Hawaii I damn near shit a brick, why in the hell would he take me to Hawaii? I mean we cool and all but we've just been friends the entire time. I would've never thought he would do all this for me and take me out here. It don't matter though, I know that I'll have fun with Sebastian. I just don't know what he wants in return and not knowing that has me worried. I'm not looking for a relationship it's only been a minute since shit went down and I'm not even thinking about sex. I guess it's the company. Yeah Right!

For a minute we did the usual, site seeing all around the island, jet skiing, shooting range and shopping. I was done when he kept spending his money on me. Those prices was just too damn high and if it was up to my cheap ass, I would prefer a well crafted knock off over the real thing any day.

Not that I'm broke 'cause I'm far from it, but black people need to catch up. White people don't buy that expensive shit. They shop at your neighborhood convenience store and stack they paper for their kids. Black people stunt so damn hard, they don't care what part of their mothers sofa cushion they cut up to get the money from.

On my birthday he went all out. Massage, chopper ride, boat ride over the ocean, fun, food and laughs all night. We found ourselves sitting out looking into the ocean talking. I had to see where his head was at 'cause you don't do all this for just a friend. "Why you here with me?" "Why not?" he said trying to not answer my question. I pressed him some more and he finally told me. He was right; he did keep my spirits up. I sat there thinking then decided to enjoy the moment and let this road take me where it leads me.

I climbed on to Sebastian and looked into his eyes. I saw that he really meant what he said. Once he started kissing me I felt like I was sitting on a barrel. He tried to lift me up with him but that thing was trying to bruise me. It's been a minute for me, eight minutes or months I should say. I walked toward the water and called him in.

I laughed at the site of him damn near running down after me. He picked me up so that I wouldn't drown in all that water. I can swim but the site of nothing but water is a little too much for me. They won't find my body drifting around the sea. Headstone reads, "She could swim, just not in the ocean." Yeah okay.

Sebastian made me feel safe in his arms and I had him locked, he not going anywhere without me. When he told me he didn't have a condom we took the walk of shame back to the hotel. Everybody was pointing, whispering and laughing 'cause they know what we have been up too.

It didn't help that everybody Sebastian saw looking at us he had to speak to or make some smart remark. "What's up Bigg Dog?" "Watch out there now!" "Feel real good in the ocean tonight if you know what I mean." I tried to ignore him and get in as soon as we could. Before we could make it up he had to let it be known in the lobby first. He started asking random people for whips and chains.

After we showered I was spread eagle on the bed, he went straight for the gold. He eating like he putting in overtime with his mouth all over me. I can't inhale long enough to think about what was happening. I held my breath for what seemed like forever. It was like an instant wave came and then another, then another. I don't know how the hell he doing it. I don't give a damn either 'cause it fells too fucking good.

I had one so hard I thought I was pissing on myself. I jumped up too quick. Then my legs started to shake, I can't even stand up. I have to sit my ass on something steady and cold so I chose the floor. I can tell by the look on his face and the fact that he laughed at me that he think he won. I learned a couple tricks too. Soon as he was within arm's reach, I sat up on my knees and wrapped my mouth around just the head of his dick. I made sure it was wet.

I had it wet enough to slide my hand up and down

while I was concentrating on the head. I let my juices run all the way down his ass. I slurped it backup pulling away long enough to show him his pre cum hang from the tip of my tongue all the way to his head. Once he put his hand on my head I knew I had him. I can see his toes dance on the floor; I decided to go for his balls.

I sucked and licked them then started going back and forth spending time on his dick then back to his balls. I can feel him heat up, I know he about to blow, before I know it he pulled away. If I didn't know any better, I would've thought I bit the damn thing off the way he jumped back. I knew then I had my revenge so I threw it in his face.

I don't know why I did that 'cause he bent my ass over and I damn near shot off the other side of the bed. He didn't even make it all the way in before I was running. It was like my body wasn't willing to open up and accept him. I can feel the pressure and I wanna bear down and force it out instead of letting him in.

The more I ran the tighter his grip became. I just know I have FBI quality finger prints of his fingers on my waist. We had a great time that night and many more to follow, even after our trip ended. I was happy and I can see that Sebastian is happy too.

45 DOMINIC

Thirteen months ago.

"What the heck Terentia? Why you always come home tripping with me?"

"Why the hell you think Dominic? Why the fuck I check the account and find out thirteen thousand dollars gone?"

"What?" I tried to buy myself sometime to think of how I could explain but I know she not going to have it.

"What? Is that how you gone try and play me? Yeah, think nigga! Think!"

"Terentia gone somewhere with that. Just drop it okay!"

"I'm gone drop it all right, first thing in the morning I'm getting my own account. I don't want shit out of that one! You can have it and that'll be that." I don't know why she didn't take my advice and leave it alone, I have enough on my mind. In that moment I was not going to let her say anything else. I got up off the bed and put her right down on the floor. I put both her hands above her head and held her there kicking and screaming for me to get off her.

"You know what, ever since we been in St. Louis you been on some bullshit. Working all these damn jobs trying yo' best to stay out of sight. Now I know you 'bout think I'm getting high and smoking up *OUR* money but I'm not. You right, go ahead and get another account. It's not like you don't have several of them anyway now is it?

Yeah I know, but what you do is on you. I never asked you for shit and always provided for us and still do! You know what I think yo' problem is, you back stuck on stupid. You think I don't know about that nigga? Matter fact give, me this shit..." I broke the bracelet off her wrist then dangled it in front of her, "...yeah, Forever T DAJ, you been holding on to this nigga ever since I met yo' ass.

This the same nigga had mufuckas put a gun to yo' thick head. The same nigga that had people chasing yo' ass all across the country; you remember why we had to leave Ft. Lewis? You quite now huh? Where was that nigga at then? Where was he at when they found yo' ass?

Where was he when I sat with yo' ass at the hospital? Where was he when the unit put you on special orders to an undisclosed location? I didn't want you to leave like that; I wanted to marry you to make sure we would stay together! I was the one who left everything behind to make sure you was good! Where was he when I married yo' ass? Huh Terentia? What about when we had Shay, where was he then?

Let me tell you something baby. You my mother fucking wife and that nigga can't fucking have you! Point, blank, period! You can fuck around and keep up with this bullshit if you want to. Acting like you don't know. I told you I wanted to move the fuck from up here. We been here for almost seven months now. You want to know where the money went. It went towards a down payment on a house, FOR US!

Yeah that's right, all the shit you think I been selling or whatever the fuck you think I been doing. I been sending down to *OUR* house. So think what the fuck you want Terentia but I been good to you. I'm going to give you time to think about what you need too. At the end of the day, remember you my mother fucking wife and until I decide different, that's just what it is!"

I sat there on top of her for a minute looking into my

baby eyes. I can tell she hurt but I don't give a fuck at this point. I picked her up from the floor then laid her down onto my chest. I'm tired of fighting with her and I know she has love for that nigga still in her heart.

The only way I'm going to remove that Cancer is to move the fuck out St. Louis. I know he the nigga I been hearing about. He was the only one who called her T. Then I thought back to the ring on her bracelet and it pissed me off even more.

The nigga thought he had me with the bullshit weed he passed me. But I already had a blunt rolled before so I finished that off and went to sleep. After I woke up I couldn't find the shit. I checked my phone and heard the message Terentia left. She was at work so I couldn't ask her until she came home.

I was glad that she did what she did though, I haven't smoked since. She wouldn't know that 'cause she thinks I'm an addict or some shit, she found the weed I had before I bought that bullshit. Since then she been on my ass, I can't blame her though, I wanted to surprise her with the house. I was planning on having everything moved before she came back from one of her four days. Hell, she so paranoid she been doing one day here and there so I could only move a piece at a time trying to keep it a secret.

She sat up, eyes swollen and began telling me what she had been holding back all this time like she was reliving it all over again. "He did come when I was in the hospital. All I could think about was the day that I signed my life away to protect him in the long run."

"What are you talking about Terentia? Say it!" Then it was like her flashback began as she explained from the beginning.

> 'You ready T, got yo' permission slip?'
>
> 'Ha, ha funny man!'
>
> 'For real T, you get her to sign it in all the spots? The last thing you need to do is leave it lying around the house where she can find it.' I go in my bag and pull out the bullshit ass papers coach gave me to give my mom's to sign.

'See here it go and yes she signed on every spot that was marked so you can stop worrying. I don't even know why I need all this anyway if the tournament is downtown. Hell, I'll only be away one night.'

'Well ya'll not in a tournament.'

'Whatchu mean?'

'I had that nigga give you that and call yo' moms so you could ride with me for a minute.'

'Really, you couldn't let me in on this?'

'Naw, I didn't want you to lie to yo' moms.'

'Well I did now didn't I. Where we going anyway?'

'You'll see.'

We pull up at the airport and I was shocked 'cause we was getting on a private jet. I had a million and one questions the whole time. Deangelo ducked everything I said. Before we landed he gave me a bag with winter clothes in it and said I should change 'cause it was cold so I did. I was glad I did once we stepped off the plane.

It was cold as fuck even wrapped up in the pretty ass fur coat and matching accessory set he gave me. The driver pulled into this huge driveway. The grass was covered in snow it seemed like it would never end. The wind hit me straight in the face as he opened the window.

We made it to this large cabin like house, big windows was all I could see, and I couldn't see anything inside. Soon as we walked in the door I started looking around. Deangelo went in the opposite direction on the phone so I didn't think anything about it. We ate and he avoided my questions again. The only thing he did say was that we would be leaving in a little while, and I would be back down Gee Gee house before I knew it. I heard Deangelo go to the door, as I made my way into the room I could hear a man.

'Now you're sure Mr. Joseph you want this to be eternal? You do understand that you'll never be able to alter it. Even if something was to happen to the beneficiary it would go to that persons next of kin.' He stopped talking as I came around the corner and they both looked up at me.

'Yeah I'm sure!' Deangelo introduced me to his attorney. All I can remember is Schultz. I was too baffled about being there to even remember his first name or the lady that was with him. We all sat down as the lady turned on the camera she setup. Mr. Schultz began reading something and asked Deangelo to read the top page of the paper he held in his hand.

'I, Deangelo Alejandro Joseph...be...' Blah, blah, blah. I figured he needed me to witness, I drowned all that boring shit out and sat there.

Then I heard him say, 'I give and bequeath the following below-described sums of money or items of personal or real property, as the case may be to Terentia Treasure Waters m...' It felt like the wind was knocked right out of me, I damn near fell off the couch. I got up too damn fast and ran to the balcony; I needed some fresh air and quick.

Every bone in my body froze the moment I opened that door but I needed to get the hell out of there. I felt the fur come across my arms as Deangelo placed it on my shoulders.

'T don't be so cold, come back in here so I can get chu back to Gee Gee house.' I turned to him.

'Deangelo what the hell are you thinking? I'm a sophomore in high school! What the hell do I look like accepting all those things and all that damn money? Whatchu plan on dying and don't want me to know?'

'T I just want to make sure you good, I still have access so it's not a big deal. Besides if something did happen to me who else would I leave anything too?'

'Why me though Deangelo?'

'Come on now T you know you my buddy, I can't leave my best friend out like that.' He smiled and I couldn't get any other real answer out of him after that. I knew it had to be more than what he was telling me. But hell, it was getting colder and colder by the second. I decided to roll with it and when I had the chance I would press the issue more.

We sat back down and he began to go over the paperwork again. Mr. Schultz said something about me being underage and needing my guardian's permission. I thought I had a chance to get him to change his mind. Hell, my mom's was not going to sign shit. I damn sure wasn't going to try and explain it to her or even give it to her to sign.

'Ay T, where yo' permission slip at?'

'What?'

'You know the paperwork I asked you about earlier?' I reached into my bag. I know I saw the shit about the games and the times so I pulled it out and gave it to him. He pulled off the first couple pages then gave the rest to Mr. Schultz.

Mr. Schultz looked over it. Then he put it with some other stuff he had on the table. He started pointing to all the spots for me to initial and sign before he handed me a pen. I looked at Deangelo and he smiled and nodded his head. I grabbed the pen and started filling it out where he asked me to.

After that they all began signing, the lady stamped shit and signed then they were back out the door just as quickly as they came. The heat was just too much for me again so I went back out onto the balcony wrapped up and sat on the edge of the jacuzzi. I didn't know what I had just got myself into. Deangelo came out; he didn't say anything, we both sat as long as we could before we headed back into the house. We were out the door shortly after not mentioning a word of what had happened.

After he let me out in front of Fourteen Thirty-Four I couldn't go without asking him, 'I'm not going to regret this am I? I hope you're not getting me sucked up in this lif...'

'Come on now T, you think that mufucka gone put his shit on the line for a nigga like me if it was anything illegal? Have a little trust in yo' boy T. Just remember that whenever you think that no one has your back that you don't have to be so cold to me 'cause I do.' He smiled and so did I, we never talked about it again.

I had forgotten all about it over the years until a couple days before I left for the military, I received a letter in the mail from him.

Hey T, sorry for the way shit went down. I know you probably still mad at me and all but it was for the best. I want you to grab the keys I stashed in yo' mom's basement in the laundry room on that cabinet, they go to a safety deposit box. You'll find all the stuff you need in the package there.

If you ever want to meet up with me then let Bateador know you being cold and I'll make my way out to Minnesota to meet you. It may take a couple days for me to get word and back so don't leave before I see you. Take care T.

I couldn't believe it when I read what was in the package that Deangelo left for me. I was more afraid then I had ever been for him. I had no idea just how much he was doing in the streets. I mean it didn't have anything illegal in it.

What it did say was that I owned four houses in four different states plus a villa over in Greece. Five accounts with way too much money in each, cars and boats. Hell, I have some membership shit setup for private flights for like the next lifetime. I didn't know what the hell to do, it was too much. I decided to get another safety deposit box and leave that shit right where it was.

I didn't want any parts of it. Something was telling me to not touch any of it. It felt like if I did something would happen to Deangelo in exchange so I didn't. I continued on with my plans like nothing had ever happened."

Terentia and I barely said anything to each other after that. I decided I would head to the house and give her some space to figure it out. That was the hardest decision I've ever made in my life. I wanted to drag her ass kicking and screaming but I know that wasn't going to make it better.

She has to make a choice on who she wants to be with. I was trying to make sure she know where I stand on the situation. I just hate that I fucked up and started doing the shit behind her back. I guess if I would've known better I would've done better. I been away from my family for three months and decided that I would have to put an end to it.

"Terentia!"

"Hey."

"Hey? That's it? Let me guess you with some nigga that's why you can't say my damn name?"

"Dominic I am with someone but it's not like that and I don't have a problem saying your name. But if it'll make you feel better, yes husband Dominic, how may I help you?" Okay, I see she want me to come up there and lay my hands on her ass.

"What the hell you mean you with a nigga? You know what, it don't even matter. If I don't hear from you by the end of the night that yo' ass headed down here then we done! You hear me Terentia? You have until the clock strikes midnight to be on the first thing smoking the fuck out of St. Louis!

I'm tired of you pussy footing around on making yo' damn mind up and if you think for one second my baby staying up there you have another thing coming. Hell, yo' ass not around enough to take care of her no damn way! Don't say for a second you need the money either 'cause those accounts that nigga steady dropping dough in I know they loaded." I listen to her bicker back at me for awhile then I get tired of hearing it and cut her off.

"Yeah, yeah, yeah! You heard what I said, midnight! If not I'm gone make sure yo' ass never want to be with me again!" I hang up with her still going on.

The next day Terentia was nowhere to be found, I was devastated. I wanted to take everything I said back. But just like she says she like to keep it funky I had to keep it funky with her ass. It took everything out of me to stop myself from my original plan of dragging her ass away kicking and screaming. I spent most of my days working on my business and my nights in the clubs. Monroe had come down to go into business with me so it was just like old times.

I found a nice girl and we hit it off, nothing serious though. I was still waiting on Terentia and praying that some sense would run in her damn head. The more I was away from

Terentia the more my body began to break down. I was in and out of the hospital on a regular basis. The only thing they knew was that I had foreign chemicals in my blood. It was linked to the fire I was in before I was discharged. I had been in pain since that day. The medications wasn't doing shit so I started smoking weed to balance it out. It must've done something to my system 'cause I was hurting in more ways than one.

I was missing Terentia so I decided to head home early and jump on a flight to go see her. It wouldn't be the first time but it would be the first since my ultimatum. I don't know how she will react. I'm all ready to go so I jump in the car head to the highway. The next thing I know I'm waking up in the hospital.

I was happy to see Terentia standing by my bed with my baby in her arms. I found out I passed out from pneumonia, that's why I had been feeling like I was. I crashed my car and was in the hospital, the next morning Terentia made it down and I woke up later that night. We talked about a lot of shit and I'm starting to think that we can still work on our marriage. Hell, she has been with me damn near everyday for a month. Then just as fast as that thought came it went.

"Oh baby I just found out what happened from your mom so I came right over. I've been sick trying to find you; I was desperate so I had to go to your mom to find out. How are you feeling? What did the doctors say?"

In walked or should I say ran Janesha with her bald face lies. Janesha is a sack chaser; I found that out a couple weeks ago. Every time I'm with her she has her handout like I was supposed to pay her to be with me. Whenever I had Shay, Janesha would act like she would get infected by her. When I questioned her on it she played like I was making it up.

I was really about to put my hands on her when she popped Shay, I never told Terentia about it. I just so happened to leave out the room and Shay spilled her juice and it splashed on Janesha shoes. When I came in I saw Janesha hand come back and heard Shay scream. I snatched her up and asked what the hell she do to her. She claimed Shay threw it at her on purpose so she "tapped" her hand. I put her ass out and for two weeks Janesha did all she could to apologize for what happened.

When she came to me on some she need a new car shit, I flat out laughed at her. Yeah I can afford to get her a new car but why? Monroe had already told me she came at him. Not to mention my sister had already told me she saw Janesha at the store and told her I was in the hospital. My sister said she asked her if she could get some money from me to pay her rent. What kind of shit is that?

Janesha was coming over to my side fast. As she leaned in to kiss me, Terentia pushed her head back damn near knocking her into the blood pressure machine. Terentia didn't say a word she just looked at me, Janesha was furious and she launched at Terentia. Either the shit was going in slow motion or I was on the best dope in the world. Terentia took one step to the side out of Janesha way. Then she punched her right in the back of the head as she landed face first on the side table knocking herself out.

All the nurses came flying in to check on all the commotion. Terentia still didn't say a word, her eyes were on fire with anger and I can read her every thought. I saw a tear roll down her face. She picked up Shay who was crying at the foot of the bed, looked up at me again and was out the door. I felt bad for what happened and I knew then I had fucked up any chances with Terentia.

My body took the hit the worst though; the more I was rushed to the hospital, the more I checked the fuck out. Terentia would come sometimes and others she would just call, the last time I talked to Terentia before I hung up I told her, "Terentia, you gone miss me when I'm gone!" I sat on the couch looking through old pictures of me and Terentia. I reminisced about what we used to be. I looked at my baby girl and how beautiful she is. All I could do was close my eyes as my heart broke for the last time.

46 TREASURE

Ain't this a bitch? I can't believe his silly ass; I can't wait 'til I get home! I drove as fast as I could to make it in the house. I didn't even bother to bring my bags in from out of the car. As soon as I opened the door I started going the fuck off.

"Dominic August Xavier, have you lost your fucking mind? Every got damn day it's something with you. I'm sick and fucking tired of this bullshit. You one sneaky motherfucka, always creeping around doing dumb shit on the side! I could shoot yo' ass right here right fucking now!"

"What the h..." His ass ain't seen tripping yet, I just told his ass I could shoot him so he ain't seen tripping yet. I guess I'm going to have to put a fire under his ass, I don't know who this man is anymore. After going back and forth with Dominic I decided to let him know I was taking my name off the account and getting my own.

"What the hell are you doing? Let me go! I'm tired of yo' shit Dominic! Let me up! Get off of me!" He had me on the floor before I could even make it past the door. All I can do is kick and scream. I can't hit his ass; he got my hands pinned down. He know I was gone knock the shit out of him if he didn't.

He sat on top of me staring me in my eyes, I don't know what the hell he thinking, I know he about to tell me. He let my ass have it and then he snapped my bracelet. I realize now that I'm wrong for holding onto it the way that I have. He got real up close and personal with me and exposed every dirty little secret I thought I buried on a forgotten island.

I was shaken to the core when I was given a different view of how I was behaving. I can't look him in the eyes but he making sure that I do. Every time I turn he do the same, I'm getting more and more furious with every word he spit out in my face.

I broke down when he brought up Washington, I was ashamed by how it happened and why. He was right though, that guy had been looking for me on post, asking around about me to whoever he could. When he found me he told me he killed the dude brother that held the gun to my head that night. He also said that he wanted to take from Deangelo what he was hiding. I didn't understand who he was. By the sounds of things he thought he needed me and Deangelo in order to get whatever he wanted.

He had me for two days, and then a housekeeper came into the room. I could barely talk, I was covered in blood. All I could do was cry; Deangelo was nowhere to be found to stop it from happening. He said he would take care of it. I thought I was getting over what happened that night but Deangelo left me and look what happened. I cried and all I could think about was how Dominic was right and how I was a damn fool not to see it before this moment.

Even with all the shit he said I still don't know if I can trust Dominic. All the lying he has been doing. I cried so hard after that, he carried me to the bed and I was on his chest crying until I couldn't anymore.

I decided that I needed to tell Dominic about everything so I sat up and told him. It felt like I was right back at that day and every little detail was rolling off my tongue. I didn't know what to say to Dominic after that so I did whatever I could to stay busy. Then he came home and said he was leaving.

I wanted to beg and plead with him to help me trust him again. I didn't want him to go, all I wanted was to trust him the way I use to I just didn't know how. I watched him pull off and I cried for two days straight. I didn't know what to do with myself. I didn't know what was holding me to St. Louis. I didn't know why I couldn't leave again something was pulling me like I was gravity and it was the center of earth. At that moment I knew what it was. I just didn't know if I could leave it alone, run away, or run back to it.

It seemed like the only time I wasn't crying I was with Sebastian. I told Dominic about him and I know he didn't like what I was doing. I was losing my mind and Dominic didn't understand why. In his mind I think he thought it was simple but I know it's not simple at all. I spent all this time running and look where that has gotten me.

Once I received the call that Dominic was in the hospital, I put all that shit on the back burner and I was there for him. I spent many days and nights by his bedside praying that he would get better. I was starting to feel at peace with the right decision that I needed to make. We laughed and we cried together. I was starting to feel like we were connecting again in a way that we can only do outside of St. Louis.

After eating breakfast we sat around the bed laughing at Shay as she fumbled around Dominic. I was trying to stop her from pulling on his IV so I moved her to the foot of the bed. Then this girl came running in and soon as she said baby I stood to my feet. I can tell by the way she looking at Dominic she in the right room.

Before I know it I tried to mush her face into the wall when she went to kiss him. That bitch straight act like she don't see me and my baby sitting here. Oh well, if she didn't she do now. After she stumbled back she came around the bed like she wanted some. This dumbass didn't see the bar coming from under the hospital bed that I had my foot resting on. I moved right over I knew she would trip on it. As soon as she did I hit that bitch so hard in the back of the head I could feel my hand swell up instantly.

This bitch hit the side of the table on her way down, all we could hear was snoring and Shay crying. The nurses ran in and started shaking the bitch and shit. I look at Dominic and I can see by the look in his eyes he fucked that girl. He crossed a line that he had drawn in the sand. I hated him at that moment; I pulled up my baby and headed for the door. I didn't want his ass to see the pain in me no longer. I went straight to the airport, I left his car right out front, didn't even bother taking the keys out.

After that I found myself arguing more and more with Dominic. I was starting to believe that he was checking his self out the hospital just to get me to come back down there. I stopped going. I was tired of the constant back and forth with him; it had been almost two months since he was in the accident. And the fact that he was still talking to his girlfriend didn't help the matter much. Then one day I heard this song, *Testify* by Common that I instantly felt like was speaking to me. I heard that song like twenty times. The more I heard it the more it touched my soul. Then I received the call that turned my world upside down. Dominic was dead!

I couldn't believe it when they called me. I had just talked to him the day before and he sounded fine. When it really sank in, I was beat. I was out of control; all I wanted to do was make the pain end. He took my heart with him and I don't know how I'll continue on without him. I'm pissed that I couldn't see what was in front of me. I need to tell him just one more time that I love him. It's like that song was telling me what was happening and I couldn't read it before it was too late. All that I want to do is take all this shit back. When he left I should've been on his arm leaving with him. I'm lost now.

The next day I started receiving calls from people confirming arrangements for his burial. I couldn't deal with it though. I put the phone outside in my mailbox and told my sister to take care of it. I sat in the house the entire time depressed, lonely and crying. I didn't leave out 'til my sister came a couple hours before we had to leave out so we could make the final arrangements for the funeral.

I wasn't surprised to see a driver take us all to the airport. My family was all excited that we were flying private, half of them it was their first time flying. I was starting to get really annoyed by it. They made it seem like we were on vacation or something. The line of white Lincoln MKZ's waiting to take us to a fancy ass hotel didn't help.

The entire time I just wanted to scream with the way people were acting. The funeral was over the top. Everyone thanked me for the gift bags with some of Dominic's favorite things in them. Then when I thought I couldn't take anymore, the Pastor stopped me before I headed back to the limo.

"I would like to thank you for the large donation to the church." I looked in his hand and saw a white envelope with only the initials DAJ on the front. I knew then that my sister had little to do with this. After that the funeral director came over with the same envelope saying the same thing.

A couple weeks later Dominic's family called and left me a message thanking me for the money. Supposedly I sent them money along with seem like several other people who attended the funeral. I wasn't mad about how the funeral turned out. It was the guilt and pain that kept me from wanting to deal with anything.

I had to make a move to stop from being in the looney bin. I signed backup full time in the military and moved out of St. Louis. It was just my luck that I didn't go far; it was enough to keep me feeling better about what I had gone through. I wish that I would've listened to Dominic. The last thing he told me was that I would miss him when he was gone, he was right.

He's all I think about, I blame myself for his death. If it wasn't for me he wouldn't have been in the fire, he probably would've been in another state. If it wasn't for me he wouldn't have been in St. Louis or had to deal with the things I put him through. If it wasn't for me he wouldn't be dead. I wish I would've known better so that I could've done better. Maybe he would still be here.

47 DEANGELO

I sat staring at T ring for about an hour. All I can think of was back in the day. Every detail of what happened started playing out in my mind as I laid back on the couch.

Five years ago.

"What the hell you mean you lost her? I'm on my way!" By the time I made it to Washington, T had been found and I was sort of relieved.

"Man Bateador, what the fuck happened?"

"Tim said he saw her man walk her to her room. A couple hours later her man left so he figured she would be in for the night which was her usual. Tim say when he came back that morning at the time she would usually get out, she didn't show so he thought he missed her. He waited around still nothing, he went by her unit and found out they was looking for her too. He called me, I flew out here to see what was up then I put in word to you." All I could do was pace; I know if I see Tim I'll kill him.

"So what happened?"

"All I know Pandillero is the chick at the hospital said she was brought in with multiple injuries—"

"Bateador don't fuck around with me, what did she say?"

"Man, she been raped!" All I could do was drop my

head into my hands when I heard those three words.

"Three broken ribs, broken jaw, three fingers on her left and two fingers on her right hand are broken. Deep abrasions around her neck, wrist and ankles. A broken right foot, small burns possibly from a cigar on her inner thigh. Her face is swollen to the point that she may be unrecognizable. She's in an induced coma for the pain, maybe three days at the least."

"Get the fuck out! Bateador find who the fuck did this and make sure I see'em! Make sure her people get out her in the morning!" I can't believe this has happened to my T, I was supposed to handle this and now look where she is. I thought that my little plan worked. I know this has all to do with me and not T. After days passing by without being able to go see T I was growing impatient. Still nothing on who did this, each day we are getting closer but they locked down the post and it's getting harder to get some answers.

"Pandillero, she up! I can get her man out for about an hour but it's another girl there with her."

"I'm on my way now." The closer I get to T the more I want to help her and make her better. I never meant for this to happen to T and I can only blame myself. I made my way into the room; T was facing the window looking at a girl sitting in the chair facing me.

"Hello, who are you?"

"Hi, I'm here to see T." I didn't know if T wanted me to tell her who I was so I decided to skip right over her question.

"Is T sleep?"

"No!" I hear T say just above a whisper.

"Can I have a minute to speak with T alone?" She looked at T and I saw T hold her arm barely up like it weighed six hundred pounds are something and the girl slid closer to her.

"Harmony, please don't tell Xavier that that guy behind me is here."

"I won't Waters," was all the girl said as she came towards me.

"Here, take this for your troubles." I gave her two thousand dollars.

"No! I can't accept that, like I said I won't."

"Well use it to get T some lunch."

"From where, Mars?" She giggled and walked out the room.

"What do you want Deangelo?"

"T I'm so sorry that this happened, as soon as I found out I came out. I've been waiting on you to wake up and for Kathy nem to leave." T didn't say anything.

"T please come with me, I talked to Schultz; you remember the attorney you met? He said he can make some calls and get you released, you can stay on emergency leave until you're discharged." Still no answer, I walked around the bed, once I saw her I broke down. The pain was too much; I fell to my knees and held onto the rail.

I felt like I was hit by a train the moment I looked over at her, I wanted to die at the site of my girl. All I wanted to do was trade places with T, she didn't deserve for this to happen to her. I felt her reach for my hand, I made my way over closer I still couldn't look her in the eyes. She placed her hand on the back of my head while I tried to get my shit together.

"Look at me Deangelo." I wanted to tell her that I couldn't and it was all my fault. I continued to cry, I didn't care who heard me I was in too much pain. I couldn't do what she asked; the shame was weighing down on my soul like a mountain.

"Deangelo, I'm not going with you." All I could do was look down and plead with T.

"Please T, please don't do this, I need you to come with me."

"Look at me Deangelo." I pulled myself together and looked at T. I saw all the pain and hurt in her bruised face. Her eyes were blood clot red and barely open from all the swelling. Her face was swollen to the point that her skin was purple like the pressure behind it was about to make it explode. All I wanted was to kiss her and make it all go away, so that's what I did. I tried my best to kiss every inch of her face so that she could feel better.

"T please, just tell me what I have to do to make you happy, all I want to do is that. I know I can again if you come with me."

"I'm not going with you Deangelo. I don't blame you for anything and you shouldn't either. Go back overseas; I'm going to stay here for now. I'll be fine I just need to pay more attention to my surroundings, that's all." I wasn't about to leave T again, I was on my feet.

"Look T, I'm not going to leave you here. I should've stopped yo' ass from even signing up for this shit!" I said trying to clean my face and man up. All she did was rolled over toward the door.

"Why the hell did you do that anyway?"

"It don't matter Deangelo, I'm not going and you know I'm not."

"T you don't need the fucking money and you damn sure know you don't. I'm calling Schultz to have him make the call. I'm getting a doctor to take over your care and we out this bitch!" I started to walk toward the door.

"I'm not going Deangelo; I don't know why you not listening to me, if you want to take it there, I will." What? I know I haven't seen T in a minute but I know she didn't just put out a threat. I turned around and looked at her battered face again and I damn near lost control all over.

"Why T, you the only multimillionaire I know who live like they broke or damn near broke." The moment I said it I could hear my words echo from her friend behind me. I turned around and there she stood with her mouth wide open and her eyes big from the shock of what she just heard. All I could do was drop my head down.

"Ummm. Shit! Excuse me, Waters, umm Xavier, yeah Xavier is on his way back here, I thought you wanted to know." Then she fumbled and closed the door.

"Thanks for everything Deangelo, just what the fuck I needed, people to be in my fucking business."

"T I'm sorry I just don't understand why you doing this or why you being so damn pig headed about staying here when you don't have to be."

"It don't matter whatchu understand anymore, just leave! I'm tired Deangelo, I don't have the strength to fight with you about this." I felt the tears run back down my face at the thought of what she said. I could see that T was tired and I was determined to get her to leave. I cleaned myself backup.

"Just as long as you know you coming with me T, I'm not fucking around with you about this either." I watched as she shifted her hand under the cover, in walked the nurse and two MP's.

"Please send him away and don't let him come back in here." I looked over at T in disbelief that she would do this to me, then the MP tried to grab my arm but I stared him down.

"I'm still making the call T." I turned and walked out the door. I don't care how she feels about ending this bullshit. She's coming with me and I'm not leaving this wet, depressing ass place until she does. I went back to the hell hole of a room they had right outside the gates near the hospital. Before I could even get the key in the door I got a call from Bateador.

"We found him."

"Where you at, I'm on my way."

"Don't bother; I'll be over in a minute to let you know what happened." Before I could get anything else out he hung up the phone, what the fuck now? I wait and call Schultz and my peoples to make arrangements for T. I let Bateador in, I can see the look on his face telling me that he's not about to say anything I wanna hear.

"We found the guy but he wasn't the cat that we thought he was, this was a real hitter. The only thing I could get out him at first was he found out about her from them niggas I was looking for. I know they both sleep so I guess he the one that took care of that. But I couldn't get who sent his ass; I was putting it on him too.

Then the MP's start banging on the door so I didn't have time to do his ass before we had to get out of there. Whoever sent him know something, soon as I figure it out I'm on it. Also he took out Shaddy, Monk and Special Order before we caught up with him so I made the call already to handle that."

I already knew what he was after from T she must not have told him shit for her to still be alive. But hell, they need her more than they need me. How in the hell did they find out? I have to think about this before I can figure this shit out, then my phone ring.

"Schultz, what's the word?" This all I need, more bad fucking news.

"Let's go man; we have to get back to the hospital!" We make it to the gate and see that the damn post is on a complete lockdown. No cars going in and not one fucking car coming out.

Bateador turned the car around, "What the hell happened?"

"They moving her, Schultz said they found yo' boy, he sleep. And he couldn't get any information about her even with his connections. She probably on her way to some fucked up ass base right now. Fuck I should've rolled her hard headed ass up outta there when I had the chance."

We stayed close for a couple days to see if they would let up and I would get a chance to see T again. Schultz called back and told me that they were looking for us so we flew back. I was pissed but I knew T would be safe. All I could picture was T broken and weak lying in that hospital bed in pain every time I tried to close my eyes. It sent me on a mission to find her so I never went back to Greece. I called my agent and let him know I was done. It was a hard decision but T was my top priority. I needed to make sure she was all right and I couldn't do that over there.

48 TREASURE

Fifteen months after arriving in Ft. Lewis, Washington.

Dang I forgot about this damn inspection tomorrow, I need to go to the unit and get the rest of my shit. I left it in my damn desk, let me hurry up and make it over there. I walk out the door and head to the unit. I can see somebody coming towards me in a uniform; I didn't think anything about it.

"Hey, do you know where I can find Waters?" What the hell is he looking for me for?

"Yes Chief, I'm Waters."

"Major Bates is calling for a meeting and he asked if I could stop by and pick you up." Just what the fuck I need, I should've got the fuck off this damn post. Now I'll be stuck up in another one of these long boring ass briefings again. All they do is ask the same damn questions over and over like they can't read the slides I already gave dey asses.

"Well if you can give me a minute Chief, I can change real quick."

"No need, the meeting has already started we need to get there now. I've been looking for you for almost an hour already. So let's go, my car is over here." I was in no mood for his shity ass attitude I hate these fucking Warrant Officers. They don't do shit but walk around here bossing people around. I follow him to the car and get in; I see he's heading off post.

"Why is the briefing off post?" He didn't say anything as he makes it through the gates.

"Excuse me Chief, is the meeting off post?"

"Shut the fuck up bitch!" I turned in complete disbelief that he just said that but by the sound of his reply, I know he's not who he said he was. I grabbed the handle of the door. I was goin' jump the fuck out, I didn't care how fast he was going I know somebody will see me.

"Take your hand off the door or I'll kill you right now!" I looked over at him and he had a gun pointing right at me. Why me Deangelo, why fucking me? I know this has something to do with him. That's the only reason this punk ass nigga would be fucking with me. He stopped at this ran down ass motel not too far from the post and told me to get out. I should make a run for it; I know someone will hear the shot.

"Don't try and run or I'll make sure that little friend of yours get his next." He came around and put the gun right in my spine and guided me to his room. All I could think was please let my brother remember our pack. We said if we lose a limb that the other would make sure they pulled the plug. I know if he shoots me in my spine, if I live, I won't be able to walk. I'm not about to force my brother to kill me but he better help me do it if I need his help.

Once we were in he closed the door, I felt a hard blow to the back of my head. I thought I was dead, and then he started whaling on me like he was waiting to do it for way too long. After I blacked out I couldn't feel the pain anymore. I don't know how long I was out. When I opened my eyes and didn't see him, I hoped he was dead. I tried to move but I was tied tight to the bed. I tried to scream out but my mouth felt like it didn't want to open.

"Where you think you going? It ain't over yet bitch, we just now getting started. It took me too got damn long to get your ass here. Now you about to tell me everything I need to know. You hear me bitch? First, tell me where the fuck is that nigger stashing all the money?" I didn't say anything, shit; I couldn't if I wanted to. My damn lips are too swollen to respond so he hit me a couple more times. All I could murmur was I don't know. He hit me some more.

"I know you know, don't act like you don't, he's not having people chase your ass around the country for nothing. Where the fuck is he hiding it? You have it somewhere?" This one dumb motherfucker, yeah I keep that kinda money right in my front pocket you dick head.

"You know those niggers in St. Louis said you were one hard bitch to crack. They're some dumbasses, that's why I had to kill those niggers. See I know how to get what I want bitch." He lit a cigar and once it was good and hot, pushed it into my thigh.

"Feel that? Yeah I can see you do, so tell me what's the number to reach your man? I know he'll give up the money once he knows you're here."

I still couldn't say shit to him. Besides, all I know is to call Bateador so I could meet up with Deangelo in Minnesota. There's no way I'll last with this bitch going all the way there. So I didn't say anything again, he went at me more beating the shit out of me.

Then he climbed on the top of me and forced his self inside. The moment I felt him hit my ass I felt my body rip open and I was out again. When I woke up, I could barely open my eyes, I can feel the blood running into them. I can see a shadow standing in the doorway and I can hear someone screaming. I broke down crying 'cause I know that I've been found and that bastard was gone or maybe even dead.

I can't remember how I made it to the hospital; all my friends were standing around me. I was feeling like I had my life back and that was all that mattered. They showed me so much love. I hadn't realized just how close we've all become in the fifteen or so months we've been together. When my own family made their way to see me, they were more like strangers to me than they'd ever been. I hated that they came and saw me in the condition that I was in.

"Terentia, baby you need to come home baby. Whatever it is that you and that fool den got yoself into, we can work it out." my mother said, I closed my eyes and ignored her. That's just like my mom; anything that happens is always my fault. I was tired of them looking at me like I was a child and needed them to baby me. I managed to convince them to leave and go back to St. Louis. I damn near pushed their asses out the door and locked it behind them as they left.

"Hey baby, you need anything before I go?"

"No, where you headed?" I didn't want Dominic to leave he's the only thing keeping me from the pain I'm feeling.

"The unit just called and said they wanted us to meet with the Commander, they have questions for us. So me and Monroe on our way there now."

"All right I'll see you later then." He kissed me and walked out.

"Hey Waters, you all right? You need me to get you anything?"

"Naw Harmony, I'm fine I'm just glad you're here with me that's all."

"Girl I'm not going anywhere, I'll be here until you tell me to go." We sat there talking about the times we spent together and all the fun we had, then the door opened. I could tell by the look on Harmony face that whoever it was she didn't know them. I was too weak to look back and see.

"Hello, who are you?" Harmony said. The way her eyes lit up I knew she was looking at someone who was drop dead gorgeous. Harmony put on the "please fuck me now" face quick. This told me there was one person that would be coming to see me for her to react that way.

"Hi, I'm here to see T." Yep, it's Deangelo and by the look on Harmony face, he still as fine as the last time I spent with him. He asked Harmony to speak with me alone, I was too happy he didn't tell her who he was. Before Harmony could leave and run her big mouth off to Dominic I asked her to not tell him. I know she will at some point but I wanted to keep it a secret for as long as I can.

I know he gave her a lot of money 'cause of her Mars comment. That was the thing with Deangelo; he didn't care how much money he gave people. That's as long as he can get what he wants. I've seen it too many times and it was the money that had me in the position that I'm in.

"What do you want Deangelo?" I didn't want to hear anything he had to say. All I wanted him to do was get as far away as he could. I know that whoever that guy was he's probably still watching. Once he finds out that Deangelo is here, I'd be in even deeper than I already am. I know he must've been devastated once he took a look at me. The way he fell to the ground crying like a baby, I know that the sight of me is what caused him to react that way.

"Look at me Deangelo." He wasn't willing to look up, I know it hurt and I know that he felt like it was his fault. I just wanted him to see that no matter how I looked, I was okay and still breathing. Once he did it only hurt me in return 'cause I wanted to fuck him up for leaving me the way he did. I know that part of this is his fault but I also know that I should've been smarter. I shouldn't have gotten into the car in the first place. The unit was a short distance away. All I had to do was say I would meet him there and this whole thing could've been avoided.

Deep down I wanted to leave with Deangelo, something was telling me the time wasn't right. I was at a fork in the road. I wasn't ready to deal with his life. I didn't know if I could ever handle the shit he's doing with a good conscious. The thought of that made a part of me laugh hard and long. The best thing for me to do right now is to push him away.

"...pay more attention to my surroundings, that's all." I tried but I knew by the sound in his voice that he's not going to go away as easily as my family did. I let him get out everything he needed to say. I know he will do whatever it takes to get me to leave.

"Why T, you the only multimillionaire I know who live like they broke or damn near broke." He said through gritted teeth, I saw the look on Harmony face that she had been outside the door listening in on our conversation. The cat was out the bag and I had Deangelo to blame for that.

He was even more upset. The look on his face said he was going to do everything that he said and there was no way I could stop him. The only thing I have are the MP's that I know are outside my room. I pushed the emergency button and waited on them to come in.

"Please send him away an..." It was the hardest thing I've ever done. I didn't want to hurt Deangelo or see him in trouble with the law. I hoped that he wouldn't overreact and go at the MP's. The way he's looking at them has me on edge.

I wanted to take back what I did then he looked at me. Everything in me wanted to hold onto him and ride with him until I couldn't anymore. Then I thought about Dominic and the love I have for him and how he made me feel. The only thing Deangelo said after that was, "I'm still making the call T." And he was out the door. I cried as much as I could while Harmony sat on the side of my bed waiting on me to finish.

A couple hours later I thought that I hit the panic button again or something. My room became instantly filled with MP's, full birds and all kinda shit. They started asking me questions about what happened. Once I told them they said I was being sent to a secure location. These dumbasses thought it was some national security type shit going on.

All I could get out of what they were saying was they found a couple bodies. All to be known fugitives connected to major shit. I had clearance to some shit but it wasn't what they were thinking. I let them ship my ass to another location; I was on a flight shortly after that. Awhile after that I was told I could only contact my mother. I chose not to call her, instead I called Dominic.

49 DOMINIC

"See you in the morning Terentia."

"All right Mr. Man, don't hurt nobody in the clubs tonight."

"You silly, I told you I'm not going."

"Yeah that's what yo' mouth say."

"See you later woman."

I go back to my room and just like I thought the room was packed, people everywhere. I can hear Monroe talking shit to everybody and Harmony instigating him to keep at it.

"Man, what ya'll doing?" I can't believe they have so many people over.

"Shit, we figured we would stay in and chill out, play the game for a minute. Where Waters at?" Monroe said he think he getting over.

"In her room, she probably about to go to sleep like all you mufuckas should be doing. Ya'll know we have that stupid base run at four freaking thirty in the morning!" They all looked around like they had forgot about it. Then I see people start towards the door.

"Man, don't tell me a little six mile run, in what, six fucking hours gone kill ya'll cats."

"Hell yeah nigga, we been going hard since Friday! I'm out; I know I forgot about that shit. First Sergeant is not about to be in my ass for the rest of the week." Brickland said as he headed to the door. Seem like everybody came to their senses after that and started heading out.

"You see this baby; he came and ruined the party." Monroe said as he walked over to Harmony.

"Yeah baby but I have to go too. I forgot about the inspection we have and I know I need to get my uniform together. So I'll see you later." Harmony kissed Monroe and they both started out the door. I could hear Monroe pleading with her to stay as they went down the steps. I cleaned up my side of the room and jumped in the shower. As soon as my head touched the pillow I was out cold. We stopped by Harmony and Terentia room so we could go over to the run site together the next morning.

"Hey ya'll." Harmony said as I opened the door for her.

"Where Terentia at, she already gone?" I asked.

"Yeah she must've left out early, she have to be there before everybody else to get the guidon." Harmony said as I closed the door. Our unit was a long way back in the formation. After the run I waited around for Terentia but she didn't show.

After chow I went to check on Terentia but Harmony said she hadn't seen her so I checked the unit. They said they didn't know where she was. I started calling her phone getting no answer all day, I wondered where she was. As soon as we were released I went looking for her again and didn't know where she could be. I went back to her unit and they were asking me where she was but I didn't know. I knew they would report her AWOL in a couple more hours so I drove around to see if anyone had seen her.

But I know Terentia and she's not someone who could be tracked that easily. All I can do is wait for her to show up; the longest two days of my dang life seem like. "They found Waters, she in the hospital!" Harmony said as she came running into the room. We jumped up and all headed over to Madigan to check on her. They wouldn't tell us anything for the first day, and then they said we could go in and see her. I was traumatized when I saw Terentia; she looked like she had been to hell and back. I was infuriated and wanted to kill whoever did this to her.

She can barely talk; her mouth's puffy almost like she's deformed. I tried to get some answers from her but she's too weak to really talk. Most of the time we all just sat by her side for as long as we could before we had to go to work or the hospital put us out. They let me stay with her overnight.

Her family arrived and seemed like they were back out the door before I could even meet any of them. Terentia acted like she didn't want to be bothered with them at all. Something was telling me that they're not as close as I am with my family. "Monroe, Xavier." We both looked at the MP as he waved us out the room. He told us the unit called and we had to meet up with the Commander for questioning. I went back into the room before I left, "Hey baby you need anything before I go?" I didn't want to leave her but I was willing to do whatever I needed to make sure whoever did this will pay.

I was pissed that we made it to the unit and damn near sat around for an hour waiting on the Commander to get back. We decided we were going back to the hospital; I called Harmony and told her we're on our way. Then the Commander finally came as we were heading out the door. He said he hadn't called for us.

He called over to Terentia unit to find out if they sent for us. Next thing we know we're being taken to the MP station and questioned like we're full fledge criminals. They searched everywhere for a gun. Checked us for residue, we didn't know what was going on. Then Blair, a guy who we kicked it with, told us what he knew.

"Man this shit is crazy, I don't know what yo' girl then got into but they found at least four bodies, all linking back to Waters. They think it has something to do with her top secret clearance. You two know she's heading up the big push for the base to head overseas next year right? Then I heard some big time judge called about her. Got the base Colonel scared. They moving her now 'cause I think they said it was a bunch of niggas in town from St. Louis killing people 'cause of what happened to her."

We both looked at each other in total shock. We weren't allowed back in the hospital after that. Wherever we went we had to let the MP know and had to check in and out. Harmony called and said they moved Terentia so we waited on Harmony to come back to the room.

"She gone, they took her to another base. I don't even know if her family knows where she's going," Harmony said as I laid back in the bed. I can't believe I didn't get a chance to see Terentia before she left. My heart was broken and I didn't know what I needed to do to put it back together.

"Man this shit is crazy, I don't know. I've never seen this type of shit happen before. I ain't even seen the base Colonel before so for him to be involved, this shit is beyond me," Monroe said as he walked into the kitchen.

"X, what you think is really going on with Waters?"

"I don't know Harmony, I know just as much as we all do."

"Well I told Waters I wouldn't say anything but since she gone I might as well tell it." I sat up. I don't know what Harmony has to say but if she don't let it out I'm gone go crazy.

"So what is it," Monroe said as he waited for her to say something.

"When ya'll left a dude, I know he was from St. Louis he looked like it; he came in and talked to Waters. Then Waters asked me not to tell you that the guy was in the room. I left out but before I could leave he gave me two thousand dollars to get Waters some food."

"Yeah right! He gave you damn near half a month of a privates pay for food," Monroe said as he sat in the chair. Harmony went into her purse and pulled out the money.

"See, he did give it to me knuckle head, why I have to lie about that?"

"Just tell me what you know." I didn't feel like hearing them go back and forth.

"Well I was outside the door just in case Waters needed me. I could hear what they were saying, this dude was crying, I know he was. This guy wanted Waters to leave with him. He said he was going to call somebody and get her out. He sounded like he wasn't leaving without her, then you called and said you were on your way.

I was going back in and I heard him say she was the only multimillionaire he knew that lived like she was broke. I know he didn't know I was in the room when he said it. He dropped his head down when he realized that I was behind him. The next thing I know, Waters emergency light came on and everyone went into the room. Waters told them to not let him back in the room and he said he was making the call."

"So what you think Waters, who let me remind you just turned eighteen is a multimillionaire. A multimillionaire who's hiding in the military busting her ass everyday taking orders even though she doesn't have to," Monroe said then laughed. I don't know what to think something was up I just don't know what.

"I know Waters didn't want me to hear what he said; I also know that he was decked out from head to toe. He was fine as fuck! He had on a watch that I know was real, a Sky Moon Tourbillon. That thing cost a million easy and I remember a couple months back Waters had a package delivered to her. She didn't want to show it to me so she put it in her wall locker. I was packing her things earlier and found it. Sure enough, she has a blue one just like he had but his was a different color. So I know something up."

"You know what; her family did show up in those new Porsche Cayenne Turbo SUV's. They didn't dress all fancy or anything but I do remember her brother saying something about them taking a private flight out here," Monroe said as he looked over at me.

"I don't know about millions but Waters got some money. All this time I thought she was making it with those online businesses that she run. Plus whenever we go out, she don't spend much but what she do buy sometimes be way more than her check. Her mother did say whatever she was in they could take care of back home," Harmony said I sat back and took it all in.

Then I thought about the conversation I overheard her

mother having in the lobby. She was telling them that she knows Terentia was in something she didn't know what though. She said how else would they get a call from somebody telling them to go to the airport. Then they get a call from the Red Cross letting them know what happened when they were about to land. Something about some thug dragging her down.

None of it mattered to me; all I wanted was Terentia back. I was willing to do whatever I had too to make it happen. I was sick without Terentia I needed her; I needed to know that she was all right. I wanted to be there wherever there was to make sure of it. A couple weeks later my phone rang, "Hello, Dominic." I was so excited to hear her voice I felt a tear try and make it down my face.

50 TREASURE

When I found out I would be in Nevada for a month I told Dominic, he took leave to come be with me. We spent every day together and before he returned he asked me to marry him. He even surprised me with Harmony and Monroe. We hung out and had the wedding; it was just like old times. I was happy that he did what he did to be with me. I know that was the only way I would be able to be with him.

They had already planned on moving me again. So we had a short ceremony with just the two of us and them. It took forever for Dominic to be transferred. But when he was, he was sent to where I was at. I was happy that we were back together.

We bounced around from state to state, seemed like we were only around about two to three months before they would move us again. It didn't matter to us though; as long as we were together we were happy. Nothing was going to change what we felt for each other. After two years of moving around, I guess the military figured out that it had nothing to do with what they thought. We spent the longest we had ever stayed anywhere at a base in California.

"Baby I'm going to miss you, this is going to be the longest time we've spent apart in I don't know how long."

"Well Mrs. Xavier you can call me and you know we'll be back together before you know it. Just make sure you keep yo' tail in the house. If you need something, call next door and they'll help you out."

"I get tired of staying in this house; I don't have anything to do since I got out."

"Terentia, you need to take care of my baby and I don't want anything to happen to you or her so let them help you."

"What if Shay come before you get back?"

"Terentia don't do that, you know I'll tell them to kiss my rear and leave if my baby come and I'm not here."

"I love you baby."

"I love you too and you too my little Shay. You rest so I don't have to go AWOL, I'll be back in two weeks. I know you can hold out until then right."

"I'm going to hold out as long as Shay let me." We said our goodbyes as the long line of trucks pulled away.

We spoke on the phone almost every day. With Dominic job he was always in his own truck far away from the rest of the unit doing his thing. A week flew past with me sitting around the house doing nothing. I was expecting a call from Dominic but it didn't come. Three more days past and I didn't hear anything from him. I was starting to get worried then I heard a knock at the door.

"Who is it?" I didn't hear anything so I went closer but stood off to the side with my finger on the phone to call the police. I heard the door open and I ran my fat ass as fast as I could into the room and closed the door. I pushed the buttons on the phone. Then I saw Dominic come around the corner.

"Baby! Whatchu doing here?" He smiled at me as I ran into his arms not wanting to let him go. He picked me up so I wrapped my legs around him and kissed him like it was my first time ever doing it. He sat me down on the couch and rubbed his hands all across my belly. He put his head down and started to cry.

I didn't know what to do so I rubbed his head and waited on him to get out what he needed to. After awhile he stopped and sat up. He looked at me, kissed me again, led me to the bathroom and turned on the water. I sat on his lap while he sat on the side of the tub. His tongue sampled my mouth as the water filled up. He deepened the kiss taking off my clothes without breaking away. His fingers slipped into me until I was slushy and about to burst.

He pulled away, smiled and put his fingers that had just been in me into his mouth. We didn't say a word we sat there while he rubbed my stomach and kissed all over me. He took his time and started bathing me up and then he did his self and we got out. Still soaking wet he picked me up and carried me to the bed just staring at me. I felt kinda weird 'cause he wouldn't stop looking at me.

"I missed you baby I didn't know where you were why didn't you call me?"

"I'll tell you later Terentia; I need to take care of you first." I was done, he think he need to take care of me. I'm about to take care of him, the way my best friend pointing at me I have to go to work. I pulled his ass right onto the bed and began working my mouth up and down his cock. I know he like it wet and sloppy so I made sure I did just that. I slowly started to jerk him off while my mouth covered the tip of his penis. I took every inch of him that I could into my mouth.

He tastes like chocolate milk. My mouth ran up and down his shaft, I let my tongue play with his dick and sucked on him while trying to breathe. He long and thick so I couldn't go too far but I tried my best to ignore it. I damn near choked myself trying to make him feel as good as he made me feel. I licked his balls and stroked him more.

I wanted to extract every last drop of him into my mouth. I went back to his dick and played with his balls as he filled my mouth with his hot shake. I cleaned him off swallowing back every bit of his load. He laid there for a second as I made my way backup to him and kissed him.

I was absolutely lovely, I knew that I had mine with all the excitement from giving him his. Dominic had other plans for me. He pressed his hand hard against me and played around in my moist softness. I was so hot and ready to go I couldn't wait for him to let me have it. As soon as he made his way down to my pearl I felt myself release more juices when he opened me up.

His fingers felt perfect inside of me and the way he was moving his tongue across my clit then around my pussy I was in heaven. I came over and over I don't know if I can take anymore. I wanted to feel that log he was hiding out of my view on the side of the bed.

"Please baby put it in! Stop teasing me and put it in!"

"One more then you can have it." He had his one more real quick. I couldn't hold back once he started hitting my spot and sucking my inner lips.

He kissed my thighs and released my legs from out of his grip. I kissed him while I climbed on top. I braced myself with my feet and put my hands on his chest. I clinched down on my walls and slowly slid down his pipe just enough so he could feel my flow run down his dick. I tightened even more as I came backup letting his head rest on my lips then did it again. I can tell he's in pain with what I'm doing. His hands are balled into fist as I played around not letting him in.

I was so turned on I had to see how long he could take it. I pulled him back out and slid down him fast and hard and held my walls as tight as I could so he would feel all of me. His head came forward and he looked like he wanted to scream. I didn't stay there long; I moved my hips just long enough for him to fall back onto the bed.

I started all over again with this exotic torture that had him wanting more. Once I saw that he was catching on to what I was doing I stopped. I climbed off and began to capture my juices as they mixed with his right off his dick. The way he sat up I know that he's not going to be able to take it much longer.

He pulled my head up and kissed me then pulled me on the side of the bed. He placed a pillow under my stomach and put another into my hands. I was ready, I knew he was about to put it on my ass. I couldn't wait to see just how much he really missed me. He moved my legs opening up my body a little more.

I felt his tongue slide right down into my ass, I thought I was about to lose my mind. He went down to my dripping hole and fucked me good while his thumb played with my ass.

I felt him turn my world upside down as he began going back and forth teasing both my lairs with his juicy tongue.

The moment he put his head against my trap I started to bear down with all that I had. I wanted to make sure it wasn't going to be easy for him to slide the slippery slopes inside of me. He knows what I'm doing so he smacked my ass; all I could do was let up some. Every chance I had I threw it back and tightened it up.

All he would do was pop my ass again, I had to retreat and let him in. He worked me over and I was so happy that he was doing everything that I wanted him to do. He had me on my back with a pillow under my butt, my legs were spread wide open with him holding onto my ankles. He was watching hard as he slid down into me.

My lips were wrapped around him so tight that he couldn't take his eyes off the wetness. He picked up and I felt his body heat up. I felt a rush of warmth that shook my body. His men are invading me and heating me up while I let go.

He's exhausted; he laid his head down on me. He's kissing all over me asking me if I'm all right and if I'm hurt. I told him I was fine and he went into the bathroom and cleaned us up. He pulled me into his arms as we caught our breath.

"Baby tell me what happened to you. Why are you back so soon?" He didn't say anything he kissed my forehead and began to rub my stomach again.

"Dominic please tell me, whatever it is I can handle it."

"Terentia it's nothing, I'm fine I'm just happy to be here with you." He's avoiding my questions and I'm starting to think that he's hiding something from me. And whatever it is it has to be big. I tried to sit up but he held me tighter not releasing his grip.

"Terentia we had a meeting and I went, I tried to tell them that how they wanted to set up the equipment it wouldn't work. Of course no one listened so I did what I was told, I wake up and the damn truck on fire." I sat up and looked at Dominic. I hadn't noticed anything, I started checking his ass looking to see if he was burned or hurt.

"Terentia I didn't get burned calm down, this is why I

didn't want to tell you. The fire was in the back I took in a lot of smoke though. I was about three miles away so I tried to put it out but I fell out and woke up in the hospital." I was still looking at my baby trying to make sure that he was okay.

"Why didn't they call me?"

"I told them not too. Plus it wasn't my unit that I was with so it was easy to get them not to call you."

"Why would you do that, what if something would've happened?" I wanted to cry, I could feel the tears rushing to my eyes the more I thought about losing Dominic.

"That's exactly why I didn't want them to call you. I'm fine Terentia all I want to do is take care of my babies. Stop worrying and calm down," he said as he sat up and kissed both my eyes and pulled me back into his arms.

I didn't know what to think, all I could think about was losing Dominic what would we do without him around. Dominic didn't want to talk about what happened I didn't want to keep asking. I let him fall off to sleep and I did the same. All I could dream about was how that could've been the last time I ever saw Dominic.

The last time I would've ever felt the way I just did with him. I tossed and turned I didn't know why I couldn't sleep; all I could feel was pain. Dominic held me tight; he would only give me room to turn. I didn't know if he was awake or sleep. I could hear him cough every now and then and he would pull me back in once I stopped moving. I had to get up, I couldn't lie there any longer thinking about losing him.

"Dominic, Dominic, baby, I need to get up." Damn shame I'm grown and have to ask him to get out the bed. I don't care that's my baby if he wants me to stay here for the rest of my life I will.

"Hurry up Terentia and come back," he said as he raised his arm helping me out the bed. I walked into the bathroom and all I could do was cry. The pain I was feeling was overwhelming, the room began to spin. I tried to grab a hold to the door knob, but I couldn't. I fell to the ground and screamed in pain. I heard Dominic bang on the door but I couldn't get up, the room went black. What's going on, why are all these people staring at me like that?

"Terentia can you hear me?" I can hear Dominic but I can't talk it's something covering my mouth. I start to panic and I want to pull it off but my body not moving. I'm trying my best to get it to do what I want but it's not responding. I was tired I had to sleep. I woke up and the thing was no longer over my mouth. The doctor was playing with my foot and I wanted to kick the shit out of him.

"Mrs. Xavier how do you feel?" How the hell he think I feel, sleepy. All I want to do is sleep but I have to find out what's going on.

"I feel, okay." I don't know what he said after that I was back sleep and dreaming of Dominic being in that fire again.

"Terentia, wake up! I know you hear me, wake up baby."

"Dominic, hey baby you all right?" He was looking so good I don't know what made me so horny. I wanted to pull him into the bed with me. He climbed in bed and held me. I realized that he had his arm on my stomach and I couldn't see my baby. I reached down and my stomach was flat.

"What happened? What happened to Shay?" I jumped up then I felt a pain in me that I've never felt in my life. It hurt so bad I screamed and passed the fuck out.

"Hey wifey how you doing?" I was feeling so much better but I had to find out about Shay and if she was okay.

"Where is Shay baby? Where is she?"

"She's fine baby, they have her in the nursery. I'm worried about you though. You need to stay still so you won't tear out your stitches again."

"Come here baby please come here." He climbed back in bed with me and held me close again.

"Tell me what happened." After Dominic told me everything that happened I felt exhausted. I wanted him to hold me while I slept and he did. I spent almost a month in the hospital due to all the complications with giving birth. Once I went back home with Dominic I started to feel better.

"I'm surprised that yo..."

"Sing it daddy!" I yelled out to my baby as he walked in the front door.

"Whatchu so happy about?" I said as I gave Shay her bottle then set her rocker on a low speed.

"I'm just happy to see my wife," he said as he came over and pulled me close to him. He sang some more as we danced around having a good time.

"For real, what's up?"

"Where you wanna go baby?"

"Whatchu talking about Dominic?"

"Where you wanna move Mrs. Xavier? We can go wherever you want, just say the place and we're there!" All I could think about was home; I was missing my family and the Lou.

"What, you out?"

"Yep! So wherever you want to go that'll be our new home." He picked me up and spun me around the room and I laughed as he sang even louder.

"I kinda wanna go home? Not for long I think but for a little while." I didn't know what Dominic was going to say with all the shit that had happened.

"You sure?"

"I think."

"Well we have about a month to find a spot then we're out of here." I was so happy I pushed my baby back on the couch and gave him a real good head job. We ran into the bedroom so he could finish me off.

51 DOMINIC

"Terentia, are you okay?"

"Yes, I'm all right how are you doing?"

"Baby I'm so much better now that I hear your voice, where are you? Can I come see you? Are you coming back?"

"I'm glad you're okay Dominic, I wish I could've seen you before I left but as long as you're okay that's fine with me."

I had so many questions for her; she could only give me bits and pieces 'cause she was constantly on the move. Then after about four months she told me that she would be in Nevada for a month so I put in leave and headed out to see her. Once I stepped off that plane and saw my boo, I dropped my bags and fell in love all over again when she came to me. I held her in my arms and spun her around. I was all in and my nose was wide open, I knew then that I couldn't let her go.

We spent the first couple nights in the bed catching up on our love making. I didn't know if I would hurt her so I took my time. I could tell Terentia was in pain so I stopped. When I did, she took over so I let her lead the way. After that she didn't want to stop.

She enjoyed pushing me to my limits, teasing me and giving it to me, I can't lie, I was lovin' it. Half way into my trip, I called Monroe and told him my plans. A week later I took Terentia to her favorite restaurant there. We sat on the deck overlooking the lake.

After the waiter took our plates I walked over to her and got down on one knee and asked her to marry me. When she said yes I was the happiest man in the galaxy. Everyone cheered; she was surprised to see Monroe and Harmony come from behind her. We all laughed and had a great night. A couple days later we made it official with Monroe and Harmony standing by our sides.

After Harmony and Monroe left, I was too aware that I would be heading back in a couple days. I want to stay with my wife and make sure she's taken care of. I'm dreading having to leave her. I made as many calls as I could to get a transfer. I was told that I have to go back to the unit if I want to get a rush on it. I spent every day that I could with Terentia and I was happy that she was happy. I wiped her tears away as I headed to the concourse. It hurt me to see her cry but I know that I'll be back with her soon.

It took about three months before I could get the transfer in, Terentia had already been moved. They sent me to her location and it was just like the first time we had seen each other all over again. We jumped from Idaho to Maine, to Florida, to Georgia, to Ohio; we were all over the place every couple months. It was to the point that we didn't even bother unpacking, we went to work and back home.

All that matters to me is that I have my wife and I'm not letting her go. They decided to send us to California for the remainder of her tour. We spent almost a year there before we were pregnant. I didn't think it could get any better. I called everybody I could think of, hell I even called people that I had not talked to in years and told them. My baby was having my baby and I was good.

"Hey baby I won't be here when you get off I have an appointment so I'll be back after that."

"You sure you don't want me to go with you Terentia?"

"No thanks, it'll be quick so have a great day at work."

After work I couldn't wait to get home, I got off a little early 'cause we had to pack. They wanted us to be ready to roll out on Monday. While I was packing I saw a package in the back of the closet. I didn't think anything of it until I moved it over and a key fell out. I opened the envelop to drop the key back inside and saw a letter addressed to T so I read it.

"Hey T, sorry for the way shit went down. I know you probably still mad at me and all but it was for the best. I want you to grab the keys I stashed in yo' mom's basement in the laundry..."

I didn't see anything else inside of it but a couple banking slips from different banks. I put everything back where I found it and let it go. Whatever it was that she kept buried in the back of the closet was right where it needed to be. I continued doing what I was doing and didn't bother to ask her about it. The weekend flew past and I know Terentia will miss me 'cause I'm going to miss her just as much.

"Baby I'm going to miss you, thi..." I tried to comfort her as much as I could. All I wanted was for her to be safe and wait until I returned home before she had our baby. I was mad as all out with the unit for sending us in the first place with her due date being so soon. I had to do what I had to do and go.

We talked every day since I was always sitting so far away from anyone else. When they did call me down it was for some bullshit. You always have some Officer making shit up when in the real world it made no fucking sense. I did what they wanted; I knew that the system wouldn't be able to hold as much as they wanted.

Hell, who am I to tell them anything besides the only one who could run the shit. It's times like this I hate that I have no choice on where I go because of my transfer to be with Terentia. The unit I'm with now trains Officers who think they know everything. My previous units I was top dog on the enlisted side and didn't do anything for real.

It was holding up so I went to sleep in the truck, then I couldn't catch my breath. When I opened my eyes the back was covered in flames. I know it had to be burning for a long time 'cause I was smoking once I made it out. My body was covered. It was pitch black and all I could see was smoke and a bright orange blaze.

The more I tried to put out the flames and breathe the more I couldn't. I woke up early that morning in the hospital. I was praying they didn't call Terentia but these dumb reservist wouldn't know protocol if it smack them in the face. I stayed in the hospital for two days then they sent me home.

I had a key but I knocked on the door so I could surprise Terentia with my early return. I heard her answer but I didn't say anything. Then it dawned on my dumb self that she might be scared seeing all that she had been through. I used my key and let myself in. I could kick myself in the tail when I saw how afraid she was when I turned the corner.

"Baby! Whatchu doing here," she said as she came from around the door.

I took the phone from her and walked to the couch with them in my arms. I was so happy that I had my family with me that I let my tears fall while I held my babies tighter. We hit the tub and made love. Terentia put it on me; I wanted to make her feel just as satisfied. I had to tell Terentia what happened and I know that she'll get worked up about it. I need her to be all right so I held on to my babies not letting them go.

"Dominic, Dominic, baby, I need to get up." I heard Terentia say, I told her to hurry up and let her go. I could hear her in the bathroom. It sounded like she was crying so I got up to check on her. Then I heard her fall and I ran to the door banging on it calling for her to let me in but she didn't. I slammed into it and found her lying on the floor.

I could see blood start to pool around her so I called the ambulance. They were there before I could get her to wake up. They rushed her out and I jumped in with them. The doctors said Shay wasn't breathing. Terentia had lost a lot of blood; they wanted me to decide who they were going to save. What the fuck kinda shit is that? I told them to do their fucking job and save them both.

My world came crashing in; I didn't know what I would do without them. Once Shay was out they rushed her out the room, they were trying to resuscitate her. Terentia laid on that table with all her insides displayed like something out of a horror film.

Then all I could hear were bells and ringing she had stopped breathing. They told me to leave and I sat outside the door crying harder than I've ever cried in my life. The nurse came and took me into the waiting room. I asked how Shay was doing but she said she didn't know.

I sat there for six hours not knowing how my family was doing. I didn't know how I would feel if I lost both of them or even one of them. I prayed the entire time. Then the nurse came in and said I could go see Shay. I moved with the quickness to the NICU. They had her in this box with tubes running all out of her. I cried more at the site of her, I didn't think it would get any worse than that.

I stayed there only being able to watch her through the box. I was in my own world, the nurse kept asking me if I wanted to go home and relax. I told her I didn't want to leave, she told me eighteen hours had passed and I needed to take a break. I explained to her that I wouldn't leave and she left me, I continued to watch Shay.

A doctor came and told me that Terentia was being moved into her room. He said she would probably be sleep but she was okay and that was all I needed to hear. I rushed to the room; Terentia was in just about the same state that she was back in Washington. The thought of the pain rocked me to the bone.

"Terentia, wake up! I know you hear me, wake up baby." I wanted to hear her voice; I needed to know she was okay. All she wanted to know was if I was okay it made me feel good. I pulled myself closer to her, I didn't want to hurt her but I had to be with her. We sat for a minute then she tried to sit up not knowing that she had the baby and was cut open.

The moment she did sit up she screamed out and fell back into my arms. Everyone came running in, I watched as her white sheets turned red. I jumped up as they rolled her back out the room. I was losing my mind; I fell down to my knees just begging for a break, hoping that I would be answered.

I went back to see Shay and waited for the doctor to tell me what was going on with Terentia. I sat in a chair next to Shay. I was awakened by the nurse telling me that Terentia was out of surgery. I had no idea that it was six o'clock the following day. Two days had past me by and I had been in total misery the entire time.

"Hey wifey how you doing?" I said to her once I saw that she was coming too. She wanted to know what happened, where was Shay and if I was okay. She didn't even notice that she was chained to the bed like a slave. The doctors didn't want her to rip her stitches so they had to tie her down.

Once I told her what happened she was all right and they unhooked her, she slept in my arms for most of the day. Then they brought Shay in and we both were happy. I couldn't ask for anything else my babies were with me and they were doing okay.

We spent sometime in the hospital and I couldn't wait to get them home. I wanted to spend as much time with them that I could. My tour was coming to an end so I asked to be released a couple months early. I was surprised that they said yes.

I went home and celebrated with my family. I was even more surprised that Terentia said she wanted to go back to St. Louis. I didn't want to tell her no, she did say for a little while so I was all right with that. I had plans of my own and they didn't include St. Louis for one second, but I'm willing to make her happy.

52 SEBASTIAN

Present day.

"Treasure we've known each other for almost two years now. I know that we've been through a lot together. I love you with every bone in my body. You and Shay mean the world to me. So I wanna know if you Terentia Treasure Xavier will marry me?" After spending so much time and going through so much with Treasure I was waiting for the right time to take her back to Hawaii which was the right place to propose.

When we returned I rode with her to pick up Shay from her family out of state. I always wondered what they were like and I wanted them to know that I'll always treat Shay as my daughter. Before we picked her up Treasure stopped at a restaurant so we could eat, to my surprise she didn't order. She drank water staring out the window.

"What's wrong baby?"

"Nothing, I was just thinking that I should probably go get her now. That's all."

"You don't want me to meet them?"

"No it's not th...." I didn't have to hear anymore; I tuned her out and walked away. Once I saw Treasure get up and drive off I was furious.

The whole ride back we didn't say a word, once we

made it to her house, I unpacked the bags and made sure she was settled. Then I jumped in my car and drove back home. I don't know what's up with Treasure, she happy one minute and sad the next. Every time I think we're good we're not.

The way she started snapping on me made me feel like she was trying to push me away. I know she has some heavy shit on her mind to deal with but damn. I spent more days away then I did with her, not 'cause I wanted to but 'cause she didn't want me around. Whenever I tell her that I'm coming down she tell me she has to work or she made plans. It's getting old. I had to beg her to stop by when she did come to town. When she did, it was only for a couple hours then she was out the door.

"I'm Seabas; let me guess they called you in from another house huh?"

"Yeah, what's up I'm Thomas, people call me Drag!"

"What house you coming from Drag?"

"Two downtown off Tucker. I was told ya'll was short so dey sent me out here to help for the next week." I talked with Drag for a minute then I see Treasure pulling up. I waited as she sat in the car debating on if she would get out. Right before I was about to go see what the problem was, I see the door open and she's coming my way.

"What's up Treasure, I ain't seen you in a long time girl, give me a hug. You know the sun been looking for you the way you get gone." I watched as Drag hugged Treasure while she looks back at me.

"Hey Drag, how you doing?" I waited while they talked wondering when she was going to say something to me.

"Hey baby, I brought you something to eat." She handed me the bag.

"All right man, I'll see you inside," I said to Drag then wrapped my arm around Treasure and walked her to the car. I sat down on the hood. I watched her play with her foot and fumble around for a minute.

"So what was that all about?"

"Nothing!"

"You know him from somewhere?"

"Yeah! I grew up with him that's all." I know it's more to the story so I continued drilling her and I can tell she holding something back.

A couple days later I pull up to the engine house and see Drag talking to somebody in a white Lambo. Seems like they're watching me get my shit out the car. Hell, I can't take my eyes off the Lambo Aventador that bitch clean. White errthing from what I can see, that bitch feet sittin' right. Now that's a pretty muthafucka! I see his potna get out and they make their way to the entrance.

"What's up Seabas, back already?"

"Shit you know I am. What's up Dog I'm Seabas." I hold out my hand but he put his hands in the air.

"I'm Pandillero but I don't shake hands wit' a nigga in a uniform." We all laughed but I can tell it's something up with him. The way his Pretty Willy ass looking at me told me that he's here for a reason, I just don't know what. Right on time I see Treasure coming down the street, once again she sit in the car debating and then get out. We talk for a minute as I sat on the hood holding her pressed up against me on the side of the car. I see Drag and Pandillero walk back out the building towards us.

"What's up T?" I knew it was something with this nigga and now I know what. Treasure never looked up; she sunk her head into my chest like she's trying not to look. I held her a little tighter and waited for what she wanted to do. I can feel her release a deep breath out before she looked up at me. Her eyes looked like she wanted to scream for help.

"You know him?" was all I said, she still didn't say anything as he stood by waiting for a response.

"Hey Deangelo." She answered my question with those same two words.

"Come on T, don't be cold like that. Can I talk to you for a second? It'll only take a second Seabas I promise." I wanted to tell him, "Hell naw you can't talk to her for a second!" Before I can even say anything she replied, "Not right now Deangelo." She wrapped her arms around my waist tight and put her head back in my chest. I felt her breathing pick up and I was about to let this nigga have it, I stared the nigga down.

Before he can say anything else I slid down off the car and opened the door for Treasure, then I got in the other side. I watch as he walks back over to Drag then he walks to his car and drove off. The whole time Treasure sat there with her eyes closed and her head back against the seat rest.

"So what's up Treasure, what was that all about?"

"Nothing."

"So you grew up with him too right."

"Yep."

"What ya'll need to talk about later?"

"You!"

"Me? What the hell you mean me?"

"Do we really have to do this right now? I'm tired, you gone be here all day. I really need you to hold me while I sleep."

She thinks she pulling a fast one on me but I'm not going to let her get out of answering my questions. Besides, by the sound of things she gone be talking to that nigga at some point about me and I want to know why.

"That didn't answer my question Treasure."

"Okay, Deangelo wants to talk to me to find out who you are and why I'm talking to you. I knew he would be showing up as soon as I saw Drag the other day. I already know that if I keep running from him, he'll only keep tracking me down so I'm going to speak to him just not right now. Does that answer all your questions?"

"No! Why the hell is he tracking you down? Why the hell you act like you so scared of him? And if he has to track you down how do you know how to get in touch with him?" I'm heated, I wanna know what the fuck I stepped into and fast. Shit, maybe this why Dominic said she was dragging her feet.

"I guess I need to be asking you something don't I Sebastian?"

"What?" Treasure sat there then turned to me and began to explain the encrypted conversation she had with

Drag.

"Look, when I saw Drag I didn't want to get out the car but since you chose not to budge I did. I knew Deangelo found me when Drag told me the sun was looking for me, he was talking about Deangelo. He told me he would be here today and that I should make sure I came back. When I saw the car, I knew it had to be Deangelo.

I didn't want to talk to him in front of you. I already know that he's here to find out about you. I know if he showed up the way he did he about to tell me something about you that I don't want to know. I just wanted to hold on to you the way you are. So Sebastian, whatever it is can you please just tell me now?"

"I don't know what the hell you talking about! I just met both of them. It ain't shit he can tell you about me that you don't already know." I don't know why I lied to Treasure the way I did. I wanted to tell her everything right then, I just didn't know how to explain it to her. But like I said, I just met both of them, no way in hell they know shit about me.

The next morning I was expecting to see Treasure at my house but she wasn't there. I called her all day and for the next three days. I even went down her house and she was gone. I don't know where the hell she went. I tried her family but they act like they don't know who I'm talking about. I figured that my secret was out the bag. She was either back running from Pandillero or with him. I was starting to think that Treasure didn't want to be found.

"Hey Seabas?"

"What's up?"

"Nothing! Wanted to know if you wanted to go to the concert tonight?"

"Naw, I'm good. I'm chilling in tonight."

"You want some company?"

"Why not, come through later."

Later that night I chilled out then about three thirty in the morning I hear something coming from the front room. FUCK! Was all that came to mind as Treasure turned on the light, I'm stuck and I know it.

"Who the fuck is dat nigga?" As soon as Mike jumped out the bed and said that, Treasure screamed and made a mad dash back out the house. I didn't bother chasing after her; I know it's officially over. I put my head back under the covers and listened while Mike left shortly after.

I never saw Treasure again after that night. I know that she don't want to be with me anymore. I still needed to explain what had happened. I had to talk to her, I went by her house, she had already moved. Then I stopped by her unit, they said she was discharged.

I wish I would have known better than to get involved with Treasure. She has been through way too much and I would only hurt her in the end. I tried my best to stay away. When she left I just needed something to take my mind off of the pain that I was feeling.

53 TREASURE

I'm having a blast in Hawaii with Sebastian, we were in my favorite spot Hanauma Bay, swimming with the fishes. Why is everyone looking at us? Seem like everyone has directed their attention behind me. I turn around and see Sebastian down on one knee with a box in his hand. Why me? Was all that came to my head.

"...Terentia Treasure Xavier will marry me?" I dropped to my knees and stared at Sebastian hoping, hell begging that he would read my eyes without me saying anything. I wrapped my arms around his neck while everyone applauded.

"Sebastian, I'm not ready."

"Okay!" was all he said as he kissed me and we made our retreat off the beach. We didn't respond to the, 'What she say?' or the congratulations. I know Sebastian's hurt. He tried to pretend like he was regular old happy go lucky Sebastian for the rest of the trip. He asked me to at least keep the ring. I tried to have him hold onto it he wouldn't have it any other way.

I would on occasion stop by the fire house to spend time with Sebastian while I was in town. I decided to stop by since I hadn't seen him in a couple weeks. We'd been back from Hawaii for a month and we've spent less and less time together. What the hell is he doing here? Just my luck, the day I show up he's here? I sat in the car waiting on Sebastian to come over for a while. He stood there laughing it up with Drag. I had no choice but hear what he had to say.

"What's up Treasure, I ain't seen you in a long time girl give me a hug. You kno..."

"Well the sun doesn't have to see me Drag, I'd rather stay under the moon, you know?"

"Well the sun always gone be there, you turn enough corners you bound to run into him." I wonder if Sebastian is picking up on what Drag is telling me about Deangelo.

"You don't have to tell me, I already know but the longer I can stay out the light I'm good."

"You sure about that? I know the sun will be out the next time ol' Seabas here. Don't you think you should be here for that?" I can't believe this bastard just said that.

I want to cuss his ass out and tell him to stay the fuck out my business. I know if I do Sebastian will have more damn questions. I played it off and told him I'd be here. I talked to Sebastian about our little exchange. The next day Sebastian was scheduled to work, like Drag said I saw a souped up white on white Lamborghini sitting right out front.

I still wasn't ready for what was about to be said. I tried to make my exchange with Sebastian quick since I didn't see Deangelo standing out there. Sebastian had different plans. He came over and sat on the side of the car and pulled me into his chest as we talked. I heard the voice that I knew was there to put an end to my happiness.

"What's up T?" All I wanted to do was hold onto Sebastian and make Deangelo ass disappear.

I know he's here to fill me in on whatever Sebastian's hiding from me and it'll be true. I just can't do it so I sent his ass away. I know Deangelo wasn't having it when he told me not to be cold. His way of telling me to meet him in Minnesota to talk. After talking to Sebastian, I needed a minute to think. Instead of going back to his place where I know Deangelo's waiting I went back home.

I didn't stay long, just long enough to pack our bags and get the hell out of dodge, or try before I saw anyone that looked familiar. I took Shay to her family out of town and sat in a hotel room there for the next couple days. I sat thinking about anything that Deangelo would have to tell me about Sebastian. What would make him be so bold and out front about it?

I know it's something big, I just can't figure out what the hell it is. I always knew that something was up with Sebastian, I guess that's why I didn't say yes when he asked me to marry him. All I can do is think and I'm in the right place to do it. I sat there letting my thoughts run back in my mind.

Then it hit me, I know better! I jumped in the car and drove straight to Sebastian house. I'm going to lay it all out on the line. I'll let him know that whatever it is I'd work it out with him. I'm ready to be his wife and I'm willing to accept him if he'll accept me. I'm not about to let Deangelo cloud my mind with his tricks. I have a key to Sebastian place and I know he's home. I saw his car out front so I make my way to the bedroom. Then I see clothes heading down the hall, his and a dress then some heels.

I knew then I walked in at the right time to see what the hell Deangelo was trying to warn me about. I was furious! I hit the light on staring right into Sebastian eyes as he had already looked up into mine. He didn't move he laid there with his jaw damn near on the floor.

"Who the fuck is that nigga?" I had to do a double take 'cause I know that voice sounded like a man trying to sound like a woman. I couldn't believe my eyes when the man jumped out the bed, dick swinging confirming exactly what I thought. I screamed then I held my breath and ran out the door as fast as I could. I'm in complete and udder shock.

"Oh my god, oh my god, oh my god!" is all I can say as I tried to get to my car.

"Where the hell is my fucking car?" I screamed into the night. I looked around for it.

"It's gone T!" I turn around and see Deangelo standing there. I ran to him, he held me in his arms as I cried into his chest. I'm trying to breathe but I can't. Next thing I remember I'm waking up in a doctor office.

"It's about time you woke up T! You had me worried,"

Deangelo said as he leaned over and kissed me on my forehead. He said I had been in and out for two days. The sight of Deangelo sitting by my side made me breakdown and cry even more. He climbed over into the bed with me and held me while I finished what I had started.

"You knew didn't you?"

"Yeah!"

"How?"

"Come on T, you know I have to keep up with you. By the way, happy twenty fifth belated birthday."

"Thanks, why didn't you tell me?"

"I tried; I knew you didn't fly out to Minnesota to meet with me. I figured you'd pop up at his spot sooner or later." I sat up I know I had unprotected sex with Sebastian. On more than one occasion, I'm in trouble. Deangelo knew exactly what I was thinking.

"They already ran test on you T; the results will be back in a couple months. They said that you good for now." I broke down in his arms again; we sat there for hours while he consoled me. I was happy that he was there to help me through what I was feeling.

54 DEANGELO

"Ay Pandillero, I just got some news about Treasure old dude, you might wanna see how she doing."

"What's up Bateador, you know I'm trying to stay away, but go 'head and tell me." After Bateador told me what happened I jumped on the phone. I know I have to be there for T no matter how much she wanted me to stay out of her life. I made sure they found out as much about him so everything was good and T didn't have to lift a finger.

I was shocked when I saw her at the funeral. She looked like she hadn't eaten in hellas. It was sad to see her, like she was a zombie just trying to make it. Afterwards I gave the pastor and funeral director both checks for a million dollars each and told them it was from her.

I saw them go over and talk to her, she didn't seem like she wanted to be bothered I made my way back. It was like I couldn't get out of there without everybody trying to give me a bag with the shit my peoples put together. I didn't even care that everyone of them had a check in it from T. They all look like they hit the lottery or something.

All I wanted to do was get out before T saw me; I made my escape and headed back to the airport. I tried to keep an eye on T but she got low on me. I was back to staying out of her life again. I know she need sometime anyway so I didn't send anyone after her.

* * *

"What's up Pandillero? I found whatchu been looking for man."

"Oh really, so how it look?"

"Fire!"

"Man you silly as hell; tell me what's the stello with it though."

"Well..." I let Drag fill me in on the details about my girl; I can't believe what he said about her man. T never seemed to amaze me with the niggas she find. I don't know how the hell she doesn't already know it before she starts messing wit 'em. It's all good though 'cause if she did, what would she need me for.

I want to see what my girl been up to, I know a lot of shit has happened. I figure she probably on the rebound, that's about the only reason she with that soft ass boy any fucking way. Seem like every nigga in the Lou trying to wife her up, that nigga know damn well she ain't what he want. If I don't know anything else, I know that I'm about to get my T back for good this time. I pull up early; I know Drag said the nigga had to be there by nine. I wanted to make sure I had a chance to see what he was about myself before T came by.

"What's good Pandillero? I ain't seen you in a minute boy. Guess the only way I can track you down is by following that treasure huh."

"Man stop, you know damn well I just saw you what, couple weeks ago at the Center. What's the deal with old boy though?"

"Man soon as I got here they filled me in on old boy, say he one of them sneaky ass niggas. They said he was in Hawaii or some shit proposing to his girl. After I met him and saw yo' girl, I got the real deal on him. I was like damn, I know this nigga ain't trying to pull one over on her like that, not Treasure," Drag said as we watched him pull up, then he went on,

"I hollad at her for a minute, she wasn't having it though for real. She was trying to duck you and shit. I told her you would be here next time her man was here, she changed her mind and said she would be back. I don't know if she knows though. It didn't seem like it the way they was all hugged up and shit."

"Well shit, let's get this over with 'cause I know he a done deal after I talk to her."

I get out and go to the front of the fire house still watching as the nigga grab his bags out. I thought he was about to walk past then he stopped and did a double take at me. Lava started pumping through my blood. That nigga did that shit like one of these ho's.

"What's up Seabas, back already?" I stood by while Drag talked with the nigga.

"Shit you know I am. What's up Dog I'm Seabas." Look at this nigga I can see the twinkle in his mufuckin' eye from here. How the hell does T not know? What this nigga think I'm about to touch his bitch ass. I should punch him in his shit for even trying to touch me. And for fucking around with T heart the way he is. I figured I was just gone play it cool.

"I'm Pandillero but I don't shake hands with a nigga in a uniform." We laughed the shit off then we went in and talked while I waited for T to get here. I was done talking with that nigga anyway. Soon as I went in Drag introduced me to some of the other niggas in there. They all started filling me in on some of the shit that nigga had been doing. After talking with them for a while I see T outside talking to his ass. I didn't want to waste anymore time I went right over to them.

"What's up T?" I already know T doesn't want me to be here. I'm past that and it's no way in hell I'm just going to stand by and let this go on. She didn't say anything but this nigga muggin' the shit out me. The way he holding on to her make me wanna tell him he can let go 'cause I got her. No shit Twan, of course she know me, didn't you just hear me speak to her? He actually looked surprised like I was here just to holla at Drag or some shit.

She said hey and by the tone in her voice I wanted to snatch her ass around and tell her about her man, just to see if all she'd say to me is hey then. I don't wanna see T hurt though.

"Come on T don't be cold like that ca..." I know if I tell her that she knows it's important that I talk to her. Her body language telling me that she doesn't want to hear it. Then after she told me what she thinking the nigga put her in the car like that's gone stop me or something. I let Drag know the deal headed to the car and rolled out. Something told me she not going to the airport. I sat back and waited to hear what her next move was.

I had niggas errwhere looking out for her. I even sent a nigga to her house to see if she headed that way but she didn't. I decided that I would stay close and watch that nigga. The way she was hugged up with him I know she will show her face sometime. After leaving the hood I see T coming down Tenth Street, I know where she's headed. I followed behind and called my people. I already know the nigga has company 'cause my boys watching him. I'm in the right place at the right time.

T went in but she didn't stay long, I'm glad that I sent her car away. That way she has no choice but to ride with me. As soon as she came out I can see that T has learned a lesson that I'm not proud that she had to learn. She wanted me to stay out of her life so she had to learn this one on her own. She was looking around for her car so I jump out.

"It's gone T!" She took one look at me and came right back to daddy. I guess the lesson was hard on her 'cause she was rambling then fell out. I took her straight to Doc, I wasted no time getting her there either. T was out for a couple days. Doc said she had a panic attack and she needs to rest but she'll be okay. I sat around with T, she was in and out but they had her feeling better in no time.

"It's about time you woke up T! You had me worried." The moment she opened her eyes I was instantly feeling like I can start my life. She's crying so I kiss her and jump in the bed with her. She asked me some shit and I let her in on what I know. I was happy and sad about everything that happened to T. I was hoping she'll come back to me for good this time. With everything that we've been through all I want in this world is for T to be with me just as much as I wanna be with her.

We headed to the house and sat around for a couple days, seemed like we spent most of our time on the dock. I know she has to pick up her shorty. Before she does I know she's never seen her place over in Greece. I stayed there the whole time I was over there hoping that she'd make her way by and see me.

Of course she never did. She had the world in the palm of her hands but she never took the easy way. She had to do it her way and I praise her for that. I was ready to do that now; it's my time to take care of her my way.

"Hey T, I know you have to pick up my baby but I want you to get away with me before you do."

"Stop messing with me. I have to get her in two weeks so whatchu thinking?" I smile and we walk to the car, I pull up at the airport.

"You know we don't have anything to wear so I hope this is going to be a short trip." I look over at her.

"Here, I think this is yours." I gave her back her ring.

"What did you do to it?"

"I changed the diamonds out, whatchu think?"

"I can see that but you know I won't be able to wear this without a body guard now right?"

"T you silly, you have something better than a body guard."

We got out and boarded the plane, it was a long trip, all she kept asking was why this and why that. I played it off and changed the subject so many times she finally chilled out and we talked about a ton of shit. I wanted to know what happened back in Washington and what happened after that.

I was also wondering why she got married and had a kid. I was shocked when she told me everything that took place. She asked me about the funeral and I didn't want to lie to her. I told her the truth and let her know I had her back.

I know I want to be with T forever and that she's the only one for me. The only way I'm going to be able to do that is to tell her everything about my life. I have no plans on stopping what I'm doing. I need to make sure she's okay with that. Everything within me wants to hold back all the gruesome details.

I have to let her in my heart and my mind and hope that she'll accept me for who I am. She didn't have too much to say, she sat back and asked questions here and there. Other than that, I think she was in more disbelief than anything. Once we landed I didn't know what she was thinking with all I told her. I was willing to wait to find out; I know it's a lot to take in.

We made it to the villa and her eyes filled up once she saw where we were at. She started crying I held her and carried her inside. I felt like I was a new man once I stepped across that threshold with T in my arms. All my secrets were out and all I had to do was wait to see how T was going to react.

We sat around talking for a little bit then we headed out on the town going to different places. She acted surprised that I spoke other languages. I teased her about me being dumb but she knows I'm not. We spent the rest of the evening walking around then we made our way out to the beach.

"You know Deangelo I always thought that you would get tired of the way you live and give it up. I mean now I understand more on why you don't but if..." I let T talk and the more she did the more I knew that I had my T back.

We spent the next couple days out and about doing whatever we wanted. Those nights I held T and that's all I needed. T was getting anxious about getting back in time to pick up my baby but I persuaded her to stay longer.

I know what I want and I want T to know that I'm all in; I made some calls and set everything into motion. I needed to make one last call to get the final go ahead. This the hardest call I've ever made in my life. It took me forever to gather the courage to do it and when I was cleared it was on and poppin.'

"T you ready? You keep me waiting any longer and I'm just gone call it a night."

"I'm coming, I'm coming." I was beaming as soon as I turned around and watched T come down the steps. She was more beautiful than I'd ever seen her. She wore the hell out of a long lavender dress with just enough showing to make we want to see more. Her hair was to the back with long bouncing curls and her legs made me even more excited with the way she moved. I was buried in love with her.

"How do I look?" she said as she came down then did her turn, stopped and looked back at me over her shoulder.

"T you still crazy. You look amazing, you already know it!" I kissed her on the cheek as we left out the door. We pulled up to the restaurant and walked inside, the place packed. The moment we made it to the backroom T face lit up and she let out a scream.

"SURPRISE!" Everyone yelled.

"What? How did you do this without me knowing?" T said as she turned around to me and held on.

"Anything for you baby."

"Mommy, Mommy," my baby said as she ran over and jumped into T arms. I smiled and let her go around the room meeting everyone. I'm feeling good at the site of seeing T happy. Her family's here, her mother, father, sister, brother, I'm glad that her friend Sammy made it out to see her. I found my family so I could talk with them.

"Now you sure you wanna do this man? You know Treasure's been through a lot." my father said.

"So all those games and fast tail girls gone have to stop! You know you not gone hurt her like that." my mother said.

"I'm more than sure Pops and Momma those fast tail girls you know don't have nothing coming now that I have my T back." After talking with them I make my way over to T family, thanked her father and asked her mother for a dance. We had a great time, all laughing and partying the night away. Once our song came on, T made her way over to me as I made my way to her.

"Nice touch Mr. Man," she said as we start dancing, it seemed like all eyes were on us. No one was more important to me than T and that was all that mattered. The music went off and the room was quiet, I looked at T and got down on my knee.

"T I know that we've been through our ups and downs.

I also know that I haven't been the man you needed me to be at times. Even though a lot has happened we've made it around each bend. And no matter how many wrong turns we've made, we found our way back to each other. I hope you know that I've been in love with you all my life. I was determined to be at this point right here with you no matter how long it took for me to make it here.

I want to show you just how much I love you T, in front of all of your family and mine so that everyone knows that I'll always and forever love you. Since I know better, it's time for me to do better; Terentia Treasure Xavier will you marry me?" Before I can pull out the ring I watch T as the tears drop from her eyes. She placed her hand on the top of the box stopping me from opening it. Her knees started to give way, I thought she was about to collapse, I sat her on my knee so she wouldn't fall.

"Deangelo, YES! YES baby! YES!" I opened the box and placed the ring on her finger. I embraced her as everyone cheered.

We didn't have a long engagement, a couple months later we were all back together in Rome having the ceremony. I didn't have time to wait anyway, I have everything I want or need. We moved out the villa about a month after the wedding once we found a house.

"So T, are you having a nice one year anniversary?"

"Yes! How about you?"

"It's cool I guess?"

"What, cool you guess?" I had to mess with T; I know she'll get worked up about what I said.

"Yeah, I mean I would like to get the hell out of here and get back so I can get my dessert."

"Really? Why you wait this long, I could've gave you yo' dessert a long time ago." We both laughed, the waiter stopped and asked us if we needed the dessert menu.

"Naw man, no one has the dessert I'm looking for on their menu," I said as we laughed even harder.

"But before we go I have something for you." She pulled out a box. I thought it was a watch or something I looked inside.

"What's this?" before I could get the rest out I saw the stick that was under the fabric. I looked over at T and she had no real look on her face. I guess she didn't know how I'd respond.

"You serious? We're having a baby?" I'm too happy to hold it in. I want to jump up out my seat and run around the restaurant showing people the stick.

"Babies Mr. Man, babies." BABIES! I got up and hugged T then I realized I may be hurting her. I let go and got down putting my head onto her stomach. I don't care that everyone in the restaurant was looking at me. I want to talk with my babies and let them know that daddy waiting on them.

"Hold up T let me help you with that." I made my way around and pulled her overnight bag out the backseat.

"I had it." T said as she stood back.

"Daddy! Daddy," Shay said as she ran and jumped into my arms.

"What's up baby? You missed us?"

"Daddy I'm mad at you!"

"Now why would my princess be mad at me?"

"Daddy you said you would bring my sister and brother back with you. Mommy still fat and I don't see my sister and brother!" I had to laugh at what Shay said.

"Ooooh, you hurt mommy feelings Shay, you don't miss me," T said as she stood back on her leg.

"Yes, I miss you mommy but I'm mad at daddy!"

"Mommy tricked us that's all, so don't be mad. I think if I give mommy a treat later then she'll let us have them babies."

"Now why you say that to her silly," T said as we both began to laugh. I turned heading towards the house with Shay in my arms.

"Ugh! Ya'll just gone leave me like that? I'm the one just came from the hospital, why she getting carried?" T said.

"Mommy you too fat, daddy can't carry you!" I burst out laughing at Shay again.

"Baby girl daddy strong, can I help mommy then I'll

come down and we can get ice cream." After Shay agreed I walked back over to T.

"Look at you T, how you gone be jealous of my princess?"

"I'm not jealous." I kissed her then picked her up.

"It's okay, you my queen I gotchu."

55 TREASURE

After we left the doctors we made it out to his place in Lake St. Louis. I always loved this house; I never had the balls to move in even though I know legally it's mine. We spent a couple days just lounging around. I feel like I'm getting my buddy back and it's starting to feel like old times.

We didn't stick around long though, Deangelo wanted to take me somewhere. I wanted to pick Shay up and take her with us, then again I really need some time to let go. I know she's in good hands so I went with Deangelo. I was starting to feel like those kids from that movie, I kept asking are we there yet.

Deangelo told me things that he probably would never let anyone else hear. He let me know about everything that he had going on. I knew a little bit or should I say I guessed a little bit about him but to hear it come out his mouth. I wondered why he would trust me with the information.

I let him do most of the talking 'cause whatever it was that made him start I didn't want to interrupt him. All I wanted was for him to get it out. I was taken back a little 'cause I always imagined that if I knew everything about him I would want to run away. But that wasn't the case.

The moment we landed in Greece I fell in love with the place. It was picturesque and serene, all I wanna do is make it to the water and float the hell away. The villa is beautiful it's too much, I cried as Deangelo carried me in the house while I took everything in.

We did a ton of shopping; I was surprised that Deangelo spoke Greek. I know he speaks that Haitian shit but I figured that was it. Hell, come to find out he speaks Spanish and Italian too. By the sound of it, he's very fluent in them all. He did spend a bunch of time overseas so I guess he had to pick it up at some point. After we ate he took me to the beach and I was more excited about the water than shopping anyway so I was good. I know Deangelo was waiting on me to bring up what he told me on the ride over. I decided to put it all out there and let the dice fall where they lay.

"You know Deangelo I always thought that you would get tired of the way yo..."

After we talked I felt better about whatever we had and everything that I had to say was out. I guess I finally stepped out into traffic. With each day that passed I realized that I wasn't ready to go back. I need my baby with me though. The thought of her being so far away is really weighing down on me.

Deangelo of course eased my worries so I enjoyed my days with him. We did everything we could when he wasn't rapping on the phone like crazy. I was surprised that he didn't try and sleep with me. Hell, maybe he wasn't that into me or maybe I was just that bad in bed. Yeah right, let him try me now, he probably could say that back in the day but not now. Every night I just knew that it was the night he would come on to me. But he didn't, he was the Deangelo I knew before our first time.

He asked me out to dinner. I figured he wanted to do something special because we'll be heading back in a couple days. We've been gone for almost a month already. I changed into this breath taking long Chanel gown. It's lavender and has a slit that stopped right in the crease of my thigh and hip. The woman at the little shop hooked my hair up. It's something different and I like how the curls move. I think I'm a model.

"T you ready? You keep me waiting a..." I hear Deangelo call for me from downstairs. I tried to make it down the steps before he turned around. I can tell by the look in his eyes that tonight maybe different from the others. He can't take his eyes off me, I had to show him what he been missing. We headed to the restaurant; I can feel Deangelo's eyes constantly looking over at my leg. Seem like every chance he has he looking to see if I moved any so he can see my prize out in the open.

We moved slow through the restaurant I'm starting to think Deangelo don't know where the hell we going. We made so many damn turns I thought that place would never end. Deangelo opened the door to the other room. That look like, I know that is not my mom, look at my baby she here.

"SURPRISE!" They damn right I'm surprised.

"What? How did you do this without me knowing?" I'm so happy with Deangelo. Here it is a month together and it feels like we never grew apart. I hugged him and kissed him to show him how wonderful he made me feel. I was too out done when I saw my girl Sammy. We had a ball laughing and just having a good time. I had to go over to speak with his family. I was surprised to see them but I figured why wouldn't he bring his family out if he brought all mine.

I heard something that made me want to find Deangelo. I didn't have to look far 'cause he was already smiling coming to find me. "Nice touch Mr. Man." We danced around in our own thoughts. I put my head on him and moved with him while listening to his heartbeat. I could hear the beat pick up as the song ended. I could've continued to dance the night away if he wouldn't have stopped me.

He looked at me and smiled then he went to the floor, I couldn't believe what he was doing. I wanted to scream yes before he had even made it to the ground. "T I know that we have been through our ups and downs, I also know..." I was so happy tears just started running from my eyes.

I didn't need to see the ring. I know what my answer is already so I told him and then I told everybody in the room. Deangelo put the ring on my finger and I was good. Hell, I was more than good; I was absolutely wonderful I had my true love. Even with all the shit I've been through, all the pain and the loss. He was right; we always seem to find our way back to each other.

"T, you sure you want to marry me? I mean I know it's only been a little over a year since Dominic and a few weeks since what's his name. I don't want you to just be saying yes 'cause you getting over him." I should wack the shit out of him for saying that. I know his intentions are good and he has every right to say something but I should really wack the shit out of him right now. I moved in and pressed myself against him and put my arms around his neck, he leaned down to help me reach him.

"I love you, I hear what you saying but, there was a reason I turned him down when he asked me to marry him. It was a reason I ran into Drag that day, all of what has happened was for a reason. It's actually been nineteen months since Dominic died. Don't get me wrong, I still love Dominic and I think about him every day.

No matter what, I can't change what happened to him. As much as I wish I could I can't there was a reason h—. Like you said, I know better and it's time for me to do better. So my answer is still yes and I love you Deangelo with all my heart I love you." We made love that night like it was the first time we had ever experienced each other before.

We were married a month after that and he flew out everyone to come to the ceremony. He thought he was slick, tried to slide an invitation in the stack for Sebastian. I pulled it right out and burned it, he thought the shit was funny. I teased the shit out his ass later that night with my little freak show.

After the wedding we moved into our new house, I never went back to the states. I was in love with living abroad so I had to have a place that we could really call ours. Besides I don't know how many women Deangelo had in none of the houses I just so happened to own. It doesn't really matter but I wanted something for all of us.

I love him even more after watching him fall in love with Shay. I think he spoils her but he says she his only child and he can do whatever he want. A week away from our one year anniversary and I wasn't feeling too well. My friend, seemed like I hadn't seen her in a minute. I decided to get a test and see what the deal was, just like I thought, I was pregnant.

I mean it wasn't like it was a surprise or anything, we all know pregnancy is one hundred percent preventable. We've been going at it on a regular. I knew that this would happen eventually, I don't know what Deangelo will say. I mean he went this long without having kids and I never asked him if he wanted any.

I'm hoping that he not paying attention to my sudden need for red onions soaked in red cider vinegar. I don't know what that was all about but I can't resist. The day before our anniversary I went to the doctor to get an official answer I was shocked, they told me I was having twins. I thought I was going to lose my damn mind. I really was at a loss with how I was going to tell Deangelo after that.

I was surprised that he hadn't picked up on the weight I'm starting to gain. I tried my best to hide it, in the back of my mind I know I have to tell him sooner rather than later. I decided that I'd tell him on our anniversary. Maybe if I make it like a gift, at least he can tell me how he feels without destroying my feelings. Hell, I don't know if I can make the decision if he not for this. Who am I kidding my fairy tale will come to a complete halt if he not on board.

"So T, are you having a nice one year anniversary?"

"Yes! How about you?" I can't believe him, he just don't know if he want we can go right around the corner and he can get that dessert he want so bad. Hell naw, that crazy ass waiter think we want to order dessert he has no idea what the hell he talking about.

Okay there's no time like now, I give Deangelo the results. I wait wondering what the hell he's going to say, I'm trying my best to read his thoughts. He looks kinda happy but I really can't tell.

"You serious? We're having a baby?" Okay that's what I wanted to hear, *we*. He was more ecstatic when I told him that we're having twins. He jumped up, kissed and hugged me; everyone in the place was looking over at us. That didn't stop

Deangelo from getting down and putting his head on my stomach. Everybody started cheering; I was so uncomfortable of course. Deangelo was telling my belly that daddy was waiting. I was ready to get the hell out of there so I could show him how happy I was.

I spent my whole pregnancy pretty much in bed. Deangelo didn't want me to have any stress so he took care of whatever I needed. I was getting too spoiled and so was Shay. He gave her anything she wanted and she was loving it, they were in their own little world. Most of the time they were out with Ms. Jackson, the nanny, leaving me home. Whenever I would say something to Deangelo about it he would tell me I was jealous. I felt silly 'cause I was getting a little jealous.

The closer I came to my due date if I felt the slightest pain I was telling Deangelo to take me to the doctor. I was so fearful about being pregnant. I remember what happened with Shay and I'm not willing to go through that again. He didn't care, every time he'd just promise Shay to bring us back so we can all play. I told him that she needed to understand that we don't know if it's a boy and a girl or two girls or boys. He said she don't care and let him handle all that.

"Daddy! Daddy," Shay said as she ran to Deangelo, I stood by and listened into their conversation while the house keeper unloaded the car.

"Mommy tricked us that's all, so don't be mad. I think if I give mommy a treat later th..." I can't believe he just said that to her, I laughed and watched as they tried to leave me outside. I should've told him I was a little jealous but the way he picked me up that went all out the window.

"It's okay you my queen I gotchu." Deangelo sure knows what to say to make me happy. His treat must've done the trick 'cause I was in the hospital that next afternoon. Everything was fine with me and the babies. I stayed in the hospital a little longer than usual but Shay was too happy when we made it home. We sat around many days as a family and I can see that Deangelo was blissful and that meant the world to me.

Deangelo has not left my side really since we went to

Greece. He made some changes that he most definitely needed to make. I was surprised that he came to me for my input on stuff. I was willing to do what I needed to do to make sure he was good. Seemed like things were getting better and better and my destiny was more in tune with his than I thought. Deangelo was happy and so was I.

After we had the twin's first birthday party a couple weeks later we decided to spend some time alone. We headed out to dinner then to a little night club. We had a blast, and then I see someone that I thought I recognized. I just can't put a name with the face for the world of me.

I make my way over to where Deangelo's sitting but before I can make it, I see something in its hand. The faster I move seem like the closer it's getting to him. I know it has to walk past me to reach him so the moment I had a chance, I push its hand down hoping that it drops whatever it is in it.

I hear a shot then another. I feel burning in my stomach. It looks at me and I look at it as we both go down to our knees. Then I see Deangelo come and I can't hear anything but I see him fire until the hammer locked back. He reloads and did it again; he came over and picked me up.

"Terentia, you missed me?"

"Dominic, I miss you so much, Shay's doing well. How are you doing?"

"I'm fine Terentia; I see you're not though."

"What? Why you say that?"

The next thing I know I see a glimpse of doctors all around me but I can't move. I see Deangelo and it look like he's crying. I wanna tell him I'm okay but I can't do shit. I don't know what the hell is wrong with me. I feel fine now that I talked to Dominic. All I can think about is my family; Deangelo, Shay, Deangelo III and August. I wanted to hold them and I don't know why I can't.

As I lay here I think back and wonder where did I go wrong in my life? Why was I being punished for doing what I thought was the right thing? Do I deserve this? Is this how my story is going to play out? Either way, I know that this is the right time and most definitely the right place to put it all to rest. I can't be mad though, there are no mistakes! I hope the next time I take a breath I remember to make different choices. But then again, it was a hell of a ride.

ABOUT THE AUTHOR

Born and raised in St. Louis, MO. She spent her younger years living in the infamous Cochran Garden Housing Projects. She decided to put her stories on paper after many years of thinking about just how much life has changed since those exciting days in the Cochran.

She wrote her first novel, Lifelong Love: When you know better, you do better and took a long memorable stroll down memory lane. With the help of an over the top imagination she's been busy putting together her next piece of work. Please enjoy Just Another Day: Cochran Affair, the second book of this series which is set to release August 27, 2013. Also checkout Cargo's Flower; Universal Laws and Sins, chapters on Kindle in Amazon. Be on the lookout for the complete book set to release September 15, 2013. You can preorder both books now.